the KEEPER

KEEPER

the

LYNN MONTAGANO

Book Cover Design by Lori Jackson
www.lorijacksondesign.com

Interior Design and Formatting by:

emtippettsbookdesigns.com

ALSO BY
LYNN MONTAGANO

THE BREATHLESS SERIES
Catch My Breath
Unravel Me
Effortless

*For everyone who supported me through the
process of writing this book.
You know who you are.*

PLAYLIST

Break My Heart - Dua Lipa
Say So - Doja Cat
Lonely Together - Avicii Ft. Rita Ora
Dominos - The Big Pink
Lost With You - Far Out Ft. Ruby Chase
Fix You - Coldplay
Close My Eyes - Mariah Carey
Stay With Me - Sam Smith
Jealous - Nick Jonas
Wannabe - Spice Girls
My, My, My - Troye Sivan
Black Magic - Little Minx
Broken & Beautiful - Kelly Clarkson

LISTEN HERE

CONTENT WARNING

This book contains darker themes, including mentions of suicide and sexual assault, profanity, explicit sexual content, and past trauma. Recommended for 18+

CONTENTS

Chapter
ONE

"**Y**es, Killian. I love standing on the side of the road in a foreign country to yell at my best friend on the phone. It's my favorite."

"You're clearly unfamiliar with the old saying 'don't shoot the messenger,'" he groused with a hint of trepidation.

"Nobody else is in my line of fire at the moment," I muttered.

"Lucky me." I could hear his pout. "Look, we'll figure it out tomorrow. The property isn't going anywhere. The damn real estate agent certainly isn't going anywhere. Stop pacing and yelling and pacing and yelling."

I sighed, drawing a half circle in the gravel with my foot. "It's annoying. I was told they wanted to meet and discuss all the paperwork tomorrow not today. That's why I flew in now instead of yesterday with you guys. My mother keeps meddling and making this harder than it should be."

"I know. That's what we told the agent this afternoon. If it makes you feel any better, she was very understanding. And she's fine with meeting you out there tomorrow."

"Thank you for handling it. Sorry for all the frantic texts. I don't know what I'd do without you."

My heart swelled with undying, unconditional affection for Killian Monroe, my closest friend since childhood. The second he found out I had to fly to England to deal with a long-neglected property my family owned, he jumped at the chance to accompany me. The added bonus was that Killian and his partner, Maxim Hadley, were a package deal, so I had double the support. Plus, they never passed up an opportunity for international travel.

While it comforted me to know I had them, I was still uneasy about actually being here. This cottage I had to deal with had been sitting unused for almost twenty years. I remembered coming here for summer vacations when life was simpler and didn't have a permanent gray cloud hanging over it.

In its prime, the cottage was charming and quintessentially British, which always made me laugh since we were the typical American family. Well, we used to be.

It belonged to my dad's side of the family —his parents were from England. After they died, it fell to him. Under different circumstances, he'd have been happy to keep it. But that was then, and this is now.

When my parents divorced, Dad split our family fortune into three equal parts. He took his share, jumped on a plane and ended up somewhere in Greece.

Mom stayed with me because I wasn't old enough to be on my own. Or that's the bullshit excuse she'd told herself. She couldn't look at me without bursting into tears or lashing out. I reminded her too much of my sister and what happened. My twin's death changed everything.

The money meant for me didn't officially become mine until I turned eighteen. Once that happened, Mom married the first guy who put up with her for longer than five minutes and moved out. I lived the Ivy League dream at Dartmouth, graduated, moved to Manhattan, and threw myself into working.

"You're stuck with me," Killian declared. "Plus, I'm well versed in all things Chase Family Hysteria."

"Yeah, well, you guys shouldn't have to be mixed up in my ridiculous family drama. I mean, my mother could just as easily have sent the lawyer's letter directly to the real estate people here. The woman hasn't spoken to me in—" I stopped myself from saying the words. All I could do was continue pacing back and forth. The path I made would become a permanent fixture on the side of this road for sure.

In an attempt to quell my jittery nerves, I stopped pacing and soaked in the English countryside. The picturesque view could seduce even the most jaded traveler with its sweeping fields shuddering to life in the burgeoning spring. Weeping willow trees bent to meet the ground in grand gestures and old stone barriers protectively hugged any grass growing too close to the road. Early evening sunshine tinted everything it touched with a golden hue. If I stood still enough —which was challenging at this particular moment in time— it felt magical. Almost otherworldly.

"It looks like Middle Earth," I mused.

"Hate to break it to you, baby girl, but that was New Zealand. More importantly, Middle Earth doesn't exist. But Orlando Bloom does, and I'm hoping he's around here somewhere."

"Pretty sure he's in L.A. with Katy Perry."

The low rumble of an engine slowing down and the sound of tires rolling to a stop on gravel distracted me for half a second. I glanced over and saw a black Land Rover.

"Party pooper," Killian chuckled. "Where are you anyway? Did you get lost on all those little winding roads? Do you need us to come find you?"

"No. I didn't get lost." I kept an eye on the Rover. "And I don't need both of you to rescue me."

"We don't mind. You're out there all by yourself. Some psycho could kidnap you."

I rolled my eyes and paced again. "You watch too much Dateline. Nobody's going to kidnap me. Although, a car just did pull up."

"Seriously?" He sounded nervous.

"Yeah." I looked to see if anyone got out yet. Nothing. "Maybe they think this is one of those texting rest stops or whatever. Do those even exist in England?"

"Probably. Listen, get back in your car and get your ass over here."

"I can't. You know how I am when all this nervous energy takes over. I'll be distracted. I need to walk it off."

"You need to not be alone on the side of the road anymore."

"Oh my God, Killian. Five minutes. I just need five damn minutes." I spun around and nearly collided with someone. I blinked, trying to focus on the tall, lean figure standing in front of me.

"Is everything alright here? Do you need me to call you a tow?" An elegant baritone voice wrapped in an English accent invaded my senses.

Blue eyes and a dimple. That's all I saw at first.

I collected myself and checked out my uninvited guest, absorbing as much detail as I could in the waning sunlight. Clad in jeans, t-shirt and leather jacket, he towered over me. His exterior screamed fine-tuned athlete, or at least someone who made it a point to stay fit. Tousled, dark brown hair rustled slightly in the chilly breeze. Expectant eyes fixed on mine, waiting for an answer.

"No. I'm fine, thank you." I smiled and moved to a different spot to continue pacing.

"Who are you talking to?" Killian demanded. "Hello? Victoria?"

"The other person who pulled off the road. They wanted to see if I was having car trouble."

"Creepy? Normal? I need details."

I squeezed the phone. "Can you not play the role of overprotective best friend please? I can handle myself."

"Yeah, yeah. The great Victoria Chase needs no one. We've all seen that movie," Killian sounded annoyed.

"Killian," I yelled. "I love you to bits but I'm going to hang up. You know how I get. I haven't been here since I was sixteen. I'm less than twenty-fours away from going to the last place we vacationed together as a family because my mother…" I exhaled harshly. "This is hard for me."

I turned and crashed hard into a wall of leather. Great. This guy again.

"That's a first." His grin revealed a dimple just beneath his left cheek. "I've heard stories about people ending up in hospital from walking while using a mobile phone but I never thought I'd become a victim."

The deep, richness of his voice accomplished two things at once: it soothed my nerves in a way I couldn't explain while giving me an uncontrollable urge to pull all his clothes off.

"I'm so sorry" was all I could think to say once I regained my ability to speak.

"Don't let it happen again," he teased.

"Victoria Chase you better tell me who that is." Killian's voice blared.

"Hang on, hang on," I mumbled into the phone.

There was something about this guy. I allowed myself to study the handsome stranger's features. The arch of his eyebrows, the aristocratic nose carved right from a Greek statue, the strong, rugged angle of his jaw. The jagged scar above his left eye. And that mouth. Full and sultry with a slight pout. Not a sulky pout. A sexy, enticing pout. It was made for promises and sin, and not necessarily in that order. I could say the same about his striking sapphire eyes. So many promises fringed by long lashes. He appeared to be around my age. Maybe a few years older.

"Just a mildly hot mid-life crisis," I blurted, staring straight at him.

An amused smile crossed his lips.

My gaze remained fixed on this man's mouth. He folded his arms, bringing up one hand to stroke his jaw. A silver ring glinted off his thumb when he ran it over his lower lip. My knees almost gave out watching the slow, deliberate movement.

Okay. Side of the road flirting it is.

I was not subtle as I checked him out from head to toe. Was that a tattoo peeking out from the neckline of his shirt? Of course it is.

Despite the casual attire, he exuded a well-bred pedigree. I'd grown up around boys and men like this. The slight air of indifference. The inevitable bursts of charm. He either came from money, made lots of money, or some combination of the two. With that athletic build I'd be willing to bet he played professionally. Probably soccer. Maybe rugby.

But beneath his curated outer layer was something else. I sensed it from the obvious way he stroked his lip and watched my reaction. There's something about him that's much more rough around the edges. And it piqued my curiosity.

Killian's concerned voice broke through the heady fog that'd wrapped around me.

"Tori, it's getting dark. And—"

"Hold on."

Tall, dark and mildly-hot walked back to his Land Rover and leaned against it. His inquisitive stare remained focused on me. I lowered the phone, letting Killian's protests get caught up and swept away on a gentle breeze.

"Everything alright?" the handsome stranger asked again, motioning toward the phone. "Sounded like a pretty intense conversation."

"How long have you been listening?"

"Not long. But you were doing such an impressive job carving a walking path that I didn't want to interrupt. I'm assuming you're not having car trouble. Relationship issues?" His dimple appeared.

Oh, this one thinks he's smooth. I forced a sweet smile. "Nope. No car trouble. No relationship trouble either. Everything is fine. Thanks for stopping."

"Everything is fine," he mimicked. "In my experience, when a person says that they mean the complete opposite."

"In my experience, indulging in a conversation in the middle of nowhere with a complete stranger is —on a scale of 'bad idea to run for your life'— not the smartest thing in the world to do."

"Can't argue with that I suppose." He shrugged. "For the record, I don't like the idea of leaving someone stranded on the side of the road."

Handsome *and* good manners. I blinked. Maybe it was the jet lag. Or the weight of all the crap I'd been dealing with the last few weeks. His sincerity found its way through the limited number of cracks in my well-crafted outer shell, affecting me almost as much as his calming tone.

"I'm not stranded." I felt my shoulders relax and the urge to pace subside. "I'm in the middle of an annoying situation and thought it best to pull over so I don't wrap the car around a tree."

"I like this answer better than 'everything is fine.' And see?" He spread his arms open and smiled. "It didn't end with any warped side of the road kidnap plot."

A small laugh managed to squeak out of me before I could compose myself. If I'd met this guy under different circumstances, I'd one hundred percent spend a significant amount of time flirting with him. And more. But that's not what this trip is about. Plus, I promised myself I'd ease up on the revolving door of instant physical gratification.

"Do you live around here or do you just drive up and down this road looking for potentially stranded drivers?"

He ran a hand through his hair and smiled. This smile was almost too pretty to be real. Pretty, but not perfect. It was a little crooked which made it even more attractive and seductive. And there was an arrogance behind it that intrigued me. He smiled like he knew I'd be enchanted, like he knew I wouldn't be able to resist his charm.

"I do live around here occasionally," he drawled in a tone reserved for expensive boarding schools. "You're the first person I've ever pulled off the road for though."

"Lucky me."

Something shifted in the air between us when our eyes locked. My pulse quickened the longer I held his cobalt stare. In that exact moment, he saw me. Really saw me. I self-consciously touched my hair which I'd thrown into a messy bun on the plane. I wish I'd worn something other than my favorite, most comfortable travel outfit — gray yoga pants, white tank top and gray hoodie. He ran his thumb along his lip again in such a way that I felt it at my core, setting off an unexpected wave of sparks.

He checked out my ensemble one more time, let out a breath, and made eye contact. "Did you just arrive here?"

I nodded, more annoyed at the fact I couldn't articulate an answer than at the actual question.

"Are you staying long?"

Speak out loud, Victoria. Use your damn media relations skills.

"No."

Yay. A word.

"Well, I hope I've given you a decent first impression of the area."

Oh he's good with the flirting. Really good. I grinned. "I'm well acquainted with this area but thanks for giving me something new to appreciate."

He opened his mouth to say something, then snapped it shut. The dimple emerged with his wide smile. To anyone else, this would come across as warm and friendly. But I knew this type of smile. I've seen it many times before on other guys and recognized the fatal charm beneath it. The major difference this time was the unspoken promise it also revealed. Part of me wished this trip had room for promises and charm.

"Now that your situation has been sorted, I'll let you finish your phone call." He pushed himself away from the car. "Drive safe."

Without breaking eye contact with me, he got back into his Rover and drove off. I watched with a twinge of regret that I'd never hear his voice again. But then I did hear a voice. A tinny, panicked voice coming from my hand.

"Killian, I'm so sorry," I winced.

"What. The. Actual. Fudge."

"Still not swearing?"

An exasperated sigh vibrated through my ear. "I already wasted my allotted ten-bucks-per-week limit at the airport yesterday."

I laughed. "Maxim's going to get so rich off you and your potty mouth."

"Anyway." I could feel his disapproving eye roll. "What happened with the rando? I heard some of what you were saying to him. Is he gone? Was he weird?"

"If it makes you feel any better, he wasn't a psycho. He just wanted to see if I was having car trouble."

"I see. So the fact that he was mildly hot had nothing to do with it?"

"Not completely."

Killian's soft laugh soothed my frayed nerves. "You are a piece of work. Does he tick all the boxes for you?"

"Knock it off."

"Get your ass back here. Max and I want to go into town to the pub you're always telling us about. Plus a few others."

Back inside the car, I tossed my phone onto the passenger seat and readied myself for the remaining drive. The black ribbon of road rolled out in front of me, leading me closer to the place I never thought I'd see again. Now wasn't the time to dwell on the house or my family or my sister. I had to focus. Driving on the left side of the road always kept me more aware of my surroundings. If I let myself zone out, I'd end up in one of these pretty fields, probably inches away from a tree.

One of the last times we were all here together as a family, my dad took us out to teach us how to drive on the left.

Us.

My grip tightened on the steering wheel.

There was no more us. There was only me. And as usual, I was left to my own devices to clean up someone else's mess.

Chapter

TWO

I can't stand surprises. They don't enhance anything and to be blunt, the inconvenience is considerable. Plus, the lack of control I'd have over the situation is beyond undesirable. For example, stopping on the side of the road to help what I'd thought was someone with car trouble. That turned out to be, well, I'm still not sure what that was.

I pushed the memory out of my head and mentally prepared myself for tonight's boys night out. I'd only agreed to go since it was with my two closest mates. They promised it would be low-key and far away from London. Forty-five minutes away was the negotiated compromise. My reputation aside, this was one thing I did not want turned into the social event of the decade. Not that it would make one bit of difference to the outside world.

The night was crisp. Not cold exactly, but that weird chill when winter tries its damnedest to turn into spring. I slowed my stride to admire some of Briarcliff Village's quaint architecture. I always appreciated the inner workings of a structure.

The bare bones and stark lines begging to be fleshed out into something unique, spectacular, and memorable. I supposed being an architect's son had its benefits. Appreciating the beauty in something from its bleak beginnings. That's a trait I happily attributed to my father.

Well, happily is a strong word choice. Let's go with it's one of the better ones I'd inherited. Actually, one of the only few good ones.

"Hey, Maddox. Get your arse over here."

Cade Gallagher stood in front of the pub surrounded by at least half a dozen people. The star striker smiled with ease as he took pictures and signed autographs. My good friend enjoyed adoration and public praise almost as much as I did.

"Keeping a low profile as usual, I see." I shook his hand, clapping him on the shoulder.

"Welcome to the show." He grinned. "Gotta give the fans what they want."

The crowd grew around us, with more people clamoring for Cade's, and by default, my attention.

"We heading inside now?" I tilted my head toward the door. I turned to walk away when a blur of gray and blue crashed past me.

I jumped back, but not before getting whacked in the ribcage.

"Hey, Gallagher, you whiny, no-talent arsehole." The guy who just blew by me was in Cade's face, shaking a fist. I grabbed the back of his gray jacket and yanked him away, getting a good, strong whiff of alcohol as I did.

"Lemme go," he slurred, struggling against my grasp.

"Not a chance. Walk away. Now."

"Make me."

"Do you really want to start something with a guy who has at least six inches on you, plus about thirty pounds of pure muscle?"

"Fuck off. Go give up some more penalty shots so we can lose another championship, you washed up knob."

I clenched my jaw, swallowing back the urge to deck this guy right here on the sidewalk. I couldn't care less who he was or what stupid, drunken argument he thought he needed to have with two professional athletes.

"Hold on, Xavier," Cade focused a self-righteous gaze on the inebriated intruder. "The whiny, no-talent asshole wants to hear what he has to say."

The guy lurched forward even though I still had him in a pretty tight grip. More than a few people had their mobile phones out, no doubt taking pictures or recording what was happening. This had the potential to turn into a viral mess if it escalated. I dug my fingers into the material, pulling the guy back.

"I'm only going to tell you this one more time," I growled into his ear so only he could hear me. "Walk away or you'll be carried away on a stretcher."

He shrugged out of my grasp with a defeated grunt. By this point some of his friends made their way over from the pub where they'd no doubt been knocking back more than enough beers to last the rest of the weekend. They mumbled their apologies and led him down the street. I exhaled, muttering something about how nothing ever changes when I felt a presence behind me.

I didn't turn. At least not at first.

"Maybe we should find another place. This looks a little too chaotic," a male voice suggested.

"No way," a female voice responded. "This is the final destination. Besides, you've been dying to meet Dawn and Ray for ages. You'll love them."

Americans.

I knew this voice. It was soft and compelling in its soothing melody.

Already thrown by the sound of her, I steadied myself and turned, and felt completely knocked down by the sight of the mystery woman from the side of the road.

Long, dark lashes framed green eyes that widened in a mix of disbelief and shock the moment she looked directly at me.

Her full, gloss covered lips parted slightly, then curved in a smile. Red gloss, like a blushing rose. The things I would do to that mouth. Unlike earlier when she had it tied back, her red hair fell in loose waves over her shoulders. Her sexy body had curves for miles, begging to be explored.

As much as I enjoyed her sporty casual look earlier, this sweater dress enhanced her supple figure in so many enticing ways. I took my time exploring every curve, every piece of her that I could bite, kiss, and lick to make her squirm and scream my name. She didn't shy away from my obvious staring. In fact, her cheeks flushed a subtle shade of pink.

Fuck. So many filthy, glorious things I could do to this gorgeous creature if she'd let me.

The two men standing with her didn't notice our brief interaction. They whisked her into the pub with a flourish.

"Nothing like mixing it up with some pissed wanker," Cade proclaimed, clapping me on the back. "Let's head in. Bennet's already at the bar."

Black Rose Tavern buzzed with the low hum of conversation. For a Thursday night, it was crowded but not filled to the point where I'd have to question whether I was too old to keep coming out to places like this on purpose.

"Gentlemen," Bennet Logan greeted us with a broad smile. He was older than Cade and I by a couple of years and often played the role of big brother to our endless, but affable, bickering. Not to mention his father owned the club we played for. Another year or two and Bennet would be running the show at Royal City Athletic.

"Sorry we're late," Cade said, reaching for a beer. "Had to handle a small problem at the door."

Bennet shot us both a concerned look. "Oh?"

"Just some drunk who thought he was smarter than us." I grinned, reaching for the other beer. "You'd think they'd have better things to do than hassle a couple of washed up footballers."

"Speak for yourself, Maddox." Cade knocked his glass against mine.

I shrugged, scanning the bar area. The restlessness that had been gnawing at me all night kicked into high gear. My body thrummed, operating on a frequency higher than I was used to. I managed to swallow it back and was on the verge of recollecting myself when *she* came into view.

Leaning against the bar with a carefree smile, she engaged in a spirited conversation with Dawn Halston, the co-owner. I'd been coming here long enough to recognize not only the regular faces, but also the husband and wife team who've been running the Black Rose Tavern for decades.

Seeing this mystery woman in a more relaxed state, rather than pacing around like her life depended on it, mesmerized me. She was, quite honestly, stunning.

When she found me again with those fierce green eyes I nearly lost it. I almost looked away because my chest did the weird *thing* again. The thing it did when I was standing with her on the side of the road.

Cade let out a low whistle. "Who's that?"

"Nobody that concerns you." I finished the rest of my drink, placed the glass on the bar and walked over to her.

"Xavier," Dawn exclaimed. "Here with the boys tonight?"

The fact that she still called us boys always made me chuckle.

"Yes, ma'am. Behaving like the proper gents you've come to expect."

"Oh, you flirt," she gushed, showing off a dazzling smile. "I'll let Ray know you're all here." She turned to the redhead perched on the stool next to me. "Tell your two friends their food will be ready soon. And—" she leaned closer to her "—watch out for this one. He's a charmer."

"You flatter me, Dawn," I called after her as she walked away.

She wasn't wrong though. Charm was my weapon of choice. Well, that and other, more pleasurable weapons. Now, back to the matter of this redhead.

I pinned my stare on her, watching those intoxicating green eyes dilate. Several thoughts flashed through my mind. All of them tempting. None of them fit for public consumption. Unless, of course, she was into that sort of thing. Flames licked at the base of my spine just thinking about it.

"So, Xavier is it?" she asked.

The way my name rolled off her tongue and lingered on her lips drove me to the edge. So help me, it took all of my strength not to pin her against the side of this building and fuck her until neither one of us could move.

"Depends on who's asking."

A knowing grin curled her lips as she leaned forward. "My guess would be the brunette about to pounce from your left."

Before I had a chance to see who she was talking about, a soft body pressed into me.

"If it isn't the elusive Xavier Maddox."

I tensed, looking down into the heavily made-up eyes of Claire Miller. Once upon a time we'd had a one night stand. Two, actually.

"Hey Claire. How's it going." I offered a brisk smile but it only encouraged her to move closer and push her breasts into my side.

"Much better now that I've bumped into you." She looked up at me through her lashes, making me wonder if this was a rehearsed move. Admittedly, I did find it kind of sexy, and if she were someone else, say the American knock-out sitting right next to me, I'd be interested.

My focus strayed back to the woman I'd rather be talking to. She sipped a martini and smiled. The way her gaze lingered a bit too long emboldened me. I moved my eyes up and down her body, savoring every inch of her. As soon as I locked back onto her verdant stare, I licked my lower lip.

There it was. There was the reaction I wanted. Her mouth parted slightly as a faint shade of pink stained her cheeks. She touched her own lip as though she were imagining how it would feel if I kissed her. A self-satisfied grin spread across my face, giving her the classic Maddox dimple.

"You still owe me a drink," Claire purred, sliding a hand beneath my shirt and stroking my back. "You promised."

I winced. This was *not* the way I pictured my night unfolding. Wracking my brain for a way to shut her down without offending her too much, I half-wished Cade or Bennet would show up as re-enforcements.

No such luck.

"Xavier, aren't you going to introduce me to your friend?" my redheaded savior asked in a soft, low, almost chastising voice. If I were a betting man, I'd say she thoroughly enjoyed my discomfort.

When I didn't respond, she widened her eyes in expectation. When I continued to just stare at her, she sighed, turning to Claire.

"I'm Victoria. I heard him say your name was Claire. Nice to meet you. Sorry for his rudeness. He must be wound up so tight from all this attention."

Claire detached herself from me, placing her hands on her hips. "I didn't realize he was here with someone."

"Well, I *am* sitting with him and we were mid-conversation when you came over, so, yeah. He's with me."

Claire looked from me to Victoria and rolled her eyes. "Good luck trying to keep his attention," she muttered, walking away.

"That was fun," Victoria said with a smile. "When's the next one due?"

"You're enjoying this way too much," I grumbled.

"I am. You're welcome by the way. You know," she paused, finishing her martini and signaling for another, "I thought this trip out here was going to be annoying. If the rest of it is anything like this, I might never leave."

"And where would you go back to, if you did end up leaving?"

"Manhattan."

"Ah, a city princess." I grinned. "Looking to see how the other half lives out here in the country?"

"You don't look like a country prince."

"No? What do I look like?"

She drummed her nails on the bar and gave me a once over. "The leather jacket and jeans, and rings and tattoos don't fool me. I've seen enough of your type in high school and college." She twisted a strand of hair. "You went to boarding school. Probably went to Cambridge or Oxford. You definitely have a trendy apartment in London. You're a certified heartbreaker with that hair and that mouth. And…" her voice trailed "…you play some type of sport. How did I do?"

"That obvious, huh?" I ran a hand through my hair.

A full smile curved her lips. "It's the way you speak and carry yourself. I saw it the minute you told me you didn't feel comfortable leaving me stranded on the side of the road. You have this refined, elegant thing with manners going for you. Yes, the bad boy vibe works but I have a feeling you'd be just as hot in a suit and tie." She sipped her freshly delivered martini. "It's sexy. All those manners and tattoos."

She was still smiling at me. I wanted to kiss her smile until she pressed into me and begged for more. I moved closer to her, angling my body so there wasn't too much space between us.

"So, Victoria is it?" Oh shit. I used *that* voice. The deeper, more clipped sounding one. The one I didn't use anymore. The one that led to me saying things like *kneel* or *undress*.

A flirtatious spark lit up her eyes. "Depends on who's asking."

Careful, careful, careful. I cleared my throat. "The mildly hot mid-life crisis."

"Aw, did I strike a nerve?"

"Not really. I mean, I wouldn't exactly call thirty-six mid-life. My ego did take a hit though."

"Would you rather I be gentle with your fragile ego?" she purred, tilting her head and exposing the smooth skin of her neck.

For. Fuck's. Sake.

Nothing about me wanted to be gentle about anything with her. I inhaled slow, barely maintaining a grip on the thin line masquerading as my self-control. The visual of her wedged between my body and a wall with her dress hiked up and her legs wrapped around me made the growing ache and tightness in my pants tough to ignore.

"Not too many things about me are fragile." Again with the tone. What is going on here?

Victoria picked up on my timbre this time. Her lips quirked into a little smile. Then she proceeded to size me up. Her eyes studied me. Devoured me. Penetrated well past the parts I kept hidden.

"Of course not," she teased, her emerald eyes resting on my neck. When she leaned closer, I could smell faint traces of perfume. Not sweet or floral, but musky and warm. Her fingers traced the neckline of my t-shirt, pulling it down to expose part of my collarbone.

"Can I help you with something?" I inquired, fully intending to pull her into my arms at any second.

"Uh-uh, no." Her eyes darkened when she pulled the shirt down a little more and found what she'd been looking for. "Nice tattoo."

"I have more."

She was close enough for me to kiss her. And from the look on her face, she was thinking the same thing. She glanced at my mouth before settling back on the stool.

"I bet you do. And no, I don't want to see them right now. Maybe another time."

Yep. I liked this one. Flirting with a woman hasn't been this much fun in years.

A wry grin pulled at my lips.

Let's see how far we can go.

"Funny how you should mention another time," I said matter-of-factly. "We're going back to my place after you finish your drink."

"That's presumptuous. Why?"

I moved closer. The tops of my thighs brushed against her crossed legs, putting her knees dangerously close to the growing bulge straining at the zipper of my pants.

"Because as much as I want to, fucking you in public isn't something I'm prepared to do yet," I replied in a calm, even tone.

Her pupils dilated. Her breathing stuttered enough for me to know she's, at the very least, curious.

"What makes you think I'm that kind of girl?"

"What kind? The kind of girl who wants to be fucked in public or the kind of girl who wants a one night stand?"

She grabbed the skewer of olives from her martini, trapped one in her teeth and pulled it into her mouth. The coy way she looked down and then back at me told me all I needed to know.

I didn't come here tonight looking for a random hook up. Don't get me wrong. Running into her again pleased me in a way I didn't anticipate. And flirting with her was a major turn on. There was just something *different* about her. Something I couldn't quite figure out yet. Something keeping me on the edge of restraint and reckless taking.

"You don't even know me," she said in a low voice. "How can you assume I'd want any of that?"

I shrugged. "You're right. I can't assume." I let my hand fall between the bar counter and her thigh. Neither one of us broke eye contact. The way she looked at me with such intensity cemented my belief she also felt whatever this was building between us.

Toying with the hem of her dress, I slid my hand under the material. Nobody could see what I was doing, but she could certainly feel the metal rings I wore. Her breath hitched and her legs squeezed together slightly. It sent a surge of lust through me. She wet her lips just as her eyelids fluttered shut.

So fucking beautiful.

I didn't move any closer. I only watched her while I continued feeling my way along her thigh. A faint, dreamlike smile crossed her lips.

Don't think I needed to assume anymore.

"How long are you here for?" I asked, removing my hand from her leg.

The sudden loss of contact seemed to rouse her from wherever she'd disappeared to. She pressed her hand to her flushed cheek, taking a deep breath. "Oh, um, not long. Just a few days."

"Are all those days spoken for? Or do you have any free time?"

Her eyes lit up with the same flirtatious spark I saw earlier. "They're spoken for. So if you were going to ask me on a date, I'm afraid this is it."

I laughed. "Wow. Who's being presumptuous now?"

She laughed with me. It was light and melodic and I never wanted to stop hearing it.

"You're a fun one, Xavier Maddox." She paused, biting down on her lip. "I should probably get back to my friends though."

"That's a shame, Victoria…" I let the last syllable trail up in a question.

"Chase."

"Chase," I repeated with a smirk. "Is that what I'm supposed to do now? Chase you?"

She did this adorable head tilt. "And you were doing so well with the flirting."

"Was I?" I lowered my eyes to her legs. "I'd like to think so."

When I looked up she had another dreamlike smile. She was also staring at my mouth. Really staring at it. I parted my lips, just to see what she'd do. Her eyelids hooded.

Okay, I could at least *try* for a friendly kiss. Or not so friendly.

I leaned closer. Her chest lifted on an inhale when she parted her lips. I really wanted to mess up this rose-colored gloss with my mouth.

But I shouldn't be doing this. I'd sworn off one night stands and reckless taking. It's just…there was something about her. *Something…*

Her palms flattened against my chest. "We can't."

"It's just one kiss," I whispered, doubting my own intentions.

"No. It won't be."

I snapped back to reality.

The barrier she'd created with her hands wasn't at all convincing but it kept me at bay. As much I wanted to know how she felt pressed against me, what she tasted like, what she sounded like, I wasn't about to force her to do anything she wasn't ready for.

Besides, she was right. It wouldn't stop at one kiss. I wouldn't stop. There's a reason I have the reputation I do and as selfish as I've been with her tonight already, I wouldn't let myself go further.

"It was nice meeting you," she said with a melancholy smile. "Too bad timing wasn't on our side." She stood up.

"Wait." My abrupt tone shocked even me. I don't give orders like this anymore.

Careful.

She paused, watching me curiously.

"I hope I didn't come on too strong," I said, my voice gentler. "Don't want to ruin the new appreciation you have for the area."

She smiled and my heart raced. "My appreciation remains firmly intact. Have a good night, Xavier."

Victoria walked back to her friends, giving me a small wave. The first thing I noticed was how tangible her absence was, how different the air felt. How empty. How much I liked being near her. How good it made me feel.

I wanted to be near her again.

Surprise.

Chapter
THREE

"There it is."

Killian rolled the car to a stop at the stone wall with *Briarcliff Cottage* etched into it. All I could see was a huge rundown house that was a shell of its former self.

Just like the Chase family.

"How does it feel to be back here?" Maxim asked.

"I don't know yet." I clenched my jaw.

"Do they call this a cottage to be cute? It's like one of those mansions in Newport. Summer cottages my ass," Killian exclaimed, getting out of the car.

"That'll be a dollar," Maxim laughed.

"Christ Almighty."

"Another one."

"Are you two finished?" I put my hands on my hips. "Do you need a timeout?"

The realtor appeared from the front door. She was on the phone but waved us over. I sighed, reluctant to face what I knew was coming.

"We got you, baby girl," Killian said, wrapping me in a comforting hug. "Charlotte does too. She's watching from wherever she is."

I swallowed hard, squeezing him tight.

The closer we got to the house, the more I could feel the weight of the past pressing down on me. Each step brought a wave of emotion so intense, I almost turned around and ran. Maxim and Killian flanked me, holding my hands to keep me steady.

Nineteen years.

That's how long it'd been since I laid eyes on this house.

One of the last times my entire family was intact.

The last summer my twin was still alive.

Anger and guilt slowly rolled through me as I thought again about all the milestones she'd missed.

High school graduation. College graduation. First love. Turning twenty-one. Turning thirty. Becoming the spectacular young woman she was meant to be.

Fighting off the memory of the day everything changed when we were sixteen, I focused on the cheery smile plastered to the realtor's face.

"Yes, yes. The owner's just arrived now. We'll be waiting." She ended the call and stuck out her hand. "Lovely to see you, Ms. Chase. Thanks for coming all this way."

"I didn't have much choice," I replied with a smile, shaking her hand. "Hopefully we can all agree to terms."

"I've no doubt we can. The buyer is quite excited. They should be here soon, so if you want to wait inside, feel free."

Wait inside.

I'd rather be dipped in honey and dropped in the middle of Yosemite National Park.

Killian's gentle tug on my hand coaxed me to look at him. "We'll go in. Maxim and I will, I mean. You can stay out here." He focused his attention on the realtor. "Would you mind giving us a tour? We've never been here before."

"Of course, of course." She smiled. "Right this way."

The realtor's animated chatter carried on the light breeze, followed by Killian's excited responses. I smiled, watching the three of them disappear through the gaping front door. I knew a cavernous foyer awaited them, fringed by a curved staircase hugging the wall as it snaked up to the second floor.

Even after all these years, I could picture the interior right down to the most intricate detail. I could still hear the epic discussions my mother and grandmother would have about throw pillows and color schemes.

My sister and I would stay hidden on the staircase, listening and giggling while they bickered.

"It's not gold, it's amber," my grandmother said in a haughty tone.

"It's obscene," my mother griped. "Nobody wants that much gold in a living space."

Recalling memories with my sister filled me with both joy and unforgivable despair. We'd always planned to keep this cottage and vacation here with our respective husbands and children.

"Remember Tori, don't marry the bad boy. Date him all you want but don't marry him."

"You're forgetting one important fact, Charlie. Bad boys are more fun. And since we're twins, you can lure them in with your sweet ways and then I'll pounce when the time is right."

"Never," she responded with a giggle. "As your big sister, I'll make sure to keep you in line."

Tears pricked at the corners of my eyes. Charlotte and I were physically identical except for a one detail. She had a small beauty mark on her right cheek. Our other differences were much more noticeable. She was gracious, reserved and unselfish. I had a fire in my soul, a loud mouth and a stubborn streak ten miles long.

I didn't realize I'd been pacing again until I tripped over a rock.

"Goddammit," I muttered, kicking it away.

It hopped and skipped a couple feet before coming to a stop near the front walk. Lavender foxgloves lined the path leading to the front door. The lawn was dull and winter-worn except for a few patches where the eager blades reached for the early spring sky in long, green grasps.

Briarcliff Cottage had a coquettish charm to it. The mix of gray and white stone exterior teased visitors with its allure of pretentiousness but would always succumb to its true nature. Warm, inviting, and comfortable. Even after all these years it stood with open arms, waiting for someone to fill it with laughter and joy, hot chocolate and fresh baked cookies, late night secrets and whispered dreams.

The only obvious sign of neglect were the rose bushes growing wild and thorny, almost cautioning potential guests that, yes, while beguiling, this house could hurt. And it could hurt in ways that lingered for years.

Leaving a home to fade away like this should fill me with sadness. Instead, it left me anxious.

"Excuse me, are you Natalie?"

The sound of an unfamiliar voice snapped me out of my reverie. I turned to face a well-dressed man holding a briefcase.

"No, I'm not. She's inside. Would you like me to get her?"

Before I needed to figure out a way to get the realtor out here without actually going inside, she appeared at the door with Maxim and Killian.

"Ben. Perfect timing," she exclaimed. "Have you met Ms. Chase yet?"

We all exchanged pleasantries. I learned Ben Arrington was an executive at a local charity called Building As One. Their main focus was refurbishing old, rundown homes and revitalizing neighborhoods that were otherwise neglected. It struck me as odd, since this neighborhood was neither neglected nor in need of revitalization. In fact, Briarcliff Village was known for being upscale and attracted many young professionals from London.

"I'm a little confused," I said. "Why would a charity want to purchase this property?"

Ben smiled. "One of our well-established benefactors likes to renovate homes like this. Upon completion, the home is put up for sale again, but at a more affordable price point. Briarcliff Cottage has been at the top of their list for years. You can imagine their pleasure upon hearing the owners no longer wanted to retain the property."

"So, you're going to renovate it and then sell it again?" I regarded this Ben guy with a hint of suspicion. "You're basically flipping the house. And why would you resell it at a lower price point? This area is wealthy. I'd assume you'd want to make a profit, not take a loss."

Killian stepped closer to me, resting his hand at the small of my back. He knew even though I didn't want to deal with this house or any of the memories that came with it, I'd rather not see it become some low-quality flip.

"I can assure you, our benefactor takes great pride in their work. No corners will be cut. This home will keep its dignity and charm intact."

I bristled at this guy's tone. "And who is this benefactor?"

"They prefer to remain anonymous."

"Convenient," I scoffed. "That's not happening. If this person wants to gut my family's home, I want to know who I'm dealing with."

"All due respect Ms. Chase, that's not really how this works."

"All due respect Mr. Arrington, this house belongs to me. I get to decide what happens to it."

I silently cursed out my mother for being so hasty with her decision to sell to the highest bidder. She didn't need the money. None of us did. For all the emotional ups and downs I'd had since receiving the lawyer's letter, there was still some part of me that desired to hold onto at least one memory.

I'd been so quick to let everything else go: the main house in Westchester County, the beach house, the winter home in Tahoe.

All of it seemed frivolous and trivial after Charlotte died. And I'd been so eager to shed any and all physical traces of the Chase family from my life I let it happen without a second thought.

Why not? My parents were just as eager to strip themselves of any guilt or connection to what happened. They let it all fall to me. Especially my mother.

But this cottage. This felt different. I wouldn't let it become some project to be gutted and sold.

"Why don't we go inside and talk all of this out. I'm sure we can come to a compromise," Natalie suggested.

I glanced up at Killian and over at Maxim. Both had unreadable expressions. I had a feeling they could both sense what was coming next.

"No deal." I squared my shoulders. "Thanks for the interest but I'm not selling."

✦✦✦✦✦✦✦✦

"Maybe this will help." Max slid a steaming plate of shrimp Alfredo fettuccine in my direction.

We'd arrived back at our rental home about an hour ago after the debacle at Briarcliff Cottage. I was actually pretty hungry, so food was a welcome sight.

"You didn't have to make this." I scooped a serving for myself.

"Sure. Because you'd be just fine if I offered you a frozen pizza and a juice box." Maxim pursed his lips and gave me a healthy dose of side-eye before settling into a chair next to Killian.

I shrugged. "I'm not above heating up a frozen pizza. Have you already forgotten the blizzard?"

A couple months ago New York was hit with the worst blizzard in fifty years. The dramatics of that statement always sounded much better coming from a meteorologist's mouth.

"You mean snowmageddon? I gained twenty pounds that weekend." Max recalled between mouthfuls.

"The drama with this one. It wasn't that bad." Killian shook his head.

"The worst part was I didn't miss any work. If we're going to get the storm of the century, it could have at least happened on a Monday."

"Says the guy whose job it is to plan swanky events on the regular."

I smiled watching the two of them quibble back and forth. They were complete opposites physically. There's Killian, with his lean frame, pale skin, white-blond hair and gray eyes. We'd always tease and fuss over who was prettier; Killian or Taron Egerton. In my opinion, both were equally pretty.

And then there's Maxim. Tall, muscular, and dark-skinned with brown eyes and hair. And yes, we had the same 'who's prettier' discussion with him. Killian and I both agreed Maxim could rival Regé-Jean Page all day, every day.

But at their core, they were alike in so many ways. Both were caring and empathetic. Both were fierce in their loyalty. And both of them would drop whatever they were doing for the people they loved the most.

"Speaking of swanky events," I said, grinning. "How's the planning for the influencer's birthday party going?"

Max groaned. "You know how it is. Everyone has their own vision of what the theme should be and you fight about it for six months until there are only two weeks left before the event and nobody has made one damn decision."

"So, right on schedule then?" I deadpanned.

"I see you forgot to check your sarcasm at the door again," Max teased.

I laughed. "Well, at least the location is finalized. It's at Employee's Only, right?"

"Yep. Great space. The vibe is so retro and intimate. Now if the guest of honor would only cut her guest list down, it would be perfect."

"Why not just use a bigger venue?" I asked.

"She wants it to be small." He made air quotes, "Ultra exclusive."

Killian exhaled one of his oh-you-poor-thing-tell-me-more sighs.

Max gave him an exasperated look. "This place only holds about seventy-five people so the biggest challenge will be working on the guest list."

Killian appeared thoughtful for a second. "Max, should we start the interrogation now?"

Maxim answered him with a hint of mischief, "I'd thought you'd never ask."

They looked at one another and leaned toward me on their elbows in unison. The synchronization was impressive.

"We chose to let it slide last night but it's been almost a full day." Killian paused for dramatic effect. "Who was the hot guy at the bar? You both looked like dogs in heat from where we were sitting."

"The man is a, what do the kids say these days, snack," Maxim chimed in.

I shrugged. "Nobody."

Killian sized me up from across the table. His astute gray eyes studied what I thought was an unbreakable neutral expression. "Victoria Ava Chase, stop your lying this instant."

"It was just some guy."

"I call bullshit. We noticed him with two other obnoxiously attractive men while you were speaking with Dawn. That man saw you and beelined right over. How do you know him?"

"Fine," I relented. "It was the guy who pulled over to see if I was having car trouble. Happy now?"

Two sets of eyes widened in curiosity. "Mildly hot?" they asked at the same time.

"Do you share a brain?" I muttered. "Yes, the mildly hot mid-life crisis. Well, no so mid-life. He's thirty-six. He was there with friends and apparently saw me. We talked. The end."

"You," Killian made air quotes, "talked? That's a bowl of bullshit. You two were so close to each other there wasn't room for the Holy Spirit."

"If we could not quote the nuns from high school, that would be great," I chided.

"You know what I mean. What was going on? It's not loud in there. You could hold a conversation from a normal, personal space distance."

I felt my cheeks flush. "Nothing was going on."

Max leaned back in his chair. The poor thing knew Killian was about to get into it with me.

"You're literally blushing in front of us." Killian lifted an eyebrow. "And your face last night said it all. You had this weird, dopey smile going on." His jaw dropped. "Did he diddle you at the bar?"

Max snort-laughed and kept eating his pasta.

"Oh my God." I slumped in the chair. "You're unbelievable. No. He did not get me off at the bar. This isn't Cinemax After Dark."

Killian eyed me. "Knowing you, it could have been."

"What is that supposed to mean?"

"I seem to remember one New Year's Eve when you and whoever the flavor of the month was at the time were going at it in the corner of my living room at the party. Like, going at it. I almost started carding people at the door. You have no shame."

"So I made out in a corner once upon a time ago." I drummed my nails on the table. "If I may, those who live in glass houses shouldn't throw stones."

"Sorry." He reached out to hold my hand. "Not to sound like a broken record but we've offered to take you to The Guild many times. You should come with us. Check it out. It's super classy there."

"I know," I sighed. "I want to go. I would just feel weird being there without, you know, someone to guide me."

"And what are we? Chopped liver?" Maxim feigned a wounded look. "We'll introduce you to the right people."

"Unless," Killian's eyes lit up, "your mildly hot guy is into it. I mean, he must be. I couldn't see where his hand was but I could tell by the look on your face he knew how to use it."

Talking about my preferences with the boys never embarrassed me. I'd been curious about many things as a teenager. Especially when I found out about all the parties the seniors threw with the paddles and the ropes. Charlotte and I would whisper about it at night. She seemed horrified. I, on the other hand, wanted to know everything.

Killian and I both fully realized our predilections at college, as one does. He experimented way more than I did though. That's not to say I didn't try a few things. More than a few things actually. I always gravitated toward the guys who had an edge or an unseen forbidden side. Guys like...

"So what's his name?" Killian asked. "We'll do a deep dive on the internet."

"No, you are not doing a deep dive."

"You don't want to know all about him? Stalk him a little on the inter webs?"

"No. I'm never going to see this guy again anyway so what does it matter."

"That's all the more reason to do it."

I slouched down in the chair again. As insufferable as this conversation was becoming, I was grateful for the small distraction from what happened at the cottage.

Lies.

This conversation wasn't insufferable. I didn't mind recalling my flirtatious encounter with one Xavier Maddox.

And let's face it. He wasn't mildly hot. He was scorching hot. I'd pictured several things I would enjoy doing with him, and to him, while he laid it on pretty thick last night. I wasn't offended by any of his suggestive talk at all. Or the tone of voice he used. Or his hand on my leg. Far from it. I wanted him to keep going.

The timing really wasn't the best though. If he'd dropped into my life when it wasn't so chaotic, I'd have taken him up on his offer. The public one.

"What's that smile for?" Killian demanded, tossing a napkin in my plate.

"Just thinking about how much I love you." I rested my chin in my hand and winked.

"Shall I call bullshit for a third time?"

The shrill ringing of my cell phone halted any further discussion. I glanced at the name and signaled for the two of them to hold on.

"Hey Glen, what's up?"

"Oh, hey, Victoria. Sorry to bother you but Ethan, er, Mr. Caldwell wanted to know if you finished those media packets for Tre Gideon. We're introducing him today."

"Yes, I did. I left them in a box next to my desk. Is everything all set for the press conference?"

"Good to go. I have to admit, I'm a little nervous."

"You'll do an amazing job. I have no doubt. Just keep Jake Kellerman in line."

Glen had been my assistant in the media relations department at the New York Legends for almost two years. His savviness earned my trust from the start, so I'd been utilizing him more as an assistant manager rather than just someone to fetch stats or schedule meetings.

Our team landed the most sought after wide receiver in the league during free agency and it was the biggest sports story to hit New York in years. That's saying a lot since the sports media there was fickle and never really *wowed* by anything. In fact, they seemed pretty bored with championship number six. But the idea of having the league's golden boy throwing touchdown passes to Tre Gideon whipped them up into a frenzy.

As media relations director, I missed being at the center of the action at work on days like today.

"One more thing," Glen said. "Mr. Caldwell wanted to know if you were free tomorrow night to attend an event in London. It has something to do with expanding the number of teams playing there in October. He'd like it if we had someone there to represent the Legends since Hannah can't make it."

Tomorrow was supposed to be a day trip to Scotland with the boys but now that the sale fell through I had my mother to deal with, which promised to be a rip-roaring good time.

Maybe going to London would be the escape I needed.

"Yeah, I'm free. Send me the info. Thanks Glen."

Killian pounced the second I ended the call. "Free for what?"

"Just some league thing in London."

"Ugh. A night with football executives. Sounds riveting."

"A little dose of predictability never hurt anyone."

Killian feigned concern, reaching across the table to feel my forehead. "Who are you and what have you done with my Tori?"

Max chuckled. "You're not one for predictability, Victoria. Even I know that."

"Wait. We're going to Glasgow tomorrow." Killian pouted. "I was really looking forward to it."

"Nobody's stopping you from going," I said. "I have to deal with Helena tomorrow anyway so it's probably better if I'm here alone."

"We don't want you to be alone. Especially here. And with the anniversary coming up." Killian's concern rolled off him in waves. They both reached across the table and grabbed my hands.

The tears came without much of a fight on my part. I didn't deserve this much affection from anyone but I was so grateful to them.

"I know," I said quietly. "And I love you guys for that but go on your trip. I'll be okay. I promise."

Killian gave me the look he's been giving me for years. The one that said *no wallowing, no dwelling, no beating yourself up over things you can't control.*

"Think of it this way," Max interjected. "Now we all have an excuse to come back and play in Scotland together."

I smiled, squeezing their hands.

"Let us know when you're going to see Charlotte when we get back to New York. We'll come with you," Killian offered.

Hearing my twin's name had the same effect it always does. Feelings of sadness, regret and guilt consumed me.

Chapter
FOUR

Warm notes of vanilla enveloped in butterscotch teased my tongue. Never has a bourbon given up its secrets to me so easily. Maybe it was because this was my fourth glass. Number five wasn't too far off in the distance. At this point. I'd do anything to erase the conversation —if one could call it that— I'd had with the woman who gave birth to me. To say it had been non-productive was putting it mildly.

For reasons known only to her, she wanted to sell the cottage to the charity and, in her words, *do away with that place.* What she failed to realize was her attitude only strengthened my resolve to hold onto it, no matter how painful the memories remained.

I relished another sip and leaned on the railing, looking down at all the executive types schmoozing and laughing. Coming to London already put me in a better mood. And this venue was a total vibe. Any place with a giant bird floating above the main bar from an ornate Victorian ceiling deserved a round of applause. It got bonus points for having three levels, giving me a perfect opportunity to watch everything from a distance.

I'd gone through the room several times already, meeting a number of Daniels, Steves, and Richards. They all seemed to blend together after awhile. We'd chatted, shared league stories, and compared notes on certain players. Of course once they'd found out which organization I worked for, they became more animated, wanting to know if we'd ever let other teams win a championship.

They knew better than to be petty. Nobody *lets* anybody else win in this league.

Owners from several soccer clubs here in London made their case for having the New York Legends play a regular season game at their stadium. Some of them introduced me to their biggest star players, both past and present, no doubt in an effort to wrap a nice little bow on their attempt to convince us.

I chatted with a couple of club owners whose teams were traveling to the States soon for an international series with five American soccer teams. One of them is coming to New York but at this particular moment, I couldn't remember which one.

In any case, tonight was about *my* football and the prospect of coming to London for a regular season game this fall.

"I don't believe I had the pleasure of meeting you downstairs," an unfamiliar voice stated from behind me.

I turned, coming face to face with a rather tall, good-looking gentleman.

Impeccable suit, broad shoulders, short dirty blond hair. A wide smile touched his lips with ease when he greeted me and extended his hand. His grasp was warm and strong.

"I'd have to agree. I'd certainly remember being introduced to the god of thunder."

The man laughed, shaking his head. "My niece will get a kick out of that. Thor is her favorite."

I lifted my glass of bourbon. "Don't mind me. One more of these and I'll go through the entire room recasting everyone as an Avenger."

"Now that is something I'd be willing to see," he grinned. "I'm Bennet Logan. Pleasure to meet you."

"Victoria Chase. Pleasure's all mine."

He regarded me with curiosity. "I don't remember seeing your name on the list of American football executives."

"I'm not actually supposed to be here," I said, pausing for another sip. "Hannah Pruitt was scheduled but couldn't make it."

"Pruitt." He looked thoughtful. "New York Legends?"

"That's us."

His amber eyes brightened. "This must be fate. We are quite interested in hosting your organization at our stadium this October. I've chatted and emailed with Ethan several times the last few months."

"So you own one of these soccer teams?"

He smiled. "My father owns Royal City Athletic. I'm the club's president and the CEO for The Logan Group, which is all very boring and stuffy to talk about at cocktail parties if you ask me."

"But a necessary evil." I laughed, appreciating his candor.

"Bennet. Mate. Why are you hiding up here?" a booming voice called from the stairs.

Another good-looking man walked over toward us.

This guy wasn't cut from same businessman cloth as Bennet. I'd bet the rest of my bourbon he played soccer. Tall, athletic build, strong thighs. Thighs like that don't just happen overnight. His light brown hair fell just so across his forehead in an effortless-but-totally-styled-floppy-hair-look. And those high cheekbones with that square jaw.

Okay, no more alcohol for me tonight.

"Just having a chat with the lovely representative from the New York Legends," Bennet answered. "She was actually the one hiding up here. I found her by accident."

A lopsided grin pulled at the newcomer's lips as he sauntered closer. I'd seen this type of walk before. Too many times to count. This guy fancied himself to be on the prowl. I bit my lip to stifle a laugh.

"Gallagher. Cade Gallagher," he said in his best 007 voice. "Renowned striker for Royal City Athletic. Often imitated, never duplicated." His hazel eyes sparkled with self-satisfaction.

"Did you rehearse all that or was this just a spontaneous eruption of verbal nonsense?" I giggled, unable to reign in my sarcasm.

Bennet turned his head to hide a smile.

"The mouth on you," Cade said with a good natured grin. "I respect that. Brains, wit, and beauty. My three favorite qualities. And you are?"

"Victoria," a sultry, baritone voice revealed my name.

I stilled. Its tone washed over me, quickening my pulse. Taking a deep breath, I glanced to my left. Getting caught up in Xavier's heated blue stare was not something I thought would happen tonight, or ever again for that matter.

Dressed in gray pants and a white button down shirt, he stood with his arms crossed. The sleeves were rolled up to expose his defined forearms. And more tattoos, just like he'd hinted at. He was motionless except for the subtle way his ring-clad thumb stroked his lower lip.

He didn't wear a tie and the shirt remained unbuttoned at the top, but my assumption that he'd look hot in a suit, or some variation of it, was correct. I finished the rest of my bourbon in one swallow and put the empty glass down.

"Nice to see you again," Xavier said with a sly grin.

"Alright, wait a bleeding second," Cade interjected. "How do you—" His eyes widened. "This is the one from the pub, isn't it? The one that got you all hot and bothered."

Bennet draped his arm over Cade's shoulders. "How about you and me go downstairs for a drink." Without waiting for a reply, Bennet guided him to the stairs, where they disappeared down into the crowd.

"You seemed pretty involved in your conversation with those two." He lifted an eyebrow. "Did I miss anything good?"

"Not as good as what just walked into the room." The words tumbled out before I could stop them. Hitting on him wasn't an option.

Or maybe it was.

Yep. It definitely was.

I'd blame it on the bourbon but that was a lame ass cop-out. He was hot and I felt more than a little frisky.

"I see." He slid his hands into his pockets and before I knew it, stood inches away from me.

He smelled so good. Not of cologne or body spray or any of the manufactured crap some men seem to think they need. Just soap, shampoo and *him*. His scent reminded me of the outdoors. Fresh and earthy, like vetiver.

"Shouldn't you be doing the rounds with your friends?" I asked.

"Not necessary."

"Are you a soccer player too?"

"Soccer," he mimicked with a grin. "Yes. I play *football*."

I bit my lip to stifle a laugh at his correction.

He leaned toward me, invading my personal space the way a five star general crosses enemy lines, with precision and a healthy serving of arrogance. I was essentially caged between him and the railing.

It took quite a bit of effort not to slide my fingers up his chest and unbutton the rest of this shirt. Or tear it open and watch all the buttons scatter.

"Did you come here with someone tonight?" he asked.

"Like a date?"

"Yes, like a date."

"No."

"Lucky me." A mischievous smile pulled at his lips. "Guess that means we're on a date now. Or at least picking up where our last date left off."

"Hardly. I'm not so sure you're my type."

"I'm everyone's type."

"I'm not everyone."

Xavier traced his thumb over my mouth. The cool, calming metal of his ring ignited a surge of lust.

"No, you're not."

The way he said it sent shivers through me. I trembled beneath his hungry stare.

"Cold? We can go sit on one of these couches. My lap is available if you'd like to warm up."

I laughed. I couldn't help myself. "I doubt you'd be much of a gentleman if I took you up on that offer."

"Oh I can be quite the gentleman, if that's what you want." Xavier kept his eyes locked on mine. "Is that your type? A gentleman who takes you in his arms, holds you close and keeps you warm. Or do you prefer the one who will do all that, plus pin you to a wall, kiss you hard and make you come with just a few rough strokes of his fingers on your needy little clit?"

His low, dark tone hit all of my hot buttons. Just like it did the other night at the pub. All I could do was stare. Stare at his eyes. His mouth.

God, that mouth.

"That guy. That's the one." I swallowed hard, leaning against the railing for more support.

"We should go find out if he exists." He lowered his lips and brushed them against mine but didn't kiss me. The soft touch ignited my craving for a night of spontaneity and bad decisions. A guy like him could fuck the anxiety and stress out of me, leaving my body sated and ravaged and wanting more all at once.

I pressed my hand to his chest, much like I'd done at the pub. He stilled. Our mouths still hovered dangerously close. I didn't actually want to stop him from kissing me. I think I just wanted to feel his chest again. Feel his heart beating. Feel each breath going in and out of his body. Why did standing with him like this feel so intimate? So invasive? So...*right*?

"Probably not the best idea to find out," I whispered against his lips.

One of his hands moved to cup the back of my neck. I felt his fingers gently scratch up into my hair. My eyelids fluttered at the sensation.

"What's the harm in knowing?" he murmured.

I looked at him. Those vibrant blue eyes devoured me. "I might want to know more."

He bent to kiss me on an exhale. To actually feel his mouth on mine lit me up in a way I didn't expect. His lips were firm and sure, parting to explore me more fully. The satin touch of his tongue didn't demand entrance. It coaxed with soft licks along the seam of my lips. I parted them, allowing it without a second thought. His tongue curled up to stroke my upper lip. He moaned, clearly tasting something he liked.

His fingers moved up through my hair, pulling it gently so my head tilted back, bringing my mouth up slightly. He sealed our mouths together, deepening our kiss. My hand remained on his chest, feeling every heartbeat, every sigh and moan vibrating inside him.

Our heated kiss was brief, leaving me shaky and yearning for more.

I felt his smile as he pulled away. His fervent gaze stayed focused on me. When he licked his lower lip, I almost lost it. He did it the same way as the other night. Slow and sensual, like he was savoring a secret that thrilled him to no end.

"Come here." He tugged my hand, pulling me toward one of the couches. At this point, I probably would have walked on water if he'd suggested it.

He patted the cushion next to him after sitting. I obliged, lowering myself onto the plush couch.

"So, what brings you to this little soiree? This isn't the annoying situation you mentioned the other day, is it?"

"No. This is an unexpected situation to be honest."

He smirked. "And here I thought you were stalking me."

"You think rather highly of yourself, don't you."

"It's been known to happen."

"Of course," I chuckled. "It all makes sense now. The over-confident flirting. The random women throwing themselves at you. I was right about you being a professional athlete." I looked up at him through my lashes and grinned.

"I'm assuming you work for one of these American football teams." He spread his arms over the back of the couch. "What do you do there?"

"You figured that out all on your own?" My sarcasm has zero filter. His eyebrow quirked up and he pinned an intense stare on me. I liked this stare. It looked like he wanted to ravage me. I crossed my legs and continued, "I'm the media relations director for the New York Legends."

"So you spend a lot of time putting up with guys like me."

"I excel at it."

"I don't doubt that." He angled toward me and reclined on his elbow. "Okay, city princess, let me see if I have you figured out yet."

"You think I'm that easy to read?"

He stroked his lip for a second. "You spend all your days around alpha males who happen to be professional athletes. And you love it." He smirked. "You're ambitious and well-educated. I suspect you went to Harvard or Princeton. You have a cozy flat in Manhattan. You're just as comfortable at one of these cocktail parties in your designer outfit as you are at a pub. How am I doing so far?"

I smiled. "That's yet to be determined."

"Ah. Okay, shall I continue?"

"Yes, please."

Apparently those two little words affected him. His pupils dilated and he inhaled a long breath. I made a mental note.

"You definitely break way too many hearts without realizing it. And," his voice lowered, "you want me to kiss you again. How did I do?"

I opened my mouth say something, anything, but nothing came out. Getting him out of my system a couple nights ago was easy since I operated under the impression I'd never see him again. This? This would be a challenge.

"Not bad."

"And the part about me kissing you again?" He looked down for a beat then looked back at me with a grin. "My lap is still available if you need it."

A vivid mental image of sitting in his lap crept into every corner of my mind. I'm not going to lie. Straddling him right now would be amazing. I suddenly wanted to feel his hands on me. Kiss his grin and tear his shirt open and…

I exhaled.

Instead, I replied, "I'm going to have to deny your request."

"A flat out denial?" He let out a low whistle. "Harsh."

"Nah. I'm sure there are plenty of things you'd deny me if given the chance."

"Doubt it," he muttered. "So if this event wasn't the annoying situation that brought you here, what is?"

Even though my lips continued to tingle from our brief, searing kiss, I chose to remain guarded. Flirting with him was one thing. Divulging more than he needed to know was another.

"I don't think it would interest you."

"Try me."

"When's your next soccer game?" I smirked, knowing he'd probably correct me again.

"You're deflecting. Answer my question."

"Maybe I don't want to answer it," I shot back.

"I think you do."

"You would be incorrect."

He moved closer, putting one arm over my shoulders. "Am I? I think you like this little game."

I had to force myself not to melt into him. Everything about him made me dizzy and clouded my judgement.

"And what if I do? Like this game, I mean," I whispered.

Xavier's eyes burned with promises of pleasures beyond my wildest expectations. He leaned forward and captured my lower lip between his teeth, gently nibbling at it while stroking his tongue on it. Then he pinched it hard between his teeth for a brief moment. So brief but so sharp and filled with unexpected pleasure. I gasped. The silkiness of his tongue soothed my lip before he kissed me.

What was it Dawn said about this guy the other night? Oh right. *Watch out for this one. He's a charmer.*

Sorry Dawn. You would also be incorrect. Charm alone would never be enough to dismantle my resistance. What Xavier possessed was a lethal combination of charm and next-level seduction tactics.

And judging by the wicked gleam in his eyes, he knew it.

"My offer is still good," he said with a grin.

"Which one? You've made several."

Instead of answering, he stood up, clasped my hand in his and led me to the spiral staircase. We walked back down to ground level, rejoining the crowd with ease. I smiled at some of the Daniels and Steves, or was it the Richards? Boisterous laughter echoed from a group to our left.

"Maddox." Cade made an *X* over his chest with his arms and shouted, "Royal City unite!"

I glanced up at Xavier in time to catch his mouth lift in an easy, familiar smile that accentuated his dimple. He squeezed my hand, then let it go to join his teammate. Their undeniable bond reminded me of the players back home.

"These two never miss a chance to shine in the spotlight," Bennet said, standing next to me. "Are you in London for a while? I'd love to have you visit the stadium, see the facilities, maybe watch a training session."

"I leave on Wednesday, so I'll have to see when I can squeeze in a field trip. That's generous of you to offer. Thank you."

"I'll have my assistant reach out to you, if that's alright. I'll just need a phone number or email, whichever is easier."

"There are these great little things called business cards." I grinned, reaching in my clutch for one and handing it to Bennet. "They're small but hold a wealth of information."

"Does everyone in the class get one?" Cade rejoined us and draped his arm over my shoulders. "I mean, we're all mates now, so it's only fair."

"You wouldn't know what to do with it, Gallagher," Xavier chimed in.

There was a crackling in the air when I met his icy blue gaze, a sense of anticipation not unlike the loaded silence between a flash of lightning and the boom of thunder. The mischievous grin on his face didn't help. It took all of my willpower not to lunge at him, kiss him senseless and strip him naked.

"I beg to differ." Cade lifted his chin in defiance. "You meeting me on the pitch tomorrow?"

"I'll be there."

"You better be. Your goal tending skills are shit these days."

"How would you know? When's the last time a ball off your foot saw the back of a net?"

"Oh, it's on pretty boy." Cade threw a couple fake punches against his teammate's chest. "C'mon. Time to hit the clubs."

"I'll pass, thanks."

Bennet lifted his hands in mock retreat and shook his head. "You're on your own. But I better not see any headlines when I wake up in the morning."

"You lot have such little faith in me." Cade turned in my direction. "Lovely meeting you. Don't do anything I wouldn't do with this one." The self-proclaimed renowned striker pointed at Xavier and left with a flourish.

"That guy is a living, breathing TMZ headline." Bennet shook his head.

"Aren't we all," Xavier muttered.

The dynamic between the three of them reminded me of siblings. Bennet definitely filled the role of the responsible, well-mannered older brother. He had the same air of mischief as the other two but it was subtle, understated. Cade was a massive goofball. And Xavier? He balanced the two out. Just as well-mannered and posh as Bennet but quick witted and ready for mischief at a moment's notice, like Cade.

There's no way I'll be able to resist him, I thought.

Bennet said his goodbyes and promised to reach out about touring the facility.

"And then there were two." Xavier reached for my hand. "What should we do now?"

"You were full of ideas when we were upstairs."

"I've already made my feelings known about what I'd like to do to you in public." His tone was low and tempting. "Would you like a more in depth demonstration in front of all these people?"

The heat radiating off him enveloped me. I *would* like a demonstration, actually. I'd like one right now. My entire body broke out in violent goosebumps.

"You know," I said, trying like hell to keep my voice steady, "I have this policy back home about dating professional athletes."

"Oh this I have to hear." A wicked smile lit up his face.

"I make it a point not to get into relationships with them. Or fuck them. Sleeping with the product is off limits."

"The product," he mimicked me again. "You make us sound like prepackaged snacks."

"Well, some of you *are* filled with empty calories."

His burst of laughter drew more than a few curious glances in our direction.

"You really want me to believe you'd prefer," he gestured around us, "this? Some dull businessman who likes it missionary and on a schedule?" He scrubbed his face with his hands and ran them through his hair.

"I'm not talking about this here."

Xavier wasn't having any more of my attempts at playing coy. Leveling a heated stare at me, he laced his fingers through mine and guided me toward the exit. Cool air washed over my exposed skin the second we walked outside, providing some relief to the scorching atmosphere I'd been subjected to on planet Maddox.

Seeing as I wasn't paying close attention to what I was doing, I bumped into someone standing on the sidewalk.

I turned to apologize. The man's chagrined expression dissipated within seconds of looking at me. His mouth fell open in shock. I'd never seen this person before in my life but he looked at me like he'd just seen a ghost. Then he noticed Xavier and all the color drained from his face. He muttered an apology and hurried off.

Chapter
FIVE

"This way." Xavier's insistent tone brought me back to the present. We walked toward a parking garage but all I could think about was the weird interaction.

That guy looked at me like he knew me. But it's not possible. I'd never seen him before in my—

Charlotte.

A cold sense of dread gripped me, taking hold of my body. Memories from the summer when we were sixteen bubbled up no matter how hard I tried to keep them locked away.

A humid August night.

Our final weekend in England before school started.

A bonfire.

Me, insisting Charlotte come to the party.

Her, adamant she'd rather stay at home.

"It's not a good idea, Tori. Mom and Dad already said no. We're too young."

"Honestly Charlie, you're never going to actually experience life if you only play by the rules. It'll be fun. We won't stay late. I promise to be by your side the whole time."

Guilt consumed me. I didn't mean to break my promise. I'd meant what I'd said. But I was young and stupid and reckless and…

"Victoria, are you alright?" The deep, soft timbre of Xavier's voice broke through my unpleasant trip down memory lane.

My present day surroundings came into sharp focus. A black Land Rover. A concrete floor. The smell of gasoline and rubber and exhaust.

"I'm fine. Everything's fine." I avoided looking at him because I knew he'd see right through my weak response. He'd had that effect on me from the start.

"Are you expecting me to believe that?"

The sobering nature of his question snapped me out of my haze.

"I'm just," I scrambled to come up with words. "Tired. It's been a long week. I have a lot on my plate for Monday. You know, just work stuff."

"You're good at deflecting. Try again."

"Says the well-rehearsed pro-athlete who knows the right things to say in any situation," I snapped.

"I could talk in circles with you like this for hours. But I'd rather you be honest with me."

His hands glided up and down my arms. An unrelenting pull consumed me. I knew what the risks were. I knew what would happen if I let him in. But I didn't have to let him in. I could do what I always did. Give him my body, take from his, and enjoy the pleasure.

Having a one night stand wouldn't be *that* bad, would it? I mean, look at this guy.

He kept touching me. Stroking my arms. My shoulders. It felt so good. Soothing. I wondered what his hands would feel like on my… No. Nope. Not going there.

I looked up. His fingers sifted through my hair, gently scratching along my scalp. Slow, sensual movements. My eyelids fluttered.

The smart, responsible thing to do would be to go back to the rental house. The boys were staying the night in Scotland, so I'd be alone.

Alone with my thoughts.

Alone with my guilt.

Fuck that.

"This feels good. What you're doing with my hair. Thank you."

"My pleasure. You're still not going to tell me are you?"

I sighed, frustrated. "It's a family thing. That's all you're getting."

A smile pulled at his lips. "Wasn't so difficult now was it?" he teased.

"Don't be cute."

"Is it against your policy to come back to my flat so we're not inhaling fumes while I do this?" He gently fisted my hair.

"I've never encountered this scenario before. I suppose I'll allow it."

Ten minutes later, we walked through the front door of his townhouse. It was quiet. Dimly lit. My heart pounded watching him. The way he moved with such fluidity hypnotized me as I followed him.

"Can I get you something to drink?" he asked, heading toward a sideboard covered in bottles and glasses.

"Sure. Whatever you're having is fine with me."

I glanced around his living room. One hundred percent bachelor pad but stylish. Large windows framed breathtaking views of London. Two large couches sat in the middle of the room. A chair and ottoman were positioned near the fireplace. I smiled to myself, picturing him sitting there at night. A huge bifold door led out to what I assumed was a patio.

I turned in a slow circle and faced a bookshelf where several medals and awards were displayed. I stood closer to admire them.

League Champions.

Man of the Match.

Player of the Month.

"Obnoxious, isn't it. All those medals."

I turned to see him grinning and offering me a glass. I smiled and thanked him.

"Not too obnoxious," I said, taking a sip. "You should see all the rings I have thanks to my team's championships."

"Those big, gaudy things?" He wrinkled his nose in mock disgust. "Wouldn't even wear them."

I swallowed the rest of the bourbon, put the glass down, and glanced at his hand. "Yours are nice."

"Just decoration." He smiled. "Would you like another?"

Yes.

"I shouldn't. I had a few too many at the event and I don't want you to think I can't hold my liquor. Plus, I should, you know, keep my wits about me while I'm here with you." My voice trailed off at the end while I studied every inch of him. I noticed the subtle way he positioned his body to fill my entire line of sight. Not that I wanted to look at anything else.

"I am a gentleman, you know." His low, sexy tone returned.

Something in his expression dared me to fire off a sarcastic response. I had a better idea.

"And what if I'm not a refined lady? What if, underneath my fancy Ivy League education, designer clothes, and successful career is just some horny girl who wants to know if the gentleman you described earlier actually exists."

The change in his demeanor was immediate, like I'd flipped a forbidden switch in him. His warm, casual smile dissolved into a curve of hungry desire. I put my hands on his chest and looked up into his eyes. A burst of icy sapphire surrounded the dark pools of his pupils.

"I thought you said—"

"I know what I said."

Screw my policy. Screw the rules. I wanted him. I wanted to stop denying myself something that would bring me pleasure beyond my imagination. And it would make me forget the real reason I had to come to England.

There's little hesitation when his mouth brushed over mine. His determined lips knew what they wanted. He flicked his tongue along the top of my lower lip, no doubt tasting the bourbon and recalling the quick bite he'd left there. A small, ragged sigh shuddered through him.

Then he fisted his hand into my hair, pulling it almost to the point of pain. He angled my head where he wanted it, his tongue invading my mouth fully. This is what I craved. This is what I needed. Aggressive. Rough. Untamed.

My back hit a wall within seconds. He pulled my skirt up and lifted me so I could wrap my legs around his waist.

I wanted to drown forever in this kiss. Taking his wild passion, giving him what he needs, losing myself in the sensation of his muscular body pressed to mine.

He broke his mouth away, slipped his hand between us and pulled my panties aside. "I've pictured this moment since running into you the other night."

"Was this the outcome you hoped for?" I arched against the wall, anticipating his touch.

That damn dimple appeared when a salacious grin curled his mouth. "One of them."

My body shook when he spread my folds open and dipped his fingers inside me, curling them to hit just the right spot. I sighed as he steadily plunged them in and out. My hips moved subtly to match his rhythm. A look of absolute ecstasy washed across his face.

"I can't wait to taste you." He withdrew his fingers and painted my lips with my own desire for him. Then he licked across them slowly and deliberately. On a groan, he molded his mouth to mine, kissing me like he'd been waiting for this moment for a long time. Like it was meant for him. Fated.

Returning his hand between my legs, he pulled his mouth away and whispered, "I won't be able to deny you anything."

The way he looked at me made my heart pound.

Xavier lowered my legs so I could stand. "Don't move." His eyes trailed up and down my body while he unbuttoned his shirt. I let out an audible gasp when he dropped it to the floor.

Yes, he was muscular. But not in the bulky way some pro-athletes are. He was lean, sculpted, powerful.

I simply stared at him. At the corrugated lines of his stomach. The expanse of his chest. How his throat worked when he swallowed. Every tendon and muscle in him braced for what was surely to come next.

And his tattoos. I sucked in a breath. They covered his upper torso from shoulder to shoulder. Some even snaked down his arms.

I placed both hands on his chest, my fingers following every curve, every detail.

He shivered at my touch. "Victoria. Are you sure you want this?"

I nodded.

"I need to hear you say it." The blue in his eyes burned like flames. Complete combustion.

"I want this." I scratched my nails down his chest. "I want you."

His mouth devoured mine again. This kiss was filled with an urgent, raw passion I'd never felt before. I matched his intensity, willing to give as much as I'd take.

We tore the rest of our clothes off without much ceremony. There was no time for sensual and slow. This was hot and greedy and breathless, almost desperate.

Xavier paused, his hand gripping my upper thigh. I felt his hard length pressed against me. I weaved my fingers through his hair, noting how soft and thick it was.

Then I heard foil tearing and looked down. He rolled the condom on with skilled quickness and lifted me so I could wrap my legs around him again.

"One more thing," I purred. "I like it rough."

His eyes shot to mine. I nodded.

"How rough?" he inquired in a forbidden tone.

"I'll tell you if it's not enough."

"You are so much more than I expected," he growled, pushing himself into me without warning.

The pleasure was so sharp I strained against him as he held me firm to the wall. He was not gentle. He was also not small. I didn't have much time to adjust to his size and quite frankly, I did not care. My entire body smacked hard against the wall every time he thrust into me. The pleasure and pain ignited a desire that dwelled deep inside me.

I tightened my legs around his waist, digging my nails into his shoulders. He was holding back for some reason. I could feel it.

"Harder," I whispered into his ear. "I need more."

Xavier groaned, gripping my backside with such force I yelped. His fingers dug into my flesh, holding me immobile while he speared his cock deep inside me without mercy, filling me deeper and faster.

Hot desire prickled over my skin. This was perfect, perfect, perfect. The beginnings of my climax twisted and knotted in my belly. My eyelids fluttered as the growing sensation spread.

"Look at me." He grit out the command.

The second I obliged, an animalistic groan rumbled through his chest. I'd never seen or felt anything so *masculine*. My body became a live wire, consumed by energy and vibration.

A faint moan escaped my lips while I watched him. What looked like a type of carnal need etched into his face. A longing that couldn't be sated no matter how hard he tried.

My orgasm hit me hard, scrambling my thoughts and seizing my body in a series of pulsing waves. He rode through it, feverishly taking every last ounce of my pleasure. A desperate sound escaped his lips, fierce and possessive. His entire body tensed. With a shudder and several final deep, hard strokes, Xavier tumbled over the edge with me.

Even though he'd finished, he was still hard inside me, his body still taut with lust. Hot, open-mouthed kisses covered my shoulders and neck. When he found my mouth, he plunged his tongue in.

Claiming. Tasting. Owning.

I shoved my hands in his hair and pulled his head back. His lips remained parted. His eyes wild with hunger.

"Again, Xavier." My voice was low and husky, almost unfamiliar to me. "Fuck me again. This is all I could think about after seeing you the other night."

The slow, deliberate way he dragged his tongue over his lower lip restarted my waning orgasm. Whatever secret he kept that thrilled him to no end reflected in his eyes. He pulled out slowly, teasing my sensitive flesh.

"Don't move." His gaze fell to my lips and his eyelids hooded when he stepped away.

I closed my eyes. My head thudded against the wall. I could hear him moving through the room. When I felt him in front of me again I opened my eyes to see him rolling on another condom.

"Tell me what you couldn't stop thinking about." He hooked my legs around his waist and pushed himself inside me.

"You," I breathed. "What you said about fucking me in public. How your…when your hand was on me. Your voice. Your face. Your eyes. They were so dark, like you wanted to take me right then and there."

He pulled out almost all the way, then rocked his hips forward, slowly filling me to the hilt. The sensation was killing me. The slow torture of pleasure. The measured control. On a moan, I clenched around his length.

"Are you leaving something out?"

I nodded.

"Tell me," he ordered.

"That…that night was the first time I got myself off thinking about you."

A dangerous, filthy smile tugged at his mouth. "You touched yourself thinking about me?"

"More than once. I didn't think I'd ever see you again. But I just… you're…"

"Did you touch yourself today? Before coming to London?"

I only nodded. I couldn't speak. His slow, torturous movements were too much.

"How many times did you make yourself come today?"

"Two."

"That's not enough," he murmured, grinding his hips into me. "Did you fantasize about seeing me again?"

"Yes."

He licked along my bottom lip before biting down on it. I went slack in his arms from the pleasure.

"Were you wet when you saw me at the event? Did you want my cock inside you in front of all those people?"

My lips parted on a silent moan.

"I've been thinking about you since I saw you on the side of the road," he rasped. "Do you have any idea how hard I was at Black Rose? I had to take the edge off as soon as I got home. Fuck. I wanted to be inside you that night."

The slow, methodical thrusts created a friction on my clit so consuming I nearly saw stars.

"Xavier." I could barely speak.

"Do you want more?" he asked.

"Yes."

His eyes flashed. "Should I go easier on you this time, dirty princess?" His voice was deeper and rougher. The sound made my arousal pool at my core.

"No," I barely whispered. "I like you untamed."

Bending his head to my ear, he growled, "You haven't seen me untamed yet." Then he thrust into me so hard and fast and deep I yelled.

"Fuck," he hissed. "This will be quick, Victoria."

He moved one hand between my legs, savagely rubbing my clit. It matched the wild intensity of his thrusts, bringing me within seconds of climaxing.

I never orgasm this fast. Never.

Not even when I'm using my own hand or toys. My second orgasm hit with the same ferocity as the first.

I cried out, scratching down his back, gasping for breath.

The involuntary grunt he expelled along with his rough breathing signaled we'd come at the same time. That's a first for me.

His sides heaved like he'd just finished running a race. Closing my eyes, I leaned my head back. His body shivered against mine on a shaky inhale as he pulled out.

"You're bloody dangerous," he declared.

"And you're addictive," I countered, looking at him.

"Perfect combination." He carefully lowered my legs to the floor. To say they were wobbly would be a gross misrepresentation. I'd had decent lovers before. But this? Him? We're talking next level.

"Feels like you marked up my back pretty good."

"What?" I panted. "Oh. Well, I mean…you…did I hurt you?"

A low, satisfied chuckle spread through his chest. "No."

His lips brushed over mine in a lush, soft kiss. When he pulled away, he held my arms, keeping me secured against the wall. My damn legs kept shaking.

"Can you walk?"

"The cheek on this one."

His serious expression almost made me regret my flippant remark. "I'm not letting you go until I know you can stand and walk."

"I can," I responded, sounding a bit more breathless than I expected. "I'm good."

Backing away as though to study his handiwork, he grinned. "Fucking gorgeous."

"Pretty sure my mascara is smudged to high hell but I'll take the compliment."

"It's not." He extended his hand. "Come with me. I need to get you cleaned up."

I gladly placed my hand in his and followed him to the bedroom. No lights were on so I could only see his face in shadows. Somehow, it was even more stunning.

He got me settled on the bed and went into the bathroom to dispose of the condom. When he rejoined me, he handed me a warm washcloth, waited for me to clean myself, and tossed it in the hamper.

Then he finally climbed in next to me. I nestled into him with my back against his chest, laying on my side. His legs tangled with mine, one arm draped over my hip. He nuzzled into my neck, nibbling at the skin. Nothing but comfort flowed through me. For at least this moment in time, I felt relaxed and whole.

His fingers traced down the side of my ribcage. I closed my eyes, hoping he wouldn't ask about the tattoo he'd no doubt already seen. He kissed it softly and let his lips linger for longer than I would have expected.

"What does this mean?"

Shit.

This was neither the time nor place for oversharing.

I shrugged. "I just liked it."

"I like mine, too, but I know what each of them means."

I swallowed. "Twin phoenix feathers made of flames. I got it when I was eighteen. It's…personal."

That seemed to satisfy him for the time being. His fingers continued caressing my skin while his mouth left warm kisses along my shoulder.

"You broke your policy for me."

I rolled over to face him, meeting his blue stare. "Looks like I did."

"How long are you here for?"

"I told you already. I leave Wednesday."

He gave me a funny look. "I'd remember that piece of vital information. You didn't say it to me."

My post-sex brain went into overdrive. I told someone. I must have. I remembered saying it earlier tonight when…

"Oh. I mentioned it to Bennet."

"Hmm." He cupped his hand over my backside. It was still sore from all his grabbing. "Confusing me with my friends? I see how it is."

"Honest mistake."

He combed his fingers through my hair, gently scratching against the scalp.

I laughed softly. "This was supposed to be why you invited me here."

"It still is."

We remained silent for a long moment. At some point I knew I had to leave but I wanted to savor this just a bit longer.

"Xavier?"

"Yes."

"I'm glad I bumped into you tonight." My eyelids became quite heavy. All the bourbon and sex finally caught up with me. "But I should probably go before I fall asleep," I mumbled.

The massaging stopped for a second. But only a second. "You don't have to go," he said quietly.

I snuggled closer to him. Five more minutes and then I'll leave. Just five minutes…

His fingers continued their slow massage through my hair.

"Feels so good." I think I said that out loud.

I woke up wrapped in Xavier's arms. The first slivers of daylight brightened the room. I squinted. He didn't have any curtains or blinds on his windows. Not wanting to wake him, I carefully disentangled myself from his embrace and got out of bed. I took one last long look at him before hunting for my clothes and redressing.

Leaving without telling him felt wrong.

But this was only a one night stand.
One night to distract myself.
It had to be.

Chapter
SIX

"**R**eady to get your ass whipped, Maddox?" Cade spun the ball in his hands before placing it on the penalty marker.

"Not in this lifetime, Gallagher." I grinned, throwing my hands up, making myself as tall and long as possible.

Cade stilled his body, letting his shoulders relax. He breathed in deep, looking just past my left shoulder. To an untrained eye, it appeared he'd kick in that direction. But I knew better. Cade's stance, while static, gave away his secrets. The way his hips tilted slightly to his left revealed that he'd kick the ball so it curved to my right.

It flew off the side of his foot with a thud, carrying small blades of grass through the air. I lunged to my right, punching it away with ease.

"Like I said, not in this lifetime. Let's go again."

Cade loved a challenge as much as I did. And holy shit, did he have a leg. Each time I punched away the ball or caught it, the velocity vibrated through my hands. He knew my weaknesses as well as I knew his, so a few balls did find the back of the net. Gallagher was talented and savvy enough to know that if he kicked it just a fraction of an inch above the span of my arms, he'd score every time.

"Hey."

We both looked to the sideline and saw one of the second team defenders, Adam Bourne, walking toward us.

Fuck me.

I scowled.

"Little brother on approach," Cade snickered. "Wasn't expecting it to be a family affair today."

"*Step*-brother," I growled. Why he'd shown up here was a mystery to me. He was, in all ways possible, a first rate twat.

"What's up, Adam?" Cade sauntered over to him.

I followed, grabbing my water bottle for a quick drink.

"Just saw you both out here. Wondering why Xavier is in goal, though."

"We're having a quick training session for when he returns. Nothing more."

Adam folded his arms across his chest, his pointed stare in my direction made my blood start to boil.

"You really think your suspension will be finished next week," he sneered. "My money's on you serving at least two more before the championship matches start."

"You really want to do this, Adam?" I asked, spreading my arms out.

"What are you gonna do? Sucker punch me like you did to Simmons? Or maybe Donovan? That bullshit doesn't belong on this pitch. Or did you forget that already?"

We were just about standing nose to nose at this point. I could flatten him in seconds if pushed that far. And I would love to do it.

"Hey, hey, whoa." Cade ran between us, separating us as best he could. "The fuck is wrong with you Adam? Back off."

Neither one of us moved. It would be a cold day in hell before

I backed down first, so I held my stance, glaring at my step-brother. Growing up with him was one thing. Having him as a teammate tested my limits daily. Wild energy coursed through my veins. It simmered just below the surface, ready to swallow me whole.

"You're nothing but a hot-tempered prima donna," he bit out. "Dad's right. You haven't changed one bit since that summer."

I swung at him without a second thought, bracing for the all too familiar feeling of flesh and bone colliding. Instead, I stumbled back a couple feet, restrained by Cade's muscular grip. He'd somehow managed to prevent my fist from connecting with the prick's face.

"Hey," he said quietly. "Let it go, mate. He's not worth it."

We exchanged the same look of knowing. Knowing what happened all those summers ago when Adam and I were always at each other's throats at youth football. The fights. The taunts. The scuffling. His jealousy over Cade and I being chosen for something he wanted never subsided.

His misfortune of getting wrapped up with the wrong people. My misguided loyalty to keep him out of trouble. And then that one night. That one fucking night.

I sucked in a breath, pushing against Cade's grip.

"Not worth it," my friend repeated. "Please."

His pleading was the only thing stopping me. I glared at Adam from behind Cade's shoulder.

"Watch that smart ass look, Xavier," Adam taunted from a safe distance.

"Or what?" I yelled, the muscles in my jaw twitching.

"Enough." Cade spun around and stood toe-to-toe with Adam. "Take your fucking face somewhere else or I'll be more than happy to provide the service for you."

Shooting one last indignant glance in my direction, Adam stormed off. I swore under my breath, grabbing my gym bag.

"Let's call it a day, yeah?" Cade asked.

I looked at my friend and pushed out a sigh.

"Yeah. Enough for today."

"Want to go downtown for a pint?"

The last place I wanted to be was London. "Let's go to Black Rose instead. I'd rather not be in the city."

Cade looked at me like he sometimes does when he can't figure me out. Our friendship has been like this since we were twelve. I'd make an off-handed, cryptic remark. He'd stare like I'd presented him with hieroglyphics. I often wondered what it was about me that both fascinated and confounded him.

"Black Rose it is," he replied. "My treat. See you there in a hour?"

"Yeah, sure," I muttered, making my way to the car park.

⁂

"You alright?" Cade asked, fidgeting with his empty beer glass. "You've seemed on edge all afternoon, even before that arse show up."

"I'll live."

"No offense, mate, but your brother can be a real prick. Everyone knows it. I'm glad you're back in goal next week. Hasn't been the same without the greatest keeper to ever wear the RCA kit."

"Again with the accolades." I smirked. "Flattery will get you nowhere."

"That's not what you said to me earlier," Dawn said in a sing-song voice, flashing one of her megawatt smiles. "You boys need a refill?"

"Dawn, you always know what we need. Marry us?" Cade grabbed her hand, kissing it dramatically. "Ray won't mind."

"The hell he won't." Ray Halston appeared beside his wife, a good-natured smile touching his lips. "You two are nothing but trouble."

"The good kind, Ray. The good kind." Cade laughed. All we needed to complete our little group was Bennet. A roar erupted from the other side of the bar.

"Looks like United just notched another win." Ray chuckled and leaned against the counter.

"Our match with them is going to be cracking," Cade exclaimed, standing up. "Next round's on me."

Another loud cheer filled the pub. Cade was notorious for being a crowd pleaser. Of course, that meant we'd be surrounded in no time.

And we were.

I drank in the attention, like I always do. So did Cade. We bantered with the fans, shared a few stories and posed for photos. This lot was much more amicable than the drunk arse from the other night.

"I always seem to miss all the big fun." Bennet sauntered over as the crowd dispersed. His casual sarcasm made Cade and I laugh.

"Maybe if you showed up on time, mate," Cade teased.

Bennet rolled his eyes and sat with us. "I've been caught up all day with my sister and the girls. Much more enjoyable than you."

"Good old Uncle Benny." Cade jumped up, ruffled Bennet's hair and draped his arms around him. "How *do* you make it look so easy?"

I thought Bennet was going to throw Cade into next Thursday. The look on his face was pure exasperation. I stifled a laugh and took a long swallow of beer.

"Leave the man alone," I scolded.

"You," Cade pointed at me and returned to his seat, "still haven't spilled what happened last night with the hot American."

I gripped the glass tighter, shooting him a dirty look.

Bennet glanced at me curiously. "The one from the Legends?"

"Ah. My third prince has arrived." Dawn flashed a warm, wide grin. "You all look like kings on your thrones."

Thank fuck she interrupted at just the right moment. The absolute last thing I planned to do was tell these two about Victoria. Just thinking about her was enough to do me in.

The part of me I'd been ignoring all day muscled its way to the forefront of my consciousness. Allowing myself to drown in thoughts of what we'd done last night wasn't just dangerous, it was fatal. Some deep, unknown part of me longed for her in ways I'd never imagined possible.

She was gone by the time I woke up this morning. No trace of her remained in my London flat, except for the faint smell of her perfume on my pillow. She didn't even leave her number. Shouldn't surprise me though. No follow up contact was one of my preferred traits of a one night stand.

And that's what I'd wanted, right? Only one night with her. One night to see how much I could take.

Boy was I wrong.

"Xavier." Dawn's voice snapped me back to the present. "What can I get you, love?"

"Do you have gorgeous, redheaded Americans on the menu?" Cade asked, looking pointedly at me. "He seems to be quite interested in those these days."

The murderous stare I aimed at him did not go unnoticed by Bennet or Dawn. Now it was my turn to fantasize about throwing him into next week.

"Watch yourself, Gallagher," I warned.

He just laughed in his Cade way. Dismissive. Unaffected. Almost as if to say *lighten up, you tosser.*

"You must be speaking about Victoria." Dawn smiled. "I saw you two flirting the other night. She's a firecracker, that one."

All three of us looked at her. She saw our expressions and chuckled.

"I've known her and her family for a long time. They used to come here while on holiday in the summer months." Sadness swept across her features. "Not anymore though. Pity." She sighed and appeared to collect herself so as not to reveal anything further. "Come let me know what you want to eat when you're ready."

I took another long swallow of beer and watched her walk away. Didn't really feel like eating anything anyway.

Bennet and Cade bickered back and forth about the match on now. Both clubs were in the bottom three. I couldn't be bothered caring about relegation or goal differentials right now. Not when every piece of me wanted something I couldn't have.

A dormant part of me had stirred the second I pulled off the road to see if she was having car trouble. It grew restless while we flirted at the pub. Her whispered demands of *more* and *harder* woke it the fuck up last night. I'd buried that part for a reason. I promised myself it would stay buried.

But then Victoria happened with her soft beauty and melodic laughter and sexy, dirty confessions. I wanted to hear all of them. I wanted to know all of her. And not just in the carnal, physical way.

I wanted to know her thoughts on random, everyday shit. How she took her tea. If she even drank tea. Probably a coffee person. If she curled up on her couch at night to binge Netflix shows. What —if anything— I had to do to impress her.

Things I couldn't easily learn from an internet search, which I have yet to do, thank you very much.

I flexed my hand. I wanted to hear her laugh. It was so pleasant and bright.

This is crazy. I'll never see her again. Last night was it.

"You're awfully quiet, mate." Cade's booming voice cut through the thoughts that slowly wrecked me.

I sighed, leaning back in the chair. "Sorry."

"No worries. Want some chips?"

"No thanks."

Bennet placed his hand on my shoulder and squeezed, a look of concern on his face. "Did something happen?"

"Other than his brother being a twat? No." Cade scowled before taking a drink. "This match is lame. Another round or should I settle up?"

I knew what Bennet meant though. It had nothing to do with football or arguments.

He checked his watch. "Settle up." He turned to me after Cade walked away. "Everything okay?"

I shrugged.

"That's not an answer. Tell me what's going on."

I almost did. I almost spilled what happened with Victoria. Almost. But that would lead to more questions.

"Nothing," I sighed, rubbing my thumb along my lip. "Same shit, different day, you know?"

"I know. And I worry, Xavier."

I bristled at his tone. "And I've told you that's not necessary."

We stared intently at one another, each trying to convince the other of something.

"Hey, you two look like you're about to fuck or fight. Which is it?" Cade sat down, folded his arms and stared at us.

"Neither," I muttered as Bennet relaxed his grip and sat back.

Cade eyed both of us. "The mood got really bloody tense. One of you needs to tell me why."

Bennet quirked an eyebrow in his posh, matter-of-fact way. Everything about him was so damn prim and proper.

"Nobody *needs* to tell anybody anything, Gallagher." Bennet's tone sharpened.

"Fine. Whatever," Cade grumbled. "You going to be at the old estate tonight Bennet? I know it's Sunday but I figured we could hang in our spot. Have a whisky or four."

Bennet's fingers tapped on his glass. "Well, I live there you muppet so yeah." He turned to me. "You plan on coming?"

Tempting. "Think I'm gonna stay here, mate. Not really feeling London tonight. Reckon I should use my house more than the flat."

"The infamous Maddox stag pad." Cade rose from his seat, knocking back the rest of his beer. "The stories that place could tell."

Bennet and I followed him out into the cool late afternoon breeze and said our goodbyes. They finalized their plans for later this evening.

Both told me to text them if I changed my mind. Pretty sure I wouldn't but stranger things have happened.

My phone vibrated the second I climbed into my car. "Cade," I muttered, looking at his text.

Cade: You really should come. Been a while since we've all been there together.

I scrubbed my face with my hands and ran them through my hair. Normally I'd just go. But for some reason I didn't feel like it this time.

Yes, *for some reason.*

A reason with silky smooth skin and soft auburn hair. A reason that smells like winter but tastes like spring. I gripped the steering wheel and started to drive.

I can't have her.

The thought made me flinch.

Maybe I should go down to London. Move on to the next one. There's always someone willing and able. I am Xavier Fucking Maddox after all.

Shit. I don't want to be that guy anymore.

I was almost home. Almost.

Don't give in, don't turn around, don't be that guy, I chanted to myself. After a couple minutes I felt a little better.

A flurry of activity in front of one of the houses on my street caught my attention. Several cars were parked near it, which struck me as odd. This particular home had been empty since I'd moved here nearly ten years ago. Every so often I'd see gardeners tidying up the lawn or clearing out the brush from all the rose bushes but that was it.

I slowed down and pulled over, wondering if whoever owned it finally put it up for sale. It's a really nice house. The kind those Hollywood types would scoop up for some Christmas-themed rom-com. The whole village could be in a movie with its little cobblestone streets and cozy shops and English charm. I laughed at myself. I always appreciated architecture but a location scout, I was not.

A man and woman engaged in a tense discussion by the front door. Out of the corner of my eye I noticed someone exit one of the cars. She stormed over toward them carrying a large envelope.

My heart stilled.

Victoria had piled her hair up in a loose bun, exposing the delicate skin of her neck. Gone was the sexy cream-colored outfit from last night's event. Instead, she wore jeans and a loose-fitting top. It was just as sexy and made my cock just as hard.

I ran my hand through my hair, debating whether or not to get out. The conversation between them appeared heated.

"Fuck it," I muttered, exiting my car.

The sound of Victoria's distressed voice carried across the yard.

"This is not happening," she proclaimed. "I can't make it any clearer. I have all the necessary paperwork from my attorney plus a full payment ready for transfer. We're done here."

"Your mother already—"

"My mother has no say in what I do anymore," she yelled. "I'm paying double what you were offered. It's done."

"That's the dumbest thing I ever heard," the man standing in front of the door exclaimed. "This offer was agreed to before you even got off the plane. Helena made it clear she'd be sending someone to finalize everything and sign the paperwork to close it out."

"Ms. Chase, please," the woman said in a soft, even tone. "I realize this is hard for you and the fam—"

"I'm not signing anything that originated with my mother or her lawyer. If you want to close on this house," she lifted the envelop, "this is the only deal you're being offered."

I paused at the edge of the lawn. Her voice was tinted with real pain. I didn't like hearing her so upset. I wanted to make it better for her in some way. Seeing her this agitated sparked a deep, non-negotiable urge to protect her. Fiercely protect her. My hands balled into fists.

"Hey, what's going on here," I demanded, stalking over to them.

When Victoria turned I had the same reaction I always did. Her beauty was strong enough to knock me down. So was the look of utter shock consuming her gorgeous features.

"This doesn't concern—" The man glanced at me with a haughty attitude before he recognized me. "You're Xavier Maddox."

"This isn't the time or place for that bullshit, mate," I growled. "I'll ask one more time. What's going on here."

This idiot practically fell over himself walking toward me. "You don't understand. I'm B-Ben Arrington," he stammered, "from Building As One. Your club has done a lot of work with us—"

"Still doesn't answer my question." I crossed my arms, staring down at him.

"We're purchasing this cottage to renovate it."

"Sounds like the lady here doesn't want that to happen."

Ben regained some of his composure. "I understand but it's not hers. It belongs to her parents." He shot Victoria a petulant look that made me want to rearrange his entire body. "They've already accepted the offer. We just need—"

"Yeah, I heard all of it from the street," I retorted, ignoring Victoria's open-mouthed stare. "Has any money actually exchanged hands between you and her family. Any promissory notes?"

"No."

"I'm no expert but it sounds like there's no actual sale yet."

"Mr. Maddox, we appreciate your interest," the woman interjected, "but this is a private matter."

"And you are?" I inquired.

"Natalie Moran. I'm the realtor."

"Perfect. What's the asking price?"

Chapter
SEVEN

Reality was an illusion.

Reality didn't exist.

Reality was meant for anyone else but me.

I lived in a perpetual state of disenchantment. Sure, I functioned like a normal adult. I went to work. Went out with friends. Went on dates. To the outside world, I was normal. Or at least whatever definition of that word fit the situation.

Yet here I stood, on the front lawn of my family's neglected home in England, feeling anything but normal and living in the complete opposite realm of what others considered reality.

The man I'd had a mind-blowing one night stand with was locked in a heated discussion over buying Briarcliff Cottage. Not only were worlds colliding, various versions of my existence and sensibilities were also on a collision course.

This wasn't going to happen.

I couldn't let this happen.

"Enough," I croaked, my voice unwilling to cooperate. I swallowed, took a deep breath and tried again. "Enough. All of you. Enough."

Three sets of eyes settled on me. Only the clear blue ones mattered. They examined me with guarded curiosity, seeing more of me than I deemed comfortable. Those eyes pierced me to my core, stripping away all the barricades I'd crafted with care. Those eyes would unravel me. That man would be my undoing.

"Ms. Chase, this is becoming tiresome," Ben expressed, glancing at his watch. "I've come here on a Sunday for what? Utter nonsense?"

"Do not speak to her like that," Xavier threatened in his low, sultry timbre. Anger and elegance all rolled into one.

"I'm sorry you both had to come out here for nothing," I said as calmly as possible. "I realize this isn't typical and seeing as my family dropped this in my lap without much thought, it's also become a huge waste of everyone's time and effort. I'm not accepting the offer. I'm not signing any agreement. There's nothing more to say."

Ben departed in a huff, muttering to himself. Natalie turned to me, placing a sympathetic hand on my arm.

"If you change your mind or if anything comes up, please call."

As if on cue, light rain started to fall as she walked back to her car. I made no effort to move. This whole trip has been one colossal clusterfuck. Getting caught in the rain felt like the perfect ending.

Xavier took my hand without saying a word and led me to the house. The front door was unlocked. Next thing I knew, we were inside. He shut the door with a hollow click and stood in front of me.

"Fuck," I murmured, leaning my head back. "I don't want to be in here."

"We'll just wait until the rain passes."

He sounded so unaffected, so unbothered. Like any normal person would be. This was the most natural thing in the world. We needed to get out of the rain. He didn't know what this place was or why it rips me to shreds from the inside out.

Sheets of rain pummeled the windows in waves, its rhythm reminiscent of the tide teasing the shoreline. The wind joined with gleeful gusts. It slammed the rain against the house harder, almost saying *you can't leave yet, I have plans for you.*

I looked at Xavier. Big mistake. He gazed at me with the whole world in his eyes. The sight of him filled me, soothing every broken part I kept hidden.

"Why are you here?" I asked, sitting on the staircase.

"I could ask you the same question."

"Pretty sure you can figure that one out on your own."

He nodded. "I live just up the road."

I wet my lips, dropped the envelope and rubbed my temples. "Of course you do."

He remained expressionless as he lowered himself next to me. His close proximity set off a chain reaction I should have expected.

Scent carried the most memory triggers, and in this moment, with him so close, with his scent invading this space, all I could think about was last night and how he felt and sounded. I'd been around him for what, a total of twelve hours combined? Maybe more? My math could be off.

Didn't matter. He smelled so good. I welcomed every image, every recollection of how he touched me, how he kissed me, how he made me feel.

"I'm just going to say it."

"Say what?"

"There's way too much gold in here." He gestured around the foyer, before getting up to walk toward a loveseat against the opposite wall. "Like this. Why?"

His tone bordered on, no wait, it *was* aristocratic. He sat down, looking like royalty in faded jeans, blue t-shirt, and bomber jacket. Arms spread out over the back of the loveseat, ankle propped up over the knee.

"You should really think about hiring a new interior designer."

"Well, that can be arranged since my grandmother was the one who picked all this out."

"Ah, the granny defense. Likely story."

"I had no idea I was sharing space with Joanna Gaines," I grinned, making my way to the loveseat to join him.

How he managed to soften my mood delighted me. He was like a drug. Losing myself in him last night cemented my addiction. The way my entire body lit up for him even now, sitting here in this house, was a craving I'd never be able to manage.

"Yes, well, that's what happens when your father is an architect and your step-mum an interior designer." He waved a dismissive hand around. "This becomes part of your DNA even though you fought against it tooth and nail."

"It's not a bad trait to have." I smiled. "Even if it makes you sound insufferably snobbish."

"I'm not wrong though. About all the gold."

"You're not. If my grandmother was still around she'd correct you and say *it's amber, my dear. Not gold.*"

He laughed. "Your family sounds lovely."

I didn't know how to respond to that without spilling all the reasons why we weren't a lovely family anymore. I did, however, want to touch him. Not in that way. I just needed to feel him.

I reached over and stroked his hair, the softness transporting me back to the intense pleasure of being pinned against him. He took my hand and held it in his lap. A roguish smile touched his lips, making my heart race.

Some men were handsome in a safe way. Not Xavier. He was handsome in a way that was too profound, too mesmerizing.

"So, this is the annoying reason why you're here."

"Yep."

"And you thought telling me this was a bad idea, why?"

"I didn't say it was a bad idea to tell you. I didn't say anything about it at all."

"I'm aware." He sounded droll, dry. "But it obviously upset you enough to pace around the side of a road."

He glanced around with his astute eyes soaking in every detail. It fascinated me how he'd study even the most mundane element as though it mattered just as much as something extraordinary. I liked watching him. Really liked it.

Knock it off, V. One time is enough.

I shifted on the cushion, painfully aware of the fact I hadn't set foot in this house since I was sixteen. Nothing had changed. The whole place was a huge time capsule, holding memories and artifacts from another life.

Xavier nudged me with his elbow. "Hello? Earth to Victoria. Did you not hear me?"

"Sorry, no," I responded sheepishly. "What did you say?"

"Lost interest in me already. I get it." He feigned a hurt expression, removing his jacket. I got an eyeful of the toned, tattooed arm sticking out of his t-shirt. This one in particular displayed a phrase on his forearm that wasn't familiar to me.

Oderint dum metuant.

"What does this mean?" I asked, caressing my hand over the words.

"*Let them hate so long as they fear,*" he answered with an amused grin. "I figured an Ivy League educated woman would know *some* Latin."

"*Potes meos suaviari clunes.*" I elbowed him. "Snob."

He laughed and shook his head. "I see. You can tell me to kiss your ass in Latin but can't translate a tattoo. I knew I liked you for a reason."

"I'm full of surprises." I grinned. "I can also swear in French and Italian."

"You're also deaf. You really didn't hear what I said, did you?"

"Nope."

"I was wondering," he angled toward me, "if you'd like to have dinner with me. Tonight."

"Seriously?" I looked him up and down. "Like a date?"

"You're too feisty for your own good." He smiled and I swear to God this man could induce an orgasm without even touching me. "Actually, I was wondering if you're more motivated to sell this place now that you know I'm your neighbor."

"And I'm the feisty one?"

He leaned in, as though he meant to kiss me, then stopped. The rhythmic pounding of my pulse filled my ears.

"Well, Mr. Maddox," I said, regaining some composure. "The real question is can you handle having me as your neighbor?"

His eyes darkened, his lips parted. He stared at me. *Through me.*

And there went my feeble attempts at staying in control.

Our playful flirting morphed into something more carnal, more insistent. And it did so with no effort. Ever since I left his place this morning, I'd felt something calling for me, tempting me, pulling me. I'd dismissed it as being overtired or maybe even feeling anxious but a deeper part of me knew what it meant.

Overcome by his scent and closeness, and with a desperate need domineering me, I leaned in, just to get a small dose to satisfy my urge.

"Careful," he warned, but even his attempt at maintaining control had been weakened, like mine. He felt it too. I knew he did.

His molten stare cut right through me and filled the atmosphere with a thick, powerful haze of need and want. The pad of his thumb whispered over my mouth. A shiver skipped up and down my spine when he pulled my hair free of the haphazard job I did throwing it up in a bun. And just like last night, he sifted his fingers through it, massaging the scalp.

So calming. So amazing.

My eyes closed from the pleasure. Until it stopped without warning. My lids popped open and there he was, staring at me. Sapphire eyes filled with promise and need and…something I couldn't quite figure out.

"Come here." He pulled me onto his lap so I straddled him.

"What are you doing?"

"Getting you to sit in my lap." His lips curled in a crooked grin. "Any objections?"

"Well, no but—"

"Good." His fingers resumed their sifting and stroking in my hair. "Is this where you'd vacation with your family?"

A violent tremor streaked through me. I tensed, sucking in a breath. "How did you know that?" I almost choked on the words.

"Dawn mentioned it. I was at Black Rose just before." His shrewd eyes studied me before he continued. "She only said you vacationed here with your family. Nothing more."

"Right." I chewed on the inside of my cheek. "Why were you talking about me with Dawn?"

"I wasn't."

"So she just walked up and volunteered information?"

"No."

"For such an eloquent speaker you're not giving me very many words right now," I muttered in frustration.

His soft laugh charmed me. Again? Still? Did it matter at this point? I was sitting in his lap.

"I was there with Cade and Bennet. Cade was being, well, *Cade*, and kept referring to hot American redheads." He looked at me. "Dawn figured out he was talking about you and just mentioned she knows you and your family." He shrugged. "That's all."

I let out the breath I'd been holding. Dawn and Ray knew what happened and why we never came back as a family. My dad returned once. But only to give the Halstons our extra set of keys to keep an eye on the place.

"Does Cade have a little crush on me?" I teased.

A flash of jealousy passed through his eyes. "No. You're too old for him. No offense."

I laughed. I could see him going for the younger ladies. His brand of flirting probably landed better with someone under thirty.

"None taken."

Xavier glanced around the grand foyer again. I followed his gaze, taking in what I already knew was there. Aside from the curved staircase and this hideous loveseat, there was a set of French doors leading to the sitting room. Beyond that, a hallway stretched to each wing of the house. The kitchen, dining room, and library were to the left, the main bedroom suite to the right. My bedroom, along with Charlotte's, was upstairs as well as two spare bedrooms and a huge bonus room.

His fingers held my chin, gently turning me to face him. "Will you show me around?"

That's quite literally the last thing I wanted to do. "Really?"

"Mmhmm. I want to see more."

"It's just a house."

A hooded, sinful stare greeted me. "Nothing about you is *just* anything. Show me. Please."

How could I say no? I stood up in a flurry of butterflies and tingling skin. He was a one night stand.

One. Night.

His hypnotic blue eyes remained on me as he stood up and started walking toward the French doors. I followed him because it's him and I didn't want to be rude.

It's just a house.

Sheets covered most of the furniture in the sitting room. There wasn't really much else to see in there. Although Xavier seemed to find interesting things to observe.

"When was this built?" he asked, running a hand over the wood panel molding.

"I have no idea. Maybe early 1900s?"

"And it belongs to your parents?"

"It does now. It was my grandparents'. On my dad's side. They're from England so this was their summer home."

"Your dad is English, too?"

"Yep. He was born near Leeds and then they all moved closer to London when he was nine or ten. He came to New York to attend Columbia University and never left."

"Another Ivy Leaguer, huh?" he grinned, studying the intricate wainscoting. "And you came here on summer holiday?"

"Every year."

"Hmm." He nodded, sliding his hands in his pockets.

"Cade actually grew up around here," he said. "Me too. My family lives a couple towns over. We played together in youth football. There's a pitch not too far from here."

He moved to one of the couches and lifted the sheet. This one wasn't gold or amber or any hue of that color, thank goodness. It was navy blue. A smile flirted with his lips as he removed the rest of the sheet and sat.

"Join me," he requested, patting the cushion.

"A break already? At this rate, we'll never finish the tour."

"Why the rush?" A lazy smile curled his mouth. "Sit with me."

He rested his head on the back of the couch and rubbed his hand on the cushion. Why was everything he did so damn seductive?

"Five minutes and then we either continue this tour or we leave." My weak attempt at putting boundaries up fell flat. We both knew I wanted to sit with him.

"Sir, yes, sir." He mock saluted me. "Now come here so I can talk to you."

I gave in because of course I'd give in. Plus, I liked his huffy little order. I sat on the far end of the sofa to guarantee some space between us. Sitting in his lap had been a challenge. This breathing room was necessary.

He looked amused. "You're so far away. Afraid I'll bite or something?"

It was the way he said *or something* that hit several of my hot buttons.

"I don't need to be on you for us to talk."

"How about," he licked his lips, "if I promise to be a gentleman. A real one this time. No funny business. Will you sit closer then?"

I noticed his cherry-picked phrasing. *A real one this time.*

This time.

Like there would be other times in the future. He rolled his head to face me and folded his hands in his lap as if to say *See? Real gentleman right here.*

I answered by sliding closer. Close enough for whatever it was he wanted to talk about but far enough so our legs and arms didn't touch. Satisfied, he rolled his head back and grinned.

Of course being this close fractured my already fragile control. And then there was his scent and the way his jeans hugged his muscular thighs. I blinked, turning my attention elsewhere. Too bad there wasn't anything else worth looking at in here.

"So, um," I stammered, "you've known Cade for a long time?"

"Since we were twelve. Like I said, we played youth football together for ages. Then we both signed with Royal City when we were eighteen. Pretty much grew up together."

"Wow. And you'd play around here?"

His head rolled toward me again. "Quite a bit." He smiled. "Maybe we met way back then without even realizing it."

"I think I'd remember you."

His smile grew wider. "I know I'd remember you. Pity. Would have been fun meeting little Victoria."

"Was little Xavier just as cocky and insufferably snobbish as grown Xavier?"

His throaty laugh filled the room, bringing some semblance of life back into it. "Yeah, he was. I learned everything I know from him."

My turn to laugh. "Oh my God. You sound so proud."

"You seem to like him." His heated stare made my cheeks flush, which then caused his breathing to stagger. So much cause and effect in our little game. I sure hope he didn't think I missed it when he splayed his hands out on his thighs. Or angled his shoulder ever so slightly toward me.

"Maybe," I conceded.

"I don't like maybes."

I glanced down at his hands. "Where are your rings?"

His eyebrows shot up in amusement. "You noticed. How cute."

"Knock it off," I smiled, shoving him playfully.

"I knew you liked them. I have more."

"That should be tattooed on you somewhere. *I have more.*"

"You'd like that, wouldn't you." He shifted closer so our thighs touched. "The rings are at home. I don't wear them at practice."

"Oh right. The soccer thing. What position do you play?"

"First, it's called football. Second, I've shown you at least one position I can play. Third," he lifted his hands, "I'm the goalkeeper."

"Are you good?"

A devilish smile appeared. "These hands don't miss."

The level of his flirting was lethal. I made a concerted effort to stay as calm and collected as possible, which was, to put it mildly, a fucking challenge.

I cleared my throat. It made his grin widen. Cause and effect.

"Did you meet Bennet when you were young as well?"

He nodded, folding his hands on his stomach. I couldn't help but look. And because I'm obvious about it, and because we're so close on the couch, he lowered his hands so they rested at the edge of his waistband. Right where someone could easily undo his jeans.

Clever.

"The three of you must have been huge troublemakers back then."

"That's one way to put it." He rolled his head so he stared straight up, answering in a tone like he was discussing the latest news headlines. "We had our share of adventures."

A dispassionate, far-away look crossed his features for a brief moment. I couldn't tell if he was annoyed or pleased. "What kind of adventures?"

He shrugged. "Usual, teenage boy shit."

"Is that how you got the scar over your eye? Usual teenage boy shit?"

His hand flew to it as though on autopilot, tracing it with his fingers. A scowl marred his elegant mouth. None of that lasted longer than a few seconds but I learned enough to know this wasn't a preferred topic of conversation.

Didn't stop me from pressing him for answers.

"What happened?"

He scowled again, looking at me. "I used to get into fights all the time when I was young. I got jumped and beat up pretty good one night. This," he touched the scar, "is from the knife they used."

"Why would someone be so violent?" I shouted. Anger simmered inside me. "Do you know who it was?"

"Hey," he whispered, holding my chin to turn my head so I faced him. "It was a long time ago."

"Doesn't mean I can't be pissed off about it."

"You are fiery." He smirked. "Want to know something else?"

"Sure."

"You're hot when you're angry." He pulled me onto his lap so I straddled him again. "Makes it hard for me to be a gentleman."

I reached up and touched the scar. His body shook.

"I'm so sorry this happened to you." On an impulse, I leaned forward and kissed it, letting my lips linger for a few seconds.

He gasped, fisting his hand in my hair. Then he pulled it hard so I leaned back. We stared at one another. Both of our breaths came hungry and fast.

"Thank you for telling me."

No matter how hard I fought it, I wanted more of him. Last night should have been enough. I should end this right now. Stand up and walk outside. Get in my rental car and drive off.

I would have if he hadn't run his tongue along his lip. Or inhaled a shaky breath. Or stared at me with such raw intensity. He didn't even have to utter a word because I could read his body language.

It said the same thing as mine.

"If we do this," he growled on a harsh exhale, "I'll never want to stop. I'll never be able to stop."

"I won't either."

Just one more time...

I slid my hands under his shirt and pulled it over his head. All I could think about was him inside me. I splayed my hand on his chest, pushing him back. He didn't seem to mind and found my hooded gaze with his own.

Leaning close, I licked the seam of his lips. "I want you like this. Please don't deny me."

"Denying you anything is impossible."

Chapter
EIGHT

The feeling of his open-mouthed kisses up and down my neck was intoxicating. Every part of me sang and arched into him. When his lips touched mine it was the most powerful thing I've ever felt. Xavier's kiss had longing, possessiveness, need, lust. And for some reason, this kiss spoke to every inch of me.

His fisted hand pulled at my hair, tilting my head. The soft touch of his tongue fluttered on mine, making me moan. His other hand worked fast to undo my jeans and maneuver between my legs. The sudden spike of pleasure hit me faster than I—

My ass vibrated. And chimes rang out. And it vibrated again. More chimes.

The sudden noise pulled us apart. My clit screamed at me for depriving it of a complete rubdown.

Xavier looked at me funny. "What is that?"

"My goddam phone." I grunted in exasperation and pulled it out of my back pocket. Text messages from Killian.

"Fuck me," I muttered.

"I was trying to."

"Don't be cute."

"Everything alright? Seems like a lot of stuff incoming."

"Yeah, it's just—"

"*Victoria.*" My shouted name echoed through the foyer. "*Tori.* Are you in here?"

I slumped in Xavier's lap. "Oh my God," I said under my breath.

The French doors swung open. Silence. And then…

"Jesus take the wheel," Killian's amused voice filled the room. "Do you want to finish? We can wait outside."

"Don't leave on our account," Xavier said.

I poked him in the side. Hard.

"Ow," he chuckled, rubbing his skin. "No poking the product."

I mouthed *sorry* and climbed off him. Buttoning up my jeans, I turned to see two sets of highly entertained eyes and two humans failing miserably at trying not to laugh.

"What are you both doing here?"

"He was literally in your pants just now, wasn't he?" Killian snorted out a laugh.

"What are you, thirteen?" I smoothed out my hair and folded my arms. "Why are you here?"

"Well, Victoria, if you must know, someone promised they'd be back by four so we could go into town for some," he looked at Maxim, "what was it? Oh right. Bonding time on our last evening here. In case you forgot, we leave tomorrow." He smirked, looking at his watch. "It's almost five-thirty. But I can see how you lost track of time."

I felt Xavier stand up behind me. Max covered his mouth and looked away. Killian stared because that's what Killian does when he sees attractive men. I turned to look at Xavier and almost lost my footing.

There it was, straining against his jeans. The outline of an erection that was beyond conspicuous. The man it happened to be attached to didn't seem to give one flying fuck about it and casually put his t-shirt back on.

"You must be the friends," he said, draping an arm over my shoulders. "Apologies for keeping Victoria later than planned."

He sounded so natural, almost blasé. Like getting caught with his thumb on a clitoris and a raging boner in his pants was just a regular Sunday. Honestly, it was a turn on.

"Yes. That's us. The friends." Killian smirked.

I rolled my eyes. "Xavier, meet Killian and Maxim. Boys, this is—"

"Mildly hot," they finished in unison.

"As usual, my reputation precedes me," Xavier quipped in a lighthearted tone. "Thank you for dropping the mid-life crisis bit. Not really sure where that part came from anyway."

Killian grinned. "I like this one. Not in that way. Well, maybe in that way because holy shit have you seen yourself."

Xavier laughed in his unaffected way, drinking in the adoration like I'd seen him do at last night's event. And then the floodgates opened and Maxim joined Killian as the three of them talked around me like I didn't even exist.

"Do you live in town?" Maxim asked.

"Yes. Just up the road a bit," Xavier answered.

"You must be loaded to live in these parts." Killian let out a low whistle. Max swatted him on the arm.

"Don't be rude," he scolded.

"How am I being rude? I'm pointing out a fact. Rich people live here."

I felt Xavier's hand go from my shoulder to my waist. "I have some savings," he said dryly. "You two are flying back to the States tomorrow?"

"First thing in the morning." Killian looked pointedly at me. "That one will have the house all to herself until she leaves."

"Subtle, Killian. Very subtle." I narrowed my eyes.

"Alright then," Max hushed all of us. "We found our girl. She's in good hands."

Killian snickered. Max elbowed him. "Enough already. We'll head back to the house and order dinner. Xavier, you're more than welcome to join us."

His fingers pressed into my waist. "I'll consider it. Thank you."

The boys left with the same zeal as when they arrived, bickering back and forth, their voices echoing until I heard the front door shut.

I let out a long sigh. "I don't even know what to say."

A soft laugh was the only response I got. I looked up at him.

"Is your dinner date offer still good?" I wondered aloud.

"All of my offers remain active until further notice."

"Good to know."

He stood in front of me. "Let me see your phone, please."

I was about to ask why when he continued, "I'm putting my number in it, just in case."

"Just in case what?"

"You'd like to text me. Or send me naughty photos." He grinned as he tapped at the screen.

"Do I get naughty photos in return?"

"Maybe." His wide, crooked grin appeared.

"I thought you didn't like maybes."

"Depends on the context."

I rolled my eyes. He glanced up and saw it. "Insufferably snobbish again?"

"*Maybe.*" I said it louder than I normally would have. It did make him laugh though.

"What does your day look like tomorrow?" I asked when he handed me the phone. I looked down, noticing he'd saved his number as Mildly Hot. "This," I laughed and held it up so he could see screen, "really got under your skin didn't it?"

"Nope. Just distinguishing myself from any other mid-life crisis you may have met here."

"Now that you mention it, I do have a couple others. Juggling all of you will be exhausting."

He tipped my chin up, brushing his thumb over my mouth. "I'd prefer it if you make me your priority."

The tinge of jealousy in his voice at my harmless banter stirred something in me.

"Is that what you expect? To be the center of my universe?"

"I expect nothing from you other than what you're willing to give me," he responded with a smirk. "C'mon. Let's finish this tour before we leave."

Before I had a chance to react, he headed for the foyer. When I caught up to him, he'd already bounded up the staircase. Dread gripped at me, knowing I'd have no choice but to follow him up there.

"Here we go," I muttered, climbing the stairs.

The second floor was more shadowed than the main level, mostly because several of the doors remained closed, blocking out any natural light. My old bedroom, along with Charlotte's, was open. I closed my eyes, sending a silent prayer to the universe, God, angels, and basically any higher power out there that he'd wandered into my room.

"Peaches and cream, huh." Xavier poked his head out from the doorway to my sister's room. "Not quite the color combination I'd imagined for little you."

Fuuuuuck. I raked my hands through my hair, watching him disappear back inside. After a few calming breaths, I followed him.

Stepping into her room felt like traveling back in time. It didn't smell like her fruity perfumes anymore but her spirit existed in every corner. I'd almost forgotten the dreamy, stylish flair she'd preferred in her decor with the soft blankets and fuzzy pillows.

"Tell me more about little Victoria," Xavier requested. He'd made himself comfortable on my sister's bed, holding what looked like a diary in his hand. "Or should I just read this?"

On instinct, I shot across the room and snatched it. My quick movement elicited a throaty laugh from him.

"That only makes me want to know everything about you even more." He tilted his head, smiling up at me. "What secrets does little Victoria have?"

The muscles in my throat worked hard to swallow back the growing panic. I wanted so much to play along with him but I couldn't. I felt her everywhere. This room was like a vacuum.

Stifling.

Suffocating.

Tears welled in my eyes.

"Oh Charlie," I whispered, sinking to my knees. The memories swept over me without mercy.

Her tear-stained face after returning home from the party I'd pressured her into going to with me.

The sound of her muffled cries late at night when she thought no one could hear her.

All the times she seemed on the verge of telling me something, then fading back into a cloud of silence. Why didn't I press her harder, when I could clearly sense she was troubled by something. I'm her twin. I should have known how to save her.

The intense pain of her loss swallowed me whole. It'd been years since these emotions consumed me this way.

It took me a few seconds to realize I wasn't crouched on the floor alone. I felt his arms first. A strong, comforting embrace. Then I was enveloped by his body and scent. My efforts to keep this part of my existence from him failed in spectacular fashion.

"You must think I'm batshit crazy," I muttered against his shirt.

"Not at all, love."

A heavy sigh rolled through me, amplifying my mental and emotional exhaustion. It relieved me to no end that Xavier didn't ask any questions or even try to say something comforting. He just sat with me, holding me, stroking my hair. I don't know how he knew this was what I needed, but he did.

After a few minutes, I sat back on my heels and wiped my eyes. As I picked up the diary, I paused. Then, without any misgivings I said, "This is my sister's. Was my sister's. Charlotte. She was my twin. She died when we were sixteen. This was her room, not mine."

He looked at me, realization dawning on his face.

"I'm…I'm so sorry. I didn't know."

"It's not really something I drop into casual conversation."

Sharing this with him shifted our dynamic. It wasn't better or worse, just heightened. My next thought was interrupted by the sound of a car door slamming. I jumped up to peek out the window.

It wasn't Killian or Max. I couldn't tell who it was through the shadows cast by the setting sun.

"Are you expecting anyone?" Xavier asked, placing a protective hand on my hip.

"No. It might be the guy from the charity again but he seemed pretty over it when he left earlier."

"Stay here."

The sound of his disappearing footsteps down the stairs echoed through the house. The person outside was already heading back to their car by the time Xavier trotted out the front door. The sight of him appeared to startle the uninvited guest. Whoever it was jumped in the car and sped off. Honestly, at this point, I was too emotionally drained to care.

I retreated from the window and grabbed Charlotte's diary before going downstairs. I paused in the doorway, glancing back into my twin's room. As painful as it'd been to be in there, I was more determined than ever to make sure this house never left my possession.

Killian pulled me close and spoke low, which for him was just regular human volume.

"Sweetie, if you want alone time with," he gestured towards Xavier, "just say the word. We'll go into town. Those Halstons are a hoot."

"I can hear you," Xavier said. He leaned against the kitchen counter and waved. "You don't have to leave us alone. I prefer an audience."

I looked at him and fought off an urge to clench my thighs together. Bringing him here for dinner seemed like a good idea on paper. He smiled at me in the sensual, dimpled way he has and helped himself to another cube of cheddar cheese.

Killian seized the opportunity. "Seems you've met your match, Tori," he practically shouted.

"So, you're a pro-athlete," Maxim changed the subject.

"Yes." Xavier responded.

"And you play soccer?"

"Football." We corrected him at the same time. Xavier glanced at me and lifted an eyebrow. I laughed.

"Oh-kay. I can see how the answering-at-the-same-time thing can be annoying," Maxim teased. "What do you plan on doing when you retire? Not that I'm suggesting you should."

"He's loaded, Max," Killian said. "The man doesn't have to do anything."

I perched on the stool next to the man of the hour, waiting for his response. He luxuriated in the attention.

"Loaded is one way to put it. I prefer financially savvy." He made it a point to graze the back of my neck when reaching for more cheese. "I have no plans on retiring yet but I've launched my own brand management company. We're having a big press conference tomorrow in London to make it official."

Killian perked right up at the mention of brand management. "Now you're talking my language. What types of brands?"

"Well, me," Xavier grinned. "It's so I can manage all my endorsement deals and any other ventures I decide to pursue."

"That's impressive," I said, nudging him with my elbow. "The product is more than just a pretty face."

"Oh God, did she give you the product line, too?" Killian groaned, rolling his eyes. "She's been hiding behind that bullshit expression for years."

"Hey," I warned. "It's a valid way to keep myself sane."

"Yah," Killian chided. "Didn't keep you away from that wide receiver though."

"We flirted. Nothing more."

"Baby girl, you know I love you. But you're a terrible liar."

A warm, muscular body pressed into me. I looked up at Xavier through my lashes. The jealousy was palpable. He didn't say anything, he only looked back at me with obvious intent filled with dirty promises and even filthier fantasies.

"You two are going to be *that* couple, aren't you?" Maxim asked.

"You boys already hold the title," I asserted.

We all sat at the table when the food was ready. Drinks flowed. Pleasant conversation beguiled all of us. We laughed, joked, teased, and enjoyed each other's company. Having Xavier with us completed a circle I didn't even realize wasn't whole. His interaction with my friends was so natural, so unforced.

"You all live in New York together?" he asked, pouring himself a whisky.

"Not together-together, but yeah, we're all in Manhattan," Killian answered.

"And you two," he gestured at me and Killian, "have known each other how long?"

"Fourth grade. Sister Mary Margaret's class." Killian smiled. "These two little redheads—" He stopped, looking at me with a concerned expression.

"It's okay," I assured him. "I told Xavier about Charlotte after you guys left the house." I gave him a look conveying *he knows I have a twin, but not why she's no longer with us.*

"Ah, okay. Well, if you can imagine two of her," Killian smirked in my direction, "in looks only. Charlotte didn't have the mouth this one does."

"Refer to me as *this one* again and I'll send you back to Manhattan courtesy of my foot."

Maxim turned to Xavier and shrugged. "Welcome to my world."

"This is nothing," Xavier said, running a finger over his eyelid. "You should see what it's like when Cade, Bennet and I all get together."

"Are those your hot friends we saw at the pub the other night?" Killian leaned in. "Max and I didn't know where to look. Them or the two of you basically dry humping at the bar."

"We weren't dry humping, you ass." I took a long swallow of wine. "We were talking."

I felt Xavier's strong hand skim up and down my back. He bent his head so his mouth hovered at my ear.

"Is that what you think it was?" he asked. "Talking?" He nibbled at my earlobe before sitting back in the chair to casually sip his drink.

"Exhibit A," Killian gloated.

"Who wants dessert?" Max stood up.

I offered to help with the plates and coffee. Separating myself from Xavier's sphere helped clear my head. He's so damn intoxicating. It's no secret I had a type but he's well beyond just an inked up hot athlete with an edge.

I caught glimpses of him talking with Killian. He appeared engaged in whatever Killian was saying. Probably more brand management talk. I made it a point to set the dessert plates down on the table so I could eavesdrop.

"…content and engagement," Killian was saying. "Way too many people go about it the wrong way. They think posting random shit everyday is enough. But if it's all boring, nobody will care."

I caught Xavier's eye and smiled. "Tea or coffee for you?"

"Tea, if it's not too much trouble."

"I don't know." I widened my eyes in mock worry. "Boiling water might be too strenuous a task."

Xavier folded his hands on the table and stared at me with dark, intense eyes. "I can think of several things more strenuous."

I swallowed. "Tea it is."

Killian, thank God, was oblivious. He'd been searching for something on his phone. He leaned in to continue his conversation with Xavier when I turned to head back to the kitchen.

Killian was all about building his brand and helping others build theirs. He loved the whole social media scene and expanding his reach. I wouldn't be surprised if he offered Xavier his expertise, although I highly doubted Xavier needed it. But he still listened politely and genuinely looked like he enjoyed the conversation.

Max and I returned to the table with coffee, tea, and dessert. Nothing too fancy, just some little cakes.

Once we'd finished, Max offered to clear the table while Killian excused himself to pack for their flight in the morning. I escorted our guest to the front door.

"Do you have plans tomorrow?" Xavier inquired, placing his hands on my hips.

"Work. I have a few things to finalize before the draft next week."

"I see." He slipped his hands under my shirt, circling them to the small of my back. "I think you should spend the day with me. Work can wait."

"Don't you have a press conference?"

"It won't take all day."

"What about practice? I know how you athletes are. Always lifting and training and pushing your bodies to perfection."

"I'd rather push limits than push to perfection." His dimple appeared. Feather-light strokes tickled my lower back. My inner resolve to resist his seduction tactics faltered.

But only for a second.

"I appreciate your tenacity but it'll be nice to have some semblance of a routine after this weekend," I said firmly.

"I'm pretty sure in this scenario *nice* and *routine* are code for boring. You're not interested in boring," he said with absolute conviction. He also pinned me against the front door, leaning his strong, muscular body on mine. "I have you right where I want you."

The clatter of dishes and silverware sent a stark reminder that all Max had to do was peek around the corner into the foyer and he'd get an eyeful.

Something in my expression registered with Xavier. He slid his hands out from under my shirt and cupped my face before saying, "We should finish where we left off on the couch."

"Right here?"

His hand skimmed down my body, pausing at the waistline of my jeans. "Right here," he murmured. "Or, we could go out somewhere."

The choices were specific and not secluded. Any shred of my so-called inner resolve dissipated. My heart raced. All the pent up sexual frustration from earlier exploded through me. I'd probably shatter in a matter of seconds no matter what I decided.

I looked up at him. He knew. He knew I was already at the edge and only needed a nudge. The sinful smile curling his lips nearly did me in.

"Where would we go?" I exhaled.

The shift in him was instant, like he'd allowed himself to *become*. Exactly what that was remained a mystery but I really, really enjoyed the way he stared at me right now. Arrogant, possessive, resolute.

He bent to kiss me, stroking his tongue along my parted lips before taking my mouth like it belonged to him. Like I belonged to him. A barrage of shivers surged through me at the thought.

His hand slid to the base of my throat, collaring it. He kissed me harder, deeper, more possessive. When he broke our kiss I grabbed onto his shirt to keep him close.

"I liked tonight," he said. His lips were still close to mine, his hand still collared my neck. "I liked being with you at your house. I liked learning more about you. Having you in my lap." He ran his nose along my jaw. "I liked how wet you were right before we got interrupted. I like how flushed and ready you look right now."

He slipped a hand under my shirt, feeling up to my breast. The pad of his thumb teased my nipple into a hard peak.

The clattering in the kitchen stopped. Xavier pinched my nipple hard and pressed his mouth to mine to swallow my shocked groan.

"Perfect," he whispered on my lips. "I know where we can go."

All at once my pulse raced and I panted like I'd been running a marathon.

A salacious smile curved his mouth. "Tomorrow."

WHAT?

"Excuse me?" My jaw dropped. "What do you mean?"

"I mean, tomorrow." His tone sounded firm and final.

"Twice." I blinked. "*Twice* in one day you brought me to the brink of an orgasm and now you're telling me I have to wait."

He grabbed my hand and placed it on the bulge in his jeans. "And what do you think this is? A sock?"

In my annoyance, I palmed his erection just because he was dumb enough to put my hand there.

He bared his teeth and moaned.

"Exactly. I can play this game, too."

"Outside," he growled, opening the door. We walked, or rather *he* walked, I stumbled, through the dark yard until we stood next to his car.

"Are we gonna do it in the backseat like horny teenagers?"

"No." He pinned me to the drivers' side door and made fast work at unbuttoning my jeans. In seconds, his thumb pressed and rubbed my sensitive bud without mercy.

"Think I can make you come before a car drives by?"

I whimpered. This was more pressure and speed than I'm used to but oh my god it felt amazing. Especially the small bite of pain entangled in all the pleasure.

"I could do this all day." His warm breath tickled my cheek. "Play with you like a little doll, make your pussy quiver whenever I want. Is that something you'd like?"

"Yes," I exhaled, reaching to undo his pants. The second I freed his cock and wrapped my hand around the velvet skin of his shaft he shuddered. The skin was so soft and warm stretched over the hardness underneath. I felt it swell and pulse in my grip when I pumped my hand.

He pressed his forehead to mine, panting and faltering slightly. I stroked him faster, harder, squeezing tighter. He thrust his hips into my hand, losing himself in the feeling. Just hearing his quick, ragged breathing was intoxicating. Empowering. His pleasure solely rested in my hand.

The pressure and pace on my clit increased.

I groaned, barely able to stand up straight.

Our eyes locked in the middle of this filthy, hot moment. I almost felt like I was having an out of body experience.

"I want you to come on me," I said, not recognizing the sound of my own voice. "Lift my shirt and come on me."

"Victoria. *Fuck.*"

The second he yanked my shirt up I knew he was at the edge.

I cried out when my orgasm commandeered my body in euphoric waves and almost lost my grip on him. His broken moan and the sound of my whispered name preceded his surrender as it coated my hand and hit my stomach in warm, roped spurts. He braced himself against the car door. His hips jerked a few more times and he drew one last, sharp breath.

Then the weight of his body leaned into mine. Neither one of us could stand under our own power just yet. Our chests heaved in satisfied, sated unison.

"You okay?" I asked.

A breathy laugh shook his body when he lifted his head to look at me. "What Ivy League school taught you that?"

"Dartmouth." I grinned.

"Money well spent."

Chilly air tickled my skin when he pulled away. I held onto my shirt with my clean hand while he dug through a gym bag in the backseat.

"Here." He handed me a towel. "So you don't walk in all messy."

I cleaned off my stomach and hand and tossed the towel back to him. I watched his face while he wiped himself off, noticing the smile that touched his parted lips. I smiled to myself and buttoned up my jeans.

He came closer and tipped up my chin. The moonlight hit his eyes just right, making them glow.

So hypnotic.

His pupils were blown as though he was drunk from me. From what we just did. But the blue…the blue was so vibrant. It surrounded those dark pools with such brightness. Such light.

"Tomorrow," he whispered.

Chapter
NINE

Sunlight glinted off the windows, forcing me to shield my eyes from the glare. Logan Tower soared above all the other buildings, a majestic structure made of steel and glass rising out of the concrete.

"Kind of obnoxious, isn't it?" Hannah Pruitt asked with a smile. "I mean, not more obnoxious than our Manhattan building. Nobody can hold a candle to the Caldwells' obsession with being the biggest, tallest, shiniest, and best, right?"

"Your grandfather does have a flair for the dramatic," I teased. "It must run in the family."

Hannah laughed, her brown eyes sparkling as she tossed her flaxen hair over her shoulder. Technically speaking, she was my boss at the Legends, even though we were the same age, give or take a few months. Hannah ran the entire communications department for the team. Some would say there's a bit of nepotism in the organization, but she's smart, savvy, and earned her place among the executives.

We walked through the automated revolving doors and checked in at the security desk, where we were instructed to wait by the reception area.

"I feel terrible I wasn't able to go to the event on Saturday," Hannah said. "Did I miss anything good?"

"Oh, just the usual bloated corporate flexing and schmoozing."

"Was Randy there?"

"I don't think so. I mean, I didn't see him. Why? I thought you two were done?"

She shrugged. "Just curious."

"You can do so much better."

"Yeah, well, *better* hasn't texted me yet."

"Oh hush," I said. "Have you met Bennet Logan yet? In person? I know you've been emailing quite a bit."

"No. Saturday was supposed to be the big in-person meet up. I can't believe I got sick on the flight over." She wrinkled her nose. "Don't tell anyone that's why I bailed. Makes me sound lame."

"Your secret's safe with me."

Professionals young and old scurried through the atrium, some talking on the phone while others deftly avoided collisions as they texted or scrolled through whatever was more important than looking straight ahead.

It was a little after two in the afternoon. Hannah and I were scheduled to see Bennet right around now. Actually, this was Hannah's meeting to discuss the Legends possibly playing here in the fall. He'd emailed me this morning to see if I was available to join.

"Ladies, there you are." Bennet's voice echoed through the atrium. He commanded the space without much effort, nodding hellos to several people. His strides were long and determined. Bennet was the archetypal vision of wealth and power in his double breasted gray suit. "Apologies for my tardiness. I seem to have double booked myself this afternoon."

"We'll let it slide this one time," I tsk-tsked with a smile.

Bennet grinned at me, then turned to Hannah and extended his hand. "Pleasure to finally meet you, Ms. Pruitt."

Hannah appeared to be a little awestruck by our host. I stifled a laugh, wondering if I should have warned her about being in the presence of the god of thunder. Bennet seemed a bit thrown himself. The extra long stare they shared put me squarely in third wheel territory.

"So, what do you have planned for us today?" I asked, trying my best to cut through the foggy layer encasing the two of them.

"Like I said, I double booked myself so we have one stop to make before we can start our meeting." Bennet's amber eyes did this little twinkle thing that instantly made me suspicious.

"I'm sure whatever you have in store for us will be fine." Hannah's normally strong, clear voice sounded almost breathy.

"Okay then, lead the way." I gestured toward Bennet, hoping to spark something other than hormones. He picked up on my cue and led us to the elevators.

I stayed a step or two behind them, observing how they interacted. Bennet seemed unsure about what he wanted to do with his hands. He kept fidgeting. Granted, I've only interacted with him once, but I'm smart enough to pick up on nonverbal cues. As for Hannah, she kept talking in a breathy voice, which is so out of character for her.

Once we got into the elevator it became abundantly clear I was now invisible. Grinning to myself, I pulled my phone out. I hadn't texted Xavier yet like I said I would. No time like the present.

Me: Hey. All recovered from your big press conference? V

I slid my phone back into my bag just as the elevator doors opened. We walked into a lobby. The name *Impact XM* hung from the wall in black metal letters.

Of course.

OF. COURSE.

Double booked, my ass.

I looked at Bennet and lifted an eyebrow. He just smiled at me and shrugged.

"The innocent act doesn't really work on you, Bennet," I muttered, looking around.

The whole space was decorated in shades of black, gray and white. A black and white photo of mustang horses running free covered an entire wall. Captivated by the photo, I walked closer to get a better look.

The animals' muscular bodies were captured mid-gallop. The lead horse in the photo was dark, most likely chestnut-colored. The image felt powerful and very masculine. Almost like…

"I'm comforted to see you've remembered how to use your phone, Ms. Chase."

I shivered when I turned. Xavier's stare zeroed right in on me while he waved his phone in my direction. I wet my lips on instinct. The corner of his mouth ticked up in a wicked grin.

"There he is." Bennet beamed as he approached his friend. "The man of the hour. So proud of you, mate."

He embraced Xavier before introducing him to Hannah. I did my best to maintain a professional smile but so help me, just being in his orbit makes it nearly impossible.

I couldn't tear my eyes away from him if I wanted to. Black jeans hugged his long, muscular legs. A black button down shirt hid his sculpted torso but I knew all too well what waited for me underneath. His left hand was clasped over his right arm at the elbow, giving me a great view of the black and silver rings adorning his thumb, middle, and ring fingers.

Hannah nudged me gently and leaned close. "How do you know him?"

I shook myself out of the daze that has been ruling my life since he pulled off the side of the road. Having my boss standing next to me while every inch of my body screamed to be touched by this man wasn't the most professional scenario. True, Hannah and I were friendly outside the office but this was a business meeting, not a night out in Vegas. And I'll be damned if he didn't know the effect he was having on me right now.

"He was at the event on Saturday." I managed to vocalize part of the truth.

A harried looking young man rushed over to Xavier. "Mr. Maddox," he stammered, "we'll need you down in the media room soon. We start in less than fifteen minutes."

"Thanks, Craig," Xavier acknowledged the young man but kept his focus on me. "Would it be alright if I borrowed Ms. Chase for a few minutes? Her media relations skills could really come in handy."

"I don't think—"

"Of course," Hannah interrupted me. "She's the best in the business as far as I'm concerned. Take all the time you need."

"Perfect. Cheers." He motioned to his left. "This way."

I turned and followed him down the hall. He led me into a room where I fully expected to see a podium with a microphone set up and maybe a handful of people waiting for the presser to start.

I was so wrong. Well, not totally wrong. There *was* a podium with a microphone. However, there wasn't a person in sight.

The door clicked shut behind me. I walked to the table positioned near the podium, steeled myself and turned around.

Xavier half-grinned, tilting his head to the side. "I have you alone again."

"Yes you do." I clutched onto the table for dear life. "So, what can I help you with?"

He moved closer, like a wolf on the prowl. "How come you waited so long to text me?"

I smirked. "That's what this is all about?"

He was in front of me now, inches away. "Not really. I knew you'd be here."

"How?"

Now it was his turn to smirk. "Bennet casually mentioned his meeting with you. Since my press conference was around the same time, I asked him to bring you here."

"Ah. You're both in on it. Good to know."

"There's no *in on it* Victoria. Just a pleasant coincidence." His hands moved to the small of my back. "I like you in business casual. I'd like it better in a pile on the floor."

"That's not a very professional thing to say in the workplace," I half-scolded.

The sound of his low, quiet laugh seared through me.

"I thought we already established the type of gentleman you preferred."

I swallowed hard, tightening my grip on the table, momentarily regretting wearing this dress instead of something more impenetrable, like pants.

A wicked gleam brightened his eyes. "Do I really make you this nervous?"

"No but someone could walk in at any moment," I warned.

"And what would they see?" His eyes darkened.

"You know what they'd see."

"And you'd love every second of it," he murmured, running his thumb beneath my lip. "Your gloss is rather sexy. Did you wear this color for Bennet?"

"Don't be ridiculous."

"Just checking." The dimple appeared.

"You're hot when you're jealous for no reason."

"And you're mine for the rest of today and all of tomorrow." He hiked up my dress and felt his way between my legs. The cool metal of his rings on my skin made me shudder.

"I love how fucking wet you are," he growled softly. "Think we can take care of this before anyone walks in?"

"Is this what you meant by *tomorrow?*"

"Not quite. But I enjoy improvising. Especially since I can't keep my hands off you."

I should pump the brakes on this. NOW.

But I really don't want to.

"So what, um, what did you need my help with exactly?"

A small smile curved his lips. "Any advice on what I should do if I get nervous in front of all those reporters?"

"You can't be serious."

The smile grew, becoming a bit more crooked. "I could just picture you naked the whole time I'm up there. I mean, I plan to anyway."

"Not quite the advice I would give."

His fingers still teased between my legs. It's hard to maintain my composure with him so close, with his hands on me, and his smile so pretty.

"You're right. Probably not the best advice. Although," he circled a finger lightly around my oversensitive clitoris, "I'm quite fond of the way you look right now. I'd love to kiss you and smear this pretty gloss all over your smart mouth."

He bent his head so our mouths just about touched. I licked my lips on instinct.

"You'll have it all over yours. The reporters will want to know what you were doing in here."

"I'll just tell the truth. A beautiful, American media relations professional was assisting me and had a few tips she wanted to share."

"Was she helpful?"

"Oh yes." His fingers slid under my panties and dipped inside me.

My eyelids fluttered. "Did she remind you to be charismatic, articulate, and authoritative? And to focus on your main message?"

Intense pleasure surged through me when he pressed his thumb on my throbbing clit, making small circles. He pulled my dress higher with his other hand, lifting and pushing my leg wider. The feel of his clothes rubbing along my skin when he rocked his hips nearly shattered me.

"She did. I know how important focusing is to her."

His thumb intensified its delicious movements. Our parted mouths hovered close while our tongues played together, slowly licking and stroking.

"I'm so close." I gasped, grabbing onto his shoulders. "Don't stop. Please."

"I told you I'd never be able to stop." He shoved his fingers deep inside me. My muscles tensed. Not once did we break eye contact. My God he felt so good.

"Do you want to come for me now, dirty princess?"

"Yes, please."

The smile that spread across his lips was more than sinful. It was sacrilegious. "Say it again."

"Yes, please."

A deep growl rumbled through his chest as his fingers meticulously teased and tantalized me. His warm breath skimmed my cheek when he whispered, "I love that you're this kind of girl."

My orgasm hit like lightning. I cried out, clutching his shirt and twisting it, pulling him close until my quivering body relaxed.

He stepped back, removed his hand from between my legs and sucked his fingers into his mouth. I almost came again.

"Xavier," I whispered, looking up at him. The way his eyes shone as he looked back at me stirred an emotion I didn't recognize.

"I thought about you last night." He pressed his forehead to mine. "After I got home. After what we did at my car." He collared my neck with his hand, caressing it with his thumb. "When I went to bed I laid there picturing you while I stroked myself. Remembering how your hand felt on me. How you sound. How you smell. How you taste. Fuck, I came so hard. So hard. And then I thought about you again this morning when I showered."

Pretty sure he meant to destroy me in this room. I couldn't breathe. He was pushing me to the brink again. Only this time, he used his words and not his hands. Those hands that do not miss.

Dangerous.

Addictive.

And so fucking hot.

It wasn't even like he was making a performance out of telling me all this. He was just telling me. And it was so him. Because it's Xavier and he's dirty and artful when he does it. How he chose his words, his inflections. How his eyes glazed over with a hypnotic mix of possession and affection and vulnerability.

"I thought about you, too," I confessed. "For a while."

"How many times did you make yourself come?"

"Three."

He reached behind me and grabbed my ass. "I shouldn't have asked. Now I want you to show me how you got yourself off and there's no time." His voice was gruff and terse.

I wanted to kiss him.

I wanted his mouth on me.

I leaned in close and licked the seam of his lips.

"Not now, love," he moaned, inhaling slow and closing his eyes.

The way he regained control over his body astounded me.

When he opened his eyes, he studied my face. Another crooked smile appeared.

"I like our prepping sessions." He pulled away, letting reality and logic pour between us. "I should hire you to be my personal media relations director."

"You couldn't afford me." I managed to say, pushing away from the table with care. "I must look a mess."

He chuckled, pulling my dress down and smoothing it. "You're beautiful."

I nearly melted into the floor.

Seconds later, the door opened and Craig walked in.

"Ready Mr. Maddox?" he inquired.

Xavier stared at me when he answered. "I'm always ready."

Hannah and I stood off to the side with Bennet while Xavier stood at the podium answering a barrage of questions from the media. He was a natural up there, talking about his vision for *Impact XM*, along with some of the new endorsements he'd already secured.

I learned quite a bit about his professional career through the back and forth with reporters. They all seemed to enjoy speaking with him and he gave a great interview.

The ease in which he handled this press conference reminded me of several of our players back home. Some pro-athletes had an innate ability to talk to the media. Xavier was definitely one of them.

"Last question, everyone," Craig called out to the room. "Brian, go ahead."

"Xavier, now that your suspension is almost over, do you have any regrets about getting red-carded and tossed from that match?"

Rapt silence spread throughout the room. I sensed from the way Bennet stiffened his posture and Xavier gripped the podium this wasn't a question they expected or wanted.

I could see the muscles working in Xavier's jaw while he paused to gather his thoughts.

"It's a passionate sport, Brian," he finally said. "Emotions were high. There was a lot going on by the goal. Lots of shoving and pushing. Lots of bodies fighting for good position. I don't really know what happened. All I know is I lost control. Deke, Zach, and I talked after." He shrugged. "We're good. No hard feelings or anything."

The room was silent for a few seconds.

"You're known to be hot-headed on the pitch. Do you regret any of your," the reported paused, "other infractions or lack of finesse in certain game situations? Would you have preferred to handle yourself in a better way?"

Xavier glared at the reporter, the tips of his fingers turning white as his grip on the podium intensified.

"Thanks for coming everyone," Craig jumped in front of the microphone. "We're really very excited about this new venture. Thanks again."

Xavier remained rooted in place while the reporters made their way out. Craig spoke to him briefly before exiting the room. Bennet excused himself and walked over to his friend.

"Do you know what that's all about?" Hannah asked me.

"No idea."

I'd been so wrapped up screwing around with this guy I didn't even stop to consider what type of athlete he could be. I've worked with many prima donnas in my career. Some with very short fuses. Hearing that Xavier could fall into this category concerned me.

Then again, he's just a casual fling, right? I don't have to worry myself about his on-field or off-field antics.

Which is why I don't fuck the product. At least not more than one time. SHIT. What am I doing?

Whatever happened, it left Xavier in an unsettled mood. His placid expression gave me pause when Bennet called us over.

"Great job, mate." Bennet remarked, placing a hand on Xavier's shoulder. "We'll meet for dinner later, yeah? There's a new spot downtown Cade's been rambling on and on about."

"Is it Noble's Paradise?" Hannah wondered. "I've heard tons about that place and was hoping to get there before I leave."

"Might be," Bennet replied. "Would you ladies be interested in joining us? Unless you have other plans, of course."

I managed to catch Xavier's eye while the two of them made dinner plans for all of us. He still seemed uneasy but softened his expression when he saw me.

"Right then. Dinner is sorted," Bennet proclaimed. "Let's get this meeting underway, shall we?"

The four of us started to walk toward the elevator when a hand gently held my arm.

"Hey," Xavier said quietly. "Thank you for being here."

"My pleasure."

A smile lit up his handsome face, erasing the discomfort dominating it. The sight kicked up a rustling of butterflies in my stomach.

Butterflies? No, no, no.

We stopped at the elevator bank and waited.

The longer he kept his hand on my arm the harder it became for me to maintain an efficient, professional barrier. Those eyes kept making dirty promise after filthy promise after I'm-going-to-do-unspeakable-things-to-you promise. My tongue and lips itched to answer with *yes, please…yes, please…Yes. Please.*

The audible gasp I heard when he kissed me in front of everyone didn't come from me. At least I don't think it did. The only sound that came from me was a whimper when he broke his mouth away.

"Tonight and tomorrow, you're mine," he murmured. "And then we'll figure out the rest."

He kissed me again. Softer but just as passionate.

I couldn't look Bennet or Hannah in the eye when I staggered toward the elevator. At least I hope I didn't stagger. I tried like hell to walk like none of this affected me in the slightest.

Xavier stood in the lobby, his eyes to glued to my every movement.

Bennet hit the button and just before the doors closed said, "Don't forget your four o'clock, mate. I'll be calling to check on you later." His tone was clipped, almost imposing.

Xavier's pissed off face was the last thing I saw as the doors shut.

Chapter
TEN

"**E**verything's great, thanks." I leaned back in the chair and watched Dr. Frances tap his pen on the notepad. "Can't complain."

"And now that we've established the bullshit portion of the session, you can answer me honestly from here on out." He looked at me and raised his eyebrows.

"You're really good at your job," I shot back. "That *was* honest."

"So, nothing out of the ordinary happened since the last time I saw you?"

Fuck you and your loaded questions. "No."

Dr. Joshua Frances was just the latest in a line of shrinks I'd agreed to see over the years thanks to Bennet always being on my ass about it. The last one couldn't find her own way out of a wet paper bag let alone figure out what goes on inside my head.

The questions were always the same.

What brings you here?

Why do you think you behave this way?

What can we do to shift your way of thinking?

How do you think you can recognize this behavior in yourself?

It's not like I could say no to this anyway. Bennet and I had an unspoken deal this is what I needed.

"Xavier."

The way this doc said my name made me want to punch a wall. Ironic, right?

"I don't give a shit who you are or what you do for a living," he continued. "That's not what I'm here for. I'm not even supposed to be doing most of the talking. You are. This is your time to say whatever you want about anything you want. Dig deep. Enough with the rehearsed bullshit."

Touché. As much as I hated to admit it, he was right. And if I was being really honest, I liked his unorthodox approach. Didn't mean I was going to spill my guts to this Indiana Jones lookalike. My inner demons or darkness or whatever fancy buzzword that's trending online these days only wanted to reveal itself to her.

Victoria.

Dark green eyes and lush, soft lips flickered through my mind day and night. She was so much more than what I'd assumed when I pulled off the road. At first blush she appeared to be a spoiled, pretty young woman on some trendy road trip through the English countryside. Shame on me for being so shallow.

Okay fine, I initially stopped because she was hot. It's a fact and I'm not too proud to admit it. And yes, there's the whole intense lust thing clouding my brain, especially after what happened this afternoon. And last night. And the night before.

But there is so much more beneath her stylish, expensive surface and the great sex. She's intelligent, raw, passionate, driven.

It's crazy to even think this way. I don't know her well. But I like *her*. I like how I feel around her. Relaxed. Whole.

Oh God. My chest did the thing again. A demanding, frantic, *thing.* I'm so fucked.

I did some internet sleuthing last night after I got home. It started out pretty innocent. I just wanted to know more about her and was curious to see pictures of Dartmouth. I did not picture her going to university in such a rural area. Lovely, yes. But she seems so metropolitan, not small town America.

Then again, I should just ask her about her life instead of always trying to shag her. Be an *actual* gentleman.

When I found her social media accounts all bets were off. I loved looking at her photos. She's always smiling. It's infectious in photos but even more enchanting in person. I can't get enough of it. I can't get enough of her.

I wonder if she's done any searching about me…

"You seem preoccupied."

Dr. Frances's observation jolted me.

He turned to look at what I was apparently staring blankly at.

"That's been in my family for years. My great-grandfather was a master at oil paintings."

I had no idea what the hell he was blathering on about. Focusing on the wall across from the couch, a painting came into view. It was intricate but there was nothing extraordinary about it. Just a landscape painting of an old, rundown farmhouse covered in snow.

"I hear you like to fix up old places like that."

"Yeah, in my spare time. I don't make a big deal out if it though."

"So I was told."

"Seems you've been told a lot about me already. No need for me to fill in any more blanks."

Frances stared at me for a beat then started writing something down in his notepad.

"Oh Jesus, not the writing." I groaned.

"Well, you're not talking so I'm just observing."

I scrubbed my hands on my face, running them through my hair. "I have nothing to say." I shrugged. "There's no big mysterious thing I'm hiding."

"Mmhmm." He kept writing for a few seconds and then regarded me with interest. "I'm giving you homework."

"Are you serious?" I snorted. "What is this, primary school?"

"No, Xavier, this is me helping you get to the root of whatever's plaguing you. I watched your press conference today. That reporter's question threw you. You haven't said one word about it yet."

I swore under my breath. The goddam fight was going to follow me to the grave. Launching my own company didn't make it disappear, though it did give the media something else to obsess over. Namely, my net worth. Twenty million pounds, thanks for asking. Next question.

"He didn't throw me. I wanted to make sure I said all the right things—"

"Like you're doing now. This isn't a press conference. Nobody is coaching you on what to say or what not to say here. This is a safe space." He paused and shook his head. "I know you don't like hearing that but it is. I'm not your opponent. I'm also not going to force you to be vulnerable but when the time comes, I'll be here to listen. No judgment."

I clenched my jaw watching him make a few more notes.

"So," Dr. Frances continued, "Your homework. If and when something else throws you off, don't dismiss it. Don't ignore it. Really feel it. We can talk about it during our next session."

I white-knuckled the steering wheel of my car driving back to my flat.

Really feel it.

Yeah, whatever.

"Not a bad view, kid," Bennet grinned, reaching for a beer. He settled into the chair facing Tower Bridge and let out a satisfied sigh.

My balcony held some of the most luxurious views of the city. "It doesn't suck," I agreed, grabbing my own drink.

"How's everything with Dr. Frances?"

I took my time sipping the beer. "For fuck's sake, mate, you went right for the jugular."

"Well, you're still going to him so that's a victory." Bennet regarded me with a thoughtful expression. "He's not your average therapist. You need someone like him."

"Yeah, I know," I scowled.

"Come on. It can't be that bad."

The cold beer soothed some of the tightness grabbing hold of my throat.

"He's fine it's—" I caught myself before saying her name.

"It's what?" Bennet's concern made me uncomfortable. He meant well. He always meant well but I'd pretty much reached my limit.

I shrugged. "No distractions, you know?"

"What's going on with you and the redhead from the Legends?"

Prick.

Leaning my head back, I rubbed my eyes with the heels of my hands. "You're full of questions today Bennet."

"C'mon. I'm not daft. I saw you with her at the pub the other night. And then at the event on Saturday. And we all saw what happened today, Maddox. I know how you are."

"And how am I?" I glared at him. "No different than you, I suspect."

He sighed. "Look, you're a grown man. I'm not about to lecture you on anything. But I know what happens when things fall apart—"

"Can't have something fall apart that doesn't exist," I interrupted, annoyed at the direction this was going. "We've spent some time together. That's all. She's leaving the day after tomorrow anyway."

"There's something different about you when she's around." He leaned forward. "I thought I saw it the other night but today confirmed it. The press conference. Did something happen before it started? Before you made a big show with her at the elevator?"

"Maybe." I rubbed a finger on my eyelid to stop it from twitching.

"You're impulsive, Xavier. You're in control most of the time but she's shaken you in some way." He shifted in the chair, resting his forearms on his thighs.

"We're not teenagers anymore. I don't need lessons from you."

"We're well beyond lessons, mate. You've been adamant about having," he made quotes, "normal relationships since you broke it off with—"

"I'm aware," I snapped.

The silence between us stretched for a minute. The more Bennet brought up or alluded to my past mistakes, the more I wanted to be left alone.

"She wasn't right for you. That doesn't mean you won't find the one who is. And if it's Victoria, then," his voiced trailed as he shrugged.

I reclined on my elbow, flexing and clenching my hand. He's not wrong. The side of me I buried all those years ago is coming back to life. I just have to be sure this time.

Bennet smiled and the warmth behind it touched his eyes. "You really do like her, don't you?"

My hand flexed and clenched. Flexed and clenched.

❦❦❦❦❦❦❦❦

"A toast." Cade raised his glass, motioning for us to do the same. "To the Legends and Royals gathered here tonight," he paused, waggling his eyebrows, "See what I did there?"

Victoria tried unsuccessfully to muffle a laugh. I reached under the table and grabbed her thigh. It stilled her, but also provided me with one hell of a sensuous glance. I kept my hand on her thigh for two reasons: one, because I liked it there and two — my earlier conversation with Bennet notwithstanding— I wanted to see how far this could go.

The lighting in this restaurant was dim enough for me to stretch her limits in public without attracting too much attention. Most important, the dress she wore was so bloody hot, I couldn't keep my hands off her if my life depended on it.

"As I was saying," Cade continued, undeterred by the not-so-subtle eye roll from Bennet, "a toast to all of us lads and the beautiful women who agreed to suffer through this dinner with us."

"That might be the worst toast I've heard," Victoria giggled. "And it includes the drunken mess of a toast my cousin delivered at his sister's wedding."

"I'm just being my authentic self." Cade looked solemn then doubled over in laughter. "That's such bollocks." He slung his arm over his date, Emma's, shoulders. She couldn't be any older than twenty-five, which for Cade, was very much on brand. She batted her lashes and laughed at everything he said. He liked them to be, at a minimum, ten years younger.

"When will your overgrown man-child friend realize he looks like he's out with his little sister, and not a date?" Victoria's warm breath tickled my ear with her question.

My only response was to drag my hand higher up on her thigh and squeeze harder.

She leaned closer and whispered, "I know what you're doing, you mildly hot menace."

"Oh yeah?"

"Mmhmm."

"Should I stop?"

"I haven't decided yet."

I grinned, sliding my fingers under the hem of her dress.

"If you two plan to shag at the table, can you at least wait until after dessert? The sticky toffee pudding here is supposed to be top notch."

Folding my hands on the table with great reluctance, I scowled at my friend. Gallagher knew what buttons to push to rile me up and as much as I wanted to rake him over the coals, I didn't want to ruin this night with Victoria.

"Cat got your tongue, Maddox?" Cade goaded me on.

"Knock it off you two," Bennet warned. "I'm not babysitting you lot tonight."

Hannah and Victoria shared a glance across the table. I wondered what, if anything, they'd discussed after disappearing in the elevator. Kissing her in front of everyone was an impulse. I regret nothing and would do it again right now.

No, you won't, you knobhead. Repeat after me, BE A GENTLEMAN.

Cade shrugged and turned his attention back to his date, who continued giggling at everything he said. Bennet resumed his conversation with Hannah, which left me to focus on the only person I wanted to talk to anyway. Victoria sipped on her wine, doing a slow once over with her eyes, drinking in every inch of me. Before I had the chance to put my hand back where it belonged on her thigh, she held it.

"No more mildly hot menace?" I questioned.

"Not right now." She turned my palm up, running her nail along my skin, then the pad of her finger. The sensation was light, fleeting, and the most powerful thing I've ever felt.

"You have nice hands," she said with a cheeky smile, "that don't miss."

When she looked up at me through her lashes it took a mountain of restraint for me not to lay her across this table and claim all of her in front of the entire restaurant. Especially looking the way she does right now, like a fuckable treat wrapped in a blue dress that's tight in all the right places. Sky-high heels. Auburn hair in loose waves. Pouty lips drenched in a dark red shine.

"They've missed on occasion," I confessed. "Ask anyone who

watched the final a few years ago. I still get yelled at on the street."

"Fans are so fickle." She chuckled. "We lost a playoff game my third year with the Legends. It was on a missed field goal. Our kicker hit the upright. It made the fun *doink* noise and everything. To this day, fans bring it up. Especially on social media."

I frowned. "I feel bad for the bloke who missed."

"Yeah, well, he's kicked quite a few winning field goals since then so don't feel too bad for him."

"All's forgiven then," I grinned. "I'm curious. How did you make the leap from Dartmouth to American football? I would have assumed you'd be running a boardroom at a bank somewhere."

"Victoria," Hannah leaned in, grabbing her attention before she could answer. "Sorry to interrupt. The fundraiser next weekend is all set. I just got an email from the event coordinator. Did you want some of the proceeds to go to your sister's charity? I'm sorry to have to ask now but they're finalizing everything and need an answer by six today. And with the time difference and everything…"

"That would be lovely, thanks," Victoria responded with a fond smile. "Is Noah behind this?"

"He is." She grinned. "I'll let them know."

Noah? Who the fuck is Noah? Ex-boyfriend? Lover? Friend with benefits?

He's apparently thoughtful and scored some points with her and made her smile like that. I swallowed my jealousy down with more scotch.

"What charity is it?" I managed to ask without sounding too predatory. I think.

Victoria fidgeted with her wine glass. "Charlotte used to volunteer at a small animal shelter where we grew up. We'd have bake sales to help raise money for them. So, now since she…I still donate money every year. And when I have time, I go help them socialize puppies for adoption."

"You can always tell a person's character by how well they treat animals," Bennet commented. "My nieces love dogs. I think it's great you and your sister are so involved with animal welfare."

I put my hand on hers and squeezed. "How often do you go?"

"Not as often as I'd like. Maybe once every few months. That's why I always make sure I send them a sizable donation every year. They're such good people."

"Makes you feel good, doesn't it?" Cade added. "Doing something that benefits someone else? Ah, I see the look of shock Queen Victoria." He laughed. "Just ask these two. I'm all about donating my time and efforts to worthwhile causes."

"He's not lying," I confirmed. "The man is a muppet but he loves giving back."

"Let me guess." Victoria flashed a playful smile at Cade. "Children's charities so you can be among your peers?"

"Mate, if you don't marry her, I will." Cade laughed with Hannah and Bennet.

Victoria looked at me with an exasperated grin that simultaneously relaxed me and made me laugh. Good to know I wasn't the only one rattled by his comment.

"Nobody's getting married, Cade," she drawled and rolled her eyes. "But thank you for the offer."

"Hate to break it to you boys," Hannah said, "but Victoria and I made a pact to get married if we're still single when we're sixty, so basically, we're already engaged." She looked across the table at Victoria and winked.

Cade lifted his hands in resignation and smirked. "I'm not going to comment for fear of being tied up and flogged by one of those two."

"Wise move." Bennet turned and looked at me. "Are you still refurbishing that old house out on Station Road?"

"Yeah but the rain slowed down some progress," I answered, grateful for the change in subject. "I did manage to gut the bathroom though. I broke through the closet wall to make it bigger."

"Some family out there in need of a place to live will appreciate it, even though they'll never get to thank you personally. It still floors me that you prefer to stay anonymous with all the great work you've done for the community."

"It's just wood, nails and sweat. I don't need anyone to pat me on the back."

I felt Victoria's inquisitive stare before her question came out. "Is it with the charity that wanted to buy my family's house?"

Bennet regarded her curiously. "What house?"

She hesitated before answering. "The summer cottage we used in Briarcliff Village when I was younger. That's actually why I'm here in England."

"Why would they being making offers in Briarcliff Village?" Bennet sat up straight. "Doesn't make any sense."

"That's my mother for you," she muttered. "It doesn't matter now. I told them I wasn't interested."

Victoria's subtle change in demeanor wasn't noticed by anyone else at the table but me. The topic of her family's house affected her deeply.

"You okay?" I asked.

"Yeah." She seemed distant. A strong urge to wrap her in my arms, take her somewhere secluded and get lost in one another overcame me. She smiled when her green eyes connected with mine. "How many houses have you helped to renovate?"

"Good question." I thought for a few seconds. "A dozen at least. I try to work on one or two every year if I can." I shrugged. "It really is no big deal. I like doing it."

I also liked the way she kept her gaze focused on me and how she leaned into the chair in this graceful, mesmerizing way. Like watching a queen prepare to receive her subjects. I felt the smallest surge of possessive pride that I'd seen this radiant, well put together woman in a much more vulnerable state yesterday.

"I told you it's not a bad trait to have," she tapped the toe of her shoe against my foot. "I should have you fix up my family's cottage."

I chuckled, ignoring the *thing* happening in my chest again. "Why would you want me to?"

"Sexy goalkeepers who renovate houses are hard to come by these days. I have one in front of me. I'd be stupid to pass up the opportunity."

I must have looked baffled because she laughed and looked at the menu. A pleasant, melodic laugh that stoked low flames in my stomach every time I heard it.

My thought process fractured into twin realities. One, where she's serious and I could actually work on the house and potentially see her again. Then the other, where she's just being flirty and teasing like the night at the pub, and will disappear from my life in less than thirty-six hours.

I didn't like the second thought at fucking all.

"I do like to keep myself busy. You know what they say, idle hands are the devil's workshop." I'd meant for that to come out lighthearted and fun.

It did not. It came out lower, more intense.

Her emerald eyes flicked back in my direction. She caught her breath when she saw my face. A slight grin pulled at the corner of her mouth.

"Is that a promise?" she asked.

I held her stare. "One I intend to fulfill."

Once dinner was finished and the bill sorted, Bennet invited all of us back to his estate for a nightcap. Cade and Emma agreed but Hannah politely declined, saying she had an early flight back to the States.

"It was very nice meeting all of you," she said, giving Bennet, Cade, and I warm hugs. "If this all works out, maybe we'll be back here in

October." She turned to Victoria. "Safe travels home on Wednesday. See you in the office."

After she was tucked safely in a taxi, Bennet asked, "Will you two be joining us?"

Victoria shrugged. "I don't mind. All I have to do tomorrow is pack, so I'm up for anything."

"See, mate. She's up for anything." Cade sounded smug.

"You're a troublemaker," Victoria laughed.

"Guilty," Cade grinned. "Join us. We can all get to know the lovely lady who tamed Xavier."

"I doubt he's able to be tamed," she said, squeezing my hand.

"That settles it then," Bennet interjected. "My place for a nightcap. See you there."

I exhaled, watching them walk away.

Chapter

ELEVEN

Bennet's invitation ping-ponged in my head as I stared at Victoria. She stood there on the sidewalk in that dress with those eyes, that hair, those legs, smiling at me in her way. Tempting me without uttering a sound.

"You sure you want to go there?" I asked.

The soft material of her dress swayed in rhythm with her hips when she walked closer. Reaching for my shirt collar, she pulled it aside.

She nodded, touching the inked section near my collarbone. "It'll be fun. I can get to know your friends." The touch of her hand on my skin was heaven. Her eyes met mine, her voice getting lost in the night air when she said, "I want to kiss you here."

"Go ahead."

The heels gave her some added height, making it easier for her to reach her intended target. I speared my fingers into her gorgeous cinnamon locks as she pressed a gentle kiss to my clavicle. Her lips lingered for a few seconds before she parted them, leaving several soft, open-mouthed kisses.

"Careful, or we'll draw a crowd," I half-scolded. But the second she pulled away, I captured her lips in mine. Her soft moan sounded so sweet, so pure. I kissed her harder, deeper, claiming her.

Victoria jumped back with a start, her face flushed with desire. Those lush, pouty lips were already swollen. I wanted to bite them. Mark her.

"Do you want to go to Bennet's?" Her inquisitive eyes searched me.

"I want to go wherever you are."

"Smooth. Seriously, what do you want to do?"

"We can go for a little while. He has this library we all hang out in. He hosts parties there, too."

"Do you go?"

"Sometimes."

"What kind of parties?" Her eyes had this faraway look, almost like she'd lost herself in some fantasy. Whatever it was, it made her eyes appear darker, more intense.

"Not as scandalous as what you're thinking." I grinned. "Although that doesn't mean everyone behaves. It's just people enjoying one another's company."

"I enjoy your company."

Her words arrowed through me. But her expression nearly killed me. She's gorgeous when she smiles but right now she's radiant. She's radiant because she enjoys being with me and that's more than I expected.

"I enjoy your company, too."

"Good. So you'll take me to Bennet's? I really want to know more about you and what you like."

"What I like?"

She bit down on her lip before tossing out one of her smart ass answers. "You had your hands on me all night at the table in front of everyone. You clearly like to push limits. I want to see how far you can push mine."

I lifted an eyebrow. "What makes you think I won't do it right here?"

Her laugh washed over me. She had no idea what she was asking. She thought this was all a game.

I took her hand in mine. "Victoria."

Wide, clear green eyes looked up at me. "Yes, Xavier?"

Hearing her hauntingly sweet voice say my name as though it's only meant to cross her lips was everything I ever wanted. I circled my fingers around her wrist and slowly ran my thumb along the underside until I felt her pulse. I made sure the ring I had on pushed into her silky skin. Goosebumps crawled up her arm.

I lifted her wrist and pressed my lips to her pulse point. "I'm not sharing you with anyone tonight."

Her mouth popped open in a small *O* shape. I grinned.

"You're adorable when you're speechless. Come."

Wrapping an arm around her waist, I kept her soft body close while hailing a cab. I only let her go to climb into the taxi but then she proceeded to torture me on the ride to my flat, kissing me on the soft spot below my ear and inching her hand up my thigh.

"Who's the menace now?" I growled, stopping her hand.

"But I can see how hard you are," she purred. "And I don't want to wait."

She wriggled her hand free from mine and gripped my erection through my pants, stroking it. Oh shit. My head fell back just as the cab driver stole a glance in the rearview mirror.

My cock felt like a rod of painful need throbbing behind the zipper.

"You're killing me," I moaned, closing my eyes, almost letting her service me right here.

Almost.

I opened my eyes to see her staring at me with liquid desire. I had to do something before I unraveled on the spot.

Moving quick, I molded my mouth to hers, loving the sounds of surprise and pleasure vibrating through her. Her hand moved away from my crotch to slide under my shirt.

She parted her lips and I chased the silkiness of her tongue with my own, until she went pliant in my arms.

"Xavier," she whispered, "why did you stop?"

"Do you want more?" My voice went dark again. Intense. The question came out more like a warning.

"Yes."

"How much more?"

"All of it."

Three simple words stirred up the old me. The me whose reputation was well known at Bennet's parties for a certain type of experience in and out of the bedroom. The me I'd buried years ago.

I pulled her close, biting down on her plump lower lip. Hard. Harder than I have before. Hard enough to leave a mark. Hard enough for her to grunt against it in shock but not stop it. When I pulled back, her dark, hooded eyes seared me. Eyes that still wanted more. I looked at her swollen, marked lip and dipped my head to lick and gently kiss the pain away.

"Is that what you wanted?"

Her satisfied smile sent a bolt of lust through me. "Yes."

There is nothing sexier than a smart, independent woman willing to surrender to her desires. Willing to trust me with them. I kissed her again, pulling her as close to me as I could, feeling as much of her as this damn backseat would allow.

"Five minutes," I whispered. "Just five more minutes."

She nestled into my side, resting her head on my shoulder. Her chest rose and fell on a contented sigh. I pulled out my phone and texted Bennet. No need for the lads to wait around for no reason.

Another sigh. God, she was all softness and warmth. My head dropped to hers and I inhaled the scent of her shampoo. Warm and sensual, just like her.

We arrived at my place not a minute too soon. I watched her curvy body as she moved through the townhouse. So graceful and elegant and alluring. I followed her into the living room toward the windows.

"That's quite a view," she murmured.

"It is."

She turned. "Did you mean me?"

Everything in me ignited. Yes, obviously. The specific view in my mind consisted of Victoria down on her knees, staring up at me with those big green eyes. I didn't say that to her. Instead, I said, "Please have a seat on the ottoman by the chair. I'll be right over."

A pink flush stained her cheeks since I'd said it in *that* voice. She eyed me with interest while she walked to where I'd directed her. I purposely watched her, waiting until she was seated before I went to the sideboard and grabbed a bottle of scotch and two glasses.

I was improvising.

Okay, I was stalling because if I didn't occupy myself with getting drinks I'd already have her bent over the couch with my cock buried deep inside her.

After I poured the scotch, I brought the glasses over. She looked up at me when I handed her the drink.

"Such a gentleman."

I rolled my eyes and sat in the chair, which was a touch higher than the ottoman. And since she's astute, she repositioned herself to sit on her knees and lean back on her heels, giving her more leverage. I fucking loved it.

"How does it feel to be back in the lion's den?" I asked, taking a long swallow of scotch.

"It feels like you might need a lion tamer," she sassed back.

"Is that what you want? To tame me?" I stroked my lip. "And how will you do it?"

She cast her eyes down, parting her lips to suck in a breath. The swell of her breasts pushed against the clingy blue material of her dress. Watching all the different ways her body reacted to me was an aphrodisiac. When she looked up at me again through her lashes, her pupils were so dilated I could barely see any green.

"You won't do it by looking at me with your fuck me eyes," I growled, taking her glass and placing it on the table next to me. I put mine there as well.

"I don't want to tame you." Her voice was low and husky and undeniably sexy.

The part I'd buried snapped fully awake. And it was *famished.* The ottoman wasn't far from the chair at all. In fact, my knees rubbed against it when I leaned forward to flatten my palms on it.

Our faces were close. Almost level. Her lips parted ever so slightly.

"Do you know what that means, Victoria? I can do whatever I want to you, wherever I want. Hike your dress up minutes before a press conference, spread your legs wide until your cunt is exposed and shag you until you can't walk. Fuck you against the wall outside the Black Rose. Take you to one of Bennet's parties and fuck you in the library so hard my friends will hear you scream my name. Bend you over my lap and spank your ass until your eyes water and you come so hard you'll forget everything except the sting of my hand on your skin."

I stood up, tilting her chin so she looked at me. "Do you still want me untamed?"

She stared at me with hungry emerald eyes and an even hungrier mouth. "Yes, please," she said hoarsely.

"Stand up," I ordered.

She complied without hesitation, swallowing hard. I moved closer, fisting my hand in her hair and kissing her. Our tongues met in a coil of dirty, silky promises.

I pulled the zipper on the back of her dress down and unclasped her bra. "Undress. But keep your heels on."

Dark red hair fell around her shoulders in messy waves as she reached behind her back. Her eyes drowned in lust when she dropped the bra and dress to the floor. She kept her blue lace panties on which will have to be dealt with shortly.

But my knees still weakened because fuck all she's perfect. I'd seen her naked only a few nights ago but the lights were dim and we were too busy shagging like mad for me to really appreciate how gorgeous she truly is. The fullness of her breasts. The ivory-pale skin. The dark pink nipples already peaked and raw. Her supple, soft stomach and the kind of hips meant for grasping.

Perfect and curved and mine.

A spark of mischief filled her eyes.

I tilted my head. "What?"

"I want to undress you. Do I need your permission?"

I smirked, sliding my hands in my pockets. "I'm not undressing." Her face fell. "But I'll allow you to unbutton my shirt. That's all."

I remained still while she loosened the buttons. Similar to when we stood on the sidewalk, she placed open-mouthed kisses on my chest.

Only this time, she moved lower.

I clenched my hands when she went to her knees and unbuckled my pants.

"That's not what I told you to do."

A coy smile curled her lips. "I know. Am I in trouble?"

Oh fuck me. She wants this. And she knows exactly what she's doing. That's a massive turn on.

"Yes," I growled. "You're in trouble. Don't move."

When I started to walk behind her, she reached up and cupped my dick. I exhaled sharply. Her feisty defiance affected me in ways I didn't know existed. I looked around the room. The ottoman was too low.

Oh, wait.

I sat in the chair. Smiling to myself, I finished unbuckling my pants, lowering them and my boxer briefs enough to free my aching cock. One hand went in my hair. I fisted myself with the other.

Victoria watched with great intensity while I stroked myself hard and rough.

The pink of her tongue darted out for a quick lick.

Fuck. Those soft lips.

They'd feel so much better on me than my own hand.

Her hand would feel better on me.

I groaned, pumping harder. All of her is right in front of me. Kneeling and waiting and watching and parting those lips and…

I stopped and pushed the ottoman away with my foot.

"Kneel here," I rasped.

I made the mistake of assuming she'd crawl over to me. But no. Not her.

She stood and walked to me, standing between my legs. I fucking loved this push and pull. I hooked a finger into the front of her panties and pulled it down so I could see the smooth rise of her pubic bone. I needed a taste. Even with my cock jutting up between us hard as steel and begging for relief I needed to taste her.

I pulled the lace down more and leaned forward. Her soft bud of flesh was visible, begging to be licked. I flattened my tongue on it and licked up slowly. *Fuck me.* That taste was everything. Clean and feminine and designed to drive men like me insane.

So I tasted again.

Hearing her soft moan made my dick twitch. I leaned back in the chair.

"Will you show me what you wanted to do in the taxi?"

She nodded.

"I can't hear you."

"Yes."

"Would you have knelt in front of me in there on the dirty floor?"

"Yes."

The corner of her mouth ticked up as she lowered herself to her knees. I've never been harder than this in my life. Never.

I reclined on my elbow again, returning one hand to my hair. The other fisted by my thigh.

"Dirty princess?"

She looked up at me.

"Show me what I missed out on."

A full smile. One that screamed smart ass comebacks and the complete desertion of all self-imposed bullshit policies about fucking pro-athletes.

She ran her nails along my thighs and flicked her tongue on my dick before looking me in the eye and wrapping her lips around it. Then she slid her mouth down, her tongue flat and warm and *so fucking soft* on my concrete shaft.

"Oh shit," I hissed.

That felt good.

Holy fuck that felt good.

I watched her head bob up and down in a sea of red waves. Exquisite. Threading my fingers through her hair, I gathered it to the side so I could see her face. The blush on her cheeks. The way her eyelashes fluttered.

Watching her was hypnotic. Feeling her was heaven. I'm enthralled and I can't explain it. I don't want to explain it. I only wanted to feel her mouth and tongue and teeth while she worshipped me.

With a growl, I thrust my hips up, filling her to the back of her throat. I had to.

She swallowed against me. Her throat squeezed the head of my cock and her tongue pressed on the shaft.

"Christ," I muttered, thrusting into her throat again, and then again. When she swallowed against me this time I lost it.

I shot my load in her mouth so hard I clutched the arms of the chair. She swallowed all of my seed down without hesitation, swirling her tongue around my pulsing length, sucking slowly, coaxing every last drop out of me.

The sensation was too much. She was too much and not enough and just right all rolled into one beautiful package. My breath left me in a rush when I pulled her lips off me.

Staring down at her absolutely fucking shredded me. Swollen, used lips. Smudged mascara. Eyes wide and glassy, shining like emeralds. Her flushed skin gleamed faintly with sweat. Seeing her like this, on her knees, vulnerable and gazing up at me was better than I imagined.

I wanted more.

Now.

"Take off your knickers and wait outside on the patio."

Her chest rose on a quick intake of air but she stood, took off her panties and went to the bifold door. She opened it without hesitation and walked outside. I followed behind, approaching her slowly.

"Hop up on the table."

She did, letting out a little yelp when her bare skin hit the surface. "It's cold," she giggled.

"Not for long." I spread her legs wide and reached behind her to pull her closer to the edge. When I pressed against her, my dick nestled against her warm, wet folds.

"You're wearing too many clothes. But you look so hot in them. Are you going to have sex with me fully dressed?"

"Yes."

She slid her hands down my chest. "Do you like having your women naked while you fuck them with your clothes on?"

"I like having you naked. No more questions."

My breathing became heavy when she reached between us to stroke me.

"Okay, no more questions," she agreed and then sassed, "Maybe if you weren't so bossy you'd be inside me already."

She pressed the head of my cock to her entrance.

Wait, wait, wait. How did she flip the script here?

"Patience," I growled, putting my hand on hers.

Her quiet laugh was punctuated by a teasing smile. Wide and sweet and sexy and fuck me there's the damn *thing* again in my chest.

Exhaling sharply, I regained composure and licked and kissed my way down to her breast. Taking her nipple in my mouth, I sucked and nibbled, then I bit down gently. She reacted how I wanted. Arching, gasping, and writhing.

When I reached into my pocket and pulled out a condom, she stopped me.

"I'm on birth control."

I've heard those words before and always ignored them, opting to use protection anyway. But hearing them come out of Victoria's mouth was a different experience. A different feeling.

For a split second, I felt like a virgin about to shag for the first time. I knew I was headed for the point of no return. And I was fine with it because the point of no return was Victoria Chase and that's all that mattered to me.

I needed to be inside her. Right the fuck now. I looked down to watch the head of my dick slide in. She felt like nothing else. I drew in long, deep breaths as I pushed farther inside. The feel of her made it difficult to be gentle. So warm and soft, like velvet. And so, so, tight.

Warding off my instinct to fuck without mercy was impossible. My body shook with the unrelenting need to drive into her. But this had to be slow to start.

Had. To.

I need to remember how this feels for the rest of my life. I buried myself in her until I had nothing left to give, until I felt her warm, wet flesh on my lower abdomen.

"Xavier, you feel so good," she moaned, tangling her fingers in my hair and pulling.

"I want to be rough with you, Victoria. Possessive," I panted. "So possessive. Tell me that's okay."

"Yes," she whispered. "Please."

"Please what?" I collared her neck with my hand, squeezing ever so slightly to feel her pulse.

"You know I like it that way." I heard a smile in her tone along with a hint of impatience. "You know that's how I want it. Be rough with me. Use me. Claim me. Don't hold back." She pulled my hair. Hard. "Please."

Instinct took over. I started fucking her in earnest now. No more slow movements. I held her hips to keep her still as I stabbed into her again and again with bruising force. Her shoes fell to the ground with a dull thud.

"More, please, more," she begged, wrapping her legs around my thighs.

I gave it to her without hesitation.

A deep, rough sound pushed out from me the second I felt her cervix wrap around the head of my cock. It was a sensation so primal I'd move heaven and earth to feel it again and again. I'd sell my own goddam soul to be inside her every day like this.

I stopped thrusting just to feel her wet, tight cunt squeeze around me.

"Don't move," I growled when she flexed her hips. "Stay still or you'll make me come before I want to."

I pressed my forehead to hers and looked down at where we were joined. I've never stopped mid-shag like this to admire how two bodies connected with such perfection.

"You're so beautiful," I said quietly, caressing her. "So beautiful."

Victoria's breathing was harsh and loud. "I can't…this is so," she panted, grabbing and twisting my shirt. "*Fuck*. Xavier. You're so hot. This is so…filthy and sexy and perfect and…I love it. I love how dirty this is. I love how you feel inside me."

I've done plenty of dirty things in the past but all of it paled compared to this moment. This filthy, hot, perfect moment on my patio with Victoria. And only with Victoria.

"I want to feel you come around me," I said, keeping our foreheads together.

"That won't be a problem," she replied, scratching her nails on my scalp. Then she did this adorable small laugh and it made her clench around me. I almost saw stars.

"Stay. Still."

Sorry, she mouthed, looking directly into my eyes. Pretty much anything she did was guaranteed to make me explode at any second.

"Try not to move," I said, sliding a hand to rub her clit.

Victoria's response was immediate. She trembled and quivered around my dick. I knew staying still was difficult for her because it was unnatural for me. We both liked it hard and fast and this was…well, this was something new.

I increased the pressure and pace.

"This is…I can't," she whimpered. "I'm trying."

"I know you are," I whispered. "You're my filthy, sexy girl aren't you. Letting me fill you like this. Keeping my cock buried inside your cunt. Out on my patio. Do you like this, Victoria? Do you like being used this way?"

"Yes," she groaned. Her head rolled to the side, exposing her silky neck.

"Do you like being my dirty princess?" I kissed her, then bent my head to bite along her neck. "I'll make you break your policy forever. I'll make you mine. And it will be so easy. So bloody easy."

I pressed my thumb on her clit. Actually, the ring on my thumb. She bucked her hips and gasped. I didn't stop her from moving this time. Instead, I withdrew my cock until only the head remained inside her, rubbing her clit faster and harder.

Her mouth opened on a silent groan. She was coming now. Her body shuddered and rolled. When her pussy spasmed around me, I slammed into her again and didn't stop, ruthlessly fucking her harder and deeper, riding through her orgasm. Biting her neck and shoulders. Holding her so tight, so tight.

A dark, primal urgency streaked up my shaft and through my belly and thighs, going right to my spine. My hips jerked and stomach muscles tensed. Her nails dug into my ass and that did it. I climaxed hard.

Vicious, throbbing ecstasy.

The pulsing seemed to go on forever. And every pulse matched the beat of my heart.

It's not lost on me how bare I am with her in ways I'd vowed never to allow again.

I kept spilling inside her, thrusting and milking every last bit of my orgasm until the pulsing subsided.

Then she looked at me with her big green eyes and smiled, sated and content. The sight nearly shattered me on the spot when my chest did the *thing*.

"You make me so weak." She kissed me, curling her hands behind my neck. "So weak. I can't control myself around you."

"You do the same to me," I admitted, holding her close.

We stayed wrapped up like this for a long moment. I would have stayed out here all night if Victoria hadn't shivered in my arms. Years of proper schooling and upbringing finally smacked me on the head and I took off my shirt.

"Put this on." I draped it over her shoulders.

"Thank you." She fastened most of the buttons. "Won't you be cold?"

"No. We're going in now. I need to get you cleaned up."

I helped her off the table, zipped myself back up and led her to the kitchen. She waited while I found a washcloth and cleaned her with warm water. The dreamy look on her face made me smile.

"That's the same smile you had last night out by your car," she mused.

"Is it?" I leaned in and brushed my lips to hers. "Wonder why."

Her eyelids fluttered closed when I deepened our kiss, licking into her mouth gently and reverently. I could kiss her like this forever.

"You know what I think?" she asked against my mouth.

"Tell me."

"I think you should fuck me again. Right now."

"**R**ight now?"

I glanced around the kitchen still trying to get a handle on my breathing from what we'd just finished doing outside. I could go again, obviously. I liked her greedy demand. Victoria is the kind of woman who could get me hard over and over. The kind I'd spend every single day shagging and still want more. I'd bend her over my kitchen counter right now but…

This sounds odd coming from me but I needed a minute to process what the fuck I was feeling.

"You look like you need a drink." She giggled. "Get comfortable on the couch, I'll bring you one."

"You don't have to.“

"I know I don't have to. I want to. Sit." She pointed at the couch with an air of finality and so I did as she requested. Or ordered? I smiled to myself and sank into the cushions.

"Can I ask you something?" Her soft voice sent shivers through me. She walked toward the couch carrying two glasses of scotch. This is a post-sex ritual I could get quite used to.

"You can ask me anything." I took a glass. "You can always ask me anything."

She knelt in front of me between my legs and reclined her forearm on my thigh. The whole thing was so graceful and intimate and natural and…

I will marry this woman.

I nearly choked on my drink.

Noooo, Xavier. What the fuck?

"I've been thinking about what you said at dinner. About renovating houses?" Her eyes widened with a hopeful glow. "Would you be willing to help me find someone who can fix up my family's cottage? I'm sure you have connections or contacts."

I cupped my hand behind her head and smiled. "I'd be happy to help."

"Really?" She looked radiant. "I can give you the keys tomorrow. That way you can go in whenever you want and…well, you can go in if you need to." She smiled and I wanted to kiss her. "Thank you. I realize we don't know each other that well, so, I just…I appreciate it."

I swallowed my drink and put the empty glass on the table. She's right. We don't know each other that well. Something I plan to rectify as soon as possible.

Victoria glanced up at me, her face thoughtful. "You look like you have something you want to say."

"I know the house means a lot to you. When I saw you upset and arguing with the guy from the charity yesterday I wanted to ring his neck. I don't care how much work I do with them, you didn't deserve to be treated that way."

She cast her eyes down. "I call it the Helena effect. When my mom gets involved in things she's like a cyclone sometimes. I'm used to it though. She's been this way since my twin died."

"What about your dad?"

"He's not as chaotic. We talk every once in a while but I can tell there's an undercurrent of heartache. I sound like her. I look like her. But I'm not her so…" Her eyes met mine again. For the first time since we've met, she looked sad. "Sometimes I wonder if they've even noticed everything I've accomplished. They only showed up at my graduation from Dartmouth because my mother said it was a," she made air quotes, "status event."

Her pretty mouth formed a tense line. Some sort of internal battle raged behind those eyes. Almost like she was telling me these things against her will.

"I didn't mean to upset you."

She squeezed my thigh before responding. "You didn't. This is my default reaction when anyone talks to me about my family."

"I bet they're very proud of the exceptional woman you've become."

"Yeah. So proud." Her laugh was bitter. "You wouldn't understand, Xavier. You didn't ruin anyone's life. You're an international soccer star. One of the top athletes to play the sport. Millions of people love you. Your parents must be beside themselves with pride."

I couldn't look at her. "Actually, my dad has zero interest in my career. And my mum died not too long after I was born. The only one who cares a little is my step-mum." I hated how flat and dispassionate my voice sounded.

"I'm so sorry. I assumed…I'm sorry." Victoria climbed onto my lap and hugged me.

I can't remember the last time I let someone comfort me.

This felt good. I held her tighter, burying my face in her neck, getting lost in her warm, vanilla scent. I wanted to comfort her just as much.

When she pulled back to look at me everything shifted. My world tilted. And then the *thing* in my chest hit me. Only it wasn't a thing anymore. It was a feeling. A feeling I've never had before. Frantic, insistent, powerful.

This can't be what I think it is, can it?

Noooo.

I've had girlfriends before. But I never felt this.

Not that Victoria was my girlfriend or anything.

I mean, she could be.

FOCUS, MADDOX.

"You're having one hell of an internal conversation with yourself aren't you?"

Victoria's amused question snapped me back to the present. The present where I had a hot woman straddling me after we had mind-melting sex out on my patio. A gorgeous woman I actually wanted for more than just a quick shag.

A smart, funny, wildly sexy woman I was starting to really care about.

"Sorry." I grinned.

"As a fellow sometimes over-thinker, you're excused." She drew lazy paths along the tattoos on my chest. "I didn't upset you, did I? When I assumed your family was normal?"

"Not really." I shrugged. "I don't generally talk about my mum or dad much so…" I shrugged again, toying with her hair. "But you can ask me about them if you want to."

"Not quite the sexy pillow talk you probably have with your other ladies, is it?"

"Ah, let me think." I rested my hands on her thighs. "I don't have any sexy pillows."

"Jackass," she laughed. "You know what I mean."

"Mmm, I do. You want the truth?"

"Always."

"This will make me sound like a cad, you know." I lifted an eyebrow.

"A professional athlete behaving badly? Pfft. Say it isn't so."

A barrage of nervous energy flowed through me which was weird because I don't get nervous with women. But it's Victoria and I wanted to impress her, not divulge anything super shitty about myself.

"I don't usually engage in pillow talk," I confessed. "I mean, not hours and hours of it. Not even five minutes worth."

"Is that a policy of yours?"

"I don't have any policies or rules." I smirked. "Stuff like that breaks too easily."

"Are you shading me, Maddox?"

"If the policy fits," I joked.

"Wow," she exclaimed, her laughter vibrating in every part of me. "And here I thought you liked me."

I do. I like you too much.

The thought winded me. So did the *thing* in my chest which is now the *feeling* in my chest.

"Not to change the subject or anything," I said, "but how would I go about making a donation to your sister's charity?"

The laughter faded. Her eyes widened in shock. "What?"

"The animal shelter. Do they have a website or something?"

I'm not too proud to admit I was partly doing this because I wanted to score points with her the same way Noah did. My stomach clenched wondering who the fuck that guy was and how he managed to get her to smile the way she did.

"Um, yeah. Yes," she responded. "They have a website. I'll text you the link." She regarded me curiously. "Why are you doing this?"

I lifted my shoulder in a small shrug. "It sounded important when you spoke about it at dinner. Do you not want me to?"

Her head tilted to the side in this adorable, frustrated movement. "They need all the help they can get, Xavier. I'm not going to turn down your generosity. You just surprised me, that's all."

"In a good way?" I leaned back into the cushion and smiled up at her.

The way she straddled my lap in such a graceful, refined manner sent an unexpected shiver up and down my spine. My shirt was much too big on her, so it hung off her shoulder, exposing just enough skin to appear tempting and flirty. Seeing her in my clothes was a massive turn on.

Her gorgeous smile lit me up inside. "Yes, in a good way," she answered. "What other surprises do you have for me?"

Stay in gentleman mode, stay in gentleman mode.

"All will be revealed in due time."

The room came to life with her sweet-sounding laugh. In all the years I've owned this flat it never felt like this. Like an actual home. A place I'd want to share with someone. Even the air feels different. And it's all because this stunning woman walked into my life.

Fidgeting with the too-long sleeves of the shirt, she looked at me with pure wonder, like she was seeing me for the first time. Can't say a woman has ever looked at me in this way before. They're usually fawning over me or wide-eyed about being in my presence or tossing out over-used pick up lines.

Admittedly, I never shied away from the attention because I liked it.

I liked it even though I knew it was superficial and they only wanted to be with me because I'm, well, Xavier Fucking Maddox.

Gentle strokes on my chest disrupted my thoughts. Victoria leaned in, pressing her lips to mine. Her kiss was soft and assured and the sexiest bloody kiss ever. She parted my mouth with her tongue, exploring and savoring me.

I fisted my hand in her hair, ready to tilt and position how I wanted her mouth. But her low moan stopped me. Odd, since I loved those sounds. They fed my natural instinct to be rough and aggressive.

This time I let her retain control and relished how she experienced me.

The sweet way she laced her hands behind my neck.

The soft fluttering of her tongue.

The sexy noises she made when I slid my hands up her thighs to cup her backside.

When she broke the kiss I wanted to grab her and keep going. Especially when she bit down on her lip and gazed at me in that wondrous way again.

Every sense memory I have of her —her taste, her smell, her touch, her sounds— skittered through me, gathering in a cloud of adoration and lust.

Right now lust was winning.

"You look like you have something you want to say," she said. "Do you?"

Fuck gentleman mode.

"Yes." I slid my hand between her legs.

VICTORIA

I surrendered at once, melting from his touch. My back hit the couch with a soft thud when he flipped me over. Xavier knelt in front of me, pulling my hips to the edge of the cushion.

"I could get used to seeing you on your knees," I purred.

"Oh really?"

"It's hot."

He stared up at me. "Quiet."

The way his rough stubble scratched my skin when he kissed his way up my thighs was better than I could have imagined.

Glancing up at me, eyes brimming with lust, he slowly licked my sensitive skin, teasing my entrance. I unbuttoned the shirt I wore —his shirt— and moved my hands to my stomach, lightly caressing myself. The combined sensations sent shivers through me.

Xavier's mouth was on mine in a searing kiss without much warning. One of his hands covered mine, sliding it lower until our fingers stroked my sex together. I moaned against his parted lips when he pushed my fingers inside. I'd done this many times on my own but never with a partner.

"Get wet for me, dirty princess."

"Like I'm not already," I breathed, massaging myself faster, tracing circles around my clit and holding his heated stare.

A low moan passed his lips when he bent his head down to watch what I was doing. He flicked his eyes back to mine. "My turn."

Returning to his knees, he lifted my hand and sucked my arousal off my fingers. The way he closed his eyes and savored what he tasted turned me on even more.

His fingers slid along my folds to the tip of my swollen clit. Then he licked and kissed it. "You taste so good," he whispered against my skin. "I want more."

He spread my legs wider, pressing his fingers into my thighs as he turned all of his attention to the one place I've been waiting for him to explore with his mouth. I squirmed when he opened me with his thumbs and teased me with his fingers.

"We have to work on your patience, love," he told me in his deep, gruff way. "I'm going to take my time with your precious cunt."

This man will most definitely destroy me with his words.

And yeah, I'm totally okay with it.

As promised, he took his time kissing, tasting, and exploring. Feeling his tongue adore and exalt me while he kissed my pussy so deep and thorough was unlike anything I've experienced. Most guys I've been with used oral sex as a gateway to get to the main event. Xavier used it as act of worship.

When he paused to look up at me, I inhaled sharply. A sultry grin curled his glistening lips before he continued taking his sweet time devouring me. I grabbed a handful of his hair and pulled.

His answering groan made my toes curl.

I felt his tongue seek out my beaded, stiff clit.

The steady licks and flickers made me whimper.

When he sucked on it, I bowed my back, causing him to flatten his hand on my stomach to keep me in place.

"I'm going to make you feel so good, love," he murmured, the feel of his breath accelerating my knotting, twisting climax.

He nibbled on it and I bucked my hips so hard I almost slid off the couch. He hooked both his arms under my thighs, holding me tight while he stroked me with his tongue.

Then he sucked my clit and I gasped.

Then—

Sharp, intense pleasure that bordered on pain shot through my body, making it impossible to breathe. I cried out, arching my back, pulling his hair, unable to still the violent tremors coursing through me. I'd never felt anything like this my life. Then I felt the softest, gentlest flicks of his tongue, soothing me and coaxing another orgasm.

My body sunk into the cushions. Sated and relaxed.

If I die now, I'll die happy.

Xavier hovered over my shattered body, licking his lips. He pressed a soft kiss to the corner of my mouth.

"Did you bite my clit?" I asked, sounding a bit delirious.

"Mmm, I wouldn't call it a bite, per se. More like an enthusiastic nibble." He smiled. "I'd ask if you liked it but you came really hard on my tongue. Twice."

"Where the hell did you learn that?"

His quiet laugh sent chills though me. I went limp when he kissed me long, slow and deep.

Chapter
THIRTEEN

Xavier slept soundly next to me. I sat up and watched him, toying with my sore lip. I wanted him to bite it some more. I wanted him to do everything some more. Kiss me, talk dirty to me, bite me, spank me. Well, he hasn't spanked me yet even though I tried to make it happen a couple of times. He totally knew what I was up to.

I felt like the one who needed to be tamed, not him.

Tamed. Held. Loved. His.

Shit.

What am I DOING?

Mind-blowing sex was not part of the plan. An aggressive, possibly dominant man was also not part of the plan. Falling in…nope. Don't even go there.

The plan was the damn house. Nothing more.

Okay fine. I liked him. He's engaging, hot, dirty, fun, mysterious to a degree, spectacular in bed. A pleasurable distraction to an otherwise annoying trip across the pond.

I reached out and touched his hair, gently running my fingers through it.

So soft.

I sifted my fingers through it again, reveling in the feeling. I'd done this so much over the last few days it should feel normal. Yet, sitting here in the dark and sneaking a touch while he slept felt forbidden. Like I was tempting fate.

So I kept tempting. Tracing the scar above his eye. Caressing down his cheek, over his stubbled jaw to his mouth. I moved down his neck to his collarbone, tracing the words *Trust Your Struggle* inked in black script. I should ask him what this meant.

I stopped when his breath hitched.

A hand encased my fingers, squeezing them. Holding my hand tight to his chest, he inhaled slow. Without saying a word, he pulled me down beside him, resting his head in the crook of my neck. He kept my hand firmly pressed to his chest, his eyes remaining closed.

"Victoria. You belong right here. With me. Always." His voice was deep and raspy, thick with sleep. The sound vibrated straight to my core. His warm breath tickled my neck on an exhale.

A powerful compulsion to imagine a future with him tempted and taunted me.

No.

I can't.

This has to end when I get on the plane Wednesday.

It has to.

"This looks ridiculous on me." I turned every which way possible to see myself at all angles in the bathroom mirror. "I'm putting my dress on instead."

I brushed by Xavier, who stood shirtless in jeans with an amused grin on his face. "You'll be in my car. Nobody can see you. Except me. And I think you look cute."

I stopped, turning on my heel to face him. "First of all, bunnies and puppies are cute." He snort-laughed. I continued, "Second, I'm literally swimming in this." I held out my arms. My hands were nonexistent thanks to how long the sleeves on this hoodie were. "And don't get me started on these pants."

He prowled over to me with a smile, led me to his full-length mirror and placed me in front of it. "What's with all the dramatics?" He stood behind me with his hands on my hips. "I like you in my clothes."

I caught his eye in the mirror. They glowed with adoration and mischief. I sighed, soaking in my temporary outfit. A royal blue zip-up hoodie with the Royal City crest sewn on the upper-left chest along with stretchy warm-up pants. He's so damn tall and muscular. I looked like a little kid in his clothes.

"I don't mind wearing this. The problem," I paused when he pressed soft kisses to my neck, "is really just these pants. They're way too long."

"I'm sure you'll sort it out." He grinned, swatted my backside, and walked away to finish getting dressed.

"Menace," I called after him with a smile. I settled on cuffing the pant legs. The fact that every inch of material I had on my body smelled like him didn't escape me. Honestly, it made me lightheaded in a way that was reserved for long-term boyfriend status.

Knock. It. OFF.

Xavier was scrolling through his phone when I walked into the living room.

"Anything good happening on your phone?"

He glanced up. "Not really. But I could take your picture and change all that."

"Don't even think about it," I paused and emphasized, *"mate"* while grabbing my dress and heels.

"I'll post it on Instagram," he teased, watching me put my heels on. "You'll go viral."

"I will end you," I threatened, half-serious. "Besides, I don't need all the unnecessary attention as much as you do."

"Gotta keep the fans happy, love," he said, leading me to the door. "You should follow me. I'll let you slide into my DMs."

I laughed as he fake moaned about only having two million followers while I bragged about my paltry twelve hundred followers that loved to see what coffee mug I used each day.

"You really think I'm going to let you drive my car?" Xavier's inquiry made me jump. I stood by the passenger door waiting for him to unlock it.

"No, I'm, oh." The realization dawned on me. The passenger side for me was the driver's side for him. "Right. Still in England."

"Americans," he muttered with mock distain, laughing at me as I shuffled to the other side of his car.

"You love me," I retorted, looking him straight in the eyes. His easy-going exterior faltered.

I had no filter when I flirted. Approaching the line but never crossing it was one of my favorite games to play. Killian could scoff at my *no sleeping with the product* line all he wanted but he knew my reasoning behind it.

No attachments. Ever.

Broken people didn't get happy endings. Especially the ones at fault for destroying an innocent person's life. Doubly so if that person was their twin. Triply so if it tore the whole family apart.

I already thought of myself as a horrible person. What others said about me could never be worse.

"Thanks for letting me borrow these." I handed the folded hoodie and pants to Xavier. I'd changed into my own clothes and started laying out the rest to pack later.

"Keep them," he offered. "Authentic souvenirs. Way better than a tea cup with the King's face on it."

"I'll pass, thanks," I laughed.

"On the tea cup? Smart move."

"You know what I mean," I grinned.

"You'll change your mind. I could tell you liked being in them."

His ability to combine cockiness, a touch of arrogance, and flirting was pretty masterful. The fact that he could do it without coming off as a complete asshole was also impressive.

"Do you plan on keeping me in this bedroom all day?" The silkiness in his tone prompted me to stop folding and look up. He leaned into the door jamb all casual and hot and boyfriend-like, exuding sex appeal with little effort.

Nope. No more sex. Maybe some kissing. Definitely some kissing but that's it.

"You're free to explore," I suggested. A sultry glow lit up his eyes, forcing me to amend my statement. "The house. You're free to explore the house."

"Smooth. C'mon. Stop fidgeting with your clothes and let's go get lunch. Remember, you're with me all day."

Food sounded like the best idea. Besides, I wanted to see Dawn and Ray before leaving. A little twinge of sadness filled me for not spending as much time with them as I'd planned. Charlotte and I loved going to the Black Rose Tavern. Dawn would always give us extra french fries with our orders. She also worked tirelessly to convince us mayonnaise tasted better on them than ketchup.

Poor thing. We never had the heart to tell her nothing topped ranch dressing.

And then there was Ray. He called us his two little ginger snaps while serving us heaping bowls of Eton's Mess. With all the empty calories we consumed there my mother would always make sure we ate nothing but fruits and vegetables once we got home.

Not too many people were at Black Rose, so we opted to sit at the bar. Dawn came over as soon as she saw us.

"This is a lovely surprise," she beamed, eyeing me warmly.

"Figured it was time to be cordial to my neighbors," Xavier said, winking at Dawn.

"Helps that she's a looker, yeah?" She reached over and ruffled his hair in a motherly way. If I didn't know any better, I'd say Xavier blushed. This man can't possibly have a bashful bone in his body.

I smiled at their interaction. Dawn was about twenty years older than me. She and Ray never had children so I considered her to be the cool aunt type. She was stylish, always ready for a joke, and had the kindest brown eyes.

"You know me," he stated. "Always the gentleman."

"You're a rogue," she declared. "I'm keeping an eye on you." Turning to me she asked, "The usual fish and chips for you, love?"

"Yes, please."

"Same for me," Xavier chimed in. "And don't hold back on the chips."

"I thought your body was a temple," she teased.

"It is." He smirked. "But the temple is closed today."

Dawn scoffed and swatted his arm gently before heading toward the kitchen. I pounced at my chance for a little fun at his expense.

"So you do have the ability to be friends with a woman you haven't slept with."

"Wow. Do you want the knife back that you just plunged into my heart?"

"Drama doesn't suit you." I rested my arm on the bar. "How long have you known Dawn and Ray?"

"Since I moved here. Ten years." He put his hand on my arm, stroking it slowly. "How long have you known them?"

"Forever." The light caresses on my arm set off a flurry of butterflies in my stomach. "I was probably nine or ten when I first met her."

"So before she owned the place?"

"Mmhmm. She worked here then. There was no Ray at the time. Well, there was. They just weren't a thing."

"A thing," he repeated quietly, turning my hand so the palm faced up. "You came here with your family often?" He glided a finger along my palm before holding my hand. I knew what he was doing. He wanted me unguarded.

"We'd come here in the summer. Usually mid-July to mid-August."

He rested his foot on the lower rung of my stool, positioning his leg so it fit between my knees. The constant feel of his body on mine helped assuage my growing anxiety. Keeping my walls up around him became more and more of a challenge. The more physical contact there was, the less resistance I had.

"Did you like coming here?"

"Very much."

He laced his fingers in mine, pulling my hand down to his lap so he could hold it in both of his. He looked at me with his brows knit together, like I was a puzzle meant to be solved. Like there was some huge secret meant to be uncovered.

"You should come back more often."

"Why?"

One shoulder lifted in a small, elegant shrug. "Just a suggestion. Besides, I need someone to swat all the ladies away like you did the other night."

I stifled a giggle. "Seriously?"

"Well, I wasn't going to mention it but yeah, that would be a big help."

"There must be hundreds of them."

"Another knife." He clutched his chest in mock agony. "I don't know whether to kiss you or leave with whatever dignity I have left."

"What happened to nothing about you being fragile? A little truth never hurt anyone."

"Maybe." He ran his tongue along his bottom lip. "I'd end up kissing you though."

"That's a relief."

"Yeah? I could kiss you right now."

I felt my cheeks flush. Sneaky flirt. "You could."

"I want to." He reached to feel my lip, which I knew was still a little bruised. The whisper-soft caress felt so good. "I won't stop if I do."

His hand fell back to his lap to hold mine while I sat beguiled by his words. By his touch. By the way his throat worked when he swallowed. The messy tousle of his hair. The flecks of midnight in his sapphire eyes. The urbane exterior that swaddled the edgy, sexy, filthy lover beneath it.

Two plates of food slid in front of us, breaking the spell.

"Alright you two, enjoy." Dawn caught a glimpse of my hand in his and smiled at me. "I told you to watch out for this one. The charm is real."

Oh, Dawn. You have no idea how real.

He released my hand so we could dig into the food. True to form, the chips were plentiful. I didn't realize how hungry I was. I'd had an apple at Xavier's place this morning but that was it. I wasn't about to make him prepare a gourmet breakfast for me. For one, that's not my style. Plus, it's not what casual flings do. It falls firmly in the long-term boyfriend column, which he was not.

Still, I was curious about so many things. I pulled out my phone and searched his name on social media. I found him pretty quick.

"Hmm. You really like to post photos of yourself diving for the ball."

He glanced over at me. The left corner of his mouth ticked up in a smile. "Checking me out, are you?"

"Well, you know. I suppose I should see what the fuss is all about."

He looked inexplicably sexy in his uniform. Maybe this wasn't as good an idea as I thought. Getting all hot and bothered scrolling through his feed while sitting next to him wasn't exactly smart.

A video of him with a young boy no older than six or seven caught my attention. They were fist bumping and posing for a photo.

"Who is this little boy?" I asked, turning my phone so he could see.

"Oh." His eyes brightened. "He's my number one fan. Theo. We spent part of the afternoon hanging out at training last month."

Another longer video showed Theo meeting other players, including Cade. They were all sitting in the locker room laughing.

I smiled. I love when professional athletes give their time in this way. There was additional footage of Xavier chatting with Theo and showing him around parts of the stadium. Looks like this little boy also got to meet the manager.

And he assisted Xavier in goal with some drills.

My heart melted. Sexy, talented, and a really *good* guy.

I'm so screwed.

"How did this all come about?"

"Funny story actually. He was imitating some of my moves in goal and his dad put together a video with a side by side comparison. It went viral. Apparently the internet thinks I'll be replaced by a six year old this season."

I laughed. "Love it."

I closed out the app and put my phone away. "So, what do you have planned for me for today?" I asked, dipping a french fry in his mayonnaise. "Aside from stopping by the cottage?"

"Do you really want to know or do you want it to be a surprise?" He pushed the mayo closer to me.

"Do you actually have a plan or is this one of your deflection tactics?"

"That's the fun of it," he said silkily. "Keeping you off guard."

"There she is," Ray bellowed, walking over to me. "I heard a rumor you were out here with this hooligan."

Xavier's pout made me laugh.

He waved off Xavier's expression with a good-natured grin and hugged me. "Just as pretty as the last time I saw you. It's been too long, Victoria."

"I know, I know."

"Thank goodness your father keeps us up to date on what you're doing."

My mouth popped open in shock. "He does?"

"Yes, yes. He comes here once a year. Tells us what you're up to. Brags about your fancy job with that American football team all the time."

"I had no idea," I said softly. "I mean, I knew he visited his cousins. I just didn't know he'd come here."

Ray smiled. "Maybe you'll be back more often, too." He looked at Xavier. "Convince her, would ya? Use some of this alleged charm my wife keeps going on and on about."

"I'm working on it."

"I like how you're both conspiring in front of me." I chuckled.

"You class this place up, Victoria," Ray declared. "Besides, Dawn and I consider you family. I don't care how many years have passed, you're always welcome here. Always."

I hugged Ray again, finding it hard to keep the tears from falling. I managed to hold them back though. I missed these people. I missed coming here every summer. I missed my sister. I missed my family. I missed so many things about how life used to be.

"Thank you." I squeezed Ray tight before letting him go. "I'll try to come back."

"You better." His gentle smile almost broke me. "I was very sorry to hear about Charlotte. She was so lovely. You two were always a joy for us every summer. I hope you know we're here if you ever need anything."

The chorus of *this is all your fault, you did this, you don't deserve anyone's kindness* bubbled up with a vengeance.

Chapter
FOURTEEN

I don't even know what else Ray said to me. He hugged me again and went on his way. I let out a harsh exhale only to come face to face with Xavier and his palpable look of concern.

"Can we go?" I stood up before he could object.

I walked out into the cool April air and paced the sidewalk.

I can do this, I told myself. *I'll go to the house, give him the keys, and then we can go on with our day.*

The second I turned around I saw Xavier advancing on me. "Are you alright?"

"I will be."

"Do you want to wait before going to the house? We can do something else. Go down to London for a bit."

I shook my head. "No. Let's just get this over with now."

The drive to the house was the longest ten minutes I've ever experienced. I couldn't shake the trepidation and nerves. When we arrived, I went straight to the kitchen to grab the extra set of keys the realtor used.

"These are for you." I handed them to Xavier. "Thank you for doing this."

He half-smiled. "Does this mean I have free reign of the place?"

"Ray and Dawn also have a spare set, so if any funny business takes place here, they'll know about it."

"I'll be on my best neighborly behavior."

I rolled my eyes. "Just make sure no weirdos show up. And if you want to wander around all judgey about the furniture or paint color or whatever, be my guest."

"That I can do." He grinned. "You never did finish giving me a tour."

"What could you possibly want to see?"

"Something I've been wondering about…" His voice trailed off as he left the kitchen.

I followed him back to the foyer and ran up the stairs after him. He passed Charlotte's room and poked his head into mine.

"Little Victoria's favorite color is yellow." The lascivious grin on his face hit me like a ton of bricks. "What else can I learn in here?"

"Shit," I muttered, chasing him.

Xavier caught me the second I ran in. He cupped my face, staring at me softly. His eyes are the perfect mix of sapphire and sky. Dark and light. They are, quite honestly, everything.

He bent to kiss me, taking my mouth gently, licking and kissing my lower lip.

"Does it hurt today?" he asked.

"Not really. It's sore. But a good sore, if that makes sense."

"It does. How about the rest of you? Feeling okay?"

"Sore." I grinned. "The good kind."

He tucked some of my hair behind my ear. "Good."

I searched his flushed face and heavy-lidded eyes. There were so many things I should say but my words were halted by the stillness of this moment. The heavy quiet of being in this house, in this room, with him.

Another kiss. This one more possessive. I felt myself go slack. His arms banded around my waist, holding me tight. There was something more than just the literal weight of his body pressed to mine. Something heavier. His head dropped to my forehead when he broke our kiss.

"Tell me what you're thinking."

"I don't know if I can," I whispered.

"Try."

So many jumbled thoughts filled my mind. All of them sparked memories of this cottage. My family. What I'd lost.

Xavier slid his fingers under my chin when I tried to look away, keeping my face angled toward his. Keeping me present. After everything we've done and shared these last few days this moment felt the most vulnerable.

Too vulnerable. Too many feelings. But standing here with him like him felt…*safe*.

"When I leave," I paused when he brushed his thumb over my mouth, "I want my last memory of this house to be of you here with me."

Some type of realization or acceptance or confirmation crossed his features. He bowed his head and swallowed before looking at me.

His lips moved over mine in a whisper of warmth and softness. He licked the seam of my lips slowly, almost asking permission to be let inside. It's so different from any kiss we've shared. There's no frantic lust. No overt possession.

This is how we'd kiss if we were actually together.

His fingers went into my hair, tugging so softly I almost couldn't feel it. He simply savored me. This kiss just might be the one that does me in. The slow dance of his tongue. The firm pressure of his mouth. This was the most tender, passionate kiss of my life.

It's everything I wanted. He's everything I wanted. Everything I dreamed about.

Everything I didn't deserve. I had to stop it. I was losing control.

I pulled away. "Xavier."

"Victoria."

"Okay good. We know each other's names." I wriggled out of his arms and paced the floor. "We need to—"

The shrill ringing of my cell phone interrupted me. Of course. Always a phone. I pulled it out of my pocket, looked at the screen and nearly threw it across the room.

Not now.

NOT NOW.

I silenced it, letting out a frustrated breath.

"Boyfriend?" Xavier lifted an eyebrow.

"Not quite," I snapped.

He held up his hands in resignation. "Alright. No need to bite my head off."

"Sorry," I grumbled, pacing the floor again. The phone rang in my hand. I stopped, looked down at it and wanted to cry. I had to answer. If I didn't, the ringing would never end.

"What?" I growled.

"Is that any way to greet your mother? You're a grown woman. I swear, your manners are nonexistent."

I held the phone so tight I thought I might crack the screen. "Sorry, Helena. Hello, how are you?"

Something caught my attention near the bed. I looked over as Xavier sat down, his eyes fixed on me.

Fan-fucking-tastic.

"I wish you wouldn't call me that," she muttered.

"It's either that or we're back to what."

I heard utensils clattering on plates. She must be having breakfast. Oh wait. Helena does intermittent fasting. She's probably having coffee. Her husband was the one who eats everything in sight. I rolled my eyes.

"You and Dan enjoying the view from your palace?" My tone dripped with sarcasm.

"We are," she gushed, missing my venom and mistaking my question for actual interest. "It's beautiful here. We're going out on the boat later. You should really move somewhere better than Manhattan. Ugh. All that concrete and exhaust."

I clenched my fist.

"Now that you mention it, there's a house for sale in the English countryside. I'm standing in it right now. Empty, messy, broken, sad. Sound familiar?"

My pacing path crossed where Xavier was seated. I glanced at him. He looked stoic. His expression was unreadable. But those eyes remained glued to me, following every move I made. I turned and walked into the hallway. Having him watch me so closely added to my rising anxiety.

"That's why I'm calling. Why are you being so stubborn about the damn house? I want it gone."

"What about dad? What does he want?"

"Your father wants to enjoy his life in Ekali and spend long weekends in Mykonos. He doesn't care what happens to it."

Xavier's shadowed figure appeared in the doorway while I continued to pace up and down the hallway. I shot him a deadly look, hoping he'd get the message. The last thing I needed was an audience.

"Then if he doesn't care, why do you?"

"You know why, Victoria," she spat. "That house is alive with memories. Get rid of it."

I stopped pacing and started shaking. "Alive with…you haven't set foot here in nineteen years," I shouted. "What fucking memories live in you from this house? I'm the one standing in it right now. I'm the one cleaning up your mess. I'm—"

"You're the one who caused all this." Her voice blared through my phone. "You just had to go to that party. You just had to drag your sister. Your. Sister." Glass shattered in the background. "She was just starting to feel better, Victoria. She was healing. But you're so selfish. You only think about yourself."

"I'm not selfish." I sobbed openly now. "Charlotte was my—"

"Do not say her name in my presence."

I ended the call. My hands shook uncontrollably. Tears spilled from my eyes. My whole body hurt. I couldn't breathe. I couldn't move.

The phone rang again. I dropped it like it was on fire, walked away and crumbled to the floor, burying my head in my hands. This was so messed up. Nobody in my family healed properly from this. Nobody. We all ran from it in our own ways and then attacked one another when the pain reared its ugly head.

I thought I heard someone talking. I lifted my head. The silence was deafening. My phone wasn't ringing anymore. Thank—

"Yes. I'll be buying the house. My realtor will finalize everything this week."

I looked up, horrified. What the actual fuck was Xavier doing? His whole demeanor was impenetrable as he stared at me. He almost appeared god-like in his determined stature. Tall, strong, fierce.

I scrambled to my feet, reaching for the phone. The determined look in his eyes halted me.

"You misunderstand me. It'll be in Victoria's name. It's this or nothing. Actually I can do that."

No, no, no.

"Xavier," I hissed. "Give me the phone."

He wiped the tears from my face, his gaze softening briefly. "My reasoning is none of your business. Take the offer or I'll get in touch with her father to initiate the transfer into her trust."

Everything went blurry. Too many versions of reality collided.

"I'm sure he'd be more willing to accommodate his daughter than you."

I couldn't listen anymore. I ran down to Charlotte's room. Her room was always our meeting place late at night. The safe haven. We'd lay on her fluffy rug wrapped in soft blankets and talk for hours. Dream about the future. Imagine our lives and careers and maybe families of our own.

I laid on my back, covered my face and sighed. Exhaustion consumed every muscle in my body. I longed to be in my own bed, surrounded by the familiar sounds of New York.

"Mind if I join you?"

I was too drained to be snarky. "Sure. Pull up some rug and have a lie down."

Xavier stretched out on his side next to me, placing his hand on my stomach. Keeping my emotions in check was impossible, so I curled into him for comfort. The tenderness he showed overwhelmed me. Pulling me close, he held me tight. I snuggled into his chest, listening to the steady beat of his heart.

"I'm not going to ask you," he said. "I just want you to know, you can tell me when you're ready."

I squeezed him, holding back a sob. I wanted to tell him. I wanted to unburden myself from this guilt. Unloading all of that on him wouldn't be fair. I closed my eyes, nuzzling into his neck. He responded by combing his fingers through my hair.

"Why are you doing this?" I asked against his skin.

"I can't explain it."

"Try?"

He kissed the top of my head, letting his lips linger. "Grief isn't easy. Everyone responds differently and I suspect your family is still dealing with…I don't know what happened but it's obvious nobody has fully dealt with it."

I propped myself up on my elbow. "What happened to your mom?" I regretted the question the second I asked it.

Much to my surprise, he answered, "Complications from child birth. I was only about six hours old when she died." He touched my cheek. "What happened to your sister?"

I pushed myself up, sitting cross-legged in front of him. He mimicked my movements, sitting the same way. I wanted to share and be open and let myself heal.

The fact that we're sitting here in my sister's room talking about this didn't escape me. Neither did the affectionate glow in his eyes when I looked up at him. My God, he was so handsome.

Staring at him made me want to kiss him. Kissing him led to more. More provided me with the escape I so desperately craved.

I can't keep taking from him like that.

"The anniversary of her death is this month. She…she, um, took her own life. Swallowed too many pills and…" I stopped, not willing to say more. "That's why I've been such a lunatic about this house. I haven't been here since the final summer we were all together. She died the following spring."

He was quiet for a while, holding my hand and studying my expression. The heaviness in this house became suffocating.

"I'm so sorry, Victoria," he said softly. "I don't know…I wish I knew what to say."

I half-smiled. "You don't have to say anything. Listening is enough." I laced my fingers through his. "Sorry about the whole being a lunatic thing."

"A cute lunatic." The gentle way he said it coupled with that damn crooked grin lifted my spirits.

"God," I laughed.

"Not quite. Close though." He stood up, helping me do the same. "Ready to head out?"

"Uh, no. I have questions."

"I'm sure you do."

"Sit." I pointed to the bed. "Please."

I gathered my thoughts while he did as I asked. Everything that's happened since I stepped foot off the plane has been confusing to say the least. I'm not normally one for carefully laid out plans but this trip was the one exception. This was the one thing that had to follow the outline. There was no room for detours.

And yet, all I've encountered were detours.

"What happened with my mother?"

He lifted an eyebrow. "We had a chat. Lovely woman."

"Lies." I started pacing.

"Do you always do this," he gestured his hand in a figure eight to illustrate my path around the room, "when you're stressed?"

"Yep." I stopped, putting my hands on my hips. "You're deflecting, Maddox."

"Possibly."

"So what happened? Why did you tell her you were buying the house?"

He regarded me thoughtfully, taking his time before answering, "It's the easiest way to give everyone what they want."

"What we…" I sputtered. "You have no idea what I want. What any of us wants."

"I know what I want."

"What does this have to do with you?" I snapped.

He winced at the nastiness in my tone, clasping his hands together. Unease and vulnerability seeped from him. Even though I didn't know him well, I knew enough to recognize this was an emotion he'd rather not have me witness.

"You want to hold onto," he spread his arms out, "this. As much as it hurts you, that's what you want. Your mother wants it all to disappear. I want…" He swallowed. "I want there to be a reason for you to come back here. To come back to me."

What the hell was happening? He looked so uncomfortable in his own skin I almost went over to comfort him. Almost. He wanted me to come back? I didn't need this house for that. He was reason enough.

My heart fluttered.

He was more than reason enough. He was *the* reason. He saw me. He calmed me. He reached parts of me I believed were inaccessible. He was…

My mind raced, spiraling into its own sinister thoughts.

He'll drop you the minute he finds out how worthless you really are. How broken you are. How messed up. How you get by every day hanging on by a string. Nobody wants to know the real you. They only want the version you show them.

Breathing became difficult.

My chest hurt. My lungs hurt. My heart hurt.

I'd worked myself into a panic. Pacing the room wasn't enough.

A screw tightened somewhere deep in my chest. It ground into me tighter and tighter and….why is this silence so goddam loud?

Out.

OUT.

I needed to get out.

I needed to leave.

I needed to get as far away from here as possible.

"I have to pack. Can we go?" My voice cracked.

Our eyes locked and all the feelings that came along with it surged through me. When he stood up to approach me I backed away.

If he touched me, I'd lose it. If he kissed me, I'd surrender.

I wanted it more than anything.

I can't have it.

This was a mistake.

All of it was a mistake.

We left in silence. Thankfully, the drive to my rental was quick. I hopped out of the car before he put it in park and ran to the door. His footsteps weren't far behind.

"Victoria."

The sound of his voice tightened the screw.

I opened the door to seek refuge but he was right behind me.

"Listen to me. Please." He reached for my hand, placing it to his chest. Just like last night in bed when he was groggy with sleep. When he told me I belonged here with him. Words he most likely didn't remember.

"I realize we don't know one another well. But what I do know about you," he hesitated, licking his lips, "I like very much."

"What could you possibly like about me?"

He was an exposed nerve, standing with my hand pressed tight to his chest. "Where to start. You're smart, bloody hilarious, honest. You go after what you want without apology." He held my hand tighter. "You keep it locked up, but you have a big heart. Big enough to let some arse like me in, even just a little. You have more to give than you realize."

Tears flowed from my eyes. "Give? All I've done is take from you."

He leaned his forehead to mine with a sigh. "I know, love. I've taken just as much from you."

Jesus Christ. We're so alike. And it scared me. It scared me how easy it was for him to see I took from him without regret, without any second thoughts. It terrified me that it didn't send him running.

"I don't want you to be alone tonight," he whispered.

"We can't…I can't have sex with you again."

"That's not what I'm asking."

Lines are blurring.

"Don't do that," I stammered.

"Don't do what?"

"Don't give me hope I deserve more."

He held my face in his hands in the gentle way he'd done earlier. The way that made me feel cared for, wanted, adored. The way I'd always dreamed it could be.

When I looked into his eyes, I shivered. So much raw emotion filled them.

"You do, Victoria. Let me give you more, please."

Lines are being crossed.

I could fall for him. I could fall so hard I'd never recover.

The screw tightened and tightened and tightened.

It's too much, too fast. I feel too much. I said too much.

I pulled away from him so forcefully we both gasped.

"I can't. We can't."

"We can try."

"No."

He exhaled in frustration. "Victoria."

Snap.

"Enough," I shouted. "You were supposed to be a one night stand. That's all. I fucked you to distract myself from having to deal with… with…" I threw my arms up "…all of this. We aren't anything. You're a casual fling. Nothing more. You have to go. Now. Please, Xavier."

Confusion and hurt flashed across his features. He stared at me, almost disoriented. Then, as though waking from a nightmare, his protective outer shell began to rebuild itself. His eyes dulled, his facial expression hardened.

"Okay," he responded, his tone flat and dismissive.

Any traces of the impassioned weekend we'd spent together disappeared the moment he walked out the front door without so much as a backwards glance. It slammed shut, filling the empty hallway with a hollow *crack*. I'd gotten what I wanted.

And it destroyed me.

Chapter
FIFTEEN

Killian: Party express, now boardingggggggg

I sighed, tossing my phone on the bed. Killian's texts were like DEFCON alerts. The more letters he left trailing at the end, the more impatient or excited he was for something to happen. Judging by the amount of 'g's', he was bursting at the seams.

Admittedly, I was excited too. Legends quarterback Noah Tate's annual fundraiser started in less than an hour. Every year he held it at a different venue, and this year it was at a trendy new restaurant and bar called The Roof.

I dabbed some gloss to my lips and did one last check in the mirror. Black lace dress. Red heels. Hair loose and wavy. *You clean up ok, Chase. For a horrible person.*

By the time I got down to the lobby of my building, Killian was waiting, tapping his foot. "The queen emerges," he proclaimed, engulfing me in a tight hug. "You are stunning. Stun-ing."

"Good to know you received your payment for compliments this week."

"Baby girl," he draped an arm over my shoulders, "my compliments are always free of charge. Let's go."

He led me out to the waiting limo, where Maxim was already seated with a glass of champagne.

"Beautiful girl on approach." He let out a low whistle and handed me a glass. "Welcome home."

"Good to be back."

We toasted as the car pulled into Manhattan traffic. I'd been home from England for a few days but this was our first night out together. I'd thrown myself into working to keep my mind off what happened with Xavier. I felt tremendous guilt for treating him like shit.

My anxiety hasn't reared its ugly head like that in years. I should reach out to him.

But every time I wanted to text him, I chickened out. What could I possibly say? I called him a casual fling and kicked him out of my rental house. Not my best moment.

I drained the glass, swallowing any and all emotions down with it. Tonight was for fun and shenanigans. I'll try to keep the self-pity and wallowing to a minimum.

The upcoming week promised to be a busy one with the draft in town. Noah's fundraiser wasn't an official part of the festivities but it certainly helped set the tone. There were so many events to look forward to. It's like Christmas for the football league. Aside from winning the championship, of course.

Camera crews lined the sidewalk outside the restaurant. They were cordoned off behind some barriers to give the players space as they arrived.

Killian whipped out his phone. "Selfie time, story time, live stream time."

I laughed at my best friend's ability to turn any situation into an opportunity to grow his audience. He pointed the phone at me as we entered the restaurant.

"I'm here with Manhattan socialite and media relations goddess, Victoria Chase, to unofficially kick off Draft Week," he said in his best tabloid reporter voice. "Ms. Chase, how do you think the Legends will fair this year?"

I giggled, pulling Maxim into the frame with me. "I don't know, Mr. Monroe, but this hot guy and I are looking forward to the open bar inside."

Killian turned and held up his phone so we all fit in the screen. "Coming in hot," he exclaimed.

I loved when Killian acted ridiculous like this. Sure, we probably weren't acting our age but who cares. Nobody else's opinion mattered. And to be honest, a little frivolity never hurt anyone.

"This restaurant is the shit," Maxim declared.

"That'll be a dollar," Killian shouted with a laugh.

Maxim wasn't wrong. This restaurant was a vibe. It looked and felt like we'd stepped out onto a rooftop deck. A very fancy one.

Since this building used to be an old warehouse, the sky-high ceilings gave off the impression we really were outside. The ceiling even had twinkling lights embedded in it to look like stars. A huge bar was located in the center with all the tables scattered around it. String lights crisscrossed above the bar out to several columns. Plush couches lined the walls for anyone who just wanted to sit and enjoy a few drinks or appetizers.

A good majority of our team and other players from around the league showed up for Noah's event. He was not only highly respected by all his teammates and coaches, but by players from opposing teams as well. He held court near the bar, no doubt retelling the story of the Legends' most recent championship victory to an enamored group of party-goers.

"Victoria. Nice to finally see you."

I looked over to see Tre Gideon, our newest asset, approaching. The wide receiver made waves after leaving Denver to become a free agent. He was rather vocal on social media about where he wanted his landing spot to be.

Fortunately, the Legends were open for discussions. And here we are.

"How long has it been?" he asked, hugging me. "Last time you guys were in Denver, it wasn't a pretty game."

"Nope. Not for you it wasn't." I grinned, remembering the blowout loss we handed his team. "But now you're with the good guys."

"Or the evil empire, depending on who you ask."

"Mind if I grab a photo of you two?" Scott, the team's official photographer stopped in front of us and raised his camera.

"Not at all," Tre replied. I sidled up next to him and smiled for the camera.

"Thanks. Enjoy the event." Scott meandered off toward the bar.

"I might as well get one too. I need to freshen my feed anyway," Killian smirked, whipping out his phone.

I shot Killian a look. "Sure. Tre, that's Killian, my pain-in-the-ass best friend."

Tre laughed and kept me snug against his side. "New York is the place to be seen," he said. "I don't mind a few photos. Especially with this stunning lady." We smiled for him.

Tre reached out and shook Killian's hand. "Nice meeting you." A bright smile lit up his face when he turned to me. "Good seeing you again, Victoria. Catch you at the stadium soon."

I watched him saunter over to Noah and some of the other guys from the offense. A sharp poke in my side jolted me.

"Ow. Killian what the fuck," I yelped.

"You little minx." His brows slashed down in accusation. "That's the wide receiver, isn't it?"

"The one we just signed? Yeah. No need to poke me over it."

He grabbed my elbow and led me to one of the couches near the wall. "You are fully aware that's not what I mean. He walked right out of the Victoria Chase Handbook for Men. Also, he looks a little too much like Maxim. Is there something you're not telling me?"

I folded my arms and attempted to glare at him but my expression came off more as a confession than a scolding. "I don't have the hots for Max. And I'm not his type, so you don't have to worry."

"But that guy is your type times infinity."

"Okay, fine. Yes, that's the wide receiver. Happy now?"

"I knew it." The smug look on his face irked me. The last thing I needed or wanted was a lecture on my sex life. "Does anyone else know?"

"No. And I'd like to keep it that way so shut your face."

"I just don't want to see you go down the rabbit hole of—"

"It. Was. One. Time." My voice rose in frustration. "Six months ago. This is the first time I've seen him since."

Maxim curled his arms around me from behind. Great. A tag team.

"We just want what's best for you. I consider you family, too."

I sighed. "I know what you're both doing and I love you to pieces but it's not an issue. Really. If we're laying all the cards on the table, he was the last person I was with before—"

I couldn't bring myself to say his name. If I did, I'd break apart in front of all these people. What were they serving at the open bar anyway?

Killian touched my cheek. He looked at me softly, tilted his head and said in a gentle tone, "At least you can find comfort in B-O-B again."

"You're an ass," I laughed.

"Wait," Maxim let me go and looked at both of us. "Who's Bob?"

His confusion only made me laugh harder. Killian laughed himself into a coughing fit. Poor Max sat down and waited for us to collect ourselves.

"It's not a *who*. It's a battery operated boyfriend. B-O-B," I explained. "You know, a vibrator."

"You two should have your own YouTube channel," Max chuckled, shaking his head. "Does this conclude the latest chapter of *as the world spins through the days of my life?*"

"Yes," Killian and I declared in unison.

We went back to the party and didn't mention boyfriends, battery operated or otherwise, again.

This was exactly the night I needed. After a couple hours, word spread that some players and other party-goers planned to continue the festivities at The Estate, one of New York City's most exclusive clubs.

Not one to turn down an invitation, I joined them without a second thought, along with Maxim and Killian.

If the amount of people lined up in front of the club was any indication, the crowd inside promised to be huge. We were all escorted to the second level.

The VIP area circled above the main floor and was already prepped for our arrival. Bottles topped every table and the private bar was open.

"Baby girl, we need to do this more often," Killian exclaimed over the music. "I feel like I'm in my twenties again, only without all the self-loathing and insecurities."

The three of us went over to the bar where Maxim promptly ordered a round of shots. Top shelf tequila shots, no less. And he ordered six of them.

The bartender lined the shots up in front of us, along with salt and limes. We all grabbed one.

Maxim lifted his glass and started the toast, "Here's to you, here's to me."

"Best friends we'll ever be," Killian joined in.

"If we ever disagree, fuck you here's to me," I jumped in, ending with the two of them in unison.

The shots went down so easy. Too easy. I smiled, my brain becoming all fuzzy and relaxed. We sat with some of the crew from marketing and sales. Everyone was buzzing about the upcoming draft, but more importantly, all the parties. I planned to attend a couple of the events, just to do the rounds as per usual.

Hannah walked over looking stylish in her champagne-colored cocktail dress and sat down with us.

"My favorite media maven," she exclaimed, hugging me. "Are you ready for this week?"

"I'm always ready," I smiled.

"Let's get a picture," she said, pulling out her phone and snapping a selfie of us. "Bennet follows me now on social media and really enjoys when I post stuff like this. And you look so stunning. I'll tell him to show Xavier."

I have no idea how I kept a smile plastered to my face. Hannah kept babbling about Bennet and some phone call and a salacious late night video chat while she posted the photo. I grabbed whatever drink Killian had in his hand and finished it.

"Hey," he frowned. "You owe me one."

"They're free," I motioned to the bar.

Drinks flowed. Music blared. The floor vibrated from the bass, almost echoing my heartbeat. Lights spun around, flashing in various colors. We danced and laughed and drank and danced some more. Killian was right. It did feel like we were in our twenties again.

Hannah kept snapping photos. Killian kept recording videos. Max and I kept dancing until we were breathless and needed to sit.

A server appeared with another round of shots for all of us. Yes, yes, yes. The more the merrier.

"These are courtesy of your quarterback."

We all craned our necks to find Noah Tate. He was over by the railing dancing with his girlfriend.

"Noah," we shouted, raising our glasses. "Stay Legendary."

With an answering yell, he came over and squeezed his six-foot-six frame in on the couch next to me. My phone was laying on the table, so I asked the server to grab it for a photo. We all smushed together as close as we could. The server kept waving her hands together for everyone to get even closer.

"Victoria," Noah said loudly in my ear. "Don't take this the wrong way, but sit in my lap so the big guys can squeeze in. Tracey won't mind."

I hopped in his lap giving a thumbs up to his girlfriend. She returned the thumbs up and had her own phone out, documenting what was now becoming a team photo. So was Killian. I'd bet all of Noah's championship rings Killian was live streaming this moment.

Hannah ended up sitting in a lap as well. So did anyone who wasn't a linebacker, running back, wide receiver, safety, or tight end. The camaraderie in this organization ran so much deeper than just the fifty-three guys on the field. I loved working with this team. With these amazing humans.

"It's two in the morning. Do you know where your morals are?" Some drunk guy shouted to nobody in particular from the sunroof of his limo.

"I'll ask your dad when I see him in a few," Killian shouted back.

"And you say I'm the bad influence," I laughed, wobbling a bit in my heels.

We were on the hunt for some street food. The greasier and saltier, the better. I can't remember the last time I was out this late drinking and partying and generally ignoring being an adult.

The vibrant sounds of New York City were just as lively in the middle of the night as they were during the day. I loved it.

"Pretzel or hot dog?" Maxim asked, standing by a street vendor.

"Both." I replied.

"As you wish."

Scarfing down this food was priority number one, then flopping into my bed. The boys ended up ordering hot dogs and pretzels as well. We walked together down the street for a bit, double fisting our post-party snacks. Maxim managed to find some empty cafe tables for us to sit.

I yelped when the cool metal chair hit my bare legs.

"Aw, poor thing's cold," Killian teased. "Wanna sit in my lap? Noah won't mind."

His frivolous question stole my breath. In a flash, I was transported back to the event in London when Xavier said similar words to me, wrapped in a much different intention. I bit into the hot dog, gathering my emotions. These last few hours may have been the longest I'd gone without thinking of him.

"Have you decided what you're wearing to the Met Gala?" Maxim asked.

I shook my head. The gala was coming up quick and I really wanted to look amazing. I had a few options, I just needed to pick one.

"If it helps," Killian spoke between mouthfuls, "Max and I are wearing all black tuxes."

"So you're saying I should wear an all black tux as well?"

"Do you have any idea how hot you'd look in one of those?" Killian clutched his chest. "I'm dead just thinking about it."

I laughed, popping some pretzel in my mouth. "Come over tomorrow after I'm finished at the cemetery. I'll show you what I have in mind."

"Are you sure you don't want us to go with you?"

I shivered slightly in the cool breeze. "I'm sure. Thank you anyway."

"It's freezing." Max complained. "Ready to call it a night?"

We all finished our snacks and walked to the waiting limo. When we arrived at my building, both of them hugged me so hard I thought I might break. I waved goodbye, went up to my condo and got ready for bed. In an effort to ward off a potential hangover, I downed a bottle of water and took a pain reliever. Sliding under the covers and snuggling into the pillows was the best feeling after a night like this.

I grabbed my phone to see the picture from the club. I have to say, I looked happy. Everyone did. I grinned, posting it with the caption *When Legends gather, greatness follows.*

Exhaustion swept over me, blurring my vision. I scrolled through the feed, liking pictures here and there.

Killian: Home safe. Night baby girl

I responded to Killian and meant to put the phone away.

But I didn't.

I shouldn't text Xavier but I wanted to. I'm too old for all this ridiculous angst. We're both adults. I should start acting like one. I was a colossal asshole to him and I have to be the bigger person here. Whether he wanted to hear from me or not was another story.

I miss you, I'm sorry, I'm thinking of you…

Me: Sorry if I hurt you.

Chapter
SIXTEEN

The cemetery was quiet and empty. Well, almost empty. A teenage boy leaned against one of the headstones with a sketch pad. I propped myself up on my knees, leaning back on my feet. Reaching forward, I rearranged the pink roses I'd placed in front of Charlotte's grave. Seeing my twin's name etched in stone was a gut punch every single time. Tears pricked at the corners of my eyes.

"So," I sighed, "I guess you know all the shit that went down in England. Mom's always on some crusade. Did I do the right thing though? Should I have just signed the paperwork?"

I pulled on some blades of grass. The sun dipped behind a cloud, muting the sky. Not in an ominous way though.

A sparrow landed on the gravestone, twitching its head this way and that, showing off its glossy dark blue feathers. I'd read somewhere that sparrows were symbols of hope. I'd also read they were symbols of sorrow so I guess it depends on which culture's description best fit the situation.

"Xavier was unexpected, wasn't he?"

The roses rustled in the soft breeze.

"Yeah, I know."

I plucked a petal from one of the roses, rubbing its velvet softness between my fingers.

"I can't take back what I said, Charlie. As much as I want to, I can't."

A squirrel ran by, frantically searching for something. Its tail twitched when it sat upright to stare at me.

"And then there's the really great drunk text I sent him in the middle of the night."

I rolled my head back, looking up. Hitting send seemed so wise at the time. When I woke up this morning I thought it was just a dream. Then I looked at my phone. Nope, I actually sent it. The most disingenuous sounding text ever. In my inebriated head, it sounded soft and caring. On the phone, it came off as dismissive.

"No wonder he didn't respond," I muttered.

Birds chirped in the distance, interrupting the solace of the cemetery. I folded my arms, aware that I sounded like a jackass.

"I wish you were here. You were always so much smarter than me about this shit." I sighed. "Oh. Your diary. I sort of found it at the house. Well, I didn't find it. But you know that already. I haven't read it. But I am curious…"

Talking out loud to her gave me a false sense of peace. And I needed that more than anything right now.

"Excuse me," an unfamiliar, shy voice sounded near me.

The sparrow took off.

I looked up into the curious brown eyes of the boy with the sketch pad. "Yes?"

"Sorry to bother you but is this a relative?"

I blinked. "Yes. My twin sister."

"Oh," he said softly. "I drew this the other day. Would you like it?"

He handed me a beautiful drawing of Charlotte's gravestone. Hovering above it, a red butterfly.

"I had to use the red for the butterfly. It was so pretty. I'd never seen a red one before. I hope you don't mind the rest of it is still black and white."

"It's lovely. Thank you."

The boy's shy smile radiated warmth. "I'm glad you like it. I hope it captures your sister's spirit." He wandered off to another part of the cemetery.

Seconds later, the sparrow returned. It could have been a different one for all I knew but I had a weird feeling it was the same one. I glanced from the bird to the drawing and sighed.

"I'm fully aware you can't actually give me your blessing to read the diary but," I gestured around, "I feel as though…it's almost like you wanted me to find it. I never would have gone up to your room in a million years if I hadn't been chasing him."

I paused, looking at the drawing. And then at the bird. And then up at the sky.

"Right. Of course. That was the idea. I want to know what happened. Why you were so upset. And now I might have the answer."

The sparrow hopped in a circle, twitched its head back and forth, and flew off.

XAVIER

"Open up, Maddox," Bennet yelled, pounding on my front door.

I'd rather not, thanks. Sitting here on the couch will do just fine. I closed my eyes, leaning my head back. Sundays are for football, not brute force entry.

Knock, knock, knock.

Pause.

BANG, BANG, BANG.

My phone started ringing. He wasn't going to let up.

"Alright, fine," I yelled. "I'm coming. Knock it off, for fuck's sake."

I shuffled to the door, opening it in frustration.

"You look like shit," Bennet declared, pushing past me.

"Guess that means our chances of shagging are low."

"I'm not in the mood for your attitude," he grumbled. "Where the fuck have you been? You haven't answered my calls. Cade says he can't reach you." He scanned the living room before stomping into my kitchen.

"Hate to break it to you mate, nothing in there but empty take away boxes." I followed him.

"Xavier," he sighed, sitting heavily on the kitchen bar stool. "It's been three days since anyone's seen you or heard from you. I thought we had an agreement."

I shrugged. "Haven't really been in a talking mood."

"What mood are you in then? Reach out to anyone you shouldn't be talking to?" His berating tone hit me hard. Bennet rarely lost his temper. And when he did, it was usually out of frustration with something I'd done to worry him.

I stared at him, holding his penetrating gaze. "No," I finally said quietly. "I just needed to be alone. Been, you know, exercising, drinking, eating, drinking some more. All the really healthy shit."

"Except showering, apparently," he muttered.

I threw an empty soda can at him. "Rude."

"Or shaving."

"Did you come here specifically to take the piss out of me or what?"

He got up and started throwing out the empty food tins. "Are you going to tell me what happened with Victoria or do I have to drag it out of you?"

"Depends. You using a paddle or a flogger?"

He dropped the containers in the trash and glared at me. "I get it, Maddox. You don't like to divulge. But you haven't been this enamored by a woman in…ever. I also know you won't admit it out loud. Have you at least reached out to her?"

"And what fucking good would that do?"

Bennet held up his hand to shush me and started scrolling through his phone. I assumed it was work related but no. He shoved the phone in my face. I stared at a photo of Hannah and Victoria. Both looked radiant but Victoria was ethereal. Perfect. My stomach clenched.

"Scroll," he ordered.

"When was this?" I couldn't take my eyes off the screen. Victoria with her friends. Victoria with Hannah again. Victoria smiling and dancing. Victoria sitting on some twat's lap. I scowled. She looked incredible in that black lace dress and should be sitting on *me*.

"Last night. Hannah sent me a whole bunch of photos from some party." He put his hands on my shoulders. "I had to tell Hannah you two had some type of falling out because she specifically sent those to me to show you."

I looked up at my friend and sighed.

VICTORIA

"You doing okay over there? I know this past week was the anniversary and a general bucket of suck thanks to everything that went down in England but I refuse to let you sink into some black hole of mopey, depressing shit." Killian's stern, clear voice punched through my pity party. "Especially since I know it's not her you're moping about."

"I'm not moping. I'm…what are you talking about?"

He picked one of the dresses up off my bed and tossed it to me. "Do you really want me to invoke his name?"

"I'm not going to burst into flame if you do."

"Have you guys spoken?"

"Not exactly." I took off my jeans and sweater and stepped into the dress.

"You drunk texted him didn't you?"

"Maybe." I pulled the dress up and turned so Killian could zip it for me.

We both in stood in front of my floor mirror, scrutinizing the ensemble. Typical pageant style dress. Baroque pattern, sequins, deep v-neck, maxi length with a mermaid hem. I wrinkled my nose. Why did I think this would be a good choice again?

"It looks divine on you but," Killian paused, tilting his head side to side, "it's not your vibe. I'm getting real housewives or something."

"Off with this dress," I exclaimed. I only had one more option and hoped it would be the perfect one.

"So, what did you say in your drunk text?"

Sighing, I shimmied my way out of the mermaid dress. "Nothing that would impress him. Sober me had a field day with it this morning."

Killian eyed me with interest. "And what did Sober Tori say about Drunk Tori's attempt at writing while loaded?"

"It was ill advised."

"Oh come on. It can't be that bad." He handed me the final dress.

"I sounded insincere."

"Baby girl, do I have to remind you that you told him you only fucked him as a way to distract yourself? The text can't be worse."

"Yeah, well, it wasn't any better," I muttered, handing him my phone. Sometimes seeing the text in its native form was better than speaking it out loud.

"I see." He made a face. "I suppose you could have been more eloquent."

"Why haven't you answered her?" Bennet sounded incredulous.

I ran a hand through my hair, trying my best to focus on the match. United threatened with an equalizer. "No reason to."

"That's bollocks. Why is it so hard for you to admit you fancy her. A lot. And you fucked it up when you walked out instead of being there when she needed you."

"Well, she did call me a casual fling." *Among other things.*

Bennet leaned his head back in exasperation. "You just told me she was upset and very emotional about everything that happened with her mom and the house and finding out her dad visits every year. You just said you knew she didn't mean it."

"Will this conversation count instead of my session with Frances tomorrow?" I bit out.

"No. You're still going. And if you try to blow it off, I'll know."

Arguing with him would get me nowhere. I knew he was right about all of it. And he knew I'd never admit it out loud so we'd keep going in circles. But then there was Frances' homework. The *really feeling it* bullshit that got me to this point.

I swallowed.

Really feeling it hadn't been so bad. I actually quite liked it. At least until the part where it all went to shit and I acted like a complete tosser and took off.

I almost called her when I saw the message this morning. She was clearly up late when she sent it. Hearing her voice would work wonders. Yeah, it hurt when she told me I was only a distraction and we were nothing. It hurt more than normal because I knew she said it in a burst of emotion. She tries to hide things like that but I can see it. The last thing I wanted was for my default reaction to be to hurt her back. But I did.

"Hey." Bennet tossed a decorative pillow at my head. "Text her. You'll regret it if you don't."

Another pillow hit me.

"Do that again and I'll cuff you to the balcony." I growled.

"Ah, there he is." Bennet grinned. "Thought that guy was dead and buried."

"He had a bit of a resurrection."

"Text her."

Another pillow smacked me in the face.

VICTORIA

"This is the one. A vision in satin and lace." Killian placed both hands over his heart and smiled. "Perfection. Bellissimo."

I smoothed my hands over the slate gray dress and nodded in approval. "I still can't believe I'm going to the Met Gala. It doesn't feel real."

"Oh it's real, baby girl. Real and spectacular."

"You know what else is real and spectacular? A pesto chicken sandwich at The Lunch Basket. I'm starving."

After I changed back into my jeans and sweater, we walked the two blocks to our favorite lunch spot. Killian went to order the food while I grabbed a table outside. Spring felt like it was finally here to stay. And it meant people watching season has returned. I've always been fascinated by catching a glimpse of a person for a few seconds. If I paid close enough attention, I'd imagine what was going on inside their minds.

Charlotte and I used to make up stories about people as they'd walk by. Her stories were always so much more down to earth than mine. I pictured almost every person as living a secret life, and trying to keep up appearances by blending in.

A new notification popped up for the picture I posted last night. I grinned, opening the app. Noah already commented on it. So did Tre and several other guys from the team. This latest notification was from Hannah. I also gained a significant amount of new followers.

"One pesto chicken sandwich for my ginger princess," Killian arrived with our food. My stomach snarled. Day-after-drinking hunger was also real but not quite as spectacular.

We ate in silence, enjoying the warm weather. Both of our phones vibrated on the table.

"This must be His Highness checking in," Killian reached for his phone.

I laughed, grabbing mine.

Mildly Hot: You ok?

I froze mid-chew. My mind raced. Killian tapped my leg under the table with his foot.

"Mildly hot?" he asked.

I nodded, showing him the phone.

A small smile touched his face. "Brief but to the point. Now maybe you two can talk."

"Right now?"

"Now. Later. Whenever. Talk to him if that's what you want."

I chewed on my lip. The swelling and bruising were gone but I still remembered how it felt. Still craved more. I sighed. Doing this through text messages bugged me but it's now or never.

Me: I'm ok. Just out having lunch with K. You?

Mildly Hot: Getting a lecture from Bennet. And getting pillows thrown at me. Usual Sunday stuff.

Me: Lectures are a usual sunday thing? Sounds awful

Mildly Hot: Loads of fun. You should try it

Me: The pillows sound fun ;)

Mildly Hot: Bennet seems to find it endlessly entertaining.

Me: Why are you being lectured?

Mildly Hot: Sort of went into ignore life mode for a few days

Me: Please don't do that. I feel so bad about what happened.

Mildly Hot: What had you up so late last night?

Me: Nice deflection

Mildly Hot: My social media spies say there was a party. I like you in black lace

Me: Interesting since you don't follow me

@XMaddox1 is following you!

Mildly Hot: That's been sorted. You sit in that wanker's lap often?

Me: No. Should I?

Mildly Hot: Not if I can help it

Me: Does that mean you want me sitting in yours?

Mildly Hot: Yes.

Me: Really?

Mildly Hot: Yes.

Me: Even after what I said to you?

Mildly Hot: We'll deal with that in due time. But yes. Even after what you said.

Me: I really am sorry

Mildly Hot: I know. Won't change the fact your ass will be sore for a week when I get my hands on it

Me: Promise? :P

Mildly Hot: Don't get smart, city princess

Me: Whatever you say, country prince

Mildly Hot: We both know that's not what I am

Me: Fine. You're a *gentleman*

Mildly Hot: Keep sitting in that guy's lap and you'll see how much of a gentleman I can be

Me: I don't really know what to say to that…I guess we'll talk soon?

Mildly Hot: I have training all week. I'll reach out when I can.

Me: Of course. Xavier?

Mildly Hot: Yes?

Me: I'm sorry

Mildly Hot: I know, love. I'm sorry too

Chapter
SEVENTEEN

XAVIER

The drive to Dr. Frances' office should only take about fifteen minutes but in reality this would be the longest drive of my life. I knew what I'd be walking into and part of me dreaded it. Rehashing what happened with Victoria didn't rank too high on my list of things to do today. Especially after this morning's less than stellar training session. All the drinking and poor eating these last couple weeks caught up with me.

Clean slate now. Gotta get back to my routine this week and actually stick to it.

Traffic moved with too much ease for my liking. I arrived at my appointment on time. Squeezing the steering wheel to within an inch of its non-existent life did nothing to calm me. My mood soured even more the second I saw the good doctor sitting in his chair, scribbling something in his notebook.

"Ah, Xavier. Glad to see you."

I stood by the door, toying with the idea of walking out. Stripping off my armor and letting the pain run free didn't appeal to me.

"Have a seat." He pointed to the cream-colored couch. It taunted me with its broken promise of comfort. Groaning internally, I took my spot on the cushion and stared at the wall with the oil painting.

The worst thing about being here right now was the quiet. It gave my thoughts permission to relive the moment I walked out of Victoria's house. I could still hear the door slam shut behind me. Even worse, I could hear her crying.

"The longer you sit there in silence, the more I'm going to write."

My fingers dug into the arm of the couch at the sound of his voice.

"It was a long week, okay? Is that what you want to hear?"

Dr. Frances sighed, shifting in his chair. "I want to hear whatever it is you want to tell me. Avoidance gets you nowhere fast. Did you at least do the homework I asked you to do?"

A bitter laughed escaped my lips before I could suppress it. "You don't know the half of it."

"I'm all ears," he responded, leaning back in the chair. "What happened?"

"I did the whole *really feel it* thing and it bit me in the ass."

All I got for a response was a raised eyebrow. No writing, no nodding, none of that. Just a stupid raised eyebrow.

"What was it you felt?" he finally asked.

"Like shit." I snapped.

"What else?"

Covering my face, I leaned my head back, trying to erase the image of Victoria's distressed expression when she told me to go.

"Inadequate," I said without thinking.

"What triggered that feeling?"

"My general existence," I muttered.

"Walk me through what happened."

I watched him make a few notes before giving his undivided attention to me. The disquiet that's haunted me for days kicked into high gear.

"Bad week at training."

The eyebrow went up again. This guy wouldn't let me slide by any questions, no matter how hard I tried.

"If there's one thing about the last week you could change or do differently, what would it be?"

"I'd get more sleep."

"Do you suffer from insomnia often?"

"Didn't say I had insomnia, doc. Just that I'd get more sleep." I clenched my jaw, eyeing him as he folded his hands and waited for me to continue.

"What did someone need from you that you were unable to give?"

His question floored me, sending a searing pain through my chest. I crammed the surge of emotion back down where it belonged. Exhaling slowly, I chose my words with care.

"I let myself get too close to someone too fast."

"A female someone?"

"Yeah."

"I'm assuming the physical intimacy isn't the issue."

I smirked. "No. Not at all."

"What did she need from you?"

The familiar swelling of my own short-comings filled me. "I don't know."

"Do you want her to need you?"

"I think so."

"What happened?"

"She's going through something quite emotional with her family. I… when I met her I didn't know any of that so we just…there was a lot of sex."

Dr. Frances nodded and wrote down a few more notes.

"But," I paused, "I started to think maybe…" I stopped. There's no way this guy was going to hear everything. "It was just a casual fling."

"Did any of your sexual encounters involve activities you've said you wanted to avoid?"

My jaw tightened. "Somewhat."

"Was she open to it?"

I shoved a hand in my hair, pulling at it. All I could see was Victoria between my legs on her knees, looking up at me, worshiping my cock. All I could hear were her soft moans and demands for more out on the patio. All I could feel was her.

"Yes."

"How long have you known her?"

"Not long. She was only here for a few days visiting from the States."

Dr. Frances nodded, making more notes.

"Some physical relationships can be very intense," he said, tapping his pen on the pad.

"Intense is an understatement," I admitted.

"When was the last time you spoke to her?"

"Yesterday."

"And was that the first contact you've had with her since she left?"

I nodded. "I was with her a week ago. She left last Wednesday. I sort of—" I remembered how I'd phrased it to her "—ignored life for a few days after that."

"You shut down."

"Yeah."

"Is shutting down something you do often?" he asked, making more notes.

"No. Generally, when something doesn't go my way, I just move on to the next without looking back."

"But you couldn't do that this time."

He said it more as a statement of fact than a question. Maybe I wasn't as hard to read as I'd led myself to believe.

"It's not that I couldn't. I didn't want to. It didn't feel right."

Dr Frances leaned forward in his chair, regarding me with caution. "I'd like you to remain aware of how this continues to play out."

"How do you mean?"

He cleared his throat. "You have a bit of unresolved trauma. What happened to you as a teenager and the fallout from your previous relationship are still somewhat unsettled inside you. You have a pretty good handle on it but this new relationship will challenge all of that unless you get in front of it."

I sat with his words while he walked over to his desk. Relationship? Hate to break it you, doc, we both used each other for our own fucked up reasons. That's not a relationship.

"Are you willing to explore something more than just a casual fling with this new woman?" he asked, sitting down.

I stared at him, unable to speak. He made another note on his pad.

"So now what?" I sighed.

"That's for you to decide."

"Hey," Bennet knocked on the changing room wall. "Heading out soon?"

"In a bit. I have a couple things I need to tie up first."

"Everything go alright with Dr. Frances?"

"Yeah." I shoved my gloves, kit, and boots into my gym bag.

Bennet crossed his arms. "Ready to get back in goal this weekend?"

"More than you know." I studied him, wondering why he'd dropped the questioning about my session so quickly.

"At least you showered and shaved. I don't know what that creature was at your flat yesterday."

"Piss off. I haven't forgotten the pillows either, Logan. The cuffing remains an option."

"Promises." He walked over and sat, looking serious. Then again, serious was his default expression lately. Compared to Cade and I, he'd always been the more buttoned-up one of our trio but this felt different. Last time I saw him this pensive and introspective was the summer we all lived at the estate. What a cracking time that had been. Until it all went to shit.

"You're looking at me the same way Gallagher looks at you when he's trying to figure you out." Bennet smirked. "I'd hoped by now we all knew each other well enough."

"One can never be too certain."

"Ah. We're back to cryptic. Must mean this cycle of gloom you've been in since Victoria left is coming to a close."

I scowled. "There is no cycle of gloom."

"Of course." He patted my shoulder in the patronizing, older brother way he's done for years. "Will you be gracing us with your presence later this evening?"

"Depends."

Bennet's eyebrow quirked. "On?"

My hand flexed and clenched. Wouldn't be the first time I'd popped this pompous arse in the mouth. I loved him like a brother but we also fought like them. Always jostling for the alpha role. Always one-upping each other because we could.

"How desperate I am for your company," I replied, my voice low and tight.

"Lovers quarrel?" a voice chastised from the doorway.

Bennet and I looked over. Unbelievable.

"What do you want Adam?" I bit out.

My step-brother reigned in whatever smart ass comeback he wanted to say. Acting like a complete tosser in front of the owner's son wasn't his style. He preferred ass-kissing. Me, on the other hand? I'd gladly risk another suspension if it meant wringing this twat's neck.

"Adam," Bennet smiled. "I see you're in the starting eleven again for this weekend's match. You've done well defending for us this season since Pope's injury."

Christ, he's smooth. I suppressed a laugh. Bennet could be masterful when the moment called for it. He knew as well as I did that

Adam needed praise. He's always been jealous of my natural ability to play the game. His skills, while decent, weren't on the same scale as mine or Cade's.

"Happy to do what I can to give RCA a better chance to win," he beamed.

"Sure," I said, standing up. "Just keep the ball away from my goal on Saturday."

"Not a problem," he smirked. "As long as you don't throw any punches."

"Ah," Bennet clasped my shoulder to prevent me from lunging at Adam. "Xavier knows what he has to do. The season is getting tight and we have our eye on the top prize. No more room for error. Right?" He squeezed my shoulder for emphasis and looked me in the eye.

"Right," I muttered, noticing the look of satisfaction on my step-brother's face. "Was there something you needed, Adam?"

"Yeah. Mom wants to know if you'd like to come for dinner on Friday. A good luck gathering before your first match back or some shit like that."

I smiled internally. He couldn't stand that my step-mother treated me as her own son. At least someone in my fucking family did.

"You could have texted me."

"You don't answer my texts and I'd rather keep our communication limited to football."

"Fine," I sighed. "Tell her I'll be there."

Adam left without so much as a glance backward. I inhaled slow, mindlessly tracing my finger over my scar.

"You should join us tonight." Bennet's voice startled me. "It'll help you relax."

I stared at him. "I'm not interested."

"Yeah. Sure," he huffed. "You've never been one to turn down a single malt scotch. Have a glass and go sulk in a corner for all I care. Cade and I would really like for you to be there. Just like old times."

"Old times, huh?"

Flattening one palm on the wall, Bennet leaned toward me, his hulking frame dominating my line of sight. "Would you go if Victoria was still here? Would you take her?"

Two can play this game. "Would you take Hannah?" I shot back.

His lip twitched. Bingo. How does it feel, you pretentious knob.

"Does Hannah know what kind of parties you host?"

"Not yet." He smirked. "Does Victoria?"

"Sort of."

"Well, tonight is just the three of us. No more parties for the foreseeable future."

I lifted an eyebrow. "Really? What happened?"

Bennet straightened himself up, adjusting his suit jacket. "I'll tell you later." He walked toward the door, pausing just before opening it.

"Almost forgot," he turned, looking at me with a pompous smile, "I'm flying to New York on Saturday after the match. Interested in tagging along?"

Twat.

"Why are you going?"

"Dad wants to buy one of the American soccer teams. The league over there is expanding and he thinks it'll be fruitful if we have access to their talent and vice versa."

"No shit. That's why we're playing there. Why not just wait? We'll be in New York next Wednesday."

"We will, won't we?" His smile was so smug and arrogant I wanted to throw something at the wall. "You do know we're playing the match at the Legends' stadium, right?"

The muscles in my jaw twitched. "I'm aware."

"Don't tell me you wouldn't jump on the first flight over there to patch things up with Victoria."

"I'd be on one now if I could." The confession surprised us both, lightening the mood.

"Wow. You actually said it out loud. Impressive, Maddox. Or have you been cloned?"

"And now I know what to get you for your birthday. How many clones is too many?"

"Mate, I love you to bits but if I ever see more than one of you," his mouth dropped open in mock terror, "I'd run for the hills."

"Oh, I wasn't talking about me." An evil grin curled my lips.

"Cade?" he exclaimed. "Are you trying to give me more gray hairs? That's it. I'm leaving. And I'd better see your sorry arse at my house tonight."

Bennet stood at his trademark spot in front of the fireplace, staring into the flames, hands in his pockets, scotch on the mantle. Cade and I not-so-quietly referred to him as the lord of the manor when he'd stand there just to rile him up.

This library was a bigger version of the one we used as teenagers at the main house on his family's estate. It had similar antique wood panel walls, dark hardwood floors, and Tiffany table lamps. But there were also secret rooms and private corners for some of our more adventurous parties.

Bennet appeared lost in thought. The smart ass in me jumped at the chance for a good ribbing. "Looks like the lord of the manor is too good to sit with us."

He whipped his head around. An ostentatious smile pulled at his mouth.

"I should lock you behind the bookcase and throw out the key."

"Then you'd have to put up with Gallagher on your own."

He frowned. "Right. Not ideal."

"I'm right here you twit." Cade swallowed the scotch from the bottle. "And you clearly know I'm more fun than Maddox."

I laughed, leaning into the Chesterfield couch. Cade passed the bottle to me and I happily took a long swallow. So much for sticking to my routine.

"I have glasses," Bennet glowered, watching us pass the bottle around.

"We know, your grace," I replied. "Tastes better this way. Here." I held it out.

"Troublemakers." He grinned, taking it and sitting with us. "Thanks for coming tonight, Xavier. I know you'd rather be alone with your thoughts or whatever the fuck it is you've been doing."

"And miss out on this warm reception? Bennet, you spoil me."

He laughed. A hearty, deep, full-bodied laugh. Cade leaned across me to get the scotch back.

"Remember the first time we came to his estate?" he asked me.

"I do. You ran around the place like a puppy who just caught a scent. You touched everything in the room."

Cade rolled his eyes. "Apologies for not being as refined and deluxe as you."

"I didn't grow up in Downton Abbey, Cade." I poked Bennet in the arm. "He did."

"I really can't dispute that." Bennet shrugged.

Cade and I laughed. We continued passing the bottle around until we were all well and truly buzzed.

"Have you thought more about New York?" Bennet asked me, walking to the cellarette for another bottle.

"Mate, you know I can't go. I have training and several sponsorship meetings next week."

"When did you become so responsible, Maddox?" Cade teased. "You're turning down a guaranteed shag to beat the bishop?"

"Watch your mouth," I snapped.

"Whoa." Cade lifted his hands. "This girl really did you in, didn't she?"

"Fuck off." I leaned my head back and closed my eyes.

The room hushed for a few minutes. There's only the sound of flames crackling and popping. Being here without a crowd of guests was actually nice. Quiet. Last time Bennet had one of his infamous parties, I'd found a corner to slink into and be alone. Sometimes I preferred that.

I'd rather have company now, though. Specific company. Company with an American accent, waves and waves of dark red hair, and the softest, silkiest mouth known to man.

The cushion next to me dipped. I opened my eyes to see Bennet sitting next to me with a wry smile.

"You're going to want to see this," he said.

"I've seen your cock already. Too many times." My tone was dry and flippant. "Show Cade instead."

"Arse," Cade snickered.

"Not quite what I'd like to show you," Bennet said in a tut-tutty way. "Look."

He shoved his phone in my hands. A photo of Victoria and Hannah smiling together with a large group of people stared back at me. I sat up straight. According to the caption it was some league draft event. And who the fuck was Tre Gideon?

I scanned the photo. The guy standing next to Victoria had his arm around her. I recognized him. She'd been sitting in his lap in another photo. My body hummed with jealousy.

The dress she wore. Fuck. I wanted her here with me so badly it hurt. In *my* lap. With *my* arm around her.

Desire twisted tighter and tighter in my chest, squeezing around my heart in thorny vines.

Chapter
EIGHTEEN

Draft week flew by. All the pre-parties were done and dusted. And now we were already on day two. Day one had been a huge success. The Legends drafted a linebacker to help shore up the defense. He's set to arrive any minute.

I scanned through the bio I'd crafted about our newest addition.

Kevin Anderson….ran the 40-yard dash in 4.32 seconds….started games as linebacker, running back and safety for Montana State…. made all-conference as an inside linebacker and an outside linebacker in separate seasons…recorded 156 tackles this past season, six sacks, and four interceptions….unanimous Defensive Player of the Year.

Glen and I went over the social media plan. Pictures of Kevin holding up his jersey with Ethan Caldwell and Coach Montgomery on the field. Record a few quick videos saying hey to the fans and telling them how excited he was to get to work for the team.

Glen actually sat with the social media team this week and had a whole week's worth of posts for our newest first round pick all planned out.

"Have I told you lately you're a lifesaver?" I asked.

"Yep. Don't let it stop you from piling it on though," he laughed.

"Big day," Hannah sashayed into the press room. "I love when the draft picks come to the stadium for the first time. They always look so awestruck."

"Until Coach gets ahold of them," Glen said.

"Oh, he's a teddy bear," Hannah joked. "Actually, Glen, would you mind taking the lead on this visit? I need to borrow Victoria."

"Take all the time you need, ladies. I got this." He gathered the jersey and some other items before heading out of the room.

Hannah turned to me. "Grab your laptop and meet me in my office?"

I nodded, heading down the hall. My mind cycled through everything I had to finish before the second round started tonight. I loved how this week had been so busy with events leading up to the draft. There wasn't any time for me to dwell on anything else. Or any*one* else for that matter. Even though he kept liking all my photos.

This won't come as a surprise to anyone but I liked getting his attention. I posted so much from all the events, I was a little surprised he didn't comment or text me about them. I know for a fact Hannah sent Bennet several photos as well. I wondered what was going on in his head.

I did a little stalking on his account as well. Is it stalking if I follow him? Nah.

Apparently he returned to regular training sessions last week, so I, along with his two million followers, were treated to various photos and videos of him participating in drills.

And yes, I liked all of them.

When I got to Hannah's office we started to plot out the media schedule for the next month. We also coordinated with our community relations department on several upcoming events.

"Who do you have in mind to handle the media coaching for the rookies?" Hannah looked up from her computer.

"Sophie. She was great with the rookie class last year."

"Agreed. How about Tre?"

I snorted. "He doesn't need media coaching. That guy is as well-rehearsed as anyone."

"True but you know how Ethan and Coach like the players to stay on message. Tre wanders at times."

"The fans like it." I shrugged. "Especially now with social media giving them all a space to let their personalities out. Tre knows what he has to do at the podium. And if he drops a little personality in here and there, it won't hurt."

"That one is on you then," she chuckled.

"How many players are going to the Met Gala this year?" I asked, scrolling through an Excel file.

"Noah, obviously. Jax and Dante will be there as well."

"Those three," I snickered. "Is Tre going?"

"Yes, sorry, he'll be there too."

"That's a splashy group."

Hannah laughed. "Yeah. The paparazzi will love it. And those guys know how to play up to the crowd." She closed her laptop. "Alright, we're done here. What time are you staying until?"

"Probably nine. Derek and Sophie will be here late tonight, and they'll be here all weekend."

"Oh," Hannah perked up. "Do you have plans tomorrow night?"

"I'm dog-sitting for Killian and Max."

"Think the dog can handle being alone for a couple hours?" she teased.

"Depends. What do you have in mind?"

"Well," she sounded nervous, "Bennet is flying over tomorrow."

"Oh?" My eyes widened. "That's exciting for you. How long will he be here?"

"All week." She flicked her wrist in a dismissive manner. "Anyway, we're going out for drinks and I want you to come with us."

"Why?"

She shrugged. "It'll be fun."

"On what planet do you think asking someone to be the third wheel on their date is fun?"

"It's not a date, it's drinks." She lifted her hands to stop me from interrupting. "He asked me to invite you specifically."

I broke out into a cold sweat. "Is there something you're not telling me?"

"I'm not an asshole, Victoria. Xavier won't be there. Bennet is flying out after their game. Apparently it's Xavier's first match back since being suspended. Bennet told me what happened." Her eyes narrowed. "And it wasn't his first time getting carded for a fight. He's got a temper. Did you know?"

"No, not really. I mean, he mentioned he got into fights when he was a teenager but never said anything more."

"Bennet mentioned the same thing," she said softly before adding, "You do know Xavier and the rest of the team will be here for a game against the Knights next week though, right?"

"What?" My heart pounded.

"The international series. You don't remember the huge announcement in January?" She gave me an incredulous look. "Five big English clubs are going to five different American cities next week. Since the Knights use our stadium, we have Royal City. The others are going to Los Angeles, Dallas, Orlando, and Chicago." She shook her head. "You wrote the press release. Remember?"

My mouth sort of did the thing where it wants to say words but just made gaping gestures like a damn fish gasping for air. After a second, I composed myself.

"I write so many press releases, Hannah. I don't remember all of them. And if it was in January, we were in the middle of the playoffs and…I don't think a soccer game was too high on my radar."

The post-season, while routine in these parts, is always chaotic.

Relatives who want tickets, national press coverage, interviews, behind-the-scenes exclusives. I probably did write the press release. But to be fair, I wouldn't have known who or what Royal City Athletic was at the time.

That's not entirely true.

As a media relations professional in the sports world, I'd have an idea of who they were. I just wouldn't have paid much attention.

Because I wasn't banging the star goalkeeper at the time.

"Royals and Knights," I muttered. "Of course."

"See? You do remember," Hannah exclaimed. "You said it sounded like *The Canterbury Tales* or something. Royals, Knights, and Legends."

"I hope I didn't write that in the release."

Hannah's laugh echoed through her office. "No, you did not." She grinned. "I have a call in five minutes. Thanks for hashing out the schedules with me."

"Anytime." I turned and walked toward the door.

"Victoria?"

I glanced behind me. "Yeah?"

"Please come out with us tomorrow."

"I'll think about it," I promised, walking toward my office across the hall.

I sat heavily in my chair and tried like hell to focus on everything I had to finish before the draft started tonight. Instead, I scrolled through the shared files for stadium events. Yep. There it was. The announcement about five English soccer clubs coming to the U.S., including Royal City Athletic.

Even though I handled all the media requests for the Legends, I wasn't the main contact for this game. The stadium has a small media team for special events.

It struck me as odd that neither Bennet nor Xavier mentioned they'd be here. Then again, I saw Bennet a grand total of one and a half times and spent all my other time climbing Xavier like a tree.

"Good job," I mumbled.

My desk phone rang, mercifully relieving me of this thought process.

"Victoria Chase," I answered.

"Ms. Chase, hello," an unfamiliar male voice greeted me. "My name is Justin Kirby. I'm a reporter with the London Independent News. Hope I haven't caught you at a bad time."

"Not at all. What can I do for you?"

"As you know, Royal City is flying out to New York next week and I was wondering if we could set up a joint interview with some players from the Knights."

"Mr. Kirby is it?" I asked.

"Yes."

"I don't handle those requests for the Knights but I'd be more than happy to put you in touch with their media handler for the game. Do you have a pen handy?"

"Apologies. I saw your name as a contact on the stadium website."

"No worries," I said. "It happens more often than not. You'll want to talk to Kaylee Meade. Here's her number."

I recited the phone number to him, exchanged pleasantries and ended the call.

"Hey. You busy?" a voice asked from the doorway.

I glanced over. "Oh, hi Tre. Um, a little. What's up?"

He tucked his hands in his pockets and sauntered into my office. Dressed in jeans and a graphic t-shirt, he looked good. Better than I remembered when I saw him in Denver. Leaner, more muscular. Images of the night we spent together flashed through my mind.

Noooo. Girl, what is wrong with you?

I shook free from the memory and closed the file I'd pulled up on my computer. While it wasn't too unusual for a player to be in the stadium offices during the off-season, I was still surprised to see him here.

"I poked my head into Hannah's before coming over," he said. "She mentioned asking you about getting up to speed with media coaching." He shrugged. "I have the team's media guidebook. Don't really think I need more."

"You've been in the league for what, seven years? I think you know what you're doing."

He chuckled. "Yeah, yeah, but I know how particular coach can be about what we say."

I leaned back in my chair and crossed my legs. "You have all the main talking points. I don't think you have anything to worry about. Seriously. You're professional, poised, articulate, confident. And you have a way with keeping the reporters engaged and entertained. In my opinion, there's nothing more you need to do."

A dazzling smile curved his mouth. "Well, with that endorsement, I guess I'm all set. Thanks, Victoria."

"Anytime. You know you can stop by if you ever have any questions."

"Yes ma'am." Just as Tre was about to exit my office, he paused and turned. "I know it's last minute but Noah and Tracey are having a little get together at their place tonight to watch the draft and just chill. Would you like to go?"

"I can't," I replied. "Thank you though."

Tre looked me over in a subtle way that would have seemed innocuous if not for our history. His casual but flirty lean into the door jamb also gave away his intent. "Busy lady," he grinned. "Another time?"

Boundaries. NOW.

"It's best if we keep everything professional."

"I've heard that before." He licked his lips and walked away.

Uneasiness snaked through my body. Yes, I'm a huge flirt. Yes, I have a tendency to get down and dirty with hot athletes on occasion. No, I do not want that to continue. Not after what happened in England.

I stood in the draft room observing the start of round two. It wasn't as glamorous as it might sound. It was just a big conference room with phones and computers scattered on the table. Coach Montgomery was on a call. The director of player personnel stood by the giant dry erase board, studying all the moves the team has made so far. Several big television screens were mounted on the walls so everyone could see what was happening at the draft venue.

By the time nine o'clock rolled around I was ready to call it a day. Killian already texted me half a dozen times to remind me he and Max were at my condo with Winston Furchill.

His name always made me chuckle. Their dog was the cutest thing ever and I loved watching him when they'd go away or have one of their weekend adventures at the Guild.

"Victoria," Glen yelled from down the hall. "Pizza in the press room."

I waved, signaling I'd be there in a minute. Might as well grab a slice or three. I have a nice bottle of Sauvignon Blanc waiting for me at home to complete the ultimate low-key, basic single girl dinner. I went into my office to grab my things.

When I re-emerged Glen was moving fast up the hallway carrying a pizza box. He stopped, breathless and laughing. "Take the box, Victoria. I nearly lost an arm saving some slices for you. Those people are animals."

I took the box and smiled. "Thanks, Glen. You're a lifesaver, again."

"I got you, V. Enjoy the weekend."

I sent Killian a quick text as I made my way down to the parking lot. The stadium was about twenty minutes outside of Manhattan. There's always traffic in the city so it would probably take me more like forty minutes to get home. Didn't bother me too much. I turned up the radio and pulled out of the parking lot, catching glimpses of the immense steel and glass stadium as it became smaller and smaller in my rear view mirror.

One week from tomorrow we'll be hosting Royal City Athletic and the NYC Knights. And then the following Monday was the Met Gala. I blew out a sigh.

I'll worry about next week when it gets here.

Navigating the streets of New York calmed me for some reason. Everything moved in its structured, routine way surrounded by beautiful chaos. I do love this city.

The noise.

The rush.

The rich, the poor, the curious, the jaded, the humble, and the arrogant all co-existing on street corner after street corner.

The joyful echo of music filling dirty subway stations.

The pockets of calm in the parks.

I shook my head. That sounded more like something Charlotte would dream up. A warmth spread through my chest as I turned into my parking garage.

"Yeah, I know you're here," I whispered, putting my hand on my heart. "Thanks, Charlie."

The night guard waved from the security desk when I passed through the lobby. "Evening, Ms. Chase."

"Hi, Mr. Baxter. How's the game?"

He shook his head in disgust. "They need to find someone who can shoot threes. This is embarrassing."

I laughed and got into the elevator. When I arrived at my door I heard Winston barking.

"Somebody is excited to see me," I exclaimed, walking into the foyer. Winston ran over and nearly tripped me.

"Finally," Killian said with a huff.

"Seriously?" I arched an eyebrow.

"He's antsy," Max explained.

"Tell me something I don't know." I rolled my eyes and put my pizza box on the counter.

Killian hugged me from behind. "Sorry, baby girl. You know I love you."

"Mmhmm."

"Am I still cool enough to be your best friend?"

"Shut up," I laughed and turned to face him. "So what's happening at the Guild this weekend?"

"The usual. But that's not what we're doing all weekend. We'll just go there tonight and then we're leaving obnoxiously early in the morning to drive up to Lake George."

"Oh?" I grabbed a slice of pizza and a napkin. "What's going on in the Adirondacks?"

"Peace and quiet," Max said, placing his hands in a meditative position. "I need to escape this zoo before the influencer's birthday party and the Met Gala. Your boy needs to be at one hundred."

Killian let out an exaggerated sigh. "You poor thing," he teased. "Will the six figure payment make it all better?"

"Alright you two," I said through a mouthful of pizza. "Get out before I change my mind about watching Winston."

"Pfft. You'd never," Killian scoffed.

"Out." I pointed to the door.

"See you Sunday. We love you," they said in unison as they left.

I leaned against the counter and looked down at Winston. He tilted his head and whined.

"I know. You'll get some peace and quiet, too."

He wagged his tail while trotting off toward the couch. I planned to trot there myself after finishing this pizza and changing into something more comfortable. I moved around the kitchen, grabbing a glass and pouring some wine. It went down really, really nice with the pizza.

And without it.

After a few glasses, all the hectic energy from the week melted away.

While I do love the draft, it's also a welcome reprieve to decompress from the pandemonium.

Of course it also meant my mind relaxed and started to wander.

And I let it. Not that I had any power to stop it if I wanted.

The images came fast and furious. Seeing Xavier for the first time when he pulled off the road. Then again at Black Rose. How his eyes consumed me every second we were together. The dark expression on his face. The dangerous edge to his voice when he called me dirty princess.

I've replayed every interaction we had over and over since I left. Including the way I left him. Guilt rippled through me. I had enough guilt living inside me to last ten lifetimes. And yet, even with those feelings, he flipped a switch in me.

It's uncomfortable to lose myself in fantasies of being with him. Really being with him, not just a casual fuck here and there. But I liked imagining us as more than a fling.

An uncomfortable heat lingered on my skin.

Okay, not uncomfortable. Insistent.

The kind of heat only Xavier could fuel and tame…and fuel again. I wandered into my bedroom and took off my work clothes.

A tiny smile touched my lips at the memory of Xavier giving me his phone number. Just in case I wanted to send him naughty photos. I stood in front of my floor mirror, running my nails along my stomach.

The familiar urge for spontaneity and bad decisions pulled at me. Flashes of what we did at his townhouse consumed me. The way he commanded me to take off all my clothes except for my heels. The carnal look on his face when he sat in the chair and stroked himself. The first flick of his tongue on my body. The possessive way he staked his claim on me.

Hot desire crawled and scratched at my skin.

He'd want to know I've been thinking about him.

He'd want to know what I did while these indecent thoughts ravaged me.

With a devilish grin, I set up my ring light tripod and attached my phone. I placed it next to the bed and stripped out of my bra and panties. Nervousness and excitement flooded me when I set the camera timer, climbed on the bed and kneeled. I kept my body in profile, showing my left side. My hair draped over my right shoulder. I lifted my left shoulder, looked over it and flashed the camera a demure smile.

For a brief second, I considered deleting it. I mean, who am I to be sending him an unsolicited naked photo? I looked good in it though. He'd be able to see just enough.

And I wanted him to see me. I wanted him to see how taut my nipples were and how my lips parted just enough to signal what I wanted between them.

I wanted him to see just how much the thought of him turned me on.

A growing ache twisted and knotted at my core. I'd use one of my toys soon enough but it paled in comparison to how Xavier could satisfy me.

I sent the photo with the message *Want to know what I'm thinking about?*

Chapter

NINETEEN

Something warm and wet slid over my face again and again. I blinked myself awake, coming face to face with an adorable pomsky.

"Winston," I mumbled. "Good morning to you, too."

I rolled out of bed and shuffled through the darkness to the closet to grab my sneakers. The sun hadn't fully risen yet but this little guy had no concept of time and needed to go outside and then have breakfast.

"Let's go, bud."

Winston's tongue dangled out of the side of his mouth while I hooked up his leash and guided him to the elevators. My building has a fenced in dog area for residents with pets. It even had real grass. Bonus points for the doggie poop bag dispenser.

Since nobody else was down here, I let Winston off the leash to do his business. It took him a few minutes to find the perfect spot. Then I watched him run around in crazy circles. It's probably best if he got the zoomies out of the way here rather than in my living room.

He ran over, panting. His tail wagged back and forth so hard the entire lower half of his body swayed.

"Ready?"

An answering bark was all it took.

After I fed him, I went through my morning rituals. A little yoga, a little coffee, a little quiet time out on the balcony. I loved watching the sun complete its rise over the city. All the buildings came to life in bursts of pink, gold, and blue. Today promised to be a bright spring day.

A perfect day to read some of Charlotte's diary.

It's been sitting on my vanity since I unpacked it, along with the sketch of her gravestone the teen boy gave me at the cemetery. There was something so calming and comforting about the drawing.

The serenity of this moment on the balcony was broken by the chirping of my phone. I walked through the sliding doors into my bedroom and grabbed it.

Oh.

My heart pounded.

I had two missed texts. The one just now was from Hannah reminding me about tonight but the other arrived a few hours ago…

Mildly Hot sent an audio message.

Do I want to hear this? I thought maybe he'd just send an emoji or something. Or a dirty text or picture of his own.

Or nothing at all. *Yeah right. Maybe in an alternate universe.*

"Here we go." I pressed play and sat on the bed.

Silence.

Then a long, rough sigh.

"Dirty princess…"

Oh God. OH GOD.

"…I do want to know what you're thinking about. But first I'm going to tell you what I'm thinking about…"

A moan passed my lips. The dark edge to his tone ignited my desire for him in an instant.

"...and when I finish, you'll send me a video showing me exactly how many times you make yourself come."

Another rough sigh. Goosebumps pebbled my skin.

"I thought about how much I like you on your knees. It reminds me of the night you knelt in front of me and sucked me off with that Ivy League mouth. I thought about how you'd look with your wrists tied together behind your back. Is that something you'd like me to do? Will you beg me to free your hands? Will you struggle against the restraint? Or will you simply let me have my way with you and demand more when I'm buried deep inside you, fucking you, taking what's mine?"

I laid back on the bed, resting the phone next to my ear.

"I thought about..."

A long pause. My pulse raced.

"...your skin, your scent, your mouth. The way you look at me when you're coming. How you sound when you want more. How much I want to mark you and..."

Another harsh exhale. And another.

"I'm so hard right now I can't think straight."

He groaned. A deep, gruff sound. It went straight to my throbbing clit.

"Fuck. You should see what you've done to me with your photo."

I heard a rustling sound. Then another groan.

"I just thought about you, Victoria. You. And all the ways I can fucking make you mine. I expect to see a video waiting for me by the time my match is finished."

His message ended.

That can't be all.

I sat up straight and grabbed the phone, wanting more. The sharp tenor of his voice cut through me with his final order. He sounded so raw. Almost like I'd pierced him squarely at the center of some vulnerable nucleus he'd clearly not meant for anyone to breach.

Every part of me was awake. I was a live wire, charged by lust.

His soccer game.

I scrambled off the bed and jogged into the living room.

Where the hell is the remote?

Winston thought I started some secret game and followed me around.

Ah. There it is.

I turned on the TV and searched the menu. I know one of the networks carries all the English soccer games. I really pushed my luck assuming they'd air Royal City Athletic.

My phone vibrated on the coffee table. Another text from Hannah.

Hannah: Are you watching?!?! It's the second half already!

Me: What channel?

Hannah: GoalZone. Should be channel 837

Me: Got it. Thanks!

Hannah: Welcome! See you tonight

Right. Tonight. Drinks with Hannah and Bennet. That should be interesting.

Overly enthusiastic banter between the analysts filled the room. Royal City just scored a goal against West London United. Actually, it was Cade who scored the goal. He exuded so much excitement reveling in the moment with his teammates. He'd done the celebratory knee-slide on the grass to the delight of fans.

I grinned. He looked good in royal blue.

"Cade Gallagher with another monster goal for Royal City," the announcer bellowed. "He is the life blood of this club. Look at the joy he brings to the pitch. It's like watching a child in a sweet shop."

I laughed at the dramatics of what I assumed was the color commentator.

After another replay of the goal, live game action resumed. According to the commentators, if Royal City wins this match, they'll move to the top of the standings in the league. So far, they're ahead two to nothing. Which means nobody has scored on them yet.

These hands don't miss.

At the exact second I thought those words, a Royal City player's bad pass landed at the feet of their opponent. United made a run for the goal. Their forward or striker or whoever it was streaked up the field, blowing past two Royal City defenders.

I held my breath. He took a shot at the goal but it deflected off another Royal City player, curved wide to the left and went out of bounds, meaning a corner kick.

My pulse raced. There he was, waving and yelling to his teammates to position them where he wanted.

My God.

Xavier was hot in street clothes and casual business attire but in his uniform barking out orders? Lethal.

Granted, goalkeepers wore obnoxious colors that could rival highlighters but there's something about this shade of green. And if the cameraperson keeps doing these close ups of him with his gloved hand gripping the post while screaming at someone to move over, I might orgasm on the spot.

There is something primal about watching an athlete in the heat of competition. The intensity is unmatched. His eyes flared, the tendons in his neck tightened with each yell.

Once Xavier had everyone where he wanted, he reigned in any explosiveness and appeared almost bored. I'd seen him exude control over his body like this before. It will never cease to amaze me.

The ball flew off the United player's foot and landed right in Xavier's hands.

I wondered what those gloves felt like. Weird thought? Probably, but the way his gloved hand cupped the ball while he walked to kick it away hit something in me. I made a mental note to search what material they're made from. I should also commend the cameraperson on their exquisite ability to capture Xavier's every move.

Oh.

A full body shot. Xavier stood on the edge of the penalty box holding the ball. He waved his free hand, signaling he'd be kicking it past midfield.

I've seen him naked so I know what's hiding under all those clothes but wow. I never realized how form fitting a goalkeeper uniform is. I liked it. A lot. And the fact that just about every inch of him from the neck down was covered, except for his knees and a sliver of thigh? I wanted to peel those layers off and reveal what belonged to me.

Time to go make the video now.

I eyed my sister's diary. Part of me still didn't think I should read it. But I grabbed it anyway and sat on the couch.

It's been a few hours since I created quite the show for Xavier to enjoy. I made sure he could see I had the game on in the background while I showed him exactly how turned on I was and how many times I climaxed. He'd responded with another audio message. A brief one, only saying "Good girl."

Hearing those words come out of his mouth launched another uncontrollable wave of intense pleasure. I haven't masturbated this much in a long time.

I drummed my nails on the diary and chuckled. "Your little sister is having some peak experiences these days."

I did the cursory flip-through a couple times, letting the pages rustle under my fingers. We'd tell one another everything so I probably wouldn't be too surprised with what she'd written down. I opened the cover and saw *Charlotte* written in her neat penmanship. The *C* flowed out so that it underlined the rest of her name. I smiled, tracing her handwriting with my finger.

Flipping the pages, I stopped somewhere close to the middle and scanned through several musings on music, clothes, food, and….

I met a boy today. Totally Tori's type but I think I might like him.

She wasn't at the pub with me when I saw him. I was picking up lunch for us when he walked in with friends. I could tell he was the ring leader. Tall, confident, loud. Sorta the male version of my sister (except for the tall part).

I snort-laughed. Charlotte always knew how to slide in a good zinger when the opportunity presented itself.

We ended up talking for almost half an hour. He plays soccer, goes to some fancy boarding school, and just got his drivers' license. That means he must be 16. So, a little older than me but not a lot. I think he brags too much but he's cute. He has such pretty hazel eyes. I gave him my instant messenger screen name so we can chat there. We'll see if I hear from him.

His friends seem nice too. They all play soccer together at some field not too far from the cottage. Grandpa's mentioned it before. I should tell Tori. Maybe if we go together to watch them practice I won't be so nervous to talk to him.

I glanced at the date of the journal entry.

Mid-July. Not too long after we arrived.

Wait.

This is from the summer *before* everything happened at the bonfire.

A cold chill skittered down my spine. This felt wrong. Charlotte wouldn't have kept her new crush a secret from me, would she? I wracked my brain trying to remember if she ever mentioned meeting anyone. Nope. She never did. Not until the last summer we went there.

Maybe she had her reasons. Maybe it was just a little crush from afar. Maybe this wasn't even the same guy.

I closed the diary and sighed. Part of me wanted to know everything. Another part of me wanted to burn it and let Charlotte rest in peace.

"Just a few more pages." I skipped ahead to August.

Adam kissed me today.

He wasn't with his friends so we spent all afternoon together. Just the two of us. The kiss was a surprise. It was soft and sweet and I wanted it to go on forever. I especially liked it when he used his tongue. He tasted like the Eton Mess we just shared. Tori and I always talk about kissing boys like this. She hasn't done it yet though.

There's a party next weekend he wants to take me to. I mentioned bringing my sister and he laughed. Twins. He said his friends will love it. I don't think he meant anything bad by it. And we're used to it. My sister gets a kick out of the attention. She's a master at flirting. I should tell her about this party and see if she'd like to go. I'll be sure to mention all the soccer players.

But this kiss today....

It stirred something in me I know I'm not ready for. Sometimes I wish I was older and more experienced. Not experienced in the way my sister talks about. All the seniors at school throwing parties with paddles and handcuffs and rope? Hell no. Way too terrifying. She seemed really into it though. And of course Killian chimed in and said how much fun it sounded. Those two. :)

No, not experienced like that. More like the girls who whisper about backseats and hiding under the bleachers out by the football field. More like that. But not now. I'm only 15. Someday. Maybe next summer. Or the summer after. I hope he's still interested in me then.

I love talking to him. Even when he brags about some development league one of the big soccer teams in London is forming for teens. He really wants to be accepted into that.

Aside from all the sports talk, he's quite intuitive and smart. And he has the sharpest sense of humor. The only time I ever really see him annoyed is when his brother comes around. They argue all the time about stupid stuff. Like, who's a better natural athlete or who's on the first team versus the second team.

Ugh. Boys. So dumb.

It reminds me of the football players at school. He seems nice though.

The brother, I mean. I've never actually had a conversation with him or anything but we exchanged a pleasant hello once. He's always surrounded by girls. Always. And he's a huge flirt. I bet if Tori met him she'd totally get a crush on him. He's a soccer player too. A goalkeeper.

I dropped the diary like it was on fire.

Chapter

TWENTY

"**X**avier Maddox with the clean sheet," Cade bellowed, clapping his hands. A handful of people on the sidewalk stopped and stared as we walked by. "Best keeper in the league. England's number one."

"Or maybe United's striker forgot how to score," I smirked.

"Shade from the big X. Brilliant."

Winning the match was never in doubt. Not with me in goal and Gallagher kicking absolute lasers in United's box. In fact, the whole squad came together when it mattered most. Even Adam. His defending actually made my life easier. *Little prick.* I snickered.

"What's got you in such a good mood?" Cade asked while we walked toward our cars. We'd just finished a post-game meal at Black Rose, a standing ritual we've had for years.

"Feels good to be back is all."

"That's a bloody lie and you know it. You've been chuffed about something since before we went on the pitch." He stopped at his car. "Are you going to New York?"

"Nope." I kept walking and didn't turn back. All I heard was a string of profanities coming from Cade mixed in with his laughter.

What I did plan to do was watch Victoria's video again. And again. First thing I did after the final whistle was check my phone. She's something else. I was noticeably hard going into the post-match interview.

Music blared from the speakers when I started my car. I lowered it and pulled onto the road.

Wednesday couldn't get here fast enough. All I could think about was taking her in my arms. I don't know if the photo she sent last night was planned or on a whim but fuck me. Waking up to it this morning erased some doubts I had about the two of us mending our…

Our what?

Casual fling?

Sorry. I don't send orders to casual flings.

The corner of my mouth ticked up into a wicked grin as I approached Victoria's house. As far as I was concerned, it was *her* house. I pulled in front of it and stopped. The keys were sitting on the counter in my kitchen so I couldn't go inside at the moment. But I didn't need to. I remembered the foyer and the awful couch and the sitting room. The sturdy lines of the wood paneling. The intricate design of the doorways and moldings.

This house wasn't ugly at all. Not by a long shot. It just needed some attention. It needed someone to strip it bare, and restore it from the inside out.

Sexy goalkeepers who renovate houses are hard to come by these days. I have one in front of me. I'd be stupid to pass up the opportunity.

Her words came back to me in a rush. All at once a wall of need, want, and desire crashed down on me. I couldn't pull myself out from the rubble if my life depended on it.

I should have gotten on the fucking plane and gone to New York. I'd make her kneel on the bed or the floor or the couch or wherever

I damn well pleased. I'd watch her coax her pussy into an orgasm as many times as I wanted. Then I'd stand her against a wall, kick her legs open so she's fully exposed to me and shag her until neither one of us could breathe.

I reached for my phone.

VICTORIA

Why did I go out tonight?

Hannah and Bennet continued laughing about something one of the fans did at the match earlier today. I tried to pay attention. I really did. Unfortunately for them, I had dueling mental images fighting for my attention. The ghosts of Charlotte's past and the very real, very erect penis of Xavier Maddox.

Did I suspect he'd send a video along those lines after what I recorded this morning? Hell yes. Although, I wasn't expecting him to be sitting in his car. I pictured the shower or even the locker room. In any case, watching the aggressive way he stroked himself to climax was hot.

His rough breathing and low moans were so sexy. And hearing my whispered name when he came all over his hand shattered me. I especially appreciated the way he rubbed his thumb over his flared crown as it glistened with his release. I wanted lick it all off.

I sipped my water, trying to control the tingling between my legs.

And I also had my orders.

No panties.

He said he'd know if I disobeyed. I'm not clear on how that's possible seeing as the chance of me letting anyone inspect what's under my skirt is absolute zero. Not important. I liked having the distraction. Every time my mind drifted back to Charlotte's diary, a dull pain filled my stomach. I needed to know who the boy was. *And if his brother is in fact…*

"I wasn't going to say anything until the official announcement on Monday," Bennet's posh accent cracked through my reverie. "But I figure since I have two senior executives in my presence, I might as well let it spill."

He glanced from me to Hannah with a sly grin.

"Royal City Athletic will host the Legends at our stadium this fall."

Hannah didn't seem surprised at all but still squealed with joy. My jaw dropped.

"I'm meeting with Ethan first thing Monday. We are quite excited about this partnership." Bennet's mouth curved into a friendly smile as he lifted his glass. "Cheers to new beginnings."

Our glasses clinked together. Once our toast was finished he shared a knowing look with Hannah, giving her a terse nod before turning in my direction.

"So, Victoria, how have you been since we last spoke?" Bennet's stare pierced through me.

He's fishing. I knew it without a doubt. The last time we spoke was the night we all had dinner together in London. He damn well knows what happened since then. I let my glass linger at my lips before taking another sip of water.

"Busy." I responded. "The draft is always a hectic time."

He steepled his fingers in front of his mouth and studied me. "All those parties must have been fun."

"They were." I sifted my fingers through my hair. "Especially Noah's fundraiser. Those are always epic. Right Hannah?"

Before she could answer, Bennet gave her a stern look. She simply smiled at me and nodded.

Interesting. Never pegged Hannah to be the submissive type.

"Hannah was kind enough to share photos from Noah's event. And other events as well." Bennet's lips quirked into a grin. "Are you close with many of the players?"

Bennet, Bennet, Bennet. You're not as smooth as you think.

I leaned back in the chair and folded my arms. "Why do I get the sense this is the beginning of an inquisition?"

Dominance and intrigue flared in his amber eyes. Hannah tapped her foot on mine under the table. I winked at her. She knows I can hold my own with these alpha CEO-types.

"No inquisition, Ms. Chase." Bennet's tone had a dark edge similar to Xavier's.

"That's a dead giveaway," I smiled. "We're well beyond formal names. And I know that tone of voice."

Hannah kept her eyes cast down.

"What tone?" he asked, squaring his shoulders.

Oh, how I love to play games. I looked up at Bennet through my lashes. "I think you know the one, Mr. Logan. Low, dark," I leaned forward for emphasis, "dominant."

Hannah remained still. So this is how Xavier would find out if I did what he asked.

"Do you like that tone?"

Smoothing the hem of my skirt down, I crossed my legs. A thick atmosphere of control enveloped our space. Whatever else was happening in the restaurant faded into the background.

"You must know by now that I do."

"And when you hear it, do you always do as you're told?"

Bingo.

"Yes, sir," I answered with a knowing smile.

"Even tonight?"

I tilted my head and held his stare. "Especially tonight."

Without missing a beat, his kexpression softened and a relaxed smile touched his lips. "I'm glad you could find time in your busy schedule to join us. Hannah mentioned you were taking care of your friend's dog. I hope we haven't intruded on any other plans."

"My weekends aren't as exciting as you might think," I responded with just as much ease, even though my pulse raced.

"Victoria has been known to binge watch entire television series on the weekends," Hannah teased, coming back to life. "It's just rumor and hear-say though."

I laughed. "Oh okay, little miss 'let's watch every episode of Stranger Things in one sitting.' You even like to bring all the food."

"I brought cookies," she sniffed. "Killian waltzed in with pizza and tacos."

"Pizza and tacos?" Bennet frowned. "A good binge night needs curry chicken. I thought everyone knew that."

"Is that what you and the boys snack on in your fancy library?" The question came out light-hearted and without much thought behind it on my part.

"Not quite, Ms. Chase." A darker, more dangerous tone emerged.

Aaaand we're back.

"What's the point of having a fun place to hang out if you don't serve fun food?" I challenged.

Hannah didn't morph into submissive mode this time but she remained silent. Bennet leaned forward on his elbow. "There's always something good to eat."

I swallowed. Okay. Am I really ready to go toe-to-toe with a Dominant?

"Xavier mentioned you host parties there. How often do you have them?"

"Once a month."

My eyes widened. "Oh. That's pretty frequent."

Hannah shifted in her chair. I wondered if she knew about them.

"What else did Xavier tell you?" Bennet's lips twitched into a smile.

Oh, just that he'd fuck me there until I screamed loud enough for all of you to hear me.

Electricity skimmed down my spine. My thoughts fractured into incomplete fragments. I wanted to answer him honestly. I felt compelled to do so. But I wanted Xavier here to watch. I wanted him to witness this conversation and get aroused with me.

"He just told me people enjoyed one another's company."

"Is that something you like? Being around people who enjoy one another's company? Or are you the type who likes to enjoy someone's company with others around?"

All at once the reality hit me like a train. I'm being vetted. In their trio of alpha males, Bennet was the leader and he's vetting me for his friend. True, Xavier had dominant tendencies but he wasn't like Bennet. I paused before answering him.

"Xavier knows what I like."

A knowing smile. "He does to a degree. And you've been comfortable with his predilection for exhibitionism and voyeurism so far?"

This was starting to feel like a job interview. "We have similar interests."

Hannah's eyebrows went up slightly. We've discussed men and relationships on occasion but never any kinks. I looked at her and shrugged. She chuckled.

"What about limits?" he asked, stroking his finger down Hannah's arm.

"We haven't talked about limits."

"Why?"

Uneasiness snaked through me. "Well, we haven't…I mean, I didn't spend much time—"

"You spent enough time together to want to know what he likes, Ms. Chase." Bennet's sharp tone signaled the end of any frivolity on my part. "He let you know. Why haven't you discussed limits?"

He wanted me to say it. Asshole.

"You know why." My voice shook.

A venomous stare was my only reply. I can understand wanting to protect a friend but this was close to crossing a line. I refused to be scolded by this guy.

"It's none of your business, Bennet."

The tendons and muscles in his neck bulged through his skin as he swallowed. "Xavier's well-being *is* my business, Victoria. And you will answer my question. Why haven't you discussed limits?" His imposing frame matched the force behind his words.

Hannah's eyes dropped down. I was truly on my own now. This was beyond intense. It was stifling. I always prided myself on handling controlling men with my own brand of grace under pressure.

Now? I might crack.

And I did.

"I told him he was just a distraction. A casual fling." The corners of my eyes stung with tears. "I shouldn't have said those things."

"No, you shouldn't have. While it's not my place to speak on any punishments, I'm compelled to advise you on discussing your limits before proceeding in a relationship with him." His expression softened slightly. "Do you understand?"

I nodded.

An eyebrow quirked. *Oh for crying out loud.*

"Yes, I understand," I answered, fighting with all my might not to roll my eyes.

"Good. I'm not asking these questions because I think you're not good enough for him, Victoria. Or that you're going to deliberately hurt him. Quite the opposite. I've observed the two of you together, although briefly. You handle him well. He can be," he paused, "impulsive."

"No shit," I muttered, reaching for my water.

"I can see why he likes you," Bennet chuckled. "You challenge him. I'd have put you over my knee at least a dozen times by now but to each their own."

A dozen? I nearly did an involuntary comedic spit-take. *A dozen?* I couldn't get Xavier to do it once and this guy already has a dozen reasons? *What the actual…*

"I can tell you're wondering what I consider disobedience." He smirked. "You're not a true submissive, so my explaining what I think is misbehaving or defiance wouldn't work for you. And that would only make me want to lay you across my knee even more. Nobody wins."

What a fascinating piece of work he is. He's right though. I don't have a submissive bone in my body. Unlike the quiet blonde sitting across from me.

"I appreciate your honesty, Victoria. I've known Xavier for a long time. We're as close as brothers. As I mentioned before, his well-being is important to me. I won't divulge any further. I'm sure you and Xavier will have a lot to talk about this week."

Bennet put his arm around Hannah's shoulders. A delicate gesture from one of the most dominant men I've ever come across. My heart pounded, betraying the confident exterior I portrayed during our exchange. I've always been curious to know what it was like to be around a true Dominant. I hope Hannah knows what she's getting herself into.

Winston ran at full speed along the perimeter of the dog area before finding the perfect spot to pee. A cool breeze brushed over my bare arms and legs. A refreshing reprieve after spending the evening with Bennet. Don't get me wrong. I've liked Bennet since the first minute I met him in London. I figured he'd be an amicable counterpart to have for future partnerships with our teams. I still feel that way on a professional level.

Tonight's interaction left the distinct impression I was being studied. Even after his interrogation, I noticed Bennet drinking in my every move, absorbing every word I said, memorizing every reaction.

None of it made me too uncomfortable. It piqued my curiosity more than anything and I wanted to know why. Why did Bennet feel as though he had to protect his friend?

Maybe for the same reasons you should have protected your sister.

The vicious thought winded me. Shaking, I grasped the wrought iron fence and crouched down. All the answers to everything I wanted to know about the final summers we spent in England waited for me upstairs.

Chapter
TWENTY-ONE

lied.

I probably shouldn't even be writing this down but if I don't get it out of my head it'll haunt me for days and days and days. I can't even talk to my sister about it. She'll get worried and say something to mom and then I'll be backed into a corner. Again. And the questions will start and never end.

So yeah. I lied. I didn't spend the night at Millie's on Saturday.

We went to a party at some huge estate near London. Millie's friend invited us. I really wanted to go because Adam was also going to the party. Millie made me promise not to tell you Tori (sorry). I did have your voice in the back of my mind all night though. You're always telling me to be adventurous and take risks. Fine. I did it. So much for being the responsible twin.

I'm tearing these pages out as soon as I finish writing this.

The party was fine. Great, actually. It felt like one of those teen parties you always see in the movies when the parents are away and everyone goes to the popular kid's house. Only in this case it was the popular kid's CASTLE. Dancing, drinking, couples making out on couches, in hallways, in secluded corners. Everyone looked and acted so grown up.

Oh Tori, you would have loved this place.

Being there made me feel like I'd been offered a glimpse into another life.

No. That's not right.

There's this part of me that doesn't fit in anywhere. Not a whole part. Just a layer. But it's there and it eats away at me. I hide it well. I have to. I'm the student body president, the youngest one ever at school. Captain of the debate team. Straight A student. I have a certain persona and I have to make sure nobody sees what lies beneath.

It's a lot of stress for one person but keeping up appearances is mandatory.

None of these kids here know me. I don't have to pretend around them. I don't have to do as I'm told or strive to be better than the best.

I could just be. It was freeing.

I shouldn't write this part out.

Millie wanted to go outside to smoke. I told her I'd keep her company. She needed a few minutes to vent about the boy she likes who likes someone else, but he also likes her. Does this ever get easier? Or will we always be running in some hamster cage of I like you, do you like me, why do you like them?

After a while, we saw a guy walking to his car. I could only see him from the back so I don't know who it was. A few minutes later some other guys came out of nowhere and beat him up. It looked bad. They slammed his head into a car door, kicked him, punched him. I think someone slashed at his face with a key or something. I heard yelling and clearly heard someone shout "If you try something like that again, I'll take your fucking eye out."

One of the guys saw us. Millie panicked because she knew who it was so we ran inside. She told me not to say anything. I guess I didn't have to *because a couple minutes later some other boys ran outside.*

I really have to remember to tear out these pages…

We got cornered in the room by some other guy. He was big for a teenager. Handsome but his smile looked more like a threat. It made me super uncomfortable.

He told us he saw us outside when they beat up that kid. He wanted to know how much we saw. Millie refused to say anything but I did. I told him we saw the whole thing.

He stared at me. His eyes were really dark and brown and mean. I didn't care though. What they did was wrong. That guy didn't deserve to be beaten up so bad, no matter what they think he did. I told this piece of shit as much.

I didn't even flinch when he grabbed my throat and pushed me against the wall. He called me a fucking American tart and said he knew all about my family and where we lived. He said he knew I had a twin and said some really vulgar things about getting us both in a room alone. I can't write those out. What he said was too awful. I'm so sorry, Tori.

I did tell him to go fuck himself though. That didn't go over well at all.

He told me he knew how much money we had and said he'd make sure to ruin our reputation if I ever told anyone about what I saw tonight.

Then he said if I ever went to one of these parties again, he'd teach me a lesson I'd never forget.

Chapter
TWENTY-TWO

"What happened?" Killian's face dropped from happiness to concern. "Are you okay?"

I stood in his doorway holding Winston's leash. Max came over and took the dog since I was incapable of moving.

"Baby girl, you're scaring me," Killian pulled me into hug.

My arms stayed frozen at my side. My feet remained rooted to the floor. I eventually let him guide me to the couch. Killian sat next to me so I could rest my head in his lap. We'd sit like this so often it's a wonder there wasn't a head shaped indentation on his leg. The weight of everything I'd read in Charlotte's diary last night consumed me again and I sobbed.

After a few minutes I heard footsteps. Then voices.

"What could have happened?" Max asked.

"I don't know." Killian responded, stroking my hair. "But when I find out who did this to her I'm gonna strangle them."

"You think it was Xavier?"

"No. He's not even here. And from what she's told me, they barely spoke all week."

"Maybe that's it then. The lack of contact."

"Max." Air from Killian's aggravated sigh tickled my neck. "You've met Victoria, yes? Have you ever known her to bawl her eyes out over some asshole guy?"

"Point taken."

"Xavier isn't an asshole." My muffled voice elicited a giggle from both of them.

"I've never been happier to hear your sassy voice." Killian cocooned his body over mine in a hug. "Feeling better?"

"I was until you started suffocating me." I sat up and stared into two sets of concerned eyes. Their suitcases sat untouched in the middle of the room. The minute they'd arrived home I bolted over here.

Winston trotted around oblivious with a toy in his mouth. Killian tucked a few strands of my hair behind my ear. "We're listening."

I knotted my fingers together and sighed. "I started to read Charlotte's diary."

Max rushed over and sat on the other side of me. Both of them placed their hands on my legs. I wet my lips and continued.

"The stuff I've read so far isn't from our last summer in England. It's from the one before."

Killian's quizzical expression matched the one on Maxim's face.

"She obviously didn't tell me everything." I slouched. "I think she witnessed the night Xavier was beaten and scarred."

"What?" Max and Killian exclaimed in unison.

"She wrote about going to some party near London." I lifted a hand to stop Killian from interrupting. "I know, I know. It sounds out of character but…anyway. She went with this girl she'd become friendly with. Millie. I didn't know her very well. And there was a boy Charlotte had been spending time with named Adam. Apparently she had her first kiss that summer."

"Okay, okay, wait." Killian jumped in. "Boys, parties, kissing, fights. This is so not the Charlotte I knew sophomore year." He glanced at me. "Sounds more like you."

"Hey." My tone sharpened. "Yes, I went to parties but I never witnessed any violence. And I wasn't kissing random boys until junior year."

Killian cradled my face before leaving a soft kiss on my cheek. "I'm sorry. I was only teasing."

"I know." Tears welled in my eyes. "The worst part is she got threatened by someone. Some guy threatened her because she witnessed the fight. He put his hands on her, Killian. I don't know why she didn't talk to me about it."

"Oh sweetie." He pulled me into a hug. "Maybe she didn't know how to tell you."

I exhaled harshly. "He said he knew our family and knew we had money. He told her if he ever saw her at a party again he'd teach her a lesson she wouldn't forget." My throat burned. "What if he did something to her at the bonfire? She didn't want to go. I made her. What if I led her right to this guy without realizing it?"

My body shuddered into quiet sobs. I let Killian keep me in his embrace while Max caressed my back in gentle strokes. The guilt is overwhelming. All the fears I've tried to dismiss over the years paled in comparison to what I learned. Maybe my mother was right all along. I did this. I ruined everything.

The boys let me grieve for quite a while. When I finally lifted my head, I noticed the giant wet spot on Killian's shirt.

"Sorry."

"Please. If I were to allow any girl to leave a wet spot on me, it's you."

I snort-laughed. "Thanks."

"Can I ask you something, Victoria?" Maxim sounded unsure of himself.

"Of course."

"How do you know it was a fight involving Xavier?"

I wiped my eyes. "He has a scar over his eye. I asked him how he got it and he told me he was jumped when he was a teenager." I shrugged. "I don't know if it's him but the stories sound similar."

"Let me get this straight." Killian shoved a hand through his hair. "Your sister spent time with Xavier when she was fifteen?"

"No. But I think she spent time with his brother."

"What the motherfu— what? What?" Killian yelled, standing up. "I can't wrap my head around this, Tori."

"Does Xavier have a brother?" Maxim draped his arm over my shoulders.

"I have no idea. He told me his mother died shortly after he was born. He mentioned having a step-mother but never said anything about a brother or any siblings for that matter." I stood up and started pacing. "I don't know anything anymore." I threw my arms up. "All we did was have sex. A lot of really great sex. We shared some stuff about one another but…" I paused. "I told him about Charlotte. I told him she was my twin. I told him how she died. He was so…so comforting and kind about it. But he never gave off any inkling he knew her."

"Are you sure?" Killian's skeptical tone irked me.

"Yes."

"Have you talked to him at all this weekend?"

Oh boy. I fidgeted with my hair. "Sorta."

His massive eye roll resulted in a faint laugh from Max. "So what did you talk about?"

"Nothing."

"Tori."

"I'm being honest. We didn't actually talk. We, uh, well I sent him a photo and he—"

"You sent dirty messages back and forth," Killian cut me off. "Got it."

"Do not shame me for having fun with this guy."

"Nobody's shaming anyone, baby girl. You like him. He likes you. You're consenting adults. You can show him your lady parts all day if you want. But maybe you should cool it until some questions get answered."

I raked my hands through my hair and paced the floor. He's right. I should put the brakes on my extracurricular activities with Xavier. Then again, I should have done it weeks ago.

"Kinda hard to cool it when he'll be here in a few days."

"Ex-fucking-cuse me?" he shouted.

"Re-fucking-lax," I snapped.

"Guys. Knock it off." Max positioned himself between us. "Babe, you need to reel it in." He turned to me. "Victoria, I know you're going through a lot of shit right now. Take a breath, both of you."

Maxim's stern but caring way of telling us to shut the fuck up worked. He and Killian have been together for almost six years so he's quite used to our high-strung battles. Actually, he preferred to call them electric bitch fests. Max has always been the calming force when Killian and I get this way.

Except right now I didn't feel as though I deserved anyone's kindness. I just wanted to curl up on my couch and fade into nothing.

My pity party ended fast when Killian banded his arms around me. I leaned into the embrace, allowing myself to be comforted.

"I love you," I muttered into his shirt.

"Love you more," he whispered.

"If you bitches think I'm not getting in on this hug, you have another thing coming." Max declared, wrapping his arms around both of us. We all looked down when Winston barked and ran circles at our feet. What a crazy little family we are.

Sleep decided to be an elusive beast. After tossing and turning for the better part of an hour, I got up, went out on my balcony, grabbed a blanket and curled up on the lounge chair. From up here, the city simply twinkled in the night. No sirens, no horns blaring, no people laughing or talking or shouting. Just lights, glass, and steel.

I had all kinds of relaxation tools I could use to quiet my mind and get a good night's rest. Mediation apps, soundscape music, breathing exercises. They usually helped.

Despite spending most of the evening with two incredible, supportive friends, I bolstered my hearty self-loathing once I returned home by reading Charlotte's diary entry again. I wondered why she never tore those pages out. Nothing else was written about the party. In fact, nothing else was written at all. Just blank pages.

After all the back and forth I put myself through over whether or not to read it, I still didn't have any answers.

Well, that's not entirely accurate. I had a starting point.

Most of our belongings from the main house sat in storage. I know for a fact Charlotte kept several diaries here as well. Maybe I'll go after work one night this week and sift through some boxes.

Killian and Max urged me to check in with my therapist this week, too. I'd go to her sporadically over the years if I needed to talk something through about Charlotte. Last time I spoke to her was probably two months ago. So much has happened since then. Seems like now would be a good time for a chat. I grabbed my phone and sent her an email asking if she was available to see me this week.

A strange kind of numbness settled over me. I'm not used to numb. I'd rather deal with the persistent nervous energy that swirled around all things related to my sister. I could pace it off and be done with it.

Or bump into attractive soccer players on the side of the road.

My eyes closed as I wrapped the blanket around me. Xavier's face appeared clear as day, his smile with the fatal charm simmering just beneath.

I finally fell into a fitful, dreamless sleep.

The next two days passed by without incident. Monday did its Monday thing at the office with unread emails and meetings and putting out small fires. Sophie, Glen, and I handed out media training guides to the rookies. A couple of them looked slightly terrified.

The league officially announced the teams traveling to London in the fall and where they'd be holding the games. Ethan called a staff meeting to introduce everyone to Bennet. Remnants of my night out with him and Hannah colored and shaped the way I viewed him now in his impeccable suit. He already gave off an air of power and control. I'd been given a small look at what lies beneath.

I stole a glance at Hannah during the meeting. She'd be an amazing poker player. Her expression gave nothing away.

Tuesday coasted by with minimal obstruction. I turned down a dinner invitation from Hannah. Politely, of course. I wasn't quite ready for part two of the Logan Interrogation Show. Especially since the team was scheduled to arrive soon.

So I opted to stay home and watch reality TV.

Lame, I know.

By the time Wednesday morning dawned, I was an assortment of nerves and excitement topped off with a dash of friskiness. Ironically, it was surprisingly easy to stay focused at work. I spent most of the morning with the community relations manager. We finalized several charity appearances for Noah and a few other players in the upcoming weeks, being mindful of the off-season workouts that started mid-month.

In fact, I was so busy when I returned to my office, I answered my phone without checking the caller ID.

"Hey honey. I'm not interrupting, am I?"

My heart almost stopped. "Dad."

"You sound surprised to hear from me."

"I am."

He laughed softly. "I won't keep you long. I'm in New York for the next few days and would love to see you. Are you free for lunch or dinner at all?"

He'd love to see me? I haven't laid eyes on this man in, what, three years? My palm flattened on the desk. "Is everything okay?"

"Yes, love," he answered in his faint English accent. "Everything is fine. Your mom is fine. I'm fine. I just wanted to see you is all."

I grimaced at the mention of my mother. Thankfully I haven't heard from her since the day she called at the cottage. I shook myself free from the unpleasantness. "Okay. Let's plan for dinner on Thursday. Does that work for you?"

"I'm free as a bird, Tori. Thursday is perfect."

"Great. I'll make reservations and text you the information."

A brief, somewhat uncomfortable silence passed between us.

"See you soon, sweetheart."

Thank God I have an appointment with my therapist in an hour.

❦

"I'll ask the obvious question first," Dr. Whitehall looked at me. "How do you feel about seeing your dad?"

I'd spent the first twenty minutes of our session unloading as much as I could about everything that's happened in the last few weeks.

"Honestly, I don't know. Fine, I guess. I have a lot of questions for him."

She nodded. "Try not to go in guns blazing."

"You know me too well." I laughed.

"I know you sometimes let your emotions rule your behavior.

Maybe lean back and let your dad take the lead for a little bit. See how that develops."

"Yeah." I sighed. "I could try." I laced my fingers together. "I'm more nervous about seeing Xavier."

"Has the team arrived yet?"

"No. They're scheduled to land at four-thirty."

"Have you spoken to him since dinner with his friend the other night?"

I shook my head. "Any talking we do should be in person from now on."

"Agreed." She paused, regarding me closely. "Are you open to seeing where a relationship with him might go?"

"That's a loaded question," I grumbled, toying with my hair.

"It's a valid question," she asserted. "We've already talked at length about you not wanting to bed hop anymore. Is Xavier someone you could see yourself forming a meaningful relationship with?"

A frantic, squeezing feeling coursed through me. I'd felt something similar at his townhouse our final night together. I wasn't lying when I'd told him he made me weak.

"He is," I answered so quiet I could barely hear myself. "But there's always the feelings of being inadequate and undeserving."

"Purging yourself of those feelings will only start to happen if you allow someone to love you. And I don't mean the platonic love you have with Killian and Max. They are wonderful friends and bring you great joy." She leaned forward. "Pushing Xavier away won't solve anything. Unless you want to push him away."

Dr. Whitehall's words echoed in my head on the drive back to stadium. My initial reason for going to see her was to talk things through about my sister. Instead, we focused on Xavier. The digital numbers on my dashboard blared the time. Only twenty minutes until the team lands.

Chapter
TWENTY-THREE

Knock, knock, knock.

Finally.

Killian texted me almost an hour ago to let me know he and Max would be stopping by with dinner. I've been fantasizing about this pasta dish all evening.

"Coming," I called out before opening the door. "It's about damn—"

Oh fuck me.

Xavier stood holding a bottle of scotch. Glenlivet 12 to be exact. I blinked at him like an idiot. He lifted an eyebrow and grinned which made me even more flustered.

"Expecting someone else?"

No words. Nothing. I just stared at him.

"Good thing I brought this instead of a rose." His grin widened. "May I come in?"

Manners, Chase. Manners.

"Uh, yeah. Yes. Please." I moved aside and motioned for him to come inside.

Xavier walked through my luxurious, but cozy, multi-million dollar high-rise condo staring at his surroundings. He stopped in the living room.

Floor-to-ceiling windows framed panoramic views of the Hudson River and Manhattan skyline. The main living space was open floor plan so the living room bled into the kitchen. The bedrooms, bathrooms, and home office were down the hall.

His quizzical expression almost made me laugh. "I had a feeling you came from money but this?"

"What?" I smirked, regaining some semblance of my ability to form sentences. "Surprised to learn I have way more money than you? And Cade? Not Bennet though. His generational wealth wins out."

He blew out a breath. "Are you kidding me?"

"Nope. My dad was a big time hedge fund manager and made loads of money. All this," I gestured around, "is just a fraction of it."

Xavier's mouth hung open a bit as he looked around. This wasn't quite the reaction I expected. It amused me more than anything.

"So impressing you with my net worth, which is twenty million pounds by the way, won't really do it for you then."

"Not quite."

"Everyone's impressed by that."

"I'm not everyone."

A seductive smile pulled at his lips. "We've established that already. What do I have to do to impress you so this date can be better than the last one?"

"We're on a date?" I questioned, meeting his gaze.

Seeing him was like a dream even though I knew this was reality.

Chocolate brown hair still tousled to a fault. Sapphire eyes still wide and searching. Mouth still pouty and sultry and made for sins and promises. And that dimple. It dug in just below his left cheek.

The man looked like he just walked off the set of a photoshoot in his dark jeans, white t-shirt, and leather jacket. Casual, refined, and carnal all compressed in one body.

He put the bottle on the coffee table, draped his jacket on the couch and slipped his hands in his pockets before sauntering over to me.

We stood inches apart, eyes locked.

"Hi."

"How the hell do you know where I live?"

"Nice to see you, too."

"I'm serious."

"So am I." He reached for my hand. "I texted your friend Killian. He told me. He also says he's not sorry."

Little sneak.

"Why didn't you just text me? I would have told you."

"I liked this option better."

"A heads up would have been nice," I muttered.

He grinned. "And ruin the surprise?"

"How do you have Killian's—"

"We exchanged numbers the night we all had dinner together. Your friend was quite intent on helping me expand my reach on social media." He chuckled. "I just think he fancies me."

"I don't doubt it."

He moved closer, his face tight with lust. "Will it break his heart to learn I only fancy you?"

I inhaled sharply when he lifted my hand and pressed a small kiss to my wrist. Right on my pulse point, like he'd done outside the restaurant. The measured control of his movements was betrayed by the fiery passion in his eyes and his shallow breaths.

"He'll live," I whispered.

Knowing what lurked beneath the mastery he had over his own body made me shudder. I wanted him untamed. Right here, right now.

Slow down.

"I didn't want you to leave," I blurted on a shaky breath. So much for slowing down.

He bowed his head. "I know. I'm sorry I did."

"I'm sorry I made you think you had to."

"I took a lot of pillows to the face for you."

I giggled. "Did you deserve it?"

"Yeah, but don't tell Bennet."

"Your secret is safe with me."

"Good." His fingers traced along my jaw and down my neck. "How was your night out on Saturday?"

I swallowed. "Interesting."

"Bennet can be intense."

"I think you're underselling the experience."

His laugh shook his body and filled the room. He genuinely enjoyed my playful response. His wide, boyish grin and the subtle etched lines that fanned from the corners of his eyes melted me. He was achingly gorgeous. The kind of man one would stop on the street to look at and wish with all their might to grab his attention. The kind of man to hold on to forever.

The shock of his skin on mine when he pressed his hand to my cheek was enough to make me shiver. His hand slid to my jaw, then my neck. He toyed with my low ponytail, reaching for the elastic keeping it in place. My entire body sighed when he pulled it free, letting my hair fall in loose waves.

"We should talk," he said.

"About?"

"A number of things."

"Okay. Do you want to sit and—"

"I do, but first I want," he paused, pulling me closer. "I really want to kiss you."

He pressed into me in a swirl of heat, need, and absolution.

"No more sitting in anyone else's lap," he said in his huffy way that makes me smile.

"Did it make you jealous?"

"Is that why you did it?"

"No. Have you been around American football players? They're huge. We were trying to get a picture and—"

He silenced me with a finger to my lips. "Still fiery. That's a relief."

"It's only been two weeks. I didn't have a personality transplant."

"Only two weeks," he repeated quietly, leaning closer, hovering his lips over mine. "Felt longer."

Guilt stabbed and twisted in my heart.

"Sounds like you missed me," I whispered.

"Almost as much as you missed me."

"Glad to see your arrogance is still intact."

"You know you like it," he said, scratching his fingers up into my hair.

"Maybe."

"I fucking hate maybes," he growled, sealing our mouths together on a searing slash of want and need. The feel of him was like gasoline in my blood. His hands on me. His possessive kisses.

I missed this. Craved this. Needed this.

I buried my hands in his hair. His deep groan vibrated in my mouth, throwing more fuel on the bonfire burning within me. He murmured something unintelligible against my lips when he pulled away.

I shivered when he kissed down my neck. I felt him smile before he kissed it again. "I love that you have no control over how you react to me. Lets me know exactly what you're feeling."

"Is that important to you?" I asked, staring into his eyes. "To know what I'm feeling?"

A slight restlessness moved through him. "Yes."

"I always assumed I was hard to read."

He shook his head. "Only because the wrong people were looking." His piercing blue eyes focused solely on me as his hand softly collared the base of my throat, his fingers caressing my skin. "Thank you for letting me intrude on your night unannounced. I was afraid you'd have a date or something."

I couldn't stop the smile from commandeering my lips if I wanted. His flirtatious arrogance charmed me.

"I love it when you smile."

"I love it when you touch me like this," I said, resting my hand over his. "Makes me feel like I'm yours."

The hungry glint I enjoyed seeing so much returned to his eyes. Something animalistic and possessive burned bright underneath all the control he'd been displaying.

"You are." His fingers pressed into my skin. "You have been since I saw you on the side of the road."

"Is that so?"

"Yes." A low, deep rumble vibrated through his chest. "No more sitting in random laps."

"You said that already."

"And I'll keep saying it. No more sitting in random laps."

"It was just a picture. Nothing more."

"I'll be the judge of that." His voice was low, silky.

"Alright, that's enough," I pulled away and put my hands on my hips. "I like your little bossy side but stop being ridiculous."

Something snapped awake in him. His eyes darkened. "Little bossy side, huh?" He felt around to the back of my skirt and unzipped it. "Take this off."

I didn't move. I just folded my arms and stared at him.

"Now, Victoria." His tone had the same dark, imminent edge as the night he introduced me to patio sex. I liked this tone. And gauging by the look on his face, so did he. I let the skirt drop to the floor and waited.

"What's his name?"

"Who?"

One eyebrow arched up. I stared at him for a beat. Oh, I see. He wants to play *this* game.

"Noah."

A flash of recognition registered on his face.

"Noah? The one who asked about your sister's charity?"

"Yes."

"I see." Xavier walked over to the couch and sat down. He motioned for me to come to him.

The way he sat on the cushion so regal and powerful and sexy made my heart race. I went to him without hesitation.

He hooked a finger in my panties and pulled me so I stood between his legs. "Did you like sitting in Noah's lap?" He caressed the back of my legs with whisper light touches.

"Will I be in trouble if I did?"

The caressing turned into kneading. His fingers dug into the skin just below the curve of my backside. "I haven't decided yet."

His smug smile tipped me off. He knew what I was up to. Just like the last time. Getting him to do what I wanted required subtlety on my part. I wasn't generally described as subtle so this whole thing would probably end up being a wash.

"You're not going start pacing are you?"

"I haven't decided yet," I mimicked him, accent and all.

Oh boy. The carnal look on Xavier's face was priceless. He rubbed his thumb along his lip and stopped, biting down on it with a grin. I think I just inadvertently got what I wanted.

"Take a step back."

I did because, well, yeah, this is happening now and I, for one, cannot wait. He stood up and glanced around.

"Kitchen."

That's all he said. I shivered and walked. The few times I dabbled with spanking, and I do mean few, were mostly drunken dares. Nobody knew what they were doing. Nobody was experienced.

I stood by the counter, waiting for whatever came next. Xavier advanced on me and God help me he looked ferocious. Not scary. No, no. He looked like he wanted to devour me.

"Turn around," he ordered.

I did without any qualms and braced my hands on the counter's edge. I felt him stand behind me. Then I felt his finger run up my arm to the back of my neck.

"There will be three," he told me. "Normally I would make you count but since there are so few and it's your first time, I won't. Would you like to know what they're for?"

I nodded.

"I can't hear you, Victoria."

"Yes, please."

"The first is for the night you unbuckled my pants when I told you to only unbutton my shirt."

I laughed softly. He leaned close and kissed my neck.

"The second," he continued, "is for your cheeky comeback just now about pacing. And the third," he lowered his hand to caress my backside, "is for sitting in Noah's lap. If at any time you want me to stop, say *red* and I will. When I ask if you are okay to continue, say *green*. Do you understand?"

"Yes."

"Are you sure you want to continue?"

"Yes, Xavier. I'm sure."

He sighed.

Oh shoot. "Green."

Inhaling slowly, I turned to glance at him over my shoulder. He looked as intense as he'd been the night on his patio. If not for the impending spanking experience, I'd kiss him until we both couldn't breathe.

My stare lingered a beat too long. When his eyes met mine he let out a low, satisfied groan. The sound pierced right through me.

"Look at you," he said in a low, forbidden tone. "My fiery, sexy girl. I've never seen anyone more beautiful in my life."

My eyelids fluttered as a tsunami of emotions ravaged me. He brushed a strand of hair behind my ear.

"Victoria, would you like to rephrase how you answered me over by the couch?" he asked softly. "Or are you satisfied with your cheeky comeback?"

I bit down on my lip and grinned. "I haven't decided yet."

A wicked smile curled his mouth. He flattened his palm in the space between my shoulder blades and pushed me down so I bent over the surface until the side of my face touched cold granite. I'd taken off my heels when I got home from work, so I stood on the balls of my feet. He pulled my hips back so I could stand with my feet flat to the floor.

After he made sure I was comfortable and steady, he took his time feeling his way from my shoulders to my hips and down over my thighs. Petting me and stroking me. He kept repeating those motions over and over. The anticipation might kill me. I wondered how—

Crack.

The first one came without warning. He made contact right where my upper thighs meet my ass. I gasped in surprise, clutching the counter tighter. The sensation sparked and crackled across my skin, more pleasant than painful.

"That was the first," he said. "How do you feel?"

"I'm good."

"Are you alright to continue?"

"Green."

"Okay." He caressed my skin and murmured, "Please tell me if it's too much."

The second one landed harder in the same spot. Still pleasant but the crackling on my skin was more intense. I shifted on my feet to get more leverage.

"Still okay to continue, love?"

"Yes."

"Victoria."

"Sorry." My voice sounded more breathless than normal. "Green."

I realized this was light and not really anything to write home about for people who lived this lifestyle but for me it was—

CRACK.

I cried out. The third one hurt. A lot. It was harder than the previous two and unrelenting. The sound echoed through the kitchen. Clearly, I'm not used these sensations. Stinging. Crackling. Even burning a little. But then came the parts I'd only read about. The aftershocks of pleasure rushing straight to my clit.

"Dirty princess," he whispered. "You did so well."

Xavier's light caresses on my skin enhanced the feeling. I remained bent over the counter while he soothed me with his hands and then, much to my enjoyment, his mouth. Soft kisses. So soft and so sweet.

"Don't stop," I whimpered.

His body cloaked mine, pressing me into the counter. "Do you want to come?"

My legs trembled. "Yes."

He reached down and slid his fingers into my panties. "You're so wet," he murmured, his warm breath tickling my ear. "Yes what?"

How am I supposed to answer him? Not one coherent thought formed in my mind. Words tumbled out in rapid succession, "Yes, please. Sir. Thank you."

He laughed softly, sliding a finger along my slick skin to my waiting clit and circled it with firm pressure. "You don't have call me sir. I'm not a Dominant. Though I like how it sounds coming out of your mouth." More pressure. The intensity added the small bite of pain I relished.

"Do you like when I call you dirty princess?" he continued. "It seems fitting. A dirty princess in her ivory tower who likes to be spanked and finger fucked while pinned against her kitchen counter."

The world around me blurred and faded away. I felt myself slip down, only to be secured by the firm grasp of Xavier's arm. One more firm press and my whole body undulated. He coaxed me through each wave of pleasure with his finger until I stopped quivering.

Then he turned me so I could watch him suck my climax off his fingers.

"I love the way you taste," he moaned, then kissed me slow and deep. I clutched onto his shirt, pulling him as close as possible. We broke the kiss in a haze of damp breaths and languid stares.

"I really liked number three," I whispered, kissing him again. "I liked how it felt."

He squeezed his eyes shut, resting his forehead to mine. I couldn't tell if I upset him or pleased him with my comment.

"I liked it, too," he finally said, opening his eyes and stroking my jaw. "Are you okay to walk?"

I nodded and let him lead me to the couch. When I felt him sit next to me, I curled up in a cozy, kitten-like position with my head in his lap. He resumed his soothing caresses, running his palm over the curve of my backside and down to my upper thighs. This feeling almost made me dizzy. I felt intoxicated by comfort, by him, by his touch. There wasn't room for my usual guilt or anxiety. There was only room to be present.

"How are you feeling?"

"I'm not sure I can pick just one word."

"Pick as many as you need."

I thought for a second before answering, "Relaxed for sure. Comfortable." I looked up at him. "Closer to you."

His shy smile and the way he bit down on his lip imprinted on my heart. "That might be the endorphins talking. The first time, even with something as light as what we did, can be powerful."

"And if it's not the endorphins?"

"Then it's pretty obvious there is more than something casual between us."

My heart twisted. "Is it?"

"Yes." His hand settled over my heart. "I don't feel casual about you at all."

I sat up, tucking my legs under me to face him. His adoring expression made me think of long-term things. Serious relationship things. Forever things.

"I'm not prepared for more than casual."

"Do you need to be?"

"You…I…if there's anyone I should prepare for when it comes to this, it's you."

The remark winded him. He winced, not in pain but in shock. After a few seconds, he admitted, "Guess we're both unprepared."

He motioned for me to sit closer, so I curled up against him, nestling into his side. He draped an arm around my shoulders and kissed my forehead.

"Is this okay?" he asked.

"This is mild compared to some of the stuff we've done."

Chuckling, he gave me a little squeeze which excited me and made me nervous simultaneously. I'm approaching a line I vowed never to cross. Giving my body to someone was easy. I could detach and enjoy the physical pleasure.

Giving my heart? I already felt like my chest cracked open enough for him to see my heart beating out in the open air. Exposed and messy.

But it's *him…*

"Xavier?"

"Yes, love."

"I don't feel casual about you either."

A slow breath gently filled his lungs. His hold around me tightened. The duality of never wanting this moment to end and knowing I'd probably be the one to screw it up tore me up inside. The little nagging voice in my head kept screaming I didn't deserve this. I didn't deserve him.

"You have no idea how happy that makes me," he whispered. "How happy *you* make me."

All the different versions of a once impossible reality collided, silencing my destructive inner monologue. They blended and fused into something singular. Something complete.

If this is what falling in love felt like, I can't possibly imagine how anyone could bear the weight of not surrendering to it.

I climbed onto his lap and straddled him.

"I'm sorry I fucked it up before I left." I trembled. "Being with you at your townhouse and…I loved every minute. I wish I'd told you that instead of…I wish I could take back what I said to you."

"I'm here now, aren't I?"

I nodded.

"So, we start with a clean slate." He caressed my thighs. "You and me."

"You and me," I repeated. And then I kissed him.

I kissed him until static blurred my vision and I couldn't picture a time when we weren't kissing or holding one another. I kissed him in the slowest, deepest way possible.

As rough as I like it, this moment of quiet softness felt just as powerful. The giving and taking. Delighting in the silkiness of his mouth and tongue. Savoring him.

I pulled back, admiring his drunk-with-lust expression. Hooded eyes. Parted lips. Raspy breathing. Hair untamed.

"That was incredible," he said, sounding dazed.

"You're incredible."

He smiled. "Now I know it's the endorphins talking."

"Stop it," I half-scolded.

He opened his mouth to say something and stopped. His brows knit together in thought when he looked at me. Then he cast his eyes down.

I twined my fingers through his hair and pulled it so his eyes met mine again.

When I pressed my lips to his again I felt his hunger and need. He took control, fisting his hand in my hair and tilting my head where he wanted, taking my mouth how he pleased. I could tell from his sighs and moans that he was just as far gone for me as I was for him.

"Tell me what you're feeling," he demanded quietly.

I didn't know what to say. Well, that's not true. I knew what I wanted to say but I wasn't ready. Neither of us were ready to say it or hear it.

"If you can't say it, I want you to show me. I want you now. Like this." His clipped, intense timbre returned. "Undress."

I stood up and removed the rest of my clothes, watching him watch me.

"I think you should keep yours on," I said when he started lifting his shirt. Shooting me a curious glance, he stopped.

"Do you?" He unzipped his jeans. "Any particular reason?"

"I think it's hot and I haven't stopped fantasizing about having sex with you again while you're fully clothed."

"As a gentleman, who am I to deny you that request." A devilish grin curled his lips as he lowered his pants just enough to free his fully erect cock. "Come here."

He yanked me onto his lap, guided himself inside slowly and groaned into my neck.

"Too good," he rasped. "You feel too fucking good."

I couldn't get enough of the intense pressure and fullness when he filled and stretched me. Feeling the fabric of his clothes beneath my thighs and ass set off a delicious wave of pleasure as I rocked my hips.

"What do you want to happen next, Victoria?" he asked, thrusting into me.

"I want us to be so much more than casual," I admitted, digging my fingers into his shoulders. My innermost thoughts tumbled out of my mouth, uninhibited. "I don't want this to ever stop. I want to let you in. I want to know everything about you. Everything. I…I want to be with you every day. Laughing and talking and fucking and living. Really living."

Tears streamed down my face. I stopped talking because if I continued I'd say something much too real. Even with him like this, kissing me and caressing me and thrusting into me, I couldn't say it. It was much too soon, not to mention foolish.

"I'll give you all of it," he told me, repositioning us so I was on my back. He pushed into me with hard, deep, determined thrusts. "All of it and more."

His fingers found my clit and it only took several rough strokes before I fell apart beneath him. Writhing and coming and falling, falling, falling so hard.

Chapter
TWENTY -FOUR

VICTORIA

"**W**e should talk now," Xavier said, sounding a little chagrined. He stood shirtless in my kitchen, wearing only his boxer briefs. I currently wore his shirt, and his jeans lay rolled up in a ball on the floor. Round two was much more naked than round one.

He looked thoroughly fucked in the best way as he grabbed two bottles of water from the fridge.

"Okay." I looked up at him when he handed me the water. "Let's talk."

For some odd reason Bennet's voice scolding me about limits flooded my head. Not quite what I wanted knocking around in my brain after what I'd just experienced.

But, yeah. Limits.

"Um." Xavier ran a hand through his hair, rubbing it back and forth. "I wanted to do this before we, uh, well, before."

I smiled. "Are you nervous, Maddox?"

"Nooo," he over-enunciated the word as he sat down. "I want to do this right. And I don't want there to be any misunderstandings or confusion."

"I'm listening," I said, sipping the water.

"The dinner you went to the other night," he started. "I wanted—"

"You were vetting me," I interrupted. "Or Bennet was on your behalf."

His mouth dropped open in surprise. "Well, sort of." He tilted his head. "Did it upset you?"

"Not really," I shrugged. "I didn't enjoy it but I figured you had your reasons. The biggest one being the way I left you and what I said."

Maybe it was better we had all the sex before this conversation. I felt notably relaxed and zen with a clear head.

"Do you want to take the lead on this?" An eyebrow went up.

"No. Sorry. I'm listening."

"Mmhmm. Listen quietly, love, unless I ask a direct question." His gentle command sounded so damn sexy wrapped in his English accent.

I only grinned in response.

He remained quiet for a long minute, looking down at his hands. It took an abundance of restraint for me not to reach out and touch him.

"Do you use rough sex as a way to punish yourself for how you feel about what happened to your sister?"

I froze. He stared at me with those sharp sapphire eyes, piercing through all the flimsy layers I use to protect myself.

"No." My voice cracked. I cleared my throat and tried again. "No," I answered in a firmer tone. "Why would you ask me that?"

"I have to be sure you aren't using it as a way to cope with something." His jaw flexed. "I've been in situations like that before and it doesn't end well. For both people involved. When did you know you liked it this way?"

"Charlotte was still alive, if that's what you're getting at. My curiosities started in high school. I'd heard stories about some of the seniors and the stuff they'd do at parties. Paddles, rope, handcuffs. I was a teenager. Everything sounds adventurous when you're young."

"Curiosity is one thing," he said in a low, tight voice. "When did you *know*?"

I inhaled a deep breath. "College. I dated this older guy freshman year. We'd play around with blindfolds and nipple clamps and stuff like that. One night, I let him tie my wrists together. I was on my knees bent forward with my ass in the air. He started running a feather tickler all over me until I thought I would explode. I was so turned on. And then he—"

Xavier's expression stopped me cold. Jealousy and lust commandeered his face.

"He what?"

"Well, he, uh, he started fucking me hard without warning and," I paused, consumed by the fierce, possessive energy radiating in my direction.

"Tell me."

"I liked it. A lot. I orgasmed and told him to do it again."

That last bit garnered a smile. I lifted my hand to stop him before he could ask me anything else.

"I like it rough, Xavier. I like it dirty and hot and very unladylike… and it has nothing to do with any deep emotional scarring. It gets me off. I know what I like. I know what I want. I'm not submissive…"

Another smile.

"…I'm not letting someone do these things to me because I'm punishing myself. I like it because it makes me feel strong. I'm choosing to play rough. I'm choosing to be used this way. The only thing I've ever denied myself is falling in love because I believed I didn't deserve it."

"Do you still believe you don't deserve it?"

"I don't know," I answered honestly.

"Do you think you don't deserve me?"

I couldn't look at him. I couldn't admit I'd thought those very words to myself over and over. I couldn't tell him I pushed him away because I believed I didn't deserve him or his affection. And now we're here again. Back to the thing I wasn't ready to think about or say.

"Xavier I'm…even if I do think that it doesn't change how I feel about you. How I feel when I'm with you."

Silence hung in the air for a few seconds before he continued, "Is what happened with your sister the reason you pushed me away?"

"Not that singular act, no. I was afraid if I let you in, let you get close to me, you…not just you, anyone really, would blame me for it."

His eyes widened. "Blame you for what?"

I didn't like the way my lower lip trembled. I also didn't like the way my eyes burned or the metallic taste in my mouth or how my throat squeezed itself. I did not want to cry in front of him. I'm not ready for this. Not yet. Not when I have the diary and so many confusing, unanswered questions.

A single tear fell down my cheek. I swallowed hard and looked him in the eye. "Red."

The questions stopped and I was engulfed in a hug. I clung to him like he was my only life source.

Having him comfort me felt incredible. Letting him comfort me broke through parts I thought I'd closed off for good.

"Did I use the color thing wrong?"

This is what I'm worried about? Pull it together.

Xavier kissed my forehead. I rested my hand on his chest so I could feel his heartbeat. It was strong and reassuring.

"It's okay, love. It worked didn't it?"

He held me tighter. Our bodies pressed together. I straddled him, wrapping my arms around him and trying to get as physically close as possible. He threaded his fingers through my hair, gently massaging my scalp. I don't know how long we stayed like this. I only know I never wanted it to end.

"Can I ask you something?" The sound of his voice startled me.

I leaned back. "Sure."

"What was your sister like?" He tucked my hair behind my ear. "Were you two similar in many ways?"

Before I read through her diary, this answer was simple. Now? I sighed.

"Yes and no, if that makes sense." I chewed on my lip. "She was older than me by three minutes and really enjoyed bossing me around. Or trying to."

"Ah," he grinned. "Glad it's not just me who fails miserably with it."

"Shut up."

"Nope. I got you to smile. I think I'm going to continue." He squeezed my waist. "So, she's bossy."

"Not *your* kind of bossy." I thought for a minute. "We both shared a love for all things pop music. When we discovered the Spice Girls it was like a religious experience. We'd put on concerts in her bedroom. I was Ginger Spice, she was Baby Spice and," I laughed, "Killian was Posh Spice on occasion."

"I bet he has a great pout and looks smashing in little black dresses."

"He does," I giggled. "How did you know?"

"Intuition," he smirked. "Continue, please."

"Um, we had different interests at school. Well, that's not entirely true. We both joined the debate team. I loved speaking in front of people, thinking on my feet, and really learning to appreciate two sides of an argument. So did Charlotte. She was actually the captain. She also wrote for the school newspaper and helped plan the fundraisers our class held with the parish. We went to a Catholic school, in case I didn't mention it. Um, I was homecoming queen. She was class president."

The unrelenting emptiness I've felt since the day she died tugged at me.

"She was my best friend. We shared everything. We dressed alike until we were ten. When I made the executive decision to only wear clothes that were purple, she bailed."

"That's bold."

I poked him. "No comments from the peanut gallery."

"Sorry." A soft kiss landed on my nose. "Go on."

"Charlotte would always tell me how lucky I was to be so naturally outgoing. She was much more reserved than me but just as friendly. I think she had some social anxieties but back then nobody really talked about it like now. She saw a few doctors and seemed to be doing okay."

Part of me wanted to tell him everything. The diary, the party, the bonfire. Every detail of what happened those summers in England and how all our lives changed one random spring morning. I wanted to unburden myself. I wanted to let him in.

Instead, I shrugged. "We were alike but different."

He smiled. "She sounds like a lovely person. I think I would have liked her."

A tremor streaked through my body. Maybe he never crossed paths with her that summer. Maybe it wasn't him she saw get attacked at the party.

On an impulse, I traced my finger along his scar. He flinched, snapping his head away.

"Sorry," I said, pulling my hand back.

He grabbed my hand and kissed it. "Don't be sorry. I wasn't expecting it."

"Does it bother you when I touch it?"

Something flashed behind his eyes. "Probably as much as it bothered you when I asked about your sister." He pressed his finger to my mouth when I started to speak. "But I like your gentleness. I like how it feels when you touch it, even though I don't respond particularly well to it."

Every nerve ending, every fiber of my existence yearned to get the answers I craved.

"You really don't know why those kids jumped you?"

A sullen expression washed over him and then he scowled.

Whatever memories he held still warred within him. His fingers pressed into my hips. "Something happened with...there was this," he squeezed his eyes shut and grimaced. "Red."

My heart dropped. "Xavier, I'm sorry." I held him tight. "I'm sorry."

The strength of his embrace revealed so much more than anything he could say. These might not be the types of limits Bennet had in mind when he mentioned them the other night, but they were our limits. These were the things only time and patience would allow.

I leaned back when his grip on me loosened. My fingers skimmed along his neck, down to his collarbone. I scooted back in his lap, leaned forward and kissed his chest.

"How was it playing again last weekend?" I asked, caressing him.

"Fucking brilliant," he exclaimed, his eyes alight with excitement. "I love it. Being in goal. Competing with my teammates. Hearing the fans. It's bloody amazing."

"You sound like the guys on the Legends," I smiled. "Have you always been this passionate about soccer?"

"Football," he corrected. "And yes, I have. I focus most of my time on training. Really pushing myself to be a great player. Cade, too. When we were younger he'd have to pull me off the pitch on weekends to go hang out or see a movie or whatever. I just wanted to excel."

"You wanted to be the best. A crowd pleaser. Attention grabber."

"Always," he conceded. "I wanted to be noticed."

I chuckled. "I think you've been noticed."

"Oh yeah?" He pulled me closer. "By you?"

"Maybe," I answered, stroking his shoulders.

"Hmm," he hummed. "Does that mean you're willing to break your policy for me again?"

"Pretty sure I broke it on the kitchen counter about two hours ago. And then twice on this couch."

His throaty laugh filled the room. "Yeah, I'd have to agree with you there, love."

Xavier's mouth fused to mine, his tongue pushing past my lips. I pressed my hand to his face, tilting it to the side so I could control the kiss and take him how I wanted. He let me but only for a few seconds. The raw, deep groan vibrating in his chest signaled he'd be the one in control soon.

"Victoria." He speared his fingers through my hair, grabbing and pulling it so I'd look at him. The sapphire in his irises burned bright, almost celestial. "I have to go back to the hotel soon."

I pouted. "Curfew?"

"Yeah. With the long flight and the time difference, we're under orders to be back in the rooms by ten since we have training tomorrow morning."

"You'll be at the stadium?"

He nodded. "We're using the practice field."

"What time?"

I was subjected to a rather intense, lascivious stare. "Do you want to watch?"

Goosebumps crawled up my arms. "Maybe. Will you be wearing your goalkeeper outfit?"

"Goalkeeper outfit," he mimicked. "I'll be wearing my training kit. Will that turn you on enough?"

"Smart ass." I kissed him quick. "And again, *maybe*."

A sinful smile pulled at his mouth. "I can see why Bennet wanted to drape you over his knee so much the other night."

I blanched. "He told you?"

"Mmm." The light touch of his hand on my backside sent a shock of pleasure through me. "He did. He finds you to be quite feisty. However, he's not allowed to touch you in that way. But I can always give him a demonstration. With your permission, of course."

"A demonstration?" I don't know what excited me more. The thought of being bent over Xavier's lap or the thought of being watched.

"Naughty girl. We'll talk about this another time." He squeezed my ass. "Up you go."

Reluctantly, I climbed off him. He put his jeans on and prowled over to me. "As sexy as you are in my shirt, I do need it back."

"But I'm not wearing anything underneath." I toyed with the hem and started lifting it.

"Even better."

"You'll never leave if I strip naked in front of you. And I refuse to be the reason you miss curfew." With those words, I trotted down to my bedroom, took the shirt off and slipped into my robe. When I walked back into the living room, Xavier was standing by the window. I kept waiting to wake up and realize this had all been a dream.

"Here you go," I said, holding out his shirt. I couldn't tear my eyes away from his lean figure as he moved with sleek fluidity through the room toward me. Once he was fully clothed, we walked to the door.

My back hit the wall without any warning. I gasped. He's unrelenting. Every cell in my body reached for him when he pressed himself against me.

"I'm going to think about you all night, dirty princess. How much I liked reddening your ass with my hand. How wet it made you. How beautiful you sounded coming on my fingers and my cock."

My head fell back against the wall with a distinct thud. Forget death by a thousand paper cuts. This was death by filthy words, inflections, and tone. All delivered in an elegant British accent and packaged in the most stunning man alive.

He flicked his tongue on my mouth. "Did I give you enough to reflect on?"

"Maybe."

"Greedy girl." He grinned and then bit down on my bottom lip. Hard. Almost as hard as the night in the taxi. I dug my nails into his lower back and scratched along his skin, drawing a low moan out of him. The silkiness of his tongue soothed my lip before he kissed me, reminding me who I belonged to with every deep lick into my mouth.

The change in the atmosphere was tangible when he broke our

kiss and pulled away. It's almost as though part of me peeled off and attached to him. I wanted to tell him to screw the curfew and stay with me all night. I wanted him near me. Always.

He opened the door and smiled at me.

"Sweet dreams, love."

It closed behind him with a gentle click.

Chapter
TWENTY-FIVE

"**P**ain shuttles, lads. Let's go."

The assistant training coach blew his whistle and off we went. I didn't mind sprinting from cone to cone too much. Helps with my endurance. And with all the extracurricular activities I planned to do with Victoria, this would come in rather handy.

Admittedly, I moved a little too fast at her place last night. My intention was to talk first but when she opened the door and stood there all shocked and gorgeous and real, I couldn't help it. Which is a major flaw, I know. My impulsiveness is notorious for getting me into trouble.

"Good job, Maddox. Rest up, then get in goal."

I ambled over to the sideline and grabbed some water. The pitch was pristine for a practice field. This whole facility was actually quite amazing.

"Quiet night last night?" Cade asked with a shit-eating grin on his face.

"Yep. Spent some quality time at the spa."

"Is that what you call it these days? Got a proper rubdown, did you?"

"Jealous?" I smirked and walked toward the net.

"Fucking tosser," he shouted after me with a laugh.

Cade can be obnoxious most of the time but he means well. He knew how nervous I was to show up unannounced at her place. I even had the idiot's voice in my head when I knocked on her door.

She's a good one, Maddox. Don't fuck it up.

Inspiring? No. But it gave me a laugh.

I joined our two back-up keepers for some reps in goal. All things being equal, my attention wasn't one hundred percent focused on training. Good thing Harry and Christian were on their game. Don't get me wrong. I didn't miss when my turn rolled around. My attention just kept drifting to the massive steel and glass building in the background. The Legends stadium.

I wanted her to come out and watch. I wanted to see if she could hide her desire and arousal. I'm not daft. The video she sent last weekend gave me loads of ideas. I'm ready to push her limits even more now.

Of course Bennet had something to say about that earlier. I know he pressed her pretty hard about discussing limits with me. I know why, too. It's another one of our unspoken understandings.

He's protective but also knows when to back off. Thing is, Bennet and I function differently when it comes to women and how we are behind closed doors. Or not so closed doors, depending on the situation.

"Xavier," Coach Hart yelled over to me. "Reflex drills."

I nodded. All thoughts of Victoria dissolved from my mind when the drills began. About a dozen cones lay scattered in the penalty box. I never knew which one Coach Hart would kick a ball from so I had to be focused and alert. Plus, one of the second team players stood ready to take a shot any time I punched a ball out. I always had to be ready to block.

Kick.

Block.

Reset.

Kick.

Block.

Reset.

The ball came flying back to my right a second after I punched it out. Extending my arms as far as I could, I dove for the ball, hitting it away. The force of it vibrated through my gloved hands.

"That's the one," Hart yelled, clapping. "That's the save we're looking for, Xavier. Game changing."

Honing my fitness, speed, and movement for all these years improved my ability to make fast, high-frequency saves over and over. Probably why I'm the best in the league and represent England for international matches.

Another set of drills. More kicks, more blocks, more quick reactions.

My back hit the grass when I finished.

"Get up, old man," Harry teased, offering his hand.

Panting and laughing, I grabbed it and stood. "At least I don't look as knackered as you," I retorted.

Harry flicked me off and glanced at the sideline. "What's going on over there?"

I looked to see what he was talking about. Bennet stood with our team manager and another, older gentleman. Hannah was also there. My heart stilled.

I scanned around but didn't see Victoria. Maybe she decided not to come down to the field. That's disappointing. I remembered Bennet telling me Hannah's grandfather owned the Legends, so that must be who he's standing with.

"Legends owner," I told him. "Probably wanted to come see some real football."

"Maddox, one. American football, nil," Christian joked.

The three of us walked toward the sideline to join the rest of the team before breaking for lunch. Bennet caught my eye and waved me over.

"Excuse me, gents. Time to go impress the big executives."

"Yeah, yeah," Harry chided. "Don't trip over your big ego on the way."

Cade's laughter echoed as I walked around some of my teammates. When he came into view, I prepared to fire off a sarcastic remark and—

Victoria.

She stood inches away from Cade, laughing and smiling in her demure, light brown polka dot dress. The top hugged her curves with precision while the bottom flowed out to just above her knees in a delicate, soft way that made me want to yank it up over her hips. Her hair was pulled back in a loose bun. She looked prim and professional, except for those fuck me heels and the deep red shine on her lips.

Images of her bent over the kitchen counter surged right to my dick, reigniting how wild it made me seeing her so turned on from the spanking and her version of submission, which was actually just plain old submission.

I smiled.

She must have felt my presence because she looked right at me.

Her candy coated lips curved into a grin as her eyes darkened and studied every inch of me. Especially the noticeable bulge outlined in my pants. Her teeth sunk into her bottom lip and so help me I wanted to bite it, too. And much harder.

"Xavier," Bennet's impatient voice snapped me back to reality. He leveled one of his I'm-tired-of-waiting stares at me. "I'd like to introduce you to someone. You too, Cade."

"Guess the lord of the manor decided to make an appearance today," Cade snickered.

"Don't be catty," Victoria scolded, playfully swatting his arm.

"Yes, my queen."

Cade shot me a smug look, linked arms with Victoria and walked toward Bennet. Victoria, for her part, winked at me and smiled. I liked how well she got on with my friends. I liked how well she handled herself with Bennet. I liked how good-natured she is around Cade. I liked everything about her.

I clasped my gloved hands together and followed, watching Victoria's hips sway until she stopped walking. The way she stood, positioning one leg slightly in front of the other so her hip leaned out to the side, exuded effortless grace. She's so bloody hypnotizing. I stood next to her closer than was socially acceptable for a professional setting. I don't fucking care.

Control, Maddox. Control.

"Cade. Xavier. I'd like you to meet Ethan Caldwell, owner of the New York Legends." Bennet motioned toward us as he addressed Mr. Caldwell. "Cade Gallagher is our striker. Xavier Maddox is our goalkeeper."

We all exchanged pleasantries.

"Good training session?" Bennet asked, eyeing how close I still was to Victoria.

"Always."

"Xavier Maddox?" Mr. Caldwell stroked his chin. "You're not related to James Maddox are you? I've been looking at commercial properties in the London area and his name has come up several times."

"I am, sir. He's my father."

"Does he still do architectural work or is he mainly in the development business now?"

"A bit of both."

"What are the odds you're also related to Rebecca?" he grinned, clearly knowing the answer already.

Keeping this conversation light and amicable became more difficult. I thought this was football training, not twenty questions about my family. Victoria's arm brushed mine when she shifted on her feet. I glanced down into her wide, emerald eyes. They held even more questions.

"Rebecca is my step-mother. So, I'd say the odds are pretty good."

I looked from Caldwell to Bennet to Hannah to Cade. All of them had smiles plastered to their faces for different reasons. Only Victoria remained stoic. I wondered what that was all about.

"And Mr. Gallagher," Caldwell continued. "I understand you come from a family of solicitors."

"I do, sir," Cade responded. "Came in handy when I negotiated my contract with Royal City."

Canned laughter that's usually reserved for cocktail parties or business gatherings erupted around me. It reminded me of the parties my parents hosted for their clients.

"Full disclosure," Hannah interjected. "My grandfather is a stickler for details about his players. They've all been through the family tree interrogation with him." She smiled at me and Cade. "It's all part of the experience."

Um, yay? I hoped I wouldn't have to answer any more questions about my upbringing.

"I made reservations for all of us this evening," Bennet announced. "We're having a team dinner. Mr. Caldwell and Hannah have graciously accepted my invitation." He turned to Victoria. "I know you have a previous engagement but my offer stands. I'd love it if you joined us for coffee and dessert later."

Hannah, Mr. Caldwell, and Bennet all said their goodbyes and made their way to the offices inside the stadium.

"I'm hitting the showers," Cade said. "If you two want to join me, feel free."

I shot him a dirty look before he jogged off. I could hear him laughing. Most of our teammates were gone by now to break for lunch. Only the equipment staff lingered on the pitch gathering cones and balls.

Victoria hadn't moved. Her demeanor seemed tense, like she was deep in thought about something unpleasant.

"You have plans tonight?" I asked, feeling rather awkward for some reason.

"Yeah," she responded. "I'm having dinner with my dad, if you can believe it."

I turned to fully face her. "Are you looking forward to it?"

She crossed her arms and shrugged. Pieces of her hair fluttered in the breeze. I didn't like how closed off she'd become.

"Are you alright, love?" When I reached for her she backed away. The rejection needled at my heart. "Victoria," I said, my voice more strained than I expected. "Look at me."

She studied me for a few seconds. "I'm okay."

"Are we going to do the talking in circles thing again?"

"No," she sighed. "I'm okay. Really. I just have a lot of crap on my mind."

"Have you heard from your friend Killian?" I asked, trying to get her in a better mood.

"As a matter of fact I did." Her face lit up. "I told him you'd love to hire him as your personal brand manager."

My jaw dropped. I couldn't tell if she was messing with me or not. "You did?"

"No." She laughed. "I just wanted to see the look on your face. It did not disappoint."

I grinned. "You're lucky I like it when you tease me."

"Is that so?" The white of her teeth dug into the dark red staining her plump bottom lip. So damn sexy.

"What are these made from?" she asked, reaching for me and running a finger down my gloved palm.

"That side? Latex mostly." Half a dozen filthy thoughts raced through my mind. "Why do you want to know?"

A coquettish glint sparked in her eyes. "I liked watching you practice."

"Oh?" I clasped my hands together below my stomach. "What did you like about it?"

"The way you move. You have this ability to control your body in ways I've never seen before. One minute you're ferocious. The next, calm. It's fascinating."

She turned and faced the goal. A stronger breeze blew between us, fusing the side of her dress to her body, accentuating her curves. The delicate hem floated up exposing the supple arc of her backside.

Her bare backside…

"Dirty princess," I spoke in a dangerous tone, approaching her. "Turn toward me."

She failed at hiding a smile when she did as I asked, which should have annoyed me. But since it's her it only succeeded in turning me on. I removed one glove and slid my hand under her dress, finding nothing but smooth skin.

"No knickers?"

"Not right now."

I squeezed her ass. "What does *not right now* mean?"

Her eyes flashed with passion, defiance, and arousal. "It means I took them off before coming outside to watch you."

Oh *fuck* this woman is so uninhibited and sexy and I love it. Now we were truly the only ones left on the pitch. Everyone else was gone, including the equipment crew.

"You did this on purpose?"

A single nod.

My fingers dug into the soft flesh of her backside. "Naughty girl. What if your dress had blown up in a breeze with everyone standing around?"

"I wasn't worried about it."

"You should be." The danger in my tone was unmistakable now. I slid my hand around to see if my suspicions were true.

Oh yeah, they were. She was soaked. I cupped cup her hot, wet pussy. "Is this from watching me practice or from standing here in a crowd of people with your cunt exposed?"

"From both, Xavier," she replied in the softest, sweetest sounding voice.

I bent my head so my mouth hovered at her ear. "I get to choose who sees what belongs to me." She shuddered when I teased her folds with my fingers. "Filthy, filthy girl. So wet and ready for my cock. Or do you want my fingers? What about my tongue?"

She was holding onto my arms now, digging her nails into the fabric of my shirt. I had to be careful I didn't let this go too far. The edge of restraint and reckless taking is more and more blurry these days.

"Does it drive you wild?" she asked in an urgent tone. "Knowing I'm exposed under this dress with your teammates around? With your best friend standing next to me?"

I stopped teasing her cunt.

"Will it drive you mad wondering how I'll get myself off when I go back to my office? How deep I'll shove my fingers inside myself? What I'll be thinking about when I play with my clit?"

"Victoria." Her name came out of my mouth in a strangled breath. "Enough."

"Does it make you hard? Untamed?"

I grabbed her hands and pinned them behind her back. Putting her in this position pressed her body into mine. "Yes it does. And if you keep teasing me like this I'll take you over my knee right here and spank your ass until you either learn to behave or scream my name while you come. Or both."

Her soft moan went straight to my aching dick. The green in her eyes exploded around her dilated pupils. I collared her delicate throat with my gloved hand, feeling the velocity of her pulse. I was about to lose my mind if I didn't shag her right this second.

And then she smiled.

A fucking gorgeous, full smile that rendered me useless and allowed the roughest part of me to take over.

"Just checking," she purred.

I sucked in a breath and exhaled harshly. The entirety of the earth's gravity could just about hold me back from ravaging every inch of her body on this grass.

I clamped my eyes shut. "Fuck," I said through clenched teeth. "I don't know what it is about you, Victoria, but you bring out the absolute beast in me."

I opened my eyes to her smile. Wide and teasing and sweet and sexy. And then my chest did the feeling thing and so help me, I love this smile.

She cupped her hand over my erection and stroked it through my clothes. "And you bring out the dirtiest little princess in me."

Well that did it. I grabbed her arm and led her toward the changing room.

"Do you have any meetings or anything right now?" I asked, not really giving a shit if she did. Animal instinct and my cock were making all the decisions.

"No."

"Good."

I practically kicked the locker room door open and yanked her inside.

Empty.

I paused, listening for any water running in the showers.

Nothing.

I rounded on Victoria and growled, "Get on your knees."

"Am I in trouble?" she asked, a bit coyly, as she kneeled.

"Yes. Big trouble."

She smiled, crossing her ankles behind her.

Not submissive my ass.

I removed my other glove and tossed them both to the floor, noticing the slight pout on her lips.

"Don't look so disappointed," I said. "Or I won't use them at all."

"Oh. Okay, I can wait," she breathed. "Do you want me to suck you now?"

I ran my thumb along her full lower lip, pulling it down. "No. I want this gloss smeared all over my cock while I fuck your mouth." I jerked my chin down toward my pants. "Take them off."

The second she reached for the waistband I heard a noise coming from the small office in the back.

"Nobody else is using this part of the facility this week, right?" I asked, placing a protective hand on her head.

"No. Just you guys. This is the visitor's room. Nobody else is scheduled for another two weeks."

"Stand up," I said. "I'm going to have a look around."

"I thought you liked having an audience," Victoria teased, getting to her feet.

"You're already in enough trouble, love." I put my finger to her lips. "Don't make it worse."

Her laughter had its desired effect on me. I couldn't get enough of how melodic it always sounded.

A scratching or dragging noise came from the office, followed by a loud thud. We both looked at one another. I put my finger in front of my mouth, signaling silence.

The blinds on the window facing into the changing room were shut. I approached the side door and looked through the glass.

You've got to be kidding me.

"What the fuck are you doing in here?" I shouted, opening the door.

My step-brother spun around, pale as a ghost.

"Jesus, Xavier. Are you trying to give me a heart attack?"

"Not at this particular moment, no. What are you doing in here?"

"If you must know," he huffed. "I'm unpacking a few things for Graham. Moving these chairs around a bit. Putting this dry erase board in a better spot. He asked me to set out some game plans for Saturday."

"Are you his lackey now? More arse kissing to get more time on the pitch?"

"Sod off," his voice rose. "Not everyone is perfect like you. Maybe I'm aiming to be a manager someday."

"Oh that's rich," I taunted. "A manager."

"Wow," he snickered. "Already pulling birds in the States. Were you about to shag her in there?"

In all the commotion I didn't see Victoria come up next to me. But Adam did.

He glanced dismissively in her direction. "You should check to see where his cock's been before he sticks it in you and buggers off."

Nothing but red rage filled my vision. If not for Victoria's quick movement to get in between us, I would have slammed his face into the floor.

"Hey," she shouted. "I will not have this in my stadium. Enough. Both of you."

I scowled and folded my arms. Adam stopped rearranging the white board and looked at Victoria. Really looked at her. His face morphed from annoyance to recognition to disbelief.

"Charlotte?" he whispered.

I barely caught Victoria before she hit the ground.

Chapter
TWENTY -SIX

So many things come into focus once a person opens their eyes and really sees. I knew that now as my head continued to pound and Hannah continued to fuss around me. I was back in my office, nursing a bottle of water. She and some Royal City trainer were caring for me when I regained consciousness.

William. That was his name.

Nice guy. Kept checking my pulse and listening to my heart.

He also kept asking if I'd eaten enough and if I was dehydrated.

The cause of my fainting spell wasn't lack of food or water. It was ghosts. Ghosts I didn't know existed one month ago but were now front and center in my life.

The whole ordeal played in my mind like a bad movie.

Someone thought I was my dead sister. Darkness. Voices. The feel of warm material on my legs. More voices. Footsteps. Silence. Then I opened my eyes.

"You should give this back to Bennet," I said listlessly, pointing at the suit jacket on my desk. It'd been draped over my legs while I laid unconscious on the floor. Apparently Xavier was adamant about keeping me covered. How thoughtful. Too bad he wasn't as adamant about being there when I woke up.

I stood.

Oh boy.

The room spun. I took a deep breath and held onto the edge of my desk.

"Are you okay?" Hannah rushed over. "Should I call William again?"

"Nope. I'm fine."

"I want you to go home. Glen can cover the rest of the day."

Actually, that didn't sound like a bad idea at all.

My legs wobbled. Driving will be interesting.

Hannah grabbed her phone. "Hey, it's me. I'm sending Victoria home but I think— Yep. Perfect. Thank you."

She looked at me after ending the call.

"Bennet's driver will take you. Come on."

I lacked the will to argue, so I grabbed my things and followed her down to the parking lot. Forty minutes and one hell of a comfortable ride in a Bentley later, I was home. Hannah insisted on staying but I told her if she didn't leave me alone I'd quit my job. She left in a huff but promised to text me every half hour.

At least somebody would. I rolled my eyes at my own petulance but my phone has been silent since I passed out. Nothing from Xavier. Not one word. I oscillated between anger and hurt. Right now, anger appeared to be winning.

It fueled me as I paraded into the bathroom. I stared at my reflection in the mirror and scowled as my eyes filled with tears. I shouldn't be this upset. Maybe he's just as shocked and confused as I am. Maybe he needs a minute to figure out what happened, just like I do. Wiping my eyes, I undressed.

Shit.

In all the uproar, I left my underwear in my office. Now there's something a person doesn't say every day. Thankfully I'd locked them in my desk but still. Not smart or professional.

I moved through my bedroom on autopilot, sifting through the closet shelves for something comfortable to wear. After settling on yoga pants and a tank top, I flopped on the couch. Again, not smart. My head pounded. I closed my eyes, willing myself to relax.

Dinner with my father proved to be the least stressful event of the day. The most stressful prize goes to Killian and Max after I asked them to pick up my car at the stadium. Neither one would do it until I told them what happened and why.

I did, of course. They're my closest friends and know everything anyway. What's another grenade to lob into the fray? Killian pestered me about not laying into Xavier for pulling a disappearing act. I went off on a tirade to actually defend Xavier and the overwhelming shock factor of the situation. Maxim played referee, again.

I threatened to delete Xavier's number from Killian's phone if he texted him without my permission. The last thing I wanted or needed was my friend launching an offensive against my boyfriend.

My boyfriend?

Christ Almighty.

I arrived at the restaurant first and waited at the table, checking my phone every two minutes to see if I had a missed text from Xavier.

I didn't. Obviously.

I typed out a message, deleted it, typed another, deleted it. Frustrated from my own lack of conviction and ability to send even a simple text, I dropped my phone on the table. The server came over to see if I wanted anything to drink. I wisely stayed with water.

"There she is." The sound of my dad's voice transported me back to when life was uncomplicated and whole. "Sorry I'm late."

Much to my surprise, I flashed him an unforced smile. "I haven't been here long."

He sat across from me and reached for my hand. His skin was tanned and soft with more defined wrinkles than I remembered. Has it really been three years? A lump formed in my throat. Why do I keep pushing the people I should be leaning on the most away?

"You look beautiful, Tori," he beamed.

My heart twisted. Killian and my dad are the only two people I allow to call me Tori. It was my sister's nickname for me and even though I complained about it non-stop when she was alive, I did secretly like it. But now that she's gone, only my dad and Killian have the privilege.

"It's the dim lighting," I joked.

He waved off my silliness. "Neither you nor your mother could ever take a compliment." His faint English accent was more pronounced.

I squeezed his hand and smiled. "Thank you."

"Better."

"What brings you to New York?"

"You."

I rolled my eyes. "I highly doubt that."

"So skeptical." He grinned. "Tell me what you've been up to at work."

Talking to my dad about work was the easiest way to get the conversation started. Plus, I actually had quite a bit to say. And it relaxed me. I could tell him things without hiding a detail or forcing an emotion.

My dad worked a lot when we were kids, much to my mother's dismay. But we lived a beautiful life and I always appreciated the sacrifice. I also absorbed quite a bit of my dad's work ethic.

My sister and I never felt neglected or like his job was more important than us. Every night, without fail, when he returned home after a long day, Dad would sit with us on the couch and ask about school or cheerleading practice or the debate team's next competition.

He was always present. Always.

Until it all fell apart.

"Ray mentioned you visit them every year to brag about me," I said, sipping my water.

"I do," he admitted. "If I don't brag about my little girl, who will?"

"Certainly not Mom," I muttered.

"Victoria Ava," he scolded. "I realize Helena isn't the easiest person to deal with but she is your mother."

I shrank in my chair. I never liked getting reprimanded by my father. Even now as an adult it made me feel like a little kid.

"I know what happened with the cottage," he continued, folding his hands. "She told me about the contentious phone call you had with her." He frowned. "I wish you'd both work on this rift. I know it's not easy but how much longer can it go on?"

I clenched my fist, unable to prevent the words from pouring out. "I'll work on it when she stops blaming me for everything."

"She doesn't blame you."

"Oh no? It must have been someone else who said I caused all this and called me selfish."

My dad shifted uncomfortably in the chair. I knew I wasn't being fair to him. This dinner is supposed to be about us, not the awful relationship I have with my mother.

"I'm sorry," I said, looking down. "It was just really upsetting. Being at the cottage brought up so many memories. I'm sorry."

His warm hand covered mine. "Your mother loves you, Tori. She doesn't have a great way of showing it but she does. You are all we have."

I didn't know what else to say so I stayed quiet. He's right. I am all they have.

After a few minutes I said, "I wish things could be different. I think that's why I wanted to hold on to something that made us all happy at one point. That's why I refused to sell Briarcliff."

"I'm glad you didn't agree to sell it. I'm sorry your mum was so harsh with you. That house holds different emotions for all of us. But I agree with you. It should stay in the family. That's part of the reason why I'm here."

My mouth popped open in surprise. I hadn't thought about the cottage this much since coming home. Surprising, since it was the root of so much anxiety and stress when I was in England.

"Who is the man your mother mentioned?" he asked with genuine curiosity. "The one who answered your phone? Is he your boyfriend?"

Of course she mentioned him. Of fucking course.

"Oh. Uh, just someone random I met over there."

"Do you know many random someones who offer to buy stranger's houses?"

A dull headache pounded between my eyes. I rubbed my temples. "No. His name is Xavier. He's a soccer player with Royal City Athletic. Do you follow the team at all?"

My dad's eyes grew wide as saucers. "Xavier Maddox? England's goalkeeper?"

"Yeah," I answered, slightly amused at his reaction.

"My daughter is dating England's number one."

"Wow. Okay. Dating is a strong word. We met randomly and spent some time together."

Omitting the obvious didn't mean my father all of a sudden fell off the turnip truck this afternoon. I'm thirty-five, not twelve. He can read between the lines. From the sardonic smile on his face, I figured he read the whole damn book.

"Regardless, he seemed to charm your mother after she got over the initial shock of speaking with him. She and I had several conversations over the last couple weeks and decided to transfer the cottage into your trust. Our attorneys finalized it on Monday. So," he reached into his jacket pocket and pulled out a small box, "these are yours now."

I opened the box, knowing what I'd find inside. Nestled on tissue paper were the original brass keys to Briarcliff Cottage. The locks had been changed years ago so these barrel keys wouldn't work in any of the doors. They were more symbolic than anything.

I pulled them out slowly, admiring the intricate design. "I haven't seen these since I was a little girl." Wistful thoughts from another life spread an unexpected warmth through me. I put them back in the box and looked across the table at my father. "Are you sure?"

He nodded. "The cottage was always going to be yours and your sister's. It's time for us to stop shedding anything and everything that reminds us we were a family. We still are a family. You, me, your mother, and Charlotte. We've all been remembering her in our own separate bubbles for too long. She may not be with us physically but we owe her the dignity of coming together for at least this one thing to keep her memory alive."

I was at a complete loss for words. Part of me worried I'd pass out cold again. Adding fainting to my repertoire of pacing and general anxiety wasn't something all too appealing.

The day Charlotte died appeared fresh in my memory. The worst home movie ever made continued to play on an infinite loop in my mind.

And now I had her diary with an endless trove of questions.

"Tori?" He reached for my hand. "What's wrong?"

I studied my father. His warm, hazel eyes. The fine lines defining his aging face. The brown hair forever being swallowed by gray and white.

"Where do I start?" I shrugged, holding back my tears.

"Start at the place where it hurts the most."

I thought of my sister and nodded.

And then I told him everything.

Pacing around my living room at two in the morning sounded super shitty on paper. In reality, it sucked even harder. I wanted to sleep. I wanted to curl up in my bed, bury my head under a pillow and succumb to the blissful nothing of unconsciousness.

But no. Sleep wouldn't allow me the honor. Plus, I was expecting company.

Knock, knock, knock.

Right on time.

I shuffled to the door and opened it. Xavier swallowed me in a hug.

"Thank you," he whispered. "I know it's late."

"I can't sleep anyway. Aren't you breaking curfew being out at this hour?"

"Yeah. It'll be fine. Come."

We walked into the living room and sat on the couch. For someone who had unmatched control over his body, he couldn't stop fidgeting.

"Can I get you a drink or something? You seem jumpy."

"I can't. Training in the morning."

"Right." I drummed my fingers on the couch. "So, what is it you want?"

He placed his hands on my thighs. "Are you okay?"

The twin flame of anger and hurt sizzled beneath my skin. All day without a word and now he wants to know if I'm okay? He sounded so sincere though. Like he always does.

"Was that guy your brother?" No reason to delay the inevitable.

Shock and disbelief ravaged his handsome features. And maybe a hint of relief. He stared at me for a beat and then answered, "Step-brother. How did you know?"

It's way too late at night, or early in the morning, for me to delve into everything. So I decided to keep it factual and brief.

"Remember the diary you found in my sister's room?"

He nodded.

"I started reading it. Charlotte wrote about a boy she'd met one summer named Adam."

Xavier's mouth parted in surprise.

"He had a brother who was a goalkeeper…"

Another shocked expression.

"…and they didn't seem to get along." I shrugged. "So it looks like my sister dated your brother once upon a time ago."

"Is there more?"

"Let's just start there, okay?"

A small nod. His own internal battle raged behind his eyes. I reached up and played with his hair, combing my fingers through. He tilted his head, relishing my touch.

"After what happened in the changing room, I had a long talk with Adam," he finally said. "He told me about your sister and how they used to see one another."

He shook his head, almost as though those words sounded unreal coming out of his mouth.

"And he told me how she never came back. He didn't know what happened to her. After a couple years passed he looked her up online and saw the death notice." Intense blue eyes met mine. "He knew she was a twin but I guess the shock of seeing you," he wet his lips, "he wasn't thinking. He wants you to know how sorry he is." This last bit came out forced, like he didn't want to pass along the sentiment.

"What else did you two talk about?"

Xavier scrubbed his face with his hands and ran them through his hair. "That was all really. I don't…he and I don't have a good relationship so I never knew about her. I never met her."

"Are you sure?" I tried to control the emotion in my voice.

"As sure as I can be. Adam and I didn't really run in the same circles. He had his friends, I had mine. If we ever crossed paths I…I wouldn't have paid much attention to what he was doing or who he was with."

"So where were you the rest of the day?" I blurted.

"With Bennet for a little while."

"Doing what?"

He pressed his fingers into my thighs, squeezing hard. "Trying to make sense of all this, Victoria. I wanted to talk to you." He looked at me. "I wanted to come right here and be with you all day but I also had to finish my preparations. I couldn't just leave. We had film analysis and then I had my individual player analysis and the team dinner."

His shoulders slumped. He looked so tired, both physically and emotionally.

"All I thought about was you," he said softly. "All I wanted to do was come to you. I hope you know that."

The twin flame of anger and hurt went out. I can't be mad at him for doing his job.

"I don't want to be a distraction for you," I murmured.

"You're not. I'm sorry if I made you feel that way."

I shook my head. "You didn't. That didn't come out right." I swallowed. "I know how demanding it is to prepare for a game. I know the obligations you all have to meet. I just meant—"

His firm kiss stopped me from continuing. I wasn't expecting it so I backed away slightly. He grabbed the back of my neck and kept me from moving, kissing me harder. Feeling how much he wants me made my head swirl.

"You," he murmured on my lips.

"What about me?"

No answer. He only pulled me close and hugged me. I relaxed into his embrace, enveloped by his scent and the strength of his arms. After everything that happened today, I think we both needed this serene moment.

When Xavier finally let me go, he leaned back and stared down at his hands.

"How was dinner with your father?" he asked after a minute, meeting my gaze.

"Started off a little rocky but ended up better than I expected."

"Yeah?" His expression brightened. "So you're glad you went?"

"I am." I paused. "He wanted to know who the guy was my mom spoke to on the phone. I told him it was you and he nearly fell out of his chair."

"Really?" He chuckled.

"Oh yeah. And then he said something about you charming my mother when you talked to her."

"I told you we had a lovely chat." The playful arrogance returned to his tone.

"Well, whatever you did worked. My parents actually talked and transferred the cottage to my trust." I spread my arms out. "Looks like we really are neighbors now."

His eyes widened, glowing with hope and fear and resolve. And, of course, mischief. "Guess that means I'll be visiting you all hours of the day and night."

"I was thinking more along the lines of you shirtless in my yard cutting the grass," I sassed.

"Mmhmm," he hummed, leaning closer. "You'd like that wouldn't you?"

I would. I'd like it a lot. For a brief moment I allowed my thoughts to go places I never let it. To the future. To him and I as a couple.

If he could read my thoughts right now, I wondered what he'd say.

I shoved my fantasy life back into the safety of my mind.

"You should get back to the hotel before they find out you're not in the room."

"It's the middle of the night," he flicked his wrist dismissively. "Nobody's checking." An intense stare focused on me. "I'm not leaving you alone right now."

The last time he said similar words to me I told him I'd only slept with him to distract myself and we were nothing. From the way he kept his eyes glued to me I could tell he was thinking the same thing.

"Okay," I said. "But promise me you won't get in trouble."

"You're worth it," he declared, gently stroking my cheek. "Bedroom?"

I nodded, standing up. There's no reason to fight this anymore. Our lives are forever entwined thanks to one fateful summer when we were both teenagers, blissfully unaware of the other's existence. And now here we are, pressed together in a gentle embrace on my bed.

He played with my hair as I slid my hand under his t-shirt to caress his skin. My earlier fantasy of us as a couple came roaring back.

I didn't stop it. I liked how it made me feel. I liked how *he* made me feel.

"Thank you," I said.

"For what?"

"This. Being here. I didn't realize how much I needed it."

He held me tighter. I curled into him, tangling my legs with his. He threaded his fingers through my hair, gently massaging my scalp.

"I'm sorry I wasn't with you today." A soft kiss lingered on my forehead.

"You don't have to apologize."

"I do. My first priority is you. I promise I won't make that mistake again."

"Don't make promises you can't keep." I nuzzled into his chest. "Especially during the season. If your schedule is anything like—"

"Victoria."

I sighed. "Yes?"

"My first priority is you," he repeated.

Propping myself up, I leaned on an elbow and admired his handsome, exhausted face. In the dim light, he appeared vulnerable.

Quiet anticipation filled what little space existed between us. I traced the curves of his lips and the slope of his nose, the sturdy angle of his jaw and the strong column of his neck. His eyes never left mine as I continued touching him, memorizing his features with my fingertips.

I watched the tension in his face melt into a relaxed peace as his eyelids became heavier and his breathing slowed to a steady rhythm.

Giving him this gift of serenity made my heart sing.

I kissed his forehead and without any pretense or forethought, I let my lips wander to his scar, pressing soft kisses along the entire jagged length. Tremors shook his body but he didn't flinch away or stop me.

So I kissed it again, each touch of my lips leaving behind an invisible mark of affection and gratitude.

Then I kissed his cheek. The corner of his mouth. And ended with a small kiss on his lips. His whole body exhaled when I pulled back.

"Show me again," he growled.

"Show you what?"

"How you feel about me," he commanded, his voice thick with emotion. "Kiss me."

I did.

Our mouths fused together with raw desire, seeking confirmation for what neither one of us can put into words. Finding it and feeling it and surrendering.

Chapter
TWENTY -SEVEN

"**W**hen's the wedding?" Killian asked, settling into the seat next to me with a heaping plate of french fries. Fans in the section to our right started singing and chanting.

I stared at the field, watching Xavier go through his warm-ups. For this particular drill all the goalkeepers juggled the ball between them without letting it hit the ground. They'd bounce it off their feet and chest. I just liked watching the way he moved.

"Shut up," I finally acknowledged Killian's question. It was Saturday evening and I was thinking ahead to my post-match plans with Xavier, not marriage.

"Mature," he snickered. "I give it three months before you're married and pregnant."

I looked at my best friend's smug smile and shook my head. "You're being ridiculous."

"No, I'm not. Because it's real now," he said plainly.

"Yeah." I stole a french fry from his plate. "It's real now. I'm still not getting pregnant or married in three months."

"Whatever." Killian's soft smile hasn't changed from the day we met as kids. "I mean, he got your parents to agree on something which is," he fisted his hands at his head, extended his fingers and pulled them away sharply while making a bomb sound.

"Wild, right?" I stole another fry.

"The house warming party is going to be lit." He moved the food away from me. "And the whole thing about his brother wasn't as nefarious as we all thought. Although you do still need to talk to him about the fight."

"I will."

The last thirty-six hours have been an absolute blur. Xavier ended up staying with me on Thursday. He managed to sneak back into his hotel room Friday morning without being discovered. I chose to stay away from their training session. I know how important routines are for athletes and my presence would only be a distraction.

Last night was another story. Xavier tempted fate again and broke curfew to spend the night with me. I tried (sort of) to convince him it was a bad idea and he should be more responsible and his team needs him and all the things one is supposed to say to a pro-soccer player the night before a game when he should be resting his body.

Xavier's impulsive side wanted to hear none of it.

We had so much sex in one night I was tempted to take a vow of celibacy for the weekend. I'm still sore from the euphoric pounding my body took. I can only imagine how his body feels.

"…vacation on the moon. The Sea of Tranquility is supposed to be great this time of year," Killian was saying. "Interested?"

"Sure," I answered in a light, dreamy voice. "The beach sounds good."

"Oh. My. God."

"What are you babbling about?" I asked, forcing my eyes away from the field.

He just smiled this dopey, sugary smile and started tearing up. I blinked at him.

"You're in love. Like, *in love,* in love."

"Don't say it out loud."

"Someone has to," he shouted to nobody in particular.

"Who's ready for a bit of English footie?" Noah Tate's bad attempt at mimicking a British accent announced his arrival.

I stood up and hugged the Legends quarterback and his girlfriend, grateful for the interruption. Several members of the team decided to attend tonight's game. Noah and Tracey sat several rows behind us. Tre arrived not too long after with Jax and Dante, our two tight ends. In fact, we had a good number of Legends players in our section. Some brought their wives and kids as well.

A few minutes later Bennet strolled over. Our seats were one row up from the field so he leaned on the padded barrier wall when he stopped in front of us.

We weren't too far away from the Royal City bench either. Well, *bench* isn't an accurate way to describe it. They had fancy soft chairs arranged beneath a curved plastic roof to keep them all cozy and safe from the elements. In this case, the elements happened to be a clear, breezy, spring evening in New York.

"Excited for your first Royal City match in person?" Bennet asked.

"First of many," Killian answered. "Many. Right, Tori?"

I wanted to strangle him in the most loving way possible.

"Yes. We're all looking forward to it," I said, noticing the warmth in Bennet's smile.

"The Knights should give us a good challenge. Maybe even score a goal or two."

"Don't let your goalkeeper hear you say that," I laughed.

"Ah. It's good for him," Bennet teased. "Keeps his ego in check." He glanced back at the field. "We'll see if he defends the goal as well as he maneuvered through the city under the dark of night."

Oh crap.

"You knew?"

Mischief and intrigue lit up his eyes. "I know *some* things, Ms. Chase. Do you really think he'd break curfew without backup?" He motioned for me to lean closer. "I told you his well-being is important to me. And that extends to you. You make him happy. If breaking one rule to spend time with you is important to him, I'll help make it happen."

I blushed. I fucking blushed and Bennet saw it and smiled. Dammit.

"You really have to start introducing me to your new British invasion friends," Killian fake-complained.

I rolled my eyes. "Killian Monroe, this is Bennet Logan, Royal City Athletic president and CEO for The Logan Group."

The two of them shook hands and I couldn't help but laugh at how different they appeared. Killian exuded frat boy charm in his distressed jeans and untucked button down. Bennet radiated power in his tailored dark blue suit. Hard to believe only a couple of years separated them in age.

"I'm also known as the god of thunder in certain circles," Bennet joked, revealing some of his own boyish charm.

"Yes," Killian exclaimed, smacking his hand down on the wall. "Did Tori call you that? She has a thing for the Avengers."

"So I've learned."

"Well I'm glad the two of you have bonded," I chuckled.

Both teams started making their way back to the locker rooms for final preparations. Fans yelled and cheered as Cade and Xavier sauntered toward the tunnel together. Many of them crossed their arms in front of their chests in an *X* shape. Cade and Xavier mimicked the pose and yelled with enthusiasm.

Bennet caught their attention and waved them over, much to everyone's delight.

Ever the crowd pleasers, the duo drank in the attention and adoration, waving to the fans. Cade looked sharp in his away whites, while Xavier smoldered in a bright bluish-teal. Bennet did the typical guy hand clasp and one-armed hug with both.

"Good luck out there, gentlemen."

"It'll be a breeze," Cade said with conviction. "No offense, Lady V."

I grinned and shook my head. "Don't get cocky until the final whistle blows."

He put his hand up for a high five, which I happily smacked. "Good luck, Gallagher."

Out of nowhere, Xavier jumped up on the wall and sat, similar to the way our players do after scoring a touchdown. The people around us went nuts, screaming for his attention.

"Hi." He smiled his sexy, crooked smile. His eyes glowed as bright as the color of his uniform. "Do I get a good luck wish from you, too?"

"Do you need luck?"

"Nope." He cupped his gloved hand behind my neck and pulled me in for a lush kiss. Pretty sure I heard a few cat calls and whistles from the crowd.

"Thank you, love."

He jumped down, waved to the fans and ran off to the locker room with Cade.

"See you after the match?" Bennet asked, walking toward the tunnel.

I nodded and waved.

Killian rested his head on my shoulder when I reclined back into the seat. "So, when's the wedding again?"

"Shut up," I smiled, stroking my tingling lips.

All talk of weddings ceased once the Knights and Royals took the field to start the game. The Knights actually gave them a run for their money, threatening on goal several times. Xavier moved like lightning for every save. Not once did they score on him. His explosive speed and agility are mesmerizing. I probably spent the majority of the game watching him.

Probably?

Fine. I spent the entire game watching him.

I nearly melted when the final whistle blew and he removed his jersey to exchange it with the Knights' goalkeeper. The long-sleeved bright blue shirt he wore under it clung to him like a second skin.

Both teams walked along the sidelines, clapping and waving to fans. The atmosphere and crowd were electric the entire time, even though the game ended in scoreless tie. I had a feeling this wasn't the last we'd see of English soccer clubs visiting the Legends stadium.

"When did you take this?" I asked Hannah, zooming in on the picture. We were standing off in a corner near the bar waiting for our drinks.

"During warm ups. Don't they look great?"

The photo of Cade and Xavier smiling and laughing was perfect. Xavier had his arm around his friend's shoulders. Cade's head tilted back like he'd been told the funniest joke ever.

"I love it."

"Thought you might."

"What do you love?" Xavier asked, sidling up behind me and wrapping his arms around my waist.

I showed him the photo. "Hannah took this when you guys were warming up. Cute, huh?"

"Cute," he laughed. "The guy in blue looks like a real pillock."

"A what?"

"Lemme see," Cade demanded, joining us. I gave him my phone. "Absolute wanker, that one. Guy in white looks minted, though."

"You're doing this on purpose." I shook my head, grabbing the phone.

"Doing what?"

"Being all British with your slang."

"Me?" Cade feigned an innocent look. "Think I'm faffing around, do ya?"

"Oh my God," I snickered.

"Cade," Xavier addressed him in a low, patronizing tone. "We don't want her to lose the plot."

"Or get cheesed off."

"You're both on thin ice." I tried to sound annoyed. "Speak English."

"We are," they said in unison before we all burst out laughing. Hannah shook her head and went back to our table with her drink. Cade planted a loud kiss on my forehead before following her.

Xavier sat on a barstool and positioned me so I stood between his legs, facing him.

"Enjoying yourself?" he asked.

"Maybe."

An eyebrow went up. "I see."

"Am I well in it now?"

A flirtatious spark lit up his eyes. "Not at the moment, city princess. But the night is young."

"Do you mind if I post the photo online?"

"Of course I don't mind."

"Want me to tag you both in it?"

"Sure."

I smiled, writing and erasing what I wanted to say in the description. After a few failed attempts I decided on *Royals gather in the house of Legends.*

Not my best work but I love this picture. I love how joyful and carefree he looked. I glanced up to see Xavier on his phone.

"What are you up to now?"

"Nothing." He put the phone in his pocket. "Just proper gentleman stuff."

"Care to elaborate?"

"So inquisitive," he muttered with a smile while pulling his phone out again. "This is what I did."

He turned the screen toward me. A picture of me smiling down at my own phone appeared on his feed. My mouth opened in surprise.

"You sneak."

"Do you want me to take it down?"

I narrowed my eyes at him before reading *Legend* in the caption. And a blue heart emoji. It already had likes and comments.

This keeps getting more and more real, doesn't it.

"No. You can leave it up." I handed the phone back and added, "Does this make us official?"

"Officially what?" he smirked.

"Internet friends."

"Oh, absolutely."

Standing like this near the bar reminded me of our encounter at Black Rose. Running into him that night had been a pleasant surprise. Flirting with him was even more fun. And now here he was, sitting in front of me.

Should I?

"So, Xavier is it?" I asked, peering up at him from under my lashes.

Confusion washed over his face briefly. Then a sinful smile pulled at his mouth. "Depends on who's asking."

I looked around to see if anyone was actually walking over. Even here in New York, he had his admirers. They were quite vocal at the stadium and since we're in a crowded bar, anyone could be here.

"There's no brunette coming up to me this time." Xavier's low, clipped tone hit all my hot buttons. His pupils dilated.

"Must be hard for your fragile ego to deal with the lack of attention."

"Nothing about me is fragile."

My lips parted slightly. I know I was blushing. I felt the heat building beneath my skin.

"Would you like to continue?" he asked.

Trembling beneath his hungry stare I answered, "Green."

The change in his demeanor was instantaneous. My heart raced.

I leaned closer, resting one hand on his thigh and using the other to tug down the neckline of his shirt so I could see his inked skin.

"Nice tattoo." I traced my nail along the base of his throat.

"I have more."

Both his hands cupped my backside and squeezed, pulling me flush against him. I was close enough to kiss him. Close enough to feel his warm breath on my mouth. Close enough to see how drunk with lust I made him.

"I bet you do." I nipped at his lower lip. "You should show me all your tattoos. Right now."

He fisted my hair with such force I whimpered. Tilting my head, he took my mouth, plunging his tongue in, claiming and owning me.

I curled my tongue to taste along his upper lip. Whisky and *him*. I moaned, licking deeper into his mouth, tasting more of him.

He tugged on my hair to the point of pain, pulling my head back. His breath tickled my ear when he asked, "Are you wet, dirty princess?"

I nodded, finding the outline of his erection through his jeans. Instead of stroking it, I traced around his length, then pushed my palm down to his inner thigh, teasing him, putting pressure there and squeezing.

"Careful," he moaned. "What makes you think I'm this kind of guy?"

"What kind of guy is that?" I held his fervent stare. This place was almost filled to capacity. We were tucked in a corner by the bar. Not quite secluded but not fully exposed to other people. They'd really have to stare to see what we were doing over here.

"You tell me." He repositioned his body a little so my hand was hidden. "Are you okay to continue?"

"Green."

The dark expression I love so much washed across his face. "I'm all yours."

Our mouths slid together, tongues entwining in a swirl of kinky, filthy demands. He cupped my face gently as I pressed my palm into his crotch and inner thigh, rubbing and squeezing. This was so dirty. So indecent. And I loved every second. I loved feeling how he controlled his body. I loved picturing others sneaking a glance to see what we were doing.

"Look at me," he groaned.

I felt the heat beneath my cheeks when I did. I'd never seen this expression before. It was insatiable. Covetous. I parted my lips, inhaling a sharp breath.

His pelvis jerked forward. "You like being this kind of girl, don't you?" he growled. "Getting me this hard in such a crowded place."

Our lips met in a brief, lush kiss. I squeezed his inner thigh when he moaned. I knew he was close.

Nuzzling into his neck, I kissed up to whisper in his ear, "I was so turned on watching you play tonight. I love how your body moves. I love how feral and competitive you are. I love how intense you look on the field. I wanted to fuck you right there."

Untamed eyes glazed with longing burned through me. The deliberate way he ran his tongue along his lower lip ignited my desire. The secret that delighted him to no end was our secret now.

"Come for me," I purred, not breaking eye contact.

His fingers dug into my arm. I kept rubbing and squeezing, mesmerized by his subtle, controlled thrusts.

He pressed his forehead to mine, a broken moan crossing his lips. I felt his body tense, his breathing stutter, then the faint rocking of his hips as he rode out his release.

"Mine," I murmured, running my fingers along the outline of his pulsing length.

"Fuck," he hissed, his pelvis jolting uncontrollably. I could stay like this all night and feel him surrender to me over and over.

I kissed him soft and slow, savoring every moan and ragged breath as his body relaxed.

"Did you like that, country prince?" I asked quietly, sliding my fingers in his hair.

"I loved it, Tori," he whispered.

I pulled back like I'd been whipped with barbed wire.

An alley. Great.

Fucking great.

I pressed my hand to the brick wall and tried to catch my breath. Did I really just run out on Xavier after giving him a hand job because he called me Tori?

Yes. Yes you did, you asshole.

"Shit," I yelled. Throwing my head back, I shouted in frustration into the night air.

What is wrong with me. I raked my hands through my hair and did the only thing I knew how to do. I paced.

I paced and paced and paced some more.

"Victoria."

The concerned way Xavier said my name stopped me in my tracks. I turned but couldn't look him in the eye. Alley trash seemed to be a more fitting option. I heard his footsteps approach and chose to stare at his shoes. He tilted my chin up. A soft smile greeted me.

He leaned down and kissed me. "Hi. I would have come out here with you sooner but, uh," he gestured to his pants, "you made a mess."

I cough-laughed, staring at his crotch. His pants looked normal. "Impressive job cleaning up."

"Took me a minute but I think I got it all."

Nothing but a relaxed, gorgeous man stood before me. No annoyance, no anger. Only concern and affection.

"It seems we've arrived at another limit," he acknowledged. "Another *red*. Am I correct in my assessment?"

Tears stung the corners of my eyes when I nodded. "You're being too kind."

"Nah. Just being me. Are you okay?"

"I will be." I blew out a breath. "You must think I'm crazy as fuck."

He chuckled, rubbing his thumb along his lower lip. "I think you're hot as fuck. Dirty as fuck. Smart and funny and loving. All as fuck, by the way."

My mouth curved into a smile with no effort. "You're not upset?"

"No." He reached for my hands. "Should I not call you by that name?"

I laced my fingers with his. "The only people who call me Tori are Killian and my dad." I swallowed. "Charlotte loved to call me that. After she died I didn't want anyone to say it."

"Is it something only for the people who are closest to you?"

My heart cracked a little. "You're close to me."

"I'm getting there, love. Come here." Xavier banded his arms around me. Nuzzling into my neck, he pressed gentle kisses against my skin.

"Sorry I ran out."

"No apologies." He kissed me. "You feeling okay about what we did in there?"

I smiled. "Absolutely."

"Good." He kissed me again. "Ready to go back and join the others?"

"Do they know?"

He grinned down at me. "Know what? That you went out for a little air? Yes. That you and I snogged like horny uni students at the bar? Yes." He traced along my lower lip. "That I came so hard I couldn't walk straight? No."

"You couldn't walk straight?"

"Not really. I think I hid it pretty well though. Weaving in and out of the crowd to get to the loo helped."

"Were they watching us the whole time?"

He toyed with a few strands of my hair. "On and off, yes. Does that make you uncomfortable?"

I shook my head. "Have you ever watched them?"

"Only at Bennet's parties. And only if they requested an audience."

"Were you alone?" I regretted asking the second I finished the question. The mere thought of him enjoying a moment as intimate as that with another woman made my stomach turn. I know I'm being irrational. I have a past, too. Pretty sure he doesn't want to know the dirty details of what I've done.

"Not always." He leaned his forehead to mine. "Not for anything but I didn't picture us having this discussion in a smelly New York alley."

"Foetorem extremae latrinae."

"I've no idea what you said but knowing you, it's probably something filthy."

"Pretty much. It basically means stench of a sewer bottom."

He inhaled and coughed. "Accurate. Let's go back inside."

"Hey." I held his arm.

He lifted my hand and kissed the pulse point on my wrist. "Yes, love."

"If you ever...I think..." I struggled with how to phrase what I wanted to say. "I liked how you said it. My nickname. I liked the way it sounded coming from you. I hope you'll say it again."

"I will." He laced his fingers with mine. "Back inside before we both smell like a sewer bottom."

Cade was in the middle of telling a story about one of their championship matches to an audience that not only included fans but also Noah Tate, Tracey Watson, and Tre Gideon. I glanced over at Hannah, my eyes wide. She laughed and shrugged, mouthing *they're all best friends now.*

"This is quite the motley crew." I waved to my team's quarterback and wide receiver. Noah jumped up and hugged me, followed by Tracey. Tre waved back, cautiously eyeing Xavier.

"It's not every day we get to hang out with some of the world's best soccer players," Noah grinned, putting his arm around my shoulders. "Did you know this guy," he pointed at Cade, "idolizes me?"

"Idolize is a strong word, mate," Cade countered. "I admire your commitment to the sport."

The table erupted into good-natured laughter.

Noah's arm still rested casually around my shoulders. I couldn't see Xavier since he was standing behind me but I could one hundred percent feel his stare.

"So many egos in one place," I said, deftly sliding away from Noah. "I don't know if I can handle it."

"Try living with it," Tracey piped up. Noah returned to his girlfriend, pressed a kiss to her mouth and sat down. I caught Xavier's eye and motioned to the empty chairs next to them.

Before he could sit with me, a blonde woman grabbed his arm and starting gushing over how talented and hot he was.

"Do you ever let anyone score on you?" she asked with obvious intent, rubbing her hand on his chest.

Ever the attention seeker, he smirked. "Scoring on me isn't easy."

I felt someone kick my foot under the table. It was Cade. He grinned at me, looked over at the blonde and said, "Scoring on Maddox is overrated. He's all show and no substance."

The girl swayed a little, holding onto his shirt. I glared at her. She really needed to stop touching him. Now.

My inability to control this envious surge surprised me. I've never been the jealous type. Then again, I've never forged an actual relationship with someone I classified as a one night stand.

"Oh, I bet there's big substance beneath all these clothes," she smiled, sliding her hand and her eyes down to his crotch.

NOT TODAY BLONDIE.

"Actually," I rose to my feet and addressed this intruder directly, "scoring on him is mind-blowing. Too bad you'll never have first-hand experience."

Noah let out a low whistle. I heard Cade snickering.

"My girlfriend is right," Xavier confirmed, removing her hand from his body. "I hope you enjoyed tonight's match though."

I couldn't process anything else. All I did was stand slack-jawed, staring at him. For his part, Xavier politely sent the blonde on her way before wrapping an arm around my waist.

Lowering his mouth to my ear he said, "You're bloody hot when you're jealous."

I sat heavily in the chair, scanning around the table. Cade had a grin on his face that screamed *I knew it* while Bennet studied me with rapt interest. I shoved the girlfriend remark out my head as best as I could in order to enjoy the rest of my night. I had to. It shook me to my core.

"I don't think we've had the pleasure of being introduced," Xavier said, sitting down and focusing on Noah.

Before I could say anything, Noah spoke. "You're Xavier Maddox. Hell of a goalkeeper, man. My little brother watches you every week." He flashed a wide smile. "Noah Tate, Legends quarterback. This is my girlfriend, Tracey."

I put my hand on Xavier's thigh and felt his muscles relax. He morphed into Attention Loving Xavier and basked in Noah's praise. He even signed a napkin for him to give to his brother.

The mood at the table was light and casual and fun. Except for Tre. He was uncharacteristically subdued. He'd engage in conversation but refrained from being his usual, animated self. I noticed him steal a few glances in my direction and glower slightly at Xavier.

I won't lie, it annoyed me.

Granted, this was a unique situation where I'm socializing with a former one night stand while nurturing a relationship with my latest.

And this is why I have that damn policy.

I brushed it off. I broke it for Xavier and have no regrets.

In fact, once we returned to my condo and climbed into bed, I made sure to break it again with him before falling asleep.

Chapter
TWENTY-EIGHT

Plans for this particular Sunday originally involved me digging through boxes in storage. Alone.

"How far away is your childhood home from here?" Xavier asked, following me down a long hallway.

Plans can obviously be modified.

"About a ten minute drive."

"Do I get to see it when we're done?"

"Sure, why the fuck not."

His throaty laugh echoed in the corridor. "Your excitement is unmatched."

I stopped in front of our unit and unlocked the door. "I sold the house ages ago. It's not like you get to go inside and critique the place."

"No gold couches?"

I shrugged. "There might be. But when I lived there? Fuck no."

"You're spicy today," his voice rumbled. "Maybe I should keep track of how many times you swear."

"Oh, okay, St. Xavier of the Virtuous Mouth. You do that."

"Hey." He turned me so I faced him. "What's going on? Talk to me."

I winced. I shouldn't be snapping at him.

"I'm sorry," I said. "Nothing's going on. I'm just a little on edge with," I gestured toward the storage unit and then squeezed his hand. "I'm happy you're here."

"Hmm."

"Don't *hmm* me. I can see you smiling."

"Must be a mirage." He leaned in to kiss me. "What are we looking for?"

"A diary," I answered, rolling the door up. Rows of boxes and plastic bins appeared in shadow. Feeling along the wall, I found the switch and turned on the lights.

Xavier let out a low whistle. "Needle in a haystack, yeah?"

"They're labeled. It shouldn't be too bad. Just pull everything with my sister's name on it." I walked in and turned. "Please."

"I was just going to say something about lack of manners," he chuckled.

I twirled a strand of hair and said in my best light and airy voice, "Thank you, Mr. Maddox."

"I want to hear you say that later when I have you bent over the couch."

"Boxes," I pointed to the stack.

We got to work grabbing everything labeled *Charlotte*. There were more boxes and bins than I remembered. Most of them had random stuff tossed inside with no rhyme or reason. Clothes, sneakers, nail polish, pillows, stuffed animals, hair clips.

"Jackpot," Xavier exclaimed.

"Did you find it?"

"No. I found this."

The opening bars to Wannabe echoed around us. The Spice Girls really wanted to tell us what they really, really want.

I jumped to my feet in time to see him reading the lyrics in the CD jacket.

"Is this what they were singing about? I never quite paid attention to the words."

Sitting on top of some bins was my old CD player. Color me surprised that it still worked.

"Pretty sure it wasn't in a box with my sister's name on it."

"Actually it was, princess. I may not have an Ivy League education but I can read." He grinned and waved another CD in the air. "What exactly is an Essential Pop Music Mix for the Ages?"

Slightly mortified, I laughed. "Put it in and find out. But just remember, you did it to yourself."

"Can't be that bad," he said, popping the disc in the player. "Besides, it's too quiet in here."

Gentle guitar notes sounded from the speakers. I grinned, recognizing it immediately. "Well, maybe I want it that way."

"Oh for fuck's sake," he griped.

"Not a Backstreet Boys fan?" I giggled, yanking another box off the pile and putting it on the floor. "I'm hearing a lot of bitching and not seeing enough searching. Get to work, Maddox."

He pulled a pillow out of the box in front of him and tossed it to me, then walked over with one of his own. "I suppose if we're going to do this we might as well be comfortable."

We put the pillows on the cement floor, sat down and started digging through my sister's stuff. Backstreet Boys faded into Christina Aguilera which then faded into Nelly.

"No Britney?" he asked, flipping through a notebook.

"She's on there."

"How about Take That? S Club 7?"

"Um, no."

He shook his head and tsk-tsked. "I'm disappointed in this alleged essential mix."

"I didn't know you were such a connoisseur of pop music."

He smirked. "I'm not. All the girls I liked were though. I did what I had to do to get a date and a proper kiss."

I threw a stuffed elephant at him. "Poser."

"What?" he laughed. "I was a teenage boy, not the prime minister." He picked up the elephant. "Be kind to animals."

Never in my wildest dreams did I think I'd be sitting in a storage facility rummaging through my sister's things and having a good time doing it. It's possible he knew I was a jumble of anxious energy deep down and was doing all of this to help keep me relaxed. Whatever the reason, I appreciated it.

"Little Xavier liked to impress the girls did he?" I winked at him. "My sister wrote that you were huge flirt."

He stopped sifting and looked at me intently. "She did?"

"Mmhmm. She said you guys never spoke but when she did see you, you were always surrounded by girls. Not much has changed."

His shoulder lifted in a small shrug. "What else did she write?"

I pulled out one of her blankets and hugged it, trying to breathe in traces of her scent. It only smelled like it'd been sitting in a plastic bin for fifteen years. "About you or in general?"

"About me."

"Your fragile ego is showing," I teased. Pausing for a second I held his pretty blue stare. "She said I'd totally get a crush on you if we met."

The shy smile tugging at his mouth delighted me. It's crazy how one innocuous sentiment written two decades ago could affect our present situation.

"Did you?" he asked.

"Did I what?"

"Get a crush on me when we met?"

Don't say it.

"Maybe." I struggled to hold back laughter. Especially after he pinned one of his devilish stares on me. He stroked his lower lip and grinned.

"We'll deal with that later as well."

After a couple minutes of quiet glances and charmed smiles while searching more boxes, I asked, "How old were you when you started playing soccer?"

"Six. My dad used to take me to one of the pitches near our house and let me kick the ball around." He thumbed through a couple of text books before continuing, "I didn't join a team until year four."

"What's year four?"

"Primary school," he explained. "I guess you'd call it third grade in elementary school here?"

"Gotcha. Did you always want to be a goalkeeper?"

"No. I wanted to be a striker, like Cade." His eyes lit up. "I actually played that position until I was eleven. Then one day our keeper got hurt and I filled in. I was really good at it, too. Really good. Poor kid never got the position back." He chuckled to himself. "I reckon the rest is history."

"No wonder you were always surrounded by girls. A striker *and* a keeper. Must have driven them crazy."

A facetious smile curved his lips. "You mean like the person Britney's singing about in this song?"

"Oh, one hundred percent." I pulled out the elastic in my hair to redo my bun. I have no idea what my face looked like but whatever expression it held caused him to check me out from head to toe, exhale, and level an impassioned cobalt stare in my direction.

"What?" I asked, sounding more nervous than curious.

"It's just…you're wearing the same outfit you had on when we met on the side of the road. You even have your hair up the same way."

I touched my hair before glancing down at my gray yoga pants, white tank top and gray hoodie. "Have I committed a fashion crime?"

The storage bay erupted with his loud, deep laugh. I loved seeing his carefree side just as much as his dark and dirty side.

"No, love." His wide, crooked smile remained. "It just made me think of that day."

"Good thoughts?"

"Yeah," he answered, looking down. Apprehension flickered across his face. It didn't last long. A mischievous glow brightened his eyes when he looked at me. "Need a new bin to dig through?"

"Yes, please."

His lips quirked up. "Something else you'll be saying to me later."

He grabbed more boxes and bins as we continued to search for the diary. I found some of her journals but they were mostly from junior high.

Xavier's genuine enjoyment while we bantered back and forth about random shit beguiled me. I learned he's a Guardians of the Galaxy guy while I'm firmly team Captain America.

Once we ventured into the topics of architecture and renovations, I couldn't get him to stop talking.

"…with a brick wall on one side and the original exposed beams in the ceiling," Xavier concluded with an animated smile. "I've been working on this house since last September. It's a bigger project than what I normally do but it really needed the work."

He paused, regarding me cautiously.

"There's something so satisfying about rebuilding something from the inside out. Maybe satisfying isn't the right word." He thought for a second. "Fulfilling. It's taking something that's beautiful but broken and making it whole again."

The way he looked at me with such affection and desire left me utterly debilitated. I wanted to freeze this moment, complete with the contradictory image of us sitting on a cement floor surrounded by my dead sister's belongings.

Beautiful but broken.

He flipped through a worn out notebook and paused. "What are these?" he asked, holding it up.

Sketches of feathers and flames filled the pages.

"Oh. Um, those were some drawings I made. Some ideas I had for my tattoo."

"Twin phoenix feathers in flames," he said softly. "For your sister?"

"Yeah. A phoenix always rises from the ashes. I thought the fiery feathers would be a beautiful tribute."

"You designed it yourself?"

"I did. I can't draw very well but thankfully I found a tattoo artist who really understood what I wanted."

He looked down at the drawings and asked, "Did you get it done here in New York?"

"No, I actually went to Boston. I was in college at the time. There weren't many tattoo artists near campus so I drove two hours away to get it done."

"Dedication," he smirked. "I like it."

"It's kind of in the middle of nowhere," I laughed.

"I know. I looked it up."

I stopped rummaging through the bin. "You did?"

"Mmhmm. Sort of surprised me you decided to go to university in such a rural place."

"Me too," I admitted. "I had my sights set on California. But, you know, best laid plans and all that."

Another veil of reflective silence fell over us. This one lasted longer than I expected.

I pushed the bin I'd been looking through away, dragged another box closer and opened it. My heart stilled. Piles of photo albums filled it. Photos and memories from a life I barely recognized but remembered so vividly. Some pictures lay scattered among the albums. One in particular brought me to tears.

Charlotte and I standing in the backyard of our beach home with red, white, and blue balloons. We each wore sundresses. Mine was blue, hers red.

I held it, brushing my thumb over our identical smiling faces. We looked so damn happy. How did it all go so terribly wrong?

"Mind if I join you?" Xavier's hesitant question broke the silence.

I nodded. He sat next to me, resting his head on my shoulder. "When is this from?"

"Our sixteenth birthday."

"It's on the 4th of July?"

"All the red, white, and blue give it away?"

He chuckled, studying the photo.

"This is you, yes?" He pointed to the girl on the left.

"How did you know?"

The warmth of his hand on my leg calmed me in a way I didn't expect. "Your smile. It lights up your whole face. Your sister's smile is just as lovely but yours," he paused, "yours is radiant. I'd know it anywhere."

I pushed out a ragged sigh. Overwhelming sadness threatened to suffocate this tender moment we shared.

"Hey." He pressed a gentle kiss to my cheek. "Are you alright?"

"I will be."

He took the photo from me and laid it on the pillow. "Do want to continue?"

I looked at him, feeling the weight of the last nineteen years pushing down on me.

"Green," I answered with a small smile.

He embraced me with more affection than I was prepared to accept. But I let him. I melted into his arms and let him hold me, let him care for me. All of a sudden, I wanted to tell him all of it. Every dark moment I've dragged with me since I was sixteen.

"I promised her I wouldn't leave her side," I blurted. "The night of the bonfire. I promised her we'd be within shouting distance the whole time. But I went off with some tattooed rugby player and ended up making out with him most of the night."

I swallowed hard. Xavier didn't say anything. He just pulled me closer.

"When I finally found her, she was upset. At first I thought she was pissed at me but then I saw her hair was all mussed up and her dress was dirty. I knew someone did something to her. I could feel it. All I could see was white hot rage. I asked her what happened. I asked her who she was with. She wouldn't tell me anything. She was never the same after that night."

I took a deep breath and continued.

"The following spring we were on school vacation. It was a Wednesday morning. Dad was at work. Mom planned to take us out for lunch in the city. I was downstairs and mom ran up to see if Charlotte was awake yet. I heard her scream. It was like a howl. I'd never heard someone scream like that before."

I shivered, reliving the panic and fear.

"You know how people talk about twins being connected? I couldn't feel her anymore. My mother ran into the kitchen and called 911. I went upstairs and…Charlotte was still in bed. It looked like she was asleep but she was so still. I saw the empty pill bottle on the floor. I knew…I knew she was gone. The rest is a blur. Sirens, paramedics, my dad coming home, police."

For several long moments I stayed quiet. The only movement was Xavier wiping the tears from my cheeks.

"My mother blamed me," I finally said, my tone flat. "She blamed me for taking Charlotte to the party. She blamed me for what happened at the party. She blamed me for not doing anything to stop it. She blamed me for tearing the family apart. She hasn't stopped blaming me."

"This goes without saying," Xavier said, tilting my chin up, "but none of it was your fault. None of it. I am so sorry you've carried this with you for so long."

Having him comfort me felt good. My parents and I splintered into our own worlds of pain after Charlotte died. It often felt like there had been no one to just *listen*. Not even Killian. As much as I loved him for being there from the beginning, he always tried to fix it.

Telling Xavier was different, like it mattered how I felt about it.

How I still feel about it.

"I think, on some level, even if my mother never said those things to me, I'd still blame myself. If I'd done one thing different that night, if I hadn't gone off, maybe she wouldn't have been alone with whoever hurt her or maybe—"

"Don't do that," he interrupted. "Please don't play the maybe game. Maybes and what ifs won't change anything. You'll just keep punishing yourself for something you could never control."

I picked up the photo of my sister and I from our final birthday together. Even though I still felt the sadness stretching through me, I also felt a sense of peace. Revealing the worst part of myself to him hadn't been as terrible as I'd built it up to be.

Beautiful but broken.

I turned to face Xavier and kissed him. "Thank you," I whispered on his lips.

"Anything for you, love."

I glanced around at the pieces of my sister's life strewn all over the storage bay.

The diary. I had to find it.

"We should get back to it," I said, caressing his cheek. "Break time is over."

"Yes ma'am."

I continued digging through this box while watching him sift through old school books and folders. He lifted a diploma cover and looked at me. It had to be mine because I was the only one who graduated.

He turned it so I could read the school name.

Dartmouth College.

"Why is this at the bottom of a box?"

"I don't know."

"Victoria."

"It's just a piece of paper."

His brows knit together in frustration when he opened the cover. "*Magna cum laude.* I know enough Latin to know what this means." He looked up at me through a dark fringe of lashes. "Aren't you proud of what you've accomplished?"

"Of course I am," I acquiesced.

"May I have the photo please?"

I handed it over. He tucked it inside my diploma and placed it on the floor next to him.

"You can't bury your life away forever," he told me.

"I know," I responded softly. "When I was out with my dad the other night, he said we owed my sister the dignity of coming together for something to keep her memory alive. He meant the cottage but I think," I stumbled over my words and emotions, "I think maybe I should do more to honor her."

"What would you like to do?"

"I've tossed around the idea of setting up a foundation in her name. Something small to start. Give the proceeds to local mental health organizations for teens and young adults. Maybe even split the donations and give some to the animal shelter." I shrugged. "I need to do something."

A soft smile curved Xavier's mouth. "I'd love to help in any way I can."

"I'd love that, too," I grinned. "Then maybe you won't be so jealous of Noah when he donates to the shelter next year."

Xavier's eyes flared. "I'm not jealous."

"Oh, okay," I laughed. "And I'm not a natural redhead."

"Yes, you are," he said in a silky tone.

My cheeks flushed. "You were so jealous at dinner that night when Hannah asked me about the charity. I thought steam was going to come out of your ears. And then last night at the bar? Come on."

"Fine," he huffed. "I was jealous. And then you sat in the wanker's lap and it made me fucking crazy. Plus, he's a bit of hugger." His voice started to rise. "He hugged you at the stadium, at the bar. He had his arm around you in another bloody photo. What is it with him always putting his hands on you?"

The fiery stare he leveled at me should have given me pause, but no.

"I've known him since he was a rookie," I said calmly. "He's been with Tracey the entire time. They're the nicest people. You saw it last night. You talked to him for almost an hour. You don't have any reason to be jealous."

"What about the other one from last night? Tre? He kept shooting me dirty looks. Do I have a reason to be jealous of him?"

Well, shit.

My little game seemed to be backfiring on me in spectacular fashion.

"Not really."

"*What does not really mean?*"

Dredging up my past sexual encounters was definitely not on my to-do list. His whole body tensed like a panther ready to pounce on its prey.

I folded my arms. "What did you mean by *not always* when I asked you about being alone at Bennet's parties?"

Realization dawned on him pretty quick. "Fair enough."

"Truce?"

"Sure."

"You're cute when you're jealous." I knew I was playing with fire at this point. He was heated and my continuous needling at his discomfort probably wouldn't end well.

The tip of his tongue slid along his lower lip. He dragged his eyes over me in a long, searing movement. All the telltale signs of his imminent switch to the untamed, dark lover I craved were falling into place.

"We'll see how cute I am when we're finished here."

"Promise?"

We spent the next half hour going through boxes and bins in silence. A heady mix of anticipation, desire, and intrigue filled the space. I kept stealing glances in his direction. He caught me looking and smirked when he reached inside a bin. A cream-colored diary was in his hand when it reemerged.

"Is this it?"

I crawled over to him and took it. Flipping through the pages I noticed it wasn't filled to the end. All the other journals I'd found so far were. My heart leapt in my throat.

"I think so," I murmured. Nervous energy spread through my veins, shocking and burning all my nerve endings.

"Okay then," Xavier said with an air finality. "Let's clean this place up and go."

Chapter
TWENTY -NINE

"**H**ot and fresh and ready to eat," Xavier looked pointedly at me while carrying a pizza box to the kitchen. "And we have a snack."

"Are you hungry?"

The slow, measured way he devoured every inch of me with his eyes made me tremble. "Not for pizza."

We'd returned to my place an hour ago and ordered some food. Spending the entire day at the storage facility wasn't exactly the plan, but at least I found what I was looking for.

"You clearly haven't had good New York pizza. This is the best delivery in the city."

Next thing I knew, I was in his arms, subjected to a classic Xavier molten stare.

"We have some unfinished business to attend to first," he murmured.

Our mouths brushed together once, twice, and then joined in a hot, intense kiss. The kind of kiss that leads to hours of dirty, rough sex.

Good thing pizza tastes just as fantastic cold as it does hot.

"What business is that?" I asked in between kisses.

"Don't be cute."

"Right." I giggled. "That's your department."

He swatted my behind in one swift, sharp slap. I shook it from side to side.

"Am I in trouble again, Mr. Maddox?"

"There aren't enough hours left in the day for all the trouble you're in."

"Do you really have to leave tonight?"

"I do." He squeezed my ass. "I've already overstayed my welcome. Plus, I have a match on Thursday."

"You haven't overstayed any welcome."

"Tell Bennet. He got an earful when he told the manager I'd be staying behind an extra day and not flying home with the team."

"Bad boy," I grinned, nipping at his lip.

"Would you prefer I stay longer?"

"Yes, please."

Our lips collided in another intense kiss. Intense and affectionate. I whimpered when he ground his hips against mine, his hands kneading my backside. I swung my legs around his waist the second he lifted me off the floor.

I loved having him with me today. I loved not feeling like an anxious, scattered mess. I want him here. Always.

"Xavier," I spoke his name on his lips. "Please stay."

A violent tremor shook his body. He slid his mouth over mine slowly as he carried me to the couch. We sank into the cushions still kissing, still touching one another. I straddled him, sifting my fingers through his hair.

He broke his mouth away, softly collaring my neck. "Let me," he breathed. "Please."

"Let you stay? Of course."

"No." His eyes burned bright. "Love you. Let me love you, Victoria."

My breath hitched as a single tear rolled down my cheek. His hand remained at the base of my throat, stroking and comforting my skin. I looked at him. Really looked at him and allowed visions of our future together to play uninterrupted.

We've known each for less than a month, and I already wanted him for the rest of my life. An invisible ribbon that bound us together tightened around my heart. If I believed in fate, I'd even venture to say the ribbon was loosely tied there by my sister when she was fifteen and sneaking around with his brother.

Xavier pressed his hand to my damp cheek, wiping away more tears with his thumb. "You don't have to say anything."

"Yes, I do."

Leaning close, I kissed his forehead and his scar, and then kissed his mouth. "I want you to love me," I admitted. "Please love me, Xavier."

His jagged exhale vibrated through me when his head rested between my breasts. I held him tight, warding off the one voice dwelling deep inside me. The one accusatory voice berating me for not keeping a simple promise to my sister the night we went to the bonfire. The one voice threatening to cut the invisible ribbon tying me to this man, blaming me for ripping apart my family.

"Did you mean what you said last night?" I asked. "When that blonde was hanging on you and you called me your girlfriend?"

"Yes." His hooded gaze met mine. "I always mean what I say." He grinned. "You were quite jealous of her."

"She kept touching you."

"Fans tend to do that. Will it be a problem for you?"

"I don't think so," I answered honestly. "Will it be a problem for you the next time Noah hugs me?"

A faint scowl marred his sultry mouth. "Suppose not."

"My first jealous boyfriend," I teased, running my hand down his chest. "Not as sexy as I thought it would be."

"No?" He looked up at me with dark eyes. "Stand up." The command came quiet and gentle, but firm.

I shivered, getting to my feet.

"Go to the window."

Dusk settled over the city in shades of purple and blue while I waited in front of it. Lights flickered to life in high-rises and along sidewalks. I heard a slow exhale before I felt Xavier remove my hoodie. It fell to my feet. Then he pulled the tank top over my head, tossed it aside and unfastened my bra.

"Do you like being undressed in front of the window?" he asked, hooking his fingers inside my yoga pants and sliding them down.

"If you're the one undressing me, yes."

"Is this sexy enough for you?"

I smiled. "Maybe."

"So much trouble," he laughed softly. "What do you think the people behind those windows are doing?"

"I don't know," I answered quietly, staring into the high-rise a few blocks away.

He stroked the edge of my panties. "What if they could see us?"

"Aren't we too far for them to see?"

Xavier's hand trailed lower, pressing and teasing my sensitive skin. Hot desire spiked fast through me. I arched my back enough to press my backside into his crotch. He was already rock hard.

"I'm curious," he whispered in my ear. "Were you this turned on last night at the bar? Would you have let me play with your cunt and come on my hand like the dirty princess you are?"

There was an answering heat in my body, as though the temperature of my blood itself had escalated. His fingers teased even more, finding their way with ease over my slick flesh before discovering the plump bud of my clit and pressing down.

"Yes," I breathed.

He cupped my breast with his other hand. My eyes fluttered closed when a deep sound of want spilled from him. I heard it the moment his fingers dipped inside me.

"You feel," he said, sounding unsteady, "like nothing else."

I pressed my hands on the window, unsure if it would be enough to keep me balanced. He kept repeating the same movements —fingers inside, curling to touch the soft textured spot that drove me wild, pulling out and toying with my clit, then back inside. When my focus shifted to the building across the way, I felt my climax knotting itself fast and hard. The very thought of being watched sent me over the edge.

Turning my head to the side so our mouths were close, I kissed him. "Yours." I covered his hand with mine, stroking his wet fingers.

"Victoria." His voice remained unsteady as he continued to pleasure my body. "What you do to me."

My legs shook. Everything from my navel to my knees clenched and crested into a wave of euphoria so consuming, so overwhelming, I could hardly stand. I scratched foolishly at the window, like it would keep me grounded while my body flew apart.

I don't even know when he slid his fingers out and turned me to face him. I only felt him paint my lips with my climax and kiss me.

"I love when you do that," I confessed when he broke the kiss.

"I know." His greedy arrogance reignited the wave of desire that still pulsed through me.

I reached up and collared his neck. "I want you. Fuck me like you want me to be yours forever."

"Is that so?" He pushed me back a step, then two, until I was pinned between him and the window. I'm not going to lie, the cold glass felt so damn good on my heated skin. His hips pressed into mine when he raised my wrists above my head and held them there.

"Don't move."

He bent down, grabbed my hoodie, pulled out the draw string and made quick work of tying my wrists together.

"Turn around," he ordered. "Keep your hands up here, just like this."

His commands alone were enough to send me over the edge. The distinct sound of a zipper opening preceded the rustling of clothes falling to the floor. He pulled my hips back, so I leaned forward and then yanked down my panties, grabbing at my ass, squeezing hard. So hard I gasped. Then I heard a low groan and felt his tongue trace its way around my clit.

I whimpered when he stopped, anticipating what he'd do next. All I could see from the reflection in the window was Xavier on his knees behind me and if that wasn't the hottest thing in the world I don't know what is.

A tingling, throbbing sensation skittered down from my hips to my legs when he bit into the soft flesh of my bottom. I laughed in surprise. Then he did it again. My knees went weak.

"Shit, that tickles," I said on a giggle.

"Should I continue?" he asked, caressing my backside in whisper soft touches.

"Yes."

He slapped one ass cheek hard. I squealed with pleasure.

"Should I continue?" he repeated in a gruff tone.

"Green."

Desire coiled at my core when I felt his tongue run along the curve of my ass, licking close to the entrance and then up to the small of my back.

When he stood, he caressed my stomach, between my breasts and stopped at my throat. He collared his fingers around it, pressing them into my skin possessively.

Everything in me stilled watching our reflections in the glass. His face was taut with intent. My eyes were wild with anticipation. It felt like I've been caught. But I never wanted to escape.

His warm breath tickled my neck before he growled, "You're fucking mine."

With a quickness and ferocity, he shoved himself inside, filling me to the hilt in one thrust. I cried out at the sudden invasion. Every nerve ending spiked with need. Over and over he drove into me.

"More," I tried to demand. "I love it, Xavier."

I could barely speak so I wasn't sure if he heard me. But he did. And he gave me what I asked. Not necessarily faster, but harder and deeper. He gripped my hips so tight I couldn't move. I was at his mercy, taking all of him.

The reflection of his impassioned face stared back at me from the window. All of his features were shadowed by the city lights but I could see him. His parted lips. His raw, animalistic stare. His hips flexing and pounding into me from behind. I bent forward even more to take him deeper.

He thrust into me so hard we both cried out. Lowering his body to mine, his rough, baritone voice filled me. "Come for me."

Heat swirled deep in my belly. I was almost there. My body ignited from the inside out.

He fucked me harder, demanding, "Give me what's mine."

I struggled to breathe as my orgasm hit with unrelenting force. I wanted to scream his name. I wanted him to hear me call out the only name I was meant to say. All I could do was shake and moan as he rode through my release. His deep grunts signaled he was close. I felt him tense, jerking his hips against me on the waves of his own surrender.

He turned me as soon as he pulled out. His cock was still hard as steel, glistening from both us.

"Kneel."

I dropped to my knees without hesitation. His sides heaved like he'd finished a strenuous workout. Looking up at him through my lashes, I leaned forward and licked under his shaft up to the flared crown. His head lolled back slightly.

"Untie me, please," I requested, leaning back. "I want to touch you."

"No." His tone matched the severe look on his face.

My lips curved in a smile. I knelt up higher, crossing my ankles behind me. It didn't take an astute observer to notice the flair of dominance behind his eyes.

He grabbed the back of my head, knotting his fingers in my hair. The covetous expression he wore at the bar last night reappeared. He tugged on my hair.

"Open," he directed.

I parted my lips, sliding my mouth down his hard shaft, flattening my tongue against it.

Both his hands pulled on my hair as he swore under his breath. Without warning, he thrust deep into my throat. I swallowed on instinct. He thrust again, harder, grabbing the back of my head to keep me from pulling away.

"Is this hard enough for you, dirty princess?" he asked, driving into my throat without apology. "Rough enough?"

I looked up at him and could only make a noise that probably sounded like a moan. My eyes started to water. All of a sudden he pulled back and blinked out of himself, inhaling a sharp breath.

"Why are you stopping?" I panted.

"I can't be that rough with you."

"Yes you can."

He broke eye contact.

What the hell is happening here?

"Xavier, look at me."

He wet his lips, taking himself in his hand. The aggressive way he stroked his cock awakened my dozing orgasm. Still, something felt off.

"Are you upset with me about all the jealousy talk?" I asked.

The muscles and tendons in his neck rippled when he swallowed. He went over to the couch and sat. "Come here."

I stood and went to him. His penis was still rigid and waiting, so I straddled him, sheathing his length until it filled me. He buried his face in my breasts, inhaling my scent like he needed it to survive.

"Talk to me," I pleaded, rocking back and forth on him.

"Give me your hands."

I waited while he untied me and kissed the faint marks on my wrists. I rested my forehead to his, running my fingers through his hair. "Why do you hide from this part of yourself?"

He grasped my hips. "I have to."

"Why? Do you think you'll insult my independent, strong female side? Do you think I'll look at you as some misogynistic asshole who talks dirty to me and wants to control me?"

"That's not it," he growled.

"Then what is it? Tell me."

"I don't want to hurt you."

"You're not hurting me. And you trust me enough to tell you otherwise. Let yourself go, Xavier."

I kissed him, licking deep inside his mouth.

"Victoria," he gasped, pulling away. "You don't understand."

"Don't understand what? You get off on being rough and possessive with me? You get hard pushing my limits in a public setting? You're jealous of other men, regardless of my history with them?"

I rocked and then rotated my hips harder, forcing him inside me deeper. "Who am I fucking right now? Who do I want more than anyone?"

I shoved my hands in his hair and pulled his head back. His mouth fell open on a low moan.

"You," I continued. "I choose to play rough. I choose to be spanked, bitten, grabbed, tied up, used in public, used in private. I choose all of it because I choose you. All of you. I'm so in love with you I can't see straight."

His lips crashed into mine in a desperate, searing kiss. The pressure of his fingers digging into my ass went straight to my throbbing clit. He stood, secured his hands on my hips to keep my pelvis pinned to his, and carried me to the bedroom.

Our bodies stayed connected when he laid me down and hovered over me. Placing one hand on each of my thighs, he pushed them open wider, sinking inside me.

I dragged my nails down his chest to his lower abdomen. When he pulled out, I circled his hard length with my fingers.

"Fuck," he hissed. "I want to be so rough and possessive with you right now. I want to fuck your history away so it's mine and mine alone." He pushed in deeper until the full weight of his body was on me.

"Do it," I breathed. "Claim me. Rewrite my past experiences with your body however you want. Starting right now."

He slid his arms under my shoulders, propping himself on his elbows. When he looked down at me, he rocked his pelvis against my clit a few times, creating a friction unlike anything I've ever felt. Then he pulled out slow, hitting my g-spot. The sensation was euphoric.

This wasn't rough but it was certainly possessive. Consuming. Over and over and over.

I couldn't breathe. I couldn't move. All I could do was surrender to the shivers running up and down my spine. My entire body was overwhelmed by energy and vibration.

Xavier buried his face in my neck, biting and kissing and licking and whispering. The methodic, repetitive motions of his pelvis rocking lulled me into an intoxicating trance. When our eyes met, his were shining with devotion. He's too perfect and beautiful in this moment.

I hooked my legs around his thighs. The change in position squeezed my pussy tighter around his length, intensifying the pressure he put on my body. He moaned quietly, never breaking his stride.

I wanted him closer. I wanted to fuse myself to him and feel this for eternity.

His intense, adoring stare locked on me and with a rough cadence to his voice, he professed, "I love you, Tori."

A sound came out of me so primal and instinctual, I didn't recognize it. My back arched as I gasped and cried out his name like a prayer and lost all control of my body, surrendering to him, to what I felt, to all the unknown moments yet to come.

With a shudder and several final deep thrusts, Xavier tumbled over the edge with me.

The sound of our heavy breathing filled the room, along with the thick fog of pleasure. I'd never felt more attuned to or more in harmony with another person. Any tense feelings swirling around jealousy or guilt or uncertainty blinked out of existence.

Xavier's quiet sigh broke the silence when he pulled out and held me close. He kissed my shoulder, moving down the side of my ribcage. He traced my tattoo in slow, gentle strokes and then covered it in soft kisses. I shivered, wondering if this is how he felt every time I touched or kissed his scar.

"Keep rising," he whispered. "I'll be with you the whole way."

I curled into him, tangling our legs together. We stayed this way for a few minutes before he got up to tend to his aftercare duties.

"You're spoiling me." I grinned while he gently cleaned me with a warm washcloth.

"Get used to it." He kissed the tip of my nose. "Don't move. I'll be right back."

I stretched like a content kitten, all arms and legs and low moans. When Xavier climbed back onto the bed next to me, I nestled into him, stroking his arms, his chest, his thighs.

All mine.

"You keep breaking your policy for me," he said after several minutes, running the tip of his nose along my jaw.

"What policy?" I murmured.

He took my mouth in a soft kiss, smiling when he pulled back. "I have a confession."

"You're really some dull businessman who likes it missionary and on a schedule?"

He chuckled. "Not exactly. I'm actually quite peckish."

"*Peckish*," I repeated.

"Mmm," he hummed. "I keep fantasizing about cold pizza."

I propped myself up on an elbow and stared into his ridiculously handsome face. "I can make that fantasy come true if you want me to."

"I've heard that about you."

"Oh yeah? What else have you heard?"

The wide, crooked smile I love so much appeared, accentuating his dimple and making his eyes glow. "Feed me and I'll tell you."

"Promise?"

"Maybe." He kissed my forehead, climbed out of bed and stretched his long, toned arms over his head. All his muscles tightened and relaxed, rippling beneath his inked skin.

I watched his naked body walk toward the kitchen and flopped back on the bed for a minute.

That man loves me, I thought with a smile, getting up and grabbing something to wear from my closet. He'd already set out plates and napkins on the island counter when I sauntered up to him. He was still shirtless but had his jeans on.

"Look at you, all domesticated."

"Don't get used to it," he laughed. "This is the extent of my talents."

"I'll try keep my expectations low," I grinned, getting a couple of glasses. "Wine?"

"Not really a wine guy."

I rolled my eyes. "*Pardon* me. Would you prefer beer? Water? Bourbon? Gin? I can go on."

"Bourbon is fine. Do you have bangers and mash too? Maybe some Yorkshire pudding?"

"Do I detect sass?"

"Whatever do you mean?" A playful grin lit up his face.

"This grin," I said.

"What about it?"

"It'll get you into trouble." I walked over to plant a kiss on him.

"That didn't feel like trouble."

"No? What did it feel like?"

"Like you love me, too," he said with conviction, pulling me closer.

"I do." I kissed him again.

"Still didn't feel like trouble," he smirked, playing with my hair.

"The night is young," I said, wriggling out of his arms and grabbing a bottle of Eagle Rare.

I poured two glasses.

"I've not had this one," he remarked, taking a sip. "Oh wow."

"Right?" I smiled. "One of my favorites."

I went over to the fridge to get some ranch dressing and a small bowl from the cabinet.

This whole day had been filled with emotion and revelations. But there was still one important subject I had to address before he went back home.

I eyed the diary we'd found in storage sitting on my coffee table. I had to tell him about the fight. The man sat on a hard floor digging through boxes with me all afternoon. He at least deserved to know the whole story before I finally see what led to the end.

"What are you doing to that pizza crust?" Xavier's baffled expression was too precious.

I dunked it into the small condiment bowl filled with ranch dressing. "Giving it some personality." I grinned before taking a bite. "So good."

"May I?"

"Of course." I slid the bowl closer to him so he could dunk a little piece of his crust. The tentative way he put it in his mouth amused me. Like he wasn't sure what would happen once he started chewing.

He did this little head bob thing after he finished and took a long swallow of his drink.

"What did you think?"

"I think you have impeccable taste in bourbon."

I laughed. "Not a ranch fan? Looks like we can't be friends, then."

He looked over at me. "How will I ever survive." His tone was droll and sardonic. Peak Xavier.

"You'll manage." I dunked the rest of my crust in the bowl and ate it with zeal.

Xavier shook his head and started cleaning up. I watched him move around the kitchen, putting the plates in the sink. I smiled to myself. These regular, mundane actions felt normal. Just another Sunday at home with the boyfriend.

Thinking of him as my boyfriend filled me with hope and fear. I finished my bourbon in one swallow, enjoying the aged smoky richness as it slid down my throat while wracking my brain to think of ways to bring up what I read about the night he was attacked.

He needs to know. It wouldn't be fair to keep this from him. Besides, I didn't want us to start our relationship with half-truths and secrecy.

"Want me to take that for you?" Xavier asked.

I slid the glass across the counter to him. "Thank you."

"Maybe I am more domesticated than previously stated."

"Let's not get crazy, Maddox."

While he finished in the kitchen, I went over to the window. Hugging my arms to myself, I sighed. A peaceful warmth spread through me, not from the food or the sex or the bourbon. What I was about to do is the right thing. Closing my eyes, I said a silent prayer for my sister.

Xavier's body radiated heat from behind me. His arms encircled my waist, pulling my back flush to his chest. I raised my arm, reaching back to cup my hand behind his neck. He hugged me tighter, lowering his head so his chin rested on my shoulder.

"Still peckish?" I asked.

A small laugh vibrated through him. "No." His lips brushed against my neck. "You seem a little tense. Anything I can do?"

It's now or never.

"Yeah, there is. I have to…there's something you need to know."

I freed myself from his embrace and led him to the couch. I fidgeted with the fabric on the cushion while we sat in silence. His vibrant eyes watched my every move.

"Sounds serious. Is it?"

"I haven't told you everything about what I read in Charlotte's diary from Briarcliff."

Unease fanned from his eyes to his mouth. His lips pressed together.

I lifted my hand to quiet him before he could speak.

"Please let me say this without interrupting. Then you can ask me as many questions as you'd like. Okay?"

He nodded, taking my hand in his.

"The summer she met your brother, um, there was a," I steadied my breathing, "there was a party. She went to a party near London without telling me. It was at some big estate."

Xavier's body stiffened.

"At some point, she went outside with a friend of hers and," I squeezed his hand, "saw a guy walking to his car. Then she saw some other guys come out of nowhere and beat him up. She said it looked like one of them slashed at him with a key."

All the blood drained from his face until he was pale. Pale and stoic.

"One of them saw her. When she went back inside, another guy came up to her and threatened her. He said he knew who she was, knew who my family was," I paused, "knew who I was. Then he put his hands on her and said if he ever saw her at another party he'd teach her a lesson she'd never forget."

I inhaled. I don't think I'd taken a breath the whole time.

"Let me see it." Xavier's low, tight timbre sent a chill through me. "Let me see exactly what she wrote."

"I told you ever—"

"Victoria," he snarled. "Show me the fucking diary right now."

Chapter
THIRTY

Tears pricked at my eyes when I went to my room to get it. Maybe I shouldn't have told him. But at the same time, what the fuck with his reaction? I grabbed it and flipped to the pages he wanted to see on my way back to the living room. He stood by the couch, arms folded, eyes cold.

"Xavier," I snapped the diary away when he reached for it. "I'll show this to you but I need you to calm down. And don't ever speak to me like that again."

He collected himself on a deep breath, regaining control over his body. His eyes still flared though. Sapphire flecks of fire burned with trepidation and anger.

"I'm sorry, love," he said. "Please, let me see it?"

I gripped the journal, uneasy about letting him see my sister's words. "These are some of the last things Charlotte ever wrote," I told him, dropping my eyes to the floor. "Remember that."

"I know." His words came out gruff and unyielding. "But I need to see it."

I handed him the diary.

He sat on the arm of the couch and flipped to the final entry. He scanned through it once, swallowed, then read it again. And again. Whatever color remained in his face drained until he appeared ashen. He covered his mouth, closing his eyes. One by one, the muscles in his arms, torso, and shoulders tightened.

An inferno raged behind his eyes when he pinned his stare on me.

"I'm so fucking sorry, Victoria. Your sister didn't deserve this and I promise to fix it."

He dropped the diary and stormed over to the kitchen. Grabbing his phone, he made a call.

"Get over to Victoria's. Now Bennet. I don't give a shit what you're doing. Yeah, I'm fucking talking to you like this. Get the fuck over here now."

He ended the call and composed himself before addressing me. "Please call down to your night guard to let him know you're expecting a guest."

"What's going on?"

"We might know who did this." His eyes widened when he saw whatever expression washed across my face. "Let us handle it."

Stunned, I sat on the couch and called down to the security desk to let them know I was expecting a visitor.

Xavier prowled through my condo like a caged animal, all sinewy power and agitation. He truly looked like a lion baring down on its prey. I chose not to ask any questions even though my curiosity demanded answers.

The untamed side to him I thought I knew was only a piece of what dwells deep down. This part was more ferocious, more threatening. I wondered if this was the side he hides from, the one he didn't want me to see.

I shivered.

"Are you okay, love?" he asked, kneeling in front of me. His agitation hadn't dissipated but his tone was warm and caring.

I played with his hair. "Are you?"

"I am right now," he answered, laying his head on my lap. "Being near you always helps."

The more I touched his hair and stroked the back of his neck, the more I felt him relax. Neither one of us said another word while we waited. I said all I needed to with every soft touch. He answered with contented sighs.

Knock, knock, knock, knock, knock.

Xavier's head snapped up at the insistent banging on my door. He jogged over to answer it. At first, all I heard were hushed voices. Then he and Bennet emerged.

I've seen the two of them side by side many times but this revealed how different they truly are. Xavier stood shirtless and barefoot in jeans, his hair wild, his eyes flaring, his tattooed torso heaving with every breath.

This is definitely the first time I've seen Bennet so casual. He looked younger than his years in a long-sleeved cotton shirt and jeans but still exuded control and power.

I stood up. "Hey Bennet."

He walked over and wrapped me in a warm hug. Totally did not expect this at all. His embrace was strong and comforting and familiar.

"Are you alright?" he asked, gently holding my arms.

"I'm fine. I'm more worried about him." I tilted my head in Xavier's direction.

"Me too," he muttered. "What happened?"

The three of us sat down. I don't know how much Xavier told Bennet so I started at the beginning, with the entry in my sister's diary about meeting Adam. Bennet didn't appear overly surprised at the information so I moved on to the party and the fight.

"May I read it?" he asked.

Xavier started prowling the room again when I handed the diary to Bennet. I watched his expression as he read and re-read my sister's words. He didn't go pale but his mouth formed a hard, angry line.

"It's him," Xavier grumbled. "I always thought he was behind it."

"We don't know for sure," Bennet responded. "He covers his tracks very well and has powerful people clean up after him. You know this. Even if we could prove it, he'd walk away unscathed."

"No he fucking won't." Xavier clenched his fists. "I'll make sure of it."

"Maddox," Bennet sighed, rubbing his eyes. "You can't beat the shit out of people every time they wrong you."

"The hell I can't," he roared. "He deserved it then and he deserves it now. He orchestrated what happened to me to shut me up for walking in on him that night. What he did to—" Xavier stopped speaking and looked at me. "Victoria, I don't think you should hear this."

I hadn't moved the entire time they spoke. Trying to process what this is all about and how it relates to my sister gave me a headache. What did she get herself into?

I glanced up at him and over to Bennet. Both had the same flashes of concern in their eyes, although Xavier's mixed with pure rage.

"I want to hear it," I told him.

Bennet stepped in front of Xavier to address me. "How much did he tell you about the night he was attacked?"

"Not much." I watched Xavier while I answered. "Just that he got jumped and ended up with a scar."

"Okay." Bennet scrubbed his face with his hands. "It happened at my family's estate."

My jaw dropped.

"We all lived there one summer together," he continued. "Royal City announced a new youth training program. Xavier and Cade were chosen along with several other teens. We had a party to celebrate."

I started pacing around my living room because at this point, what else am I supposed to do? Why the hell was my sister at a party for a bunch of soccer players?

I stopped and looked at Bennet and Xavier.

"Was Adam chosen as well?"

"No," Bennet answered. "The party wasn't exclusive to the program so if your sister was dating him that's probably why she was there."

I tilted my head to look at Xavier. "What did you walk in on?"

"At the party? Nothing," he told me.

Neither one said anything further. They just stood still, exchanging knowing glances. I won't lie. It pissed me off.

"Okay," I folded my arms and glared at them. "I realize you have your little secret society shit going on with the cryptic staring at one another but I'm trying to figure out what happened to my twin." My voice got louder. "If you know who the fucking guy is you need to tell me. Now."

Bennet's serious eyes and grim set mouth didn't intimidate me at all.

"You don't understand, Ms. Chase."

"No, no, no," I clenched my fists at my side. "Don't start the Ms. Chase bullshit with me Bennet. I'm not your sub. I'm not going to kneel at your fucking feet and ask nicely and keep my eyes cast downward and call you sir. This is my family, not some game you play at your sex parties."

Bennet's whole body stiffened. I'm fairly certain people don't speak to him this way often.

Hate to break it to you, Logan. I'm not like anyone you've ever met.

Xavier placed his hand on his friend's shoulder. "Sit down, mate."

Bennet eyed me with great interest as he made his way over to the kitchen and sat on a barstool.

"Help yourself to a drink or whatever," I offered, flicking my wrist. I can still be a good hostess, right?

"Come here." Xavier held out his hand to me. I took it, letting him pull me into a strong hug. He sighed, kissing the top of my head. "What do you want to know?"

I held him close. "Why did they attack you?"

He kept me wrapped in his arms, stroking my hair. The steady beating of his heart echoed through me.

"We think a guy named Jordan McKennie threatened your sister. A few months before Bennet's party, I saw him forcing himself on a girl at another party. I pulled him off her. We got into a fight and he ended up with a bloody nose." He tilted my chin up when I pulled back. "Needless to say, he didn't like that so we think he sent his mates to even the score."

I stared at him in shock. "They cut your face and slammed your head into a car door because you gave some asshole a bloody nose? Which he deserved, by the way. What else aren't you telling me?"

"Nothing. Jordan comes from a powerful, wealthy family and never needed an excuse to act like a spoiled wanker. He doesn't like being told he can't have something. He threatened your sister because that's what he does. He intimidates and forces people to do what he wants."

"Obviously he wanted you to stay quiet, too. Did you ever report what he did to the girl?"

Xavier winced, squeezing my arms. "No, love. I wanted to. She asked me not to say anything."

"Was she a friend of yours?"

He looked over at Bennet. The two exchanged another long, knowing glance.

"Yes," he said quietly. "We were close."

His teenage love interests were of no consequence to me right now. This was about my sister, nothing more.

"Do you think this guy…Jordan…do you think he'd follow through on what he said to Charlotte? About seeing her at another party?"

Xavier's bitter laugh sent a chill through me. "Yeah. If he felt like following through, he would. Or he'd move on to some other conquest."

Keeping my arm wrapped around his waist, I turned to face

Bennet. "Your family must be just as influential as this guy's. Nobody ever thought to challenge him?"

Bennet smirked. "British nobility can be rather cutthroat, Victoria. Especially those with hereditary titles. Both our families can be traced back hundreds of years. Challenging him isn't as easy as you might think."

Well, that was unexpected. British nobility? When the hell did I walk into *Sense and Sensibility?*

"I officially have a headache," I muttered, going to sit on the couch.

All I wanted to do was get to the bottom of what happened at the bonfire. Opening this door to nobility and revenge and God knows what else exhausted me. I liked it better when Xavier was just a smoldering tattooed goalkeeper and Bennet was the Dominant who happened to be his best friend.

The two of them huddled in a secret conference at the counter. A quick internet search would tell me all I needed to know about this Jordan person.

I eyed my sister's diary on the table. If she wrote about him again, I'll know soon enough. Then maybe I'll give this asshole a call and tell him what I think of him.

Xavier and Bennet were whispering much more animatedly now. I could tell Xavier was frustrated with whatever his friend was saying. I didn't have much time left with my newly minted boyfriend before he went back to England and I'd rather not spend it like this.

"Alright you two," I said, standing up. "No more whispering. We can put this discussion on hold for now."

They both looked at me. Blue eyes filled with devotion, amber eyes filled with concern.

"What now?" I asked, exasperated.

Bennet cleared his throat and addressed me. "I'd like to, with your permission of course, provide a security detail for you. Nothing over the top. Just someone to keep an eye—"

"Whoa." I put my hand up. "I don't need a babysitter."

"Told you," Xavier snickered.

"Fine," Bennet relented. "But I hope you'll keep Maddox informed if anything out of the ordinary happens."

"Like what?" I laughed. "A shadowy figure follows me to my car? Someone calls me and I only hear heavy breathing? This is real life. Not some crime drama."

My defiance clearly ruffled Bennet's feathers. The muscles in his jaw twitched. But he also regarded me with a small dose of amusement. I could see it swirling with the concern in his eyes.

"Bennet," I said gently, placing my hand on his arm. "I appreciate you. I really do. But I doubt the ramifications of something that happened at a party twenty years ago are still in play. At least not on his part. This guy probably hasn't thought twice about it."

"Promise me," Bennet paused and amended with, "us. Promise us you won't do something silly like contact Jordan. Okay?"

I swallowed against the tightness in my throat. "I can't make that promise."

He exhaled harshly, cursing under his breath. Xavier leveled a stern look at him before turning to me.

"Tori," he spoke tenderly, caressing my cheek. "Do it for me. Please? I know you have so many questions and I vow to find as many answers as I can. Please don't try to talk to him."

"I'm not afraid of him." I asserted.

Xavier's smile lit me up from the inside out. "I know. And I also know if I say you'll be in massive trouble if you reach out to him, you'll want to do it even more."

I laughed. I couldn't help it.

"So," he continued. "I'm choosing to trust that you won't."

The weight of his statement hit me fully. Trust is as important as love and I can't deny him this. I closed my eyes and nodded.

"Alright," I acquiesced, glancing up through my lashes. "I love you."

Our lips came together in a soft, passionate kiss.

"Love you, too," he whispered.

I one hundred percent forgot Bennet was standing right next to us until he cleared his throat. I blushed in front of him. Again. Not from the kiss or even from the fact we declared our love for each other with him standing right there.

Nope.

I blushed because he looked at me like I'd managed to do something nobody thought possible.

"Looks like I've been doing it wrong all these years, Maddox," Bennet quipped.

"Nah. Just not really into kissing you, Logan," Xavier retorted.

"Do you boys need some alone time to sort out your feelings?" I asked.

Bennet's strong laugh filled the room, lightening the mood considerably. Much to my surprise, he planted a kiss on my forehead and Xavier's. It felt like such a big brother thing to do.

"I'm going to salvage what's left of my time with Hannah." He walked toward the door. "Wheels up at eleven, mate." With a final wave, he left.

Xavier pulled me into another tight hug, holding me as though he didn't ever want to leave.

"Can I ask a favor, love?"

"Sure."

He loosened his grip and leaned back to look at me. "Would you be okay reading through the diary we found today with me?"

I sucked in a breath, taken by surprise at his request. "Now?"

"Yes." He rested his forehead to mine. "I know how difficult it's been for you with the other entries and I want to be here with you for the next step. Will you let me?"

Of course I'd let him. But there's a stronger reason why.

"I need you here, Xavier," I whispered. "I need you with me for this."

Chapter
THIRTY-ONE

Tori,

I'm sorry. If I ever let you read this before I get the courage to tell you in person, I'm sorry. I should have told you what happened at the bonfire. I should have warned you about Jordan.

I should have.

I should have.

I should have.

I did it to protect you. I did it so he wouldn't come after you next. And he would have. He was hell bent on getting both of us. And he doesn't like to hear the word no.

I'm so glad you were off with that rugby player. I'm so glad you weren't anywhere near me when he came over and pulled me away from the rest of the party. You're my little sister and I would do anything to keep you safe.

Anything.

And that's why I pretended to be you. He didn't even question it.

I know you like the aggressive type but this guy was different. It was like he was entitled to it. Like my body belonged to him just because he wanted it. I had no control over anything. But I let him do it because I didn't want you anywhere near him. Adam warned me about him, too.

Poor Adam.

I wanted him to be my first.

He's so sweet, Tori. I hope I can introduce you to him next summer. You'd really like him.

I hope I haven't ruined my chance with him. I didn't see him at the bonfire. After you found me, all I wanted to do was go back home. I still haven't sent him a message yet. He must be so confused. I can't deal with all that. Not now. It's almost spring break and then finals are coming and the SATs and I have to maintain my grades and everything.

I can't let anything else slip. I've already let too many things slip.

It's so hard, Tori. I want to tell you everything. Will you hate me if I do? Will you think less of me? Will you look at me different? Will you be disappointed?

It'll be okay.

I'll be okay.

Mom made an appointment with Dr. Hainsby for me next week. Maybe she'll prescribe something to help with how I'm feeling.

You were so worried when you found me. You had this look on your face. I'd never seen you look like that before. It's like you knew something happened. I hope you couldn't feel it. I know we're able to sense each other in some ways but my God, I hope you weren't able to feel this.

Do you want to know what he said to me after he finished? He said I was the sweetest cherry he ever tasted. I wanted to throw up. And then he told me he wanted both of us at the same time. But he was glad he fucked the fun twin first. He said the other one, meaning me, wouldn't be as much fun but would still taste just as sweet.

I hate him.

I hate what I did with him.

But I love you so much, Tori.

This summer, when we're back in England, we'll make new memories. You'll meet Adam. We'll all go to Black Rose and binge on Eton Mess, and have fish and chips with mayonnaise, and tease Dawn, and dream about the future. Just like we always do.

And Jordan McKennie will fade away, like a bad dream.

Chapter
THIRTY-TWO

Three weeks, five days, twelve hours, forty minutes, and ten seconds. Not that I'm keeping track of how long it's been since I read my sister's final journal entry. Or how long it's been since I've seen Xavier. Or how long it's been since I've felt even remotely human.

I'd love to say I received closure for the years of torture I'd inflicted on myself over Charlotte's death. I'd love to say I was finally at peace and could let go of all the guilt. And yes, I yearned to say I was blissfully happy and together with the man I love.

But no.

None of that was my current reality.

I can't even say I had a fantastic time at the Met Gala. Killian and Max were so excited. They walked the red carpet and up the long flight of stairs like they were rock stars. There aren't enough words to describe how handsome they looked in their all black tuxes.

Of course they fawned over me and told me I was the prettiest girl in the world. Best friends like Killian and Max are precious. As much as I'd tried to hide what I was feeling, they knew. But I haven't told them what Charlotte wrote. I can't break Killian's heart. I just can't.

I fidgeted with the ring hanging from my necklace. Xavier's ring. The one he'd always wear on his thumb. Silver with an infinity design etched into the band.

"I love you," he told me when he gave it to me. "Wear this every day. Touch it anytime you doubt how I feel about you."

Those were the last words he said to me before meeting Bennet at the airport. I haven't heard from him since and at this point, I probably never will. He'd been so enraged after reading about the bonfire and what Jordan did to Charlotte. Even through all the anger and vitriol he spewed about him, Xavier still tried to comfort me and make sure I was okay.

But then he dropped a bomb on me.

"He's dangerous," Xavier told me, holding my hands. "He knows who you are. He knows you're with me. I never should have posted your photo the other night. It was impulsive and stupid."

"Don't be silly," I told him. "You didn't know all of this. And who cares anyway."

"I do. He'll come after you. He likes to take things that don't belong to him."

Things? I remembered looking at Xavier and wincing. "I'm not property."

"To him, you are. And I can't have you directly in his line of sight."

"What are you saying?"

I vividly recalled the way he looked at me with such devotion and love and sadness. "Protecting you is my number one priority. I can't protect you if I'm the reason he'll come for you. We can't be together right now, love. Not until I fix this."

"You're breaking up with me?"

"No, Tori. I'm shielding you."

I fisted his ring in my hand, almost pulling it off the chain. How dare he sacrifice our relationship. How dare he make decisions that affect both of our lives. The same anger I felt after reading Charlotte's words bubbled up for Xavier.

The two people I loved the most.

Both made sacrifices in order to protect me. Neither one asked if I wanted or needed their protection.

Charlotte lost her life as a result.

I couldn't bear to think what Xavier could lose.

A soft whining broke through my unpleasant thought process. I looked down at the scared puppy sitting in my lap. His questioning eyes stared at my fisted hand.

I let the ring fall gently against my clavicle and slowly pet the dog. He crawled up to nestle into my chest and licked my chin.

"Is this better?" I smiled, holding him.

I'd taken the day off from work to spend time at the Paws for Help Sanctuary. It's been way too long since I've donated my time to help socialize the puppies. And being here helped me feel closer to my sister. Or at least the version of her I thought I knew.

She loved this shelter.

It's small and run by a husband and wife team whose only goal is to provide comfort and loving homes for abandoned dogs. Many of the animals here were either dumped in parking lots or left to fend for themselves on the street. A few came from hoarded homes in other states, but this facility wasn't equipped to handle too many serious cases. That's one of the many reasons why I donated every year and appreciated whatever Noah chose to contribute from his fundraiser.

The socializing room was quiet and comfortable, unlike the kennel area. Don't get me wrong. These animals were treated like royalty. They each had their own private enclosure with beds, blankets, toys, water, and food. But there's only so much one can do with scared, barking dogs living in an echo chamber.

A puppy like the one I'm sitting with doesn't go in the main area.

He stays in a private room with other new arrivals, in his own kennel, until he's either adopted or old enough to go with the other dogs. As much as Charlotte loved helping the animals, she'd always tell me how sad it made her to see them locked in cages, waiting for someone to rescue them.

I ended up spending a couple hours with the puppies before making my way back to the city. For some reason, I chose to drive by my childhood home. The last time I came here was the day I turned the keys over to the realtor to sell it. It was my junior year at Dartmouth. My mother moved to South Carolina the summer after my freshman year, and my dad had been in Greece since I graduated from high school.

As with everything else Chase family related, I cleaned up the mess left behind.

I pulled up to the curb and stopped, staring at the gray colonial house. Too many memories flooded back too fast.

"This was a terrible idea," I muttered, putting the car in drive.

A few hours later I sipped on a happy hour cocktail with Hannah.

Spring totally flew the coop and dropped summer on all of us. Not that I'm complaining. But it would be nice to sit outside on this terrace and not feel like my legs were melting into the chair. Even the air was thick with the summer sounds of conversations and traffic and music.

"You doing okay over there?" Hannah asked.

"Great," I answered a little too cheerfully before swallowing my overly sweet excuse for a drink. "Does this place serve anything that doesn't require a gallon of syrup?"

Hannah's gentle laugh complimented her pretty smile. "We'll get you something more robust."

Her phone chimed and I knew without question it was Bennet. He texted her like clockwork. It was close to eleven in London, the night before a huge game. I knew that, too, because I watched every televised Royal City match I could find.

Pining much? You know it, buddy.

"Bennet says hello," Hannah said quietly, watching me fiddle with the ring on my necklace. "Still nothing from Xavier?"

"Who?" I finished my drink.

"That's the shitty sweet drink talking," she scolded.

"Yeah, well, maybe you could put in a good word with your Dom to have my so-called boyfriend send me a sign that he's still alive or something."

My nails drummed on the empty glass. Hannah grabbed it from me and put it out of reach.

"What's around your neck?" she asked, eyebrow arched.

"I'm not in the mood, Hannah," I snapped.

"Tough shit. That," she pointed, "is a sign he loves you. A visible, tangible sign that you fidget with all day."

She's right. I mean, I'm touching it right now. I touch it all the time because it's the only piece of him I have.

"I hate this," I growled. "Do you know how hard it is to keep my promise? To not call that asshole and rip him a new one for what he did to my sister? To not get on a plane and show up at his house and scratch his eyes out?"

"I know it's hard," Hannah soothed. "Bennet and Xavier are doing what they think is right. It sucks but it's the only option you have."

"It's a shitty option," I shouted, drawing a few curious stares in my direction. "How does Xavier removing himself from my life keep Jordan away from me? How? I mean, not even a fucking text message for three weeks? How is that keeping me safe?"

"It's hard to understand, for sure," Hannah kept trying to calm me down. "Love makes people do irrational things sometimes."

"Irrational," I repeated. "This whole damn thing is irrational. I'm not getting the whole story and it's driving me crazy. I've had it."

All the anger and hurt and guilt I've kept simmering inside me the last few weeks came to a boil.

Red.

Furious, blinding, suffocating red.

My hands clenched into fists.

"I can't do this anymore." I stood up and stormed out of the bar.

I don't even know where I wanted to go. The muted sound of Hannah calling after me did nothing to slow me down. I weaved in and out of people, pushing my way past groups of tourists who diligently waited for the walk sign to give them permission to cross the street.

Screw that.

A taxi's horn blared its displeasure as I ran through the crosswalk. I gave the driver a spirited one-finger salute and kept going.

Speed walking has never really been my thing. It's well-known that I prefer pacing in mindless circles. Or figure eights, depending on the situation. But this worked for me now.

Don't mind me, fellow people of New York City. Hurricane Victoria reached category five and made landfall somewhere between West 58th and Broadway. By the time I reached Columbus Circle I had to stop. Not because my feet screamed at me or my lungs strained to find another breath. I stopped because if I kept going, I'd end up swimming across the Hudson into New Jersey.

Okay, fine. That's way too dramatic. But in all seriousness I can't keep walking aimlessly around the city.

I miss him.

I miss him.

I miss him.

Emptiness spread through my chest, cracking open a cavernous hole. I missed his voice. I missed how rough it sounded when he'd tell me all the dirty things he wanted to do with me. I missed his deep, silky laugh. His wide, crooked smile. His dimple. The way his sapphire eyes glitter brighter than the night sky.

I missed how I felt when I was with him.

I missed the soft, comforting way he'd touch me when I was upset.

Frustrated, I found a random bench and sat down. My phone kept vibrating in my pocket. It was Hannah. It had to be.

All the missed text messages from her confirmed my suspicion when I checked. I know she's worried. And I appreciate her for being a solid friend during this confusing, annoying time.

Keeping what I'd found out from her would have been impossible since her relationship with Bennet was becoming quite serious.

And apparently I'm on this crusade now to let people into my life, even the worst parts of it.

So, yeah.

Hannah knows. She actually knows more than Killian at this point.

No, it doesn't sit well with me. But I truly cannot break his heart. Not yet.

"Nice night," an unfamiliar voice sprinkled in a gentle southern accent sounded to my left.

I glanced over to see a guy around my age sit next to me. I bristled at the intrusion. There are at least half a dozen empty benches in this area. I rolled my eyes and ignored him.

"Ah. A native New Yorker," he said. "I can tell by the inherent disinterest."

"Is there something I can help you with?" I asked, trying to remember my manners and not sound irritated. "If you're lost, there's a hotel about a block and a half that way. The concierge is quite knowledgeable."

He chuckled. A deep, unaffected, sound. "I know my way around Manhattan."

Folding my arms, I turned to look at him.

Conventionally handsome. Dark hair, dark eyes, expensive watch, crisp button down, tailored pants. Not a tourist. Just another Wall Street business bro on the prowl after hours.

"When I first moved here," he went on, not bothered by my stand-offish behavior, "women like you scared the shit out of me."

Don't engage, don't engage, don't engage.

"Women like me?" I arched an eyebrow.

He leaned back, turning toward me. "I meant no offense, ma'am. My thoughts sometimes come out faster than I can phrase them correctly."

I wasn't disarmed by his polite response at all.

"Verbal diarrhea is common in this city," I noted.

His laugh was easy, unforced. "That's a great way to put it. Mind if I steal your line?"

I sized him up one more time and turned away. I didn't want to make friends tonight. I wanted to be left alone.

"I feel like I've started this conversation all wrong," he said. "Hi. I'm Wes. Born and raised in Kansas City. The Missouri one."

Charm oozed off him, and not in a good way. This charm felt fabricated. Like he was flipping through some flirting guidebook and trying out different lines. I could practically see him in his swanky Financial District apartment, styling his hair just right, picking out the perfect cufflinks, winking and giving his reflection a thumbs up.

To prove my point, he reached up to adjust his shirt collar so I could see exactly which cufflinks he chose to wear today and then ran his hand through his perfect hair.

"Do all men from Kansas City preen in such an obvious way?" I chided.

"Only the Missouri ones," he replied a little too smoothly.

"Whatever." I shook my head.

"Most women enjoy this. Have I met my first ice princess?"

Alright. Play time is over. I stood up.

"Probably not your last either. Have a good night."

I only made it a couple feet away before I heard, "Now I know why people called you the fun twin."

Everything froze. My legs, my blood, my lungs, time.

The fun twin.

"You're easier to track down than I thought," he drawled in an English accent reserved for the Ascot races and white tie affairs at Buckingham Palace.

Steeling myself, I pivoted on my heel to face him again. He remained seated on the bench, gazing up at me like a fucking asshole prince.

"Jordan." I choked out his name through clenched teeth.

His too-wide mouth curled in a smirk. "Victoria."

All my bad ass talk about ripping him a new one and scratching his eyes out remained just that. Talk.

I studied him. Really memorizing his features, his body, his size. I imagine he would have been seventeen or eighteen the summer we went to the bonfire. I wondered if he was this big then.

Broad shoulders, big hands, muscular build. Rotten images of his hands around my sister's neck when he pushed her into the wall consumed me, rendering me breathless.

"You're a beautiful woman," he growled.

"Fuck you," I spat.

He tsked, leaning forward. "I should gag that spicy mouth of yours right now. I didn't get to do all the really kinky stuff with Charlotte."

I doubled over from the searing pain in my stomach.

No. No. No. No.

He knew. She thought she'd fooled him but he knew.

Oh, Charlie. It was all for nothing.

He's dangerous.

I clapped my hand over my mouth to muffle the wailing sob threatening to burst from me.

"Oh, come now, Victoria," Jordan patronized, standing up. "I indulged in your sister's sweetness. Did she tell you how eager she was for it? Especially when she told me she was you? I knew she wasn't. But

I didn't want to ruin her fantasy. The fantasy of being someone else, acting like someone else. It turned her on. I barely had to do any work to get her ready—"

"Shut up," I shouted. "You took advantage of her. You threatened her. You forced her—"

"I forced nothing," he countered.

"You took my sister from me." My whole body shook. "You took her innocence. You took her like you take everything else."

"Did Xavier tell you that? Did he make it sound like all I do is take things away from people? Did he tell you how he punched me and nearly broke my jaw because *his* girlfriend wanted to fuck me? Because *she* made the advances?"

"You're lying."

He scoffed. "Did he tell you how she hated it when he'd be rough with her? The fucking prick didn't know how to control his urges, no matter how much Bennet tried to teach him." His brown eyes flicked over me, pausing briefly at the ring hanging from my necklace. "Did he tell you he stole my fiancée from me?"

I staggered backward, giving myself breathing room. Jordan's imposing frame filled my sight. The things he said. I didn't believe one word. I couldn't. None of it made any sense.

"Xavier Maddox has a reputation for a reason," he glowered. "He loves the attention. Loves the footballer way with women. He's discreet, I'll give him that. You won't find many kiss and tell articles about him. But he's not what you think."

"You're lying," I repeated, my voice shaky and weak.

"Am I? You should ask him." A wicked smile pulled at his lips. "Oh, right. Xavier is being noble and righteous these days. He thinks he's protecting you by distancing himself. Classic move."

The insistent blaring of a car horn sledgehammered its way through this abhorrent conversation.

When Jordan put his hand on my shoulder I shrank away from him.

"And just so you know, I've forgiven you for not selling me Briarcliff Cottage. I was really annoyed with you there for a bit but I think this will work to my advantage anyway."

My mouth dropped open in shock. He grinned.

"Be careful, Victoria. You never know who's watching."

"Hey." I heard Hannah's loud, concerned voice. "There you are. I've been driving all over the goddam city looking for you." She approached us, holding her phone up like she'd been talking to someone. "Everything okay here?"

"Yes ma'am," Jordan replied, affecting his fake southern accent again. "This lovely woman was just giving me directions."

"Right," Hannah said, glaring at him and then looking at me. "Let's go."

I followed her back to the waiting car without glancing back.

Chapter
THIRTY-THREE

VICTORIA

My condo is pretty big. Spacious. Lots of windows and light and high ceilings.

Right now, it felt like the tiniest prison cell buried deep underground.

Hannah stood in my kitchen talking to Bennet on the phone. She kept sneaking worried glances in my direction.

"He wants to talk to you." She held out the phone.

Yay.

A conversation with Bennet. Just what I've been dreaming of these last three weeks.

I took her phone. "Hi," I said, not even trying to hide my exhaustion.

"I'm sorry." Bennet's voice sounded small, almost defeated.

"For what?"

"Putting you through this. Convincing Maddox this was the safest option. I thought we could—"

"You thought you could what, Bennet? Control the situation by playing chess with an unhinged asshole? Jordan was always going to find me." My tone sharpened. "It's not like I live in a small town in the middle of nowhere. I'm in fucking Manhattan. I'm an executive at the most successful football team in the nation. Jesus Christ, my name is listed on the stadium website. I'm not hidden. What exactly were you trying to prevent?"

A heavy sigh. The lack of response pissed me off even more.

"I know you mean well. I know you and Xavier did what you thought was best. But it's done now." I paused, fighting back tears. "I miss him. He won't talk to me because he thinks he's doing the right thing and it's killing me."

Another heavy sigh.

"I swear to God, Bennet, if you keep sighing I'm getting on the next flight to London to handcuff you to a fire hydrant."

He laughed. A genuine, relaxed laugh. "Wow. You sound like your boyfriend."

"I want to talk to him," I demanded. "You're all at the same hotel, right? Please go knock on his door so I can hear his voice."

"No," he replied. "If he finds out what happened just now, he'll lose his mind."

"Please, Bennet," I begged, playing with Xavier's ring. "If you don't, I'll just call him myself."

"Victoria." His stern tone gave me pause. "This is going to sound harsh and shallow and I apologize because you're upset but right now, his focus has to be on tomorrow's match. I think you would understand that more than anyone else."

Fuck. "I don't want to be a distraction," I muttered.

"You're not," he assured me. "We both know how impulsive he is and I don't doubt for a minute if you were to call him right now and tell him everything, he'd be on the next flight to see you."

Double fuck. "You're making too much sense," I complained.

"Well, yes. I am the club's president so I'm sort of invested in wanting the best goalkeeper in the league to help us win the final game of the season."

"And the logic continues."

Silence. And then, "I know I'm not the one you want to be talking to. I know I'm not the one who can say the right things or help you understand. He's trying to keep you safe. I'm trying to keep him out of trouble. We're all protecting one another as best we can."

The cavernous hole in my chest expanded.

"Good luck tomorrow." I ended the call.

League champions.

I sat cross-legged on the floor with the biggest smile on my face and tears streaming down my cheeks. An older gentleman presented Royal City Athletic with the trophy and announced Xavier as the Goalkeeper of the Year. Apparently, he hadn't conceded a goal since coming back from suspension, bringing his clean sheet tally to twenty for the entire season.

Honestly, that's impressive.

His teammates crowded and jumped around him, encircling him in a jubilant, bouncing huddle. He looked thrilled. And maybe a little embarrassed?

Nah.

Xavier Maddox does not get embarrassed. I can tell he loves every moment. The cheering. The fawning. The adoration.

I stroked the ring hanging from my necklace.

The camera paused in front of him when the huddle of teammates dispersed. His eyes searched the crowd for something and then focused on the camera.

It took my breath.

Those eyes stared right at me. Right through me. And yes, I know he's only looking at a camera lens but in this moment, for the first time in weeks, it felt like he was looking at me. Only me.

And then he smiled.

My smile.

The one that's too wide and too crooked and shows too much dimple. It filled the gaping abyss residing in my chest. I felt whole, if only for a few seconds.

The camera cut away to a wide-shot of the field.

The announcers kept babbling.

The team gathered together on the stage, all wearing their medals. Cade carried the trophy and took his place in the middle, next to Xavier. On a joyful count to three, Cade hoisted the trophy as they all yelled and cheered while royal blue streamers shot into the air.

On an impulse, I grabbed my phone and took a picture of them celebrating on TV. I sent the picture to Xavier with the message *I'm so proud of you.*

My phone rang immediately, giving me heart palpitations.

"Killian," I answered.

"Tori," he replied. "What are you doing tonight?"

"I have a date with some mint chocolate chip ice cream and season two of *You.*"

"Lame. Well, not the ice cream. But anyway. Max and I were invited last minute to some fundraiser and we're taking you with us."

"Last minute?" I stood up and put my empty coffee mug in the sink. "Who invites someone last minute to a fundraiser?"

"Christ," he grumbled. "You get way too caught up in the minutia of situations. It's the influencer Max planned the birthday party for. Her dad's foundation is hosting a big who's-who event. It'll be a networking extravaganza. No more questions. Grab a dress and be ready at eight. We'll pick you up."

"How fancy?"

"Fundraiser fancy."

I sighed. "So, like, cocktail dress or full length?"

"Surprise us."

The amount of money walking around this room draped in designer couture and tailored suits could sustain a small nation for at least a decade. I realize I sound like a hypocrite since my family amassed a rather impressive fortune, but still. Seeing it flaunted around like this was nauseating.

I smiled at the young woman working the complimentary bar when she handed a dirty martini to me. We'd chatted while she prepared my drink. I learned she went to NYU and wanted to become a prosecutor. And then possibly the state Attorney General. She's probably the most interesting and real person in here. I made sure to leave a generous tip in the glass she'd set up next to the napkins.

Killian and Maxim were somewhere in the crowd, schmoozing and impressing and networking. I'm glad I came with them but I wasn't quite in the mood to talk about myself or my job or oh-my-god-where-did-you-get-those-heels.

So, I took my martini and went out on the terrace.

The night air drenched me in a cool, calm quiet. I walked farther out until I found a hightop table hidden from view. Very few people were out here so I was able to claim this space just for me.

I sipped on my drink, pulling out the skewer of olives and sliding one off with my teeth. The late spring breeze played with my full length silk dress, brushing it against my skin and teasing the skirt. Killian had gushed over the high slit that climbed up my left thigh.

"You're going to give some bloated sixty-five year old millionaire a painful hard on in that," he'd said on the ride over.

Probably.

Not really my problem though.

My hand instinctually went to my neck. A brief moment of panic sliced through me when I didn't feel Xavier's ring. Then I remembered I put it on a longer chain, so it nestled closer to my cleavage. Or my heart.

Soft peals of laughter sounded behind me. I heard footsteps shuffling off toward a section of the terrace filled with small trees, shrubs, and other seasonal plants. In front of me, Manhattan shimmered and sparkled like the global superstar it is.

More footsteps, more muffled conversations.

My shoulders slumped, knowing this meant guests were starting to wander out here and my precious solitude would end. I lifted the skewer of olives from the martini again, sliding another off with my teeth.

Another set of footsteps slowed and stopped behind me. I closed my eyes, wishing whoever it was would go away.

"So, Victoria is it?"

The sound of a rich, elegant baritone voice stole my breath. I opened my eyes and turned, fully expecting this to be some sort of prank.

Striking cobalt irises framed dark pools that focused solely on me. Tousled brown hair rustled in the breeze. Light spilling down from the top of the building illuminated his handsome face and sultry, pouty mouth.

My lips parted in silence as I drank in every tuxedo clad inch of him.

A tuxedo.

Xavier Maddox, the tattooed, smoldering goalkeeper who likes to talk dirty was standing in front of me in a tuxedo. Or as he's more commonly known these days, Xavier Maddox, the Guy Who Ghosted His Girlfriend.

His hands were tucked casually in his pants pockets. An expression of absolute amusement spread across his face.

"Is that not your name?" he inquired. "Could have sworn it was."

I blinked. It took me a second before I replied, "Depends on who's asking."

He sauntered closer, standing in front of me. Now that I could smell him, this became much too real. Much too immediate and insistent and consuming.

And then he smiled and I lost it.

Three weeks worth of suppressed sadness and anger and confusion seeped out of me in the form of tears. Way too many tears.

His expression fell.

"Hey," he whispered, pulling me into a hug. "Oh, Tori. I'm so sorry."

I cried into his shoulder.

I cried in my fancy silk dress at this stupid, fancy fundraiser.

I cried and hugged him and let him comfort me.

I held him so tight. So goddam tight. He'd never leave again if I held him like this, right?

I cried until I had nothing left. But even after my breathing evened out and I stopped sniffling, he still held me. He still kept me wrapped in his muscular grip so I could inhale his scent and hear his heart beating.

Whispered words floated around me like a solemn prayer.

I love you.

I need you.

I'm sorry.

Please forgive me.

The gentle touch of his fingers sifting through my hair made me shudder. I backed away, finding it difficult to look directly at him. Of course, he could sense it and tipped my chin up.

"You're so beautiful," he murmured, wiping what I could only imagine was my smudged mascara off my cheeks.

I swallowed, shaking my head. "I am a hot mess right now."

"Yeah but you're my hot mess," he teased.

"Asshole," I muttered, shooting him an incredulous look before moving over to the high-top table to grab my clutch. I pulled out my phone, held it up and looked into the camera.

Woof.

Hot mess was too kind.

"Can you hand me the napkin under my glass?" I asked.

Once he did, I wiped the black mascara streaks and dabbed at the dark smudges under my eyes. Fortunately, I was able to blend and salvage my make up so it looked like I either failed miserably at doing a smoky eye or I was mildly drunk. The epitome of sophistication.

Xavier watched me the whole time, fidgeting with his cufflinks.

Cufflinks.

The man wore a tuxedo and cufflinks and a *BOW TIE.*

And he's here. This morning he was on my television smiling and looking into cameras and winning championships and now he's right here.

And he didn't answer my text.

Or tell me he was coming to New York.

Or tell me he'd be at this bloated fundraiser.

Or, or, or…

UGH.

I should be angry. I should be rip-roaring mad. I should break up with him for real.

But I can't. I can't because I'm in-fucking-love with him and I'd be miserable without him.

"Come here," he ordered quietly.

I went to him because how does a moth not go to a flame or a bee *not* seek out nectar?

"Tori," he rumbled, pulling me flush to his body, so my soft curves pressed into his hard muscles. "I'm sorry. I thought I was doing the right thing." His fingers dug into the small of my back. "I won't blame you if you want to dump my arse."

I slid my hands under his jacket, circling his waist. "Nobody's breaking up with anyone." *Even though I legit had this thought a mere ten seconds ago.*

Some of the tension melted from his body. Some. I could tell he was guarded.

"However," I continued, pulling his shirt out so I could put my hands on his skin. God, I missed touching him. Feeling how his body reacts to me. "You have three weeks worth of apologizing waiting for you."

"I know. I'll do anything." He tilted his head so our lips almost touched. "Anything you want."

Explanations. I want explanations and reasons and assurances this won't happen again. And then I want to make Jordan McKennie's life a living hell.

"Did Bennet tell you?" I asked.

"Yes." His grip on me tightened. "What did Jordan say to you?"

"A lot of really shitty things," I seethed. "He must think I'm a complete moron to believe the story he spun."

"Tell me."

I recounted the conversation I had with fake-Wes-from-Missouri who wound up being real-Jordan-from-England. Xavier's expression soured. Unbridled rage flashed behind his eyes.

"What a narcissist," I groused.

"I vote we don't talk about him anymore tonight."

Great idea but I had so many questions. And avoiding what happened really won't help the situation.

I sighed, pulling out of his embrace. "We have to talk about him."

"Why?"

"Well, for one thing, you fucking ghosted me because of this guy," I blurted out.

"I didn't ghost you."

"Semantics, Maddox. Anyway. We have to talk about this because…" I blew out a breath, sending a few strands of my hair up into the air. "We just have to."

"Okay."

I grabbed his hand and put it over my heart. "Will you be one hundred percent honest with me?"

"Always."

"Even if you don't like what I'm asking?"

He closed his eyes and inhaled slow. When his eyes met mine again he said, "Even if I don't like what you're asking."

"Why would he say you stole his fiancée?"

"Shit," he grumbled, scrubbing his face with his hands. "She was cheating on him with me."

"Xavier," I exclaimed. "What the hell?"

"Not that this will make it sound any better," he continued, "but she was also shagging the striker on United at the same time."

I just stared at him in shock. I mean, I figured he got around but wow. The Jordan thing was becoming an actual *thing*.

"Okay that's…a lot." I suppressed an urge to pace around the table. "But you didn't actually steal her from him, right?"

"No."

"Honest?" I blinked up at him.

Xavier's dimple appeared. "Honest. She ended up with the striker."

"Oh." I chewed on my lip. "So why did he say—"

"Because he's an entitled piece of shit who stirs up trouble." Xavier's voice rose in frustration. "Everything he told you is a half-truth wrapped in a lie. Yes, my so-called girlfriend at the time shagged him. No, I did not almost break his jaw. I wanted to, trust me. But I did give him a bloody nose because he was forcing himself on your sister's friend Millie."

Stunned silence hung in the air, thick and heavy. I started to say something and stopped. Xavier swore under his breath and clasped his hands behind his head.

"Millie," I repeated. "You two were close?"

Xavier folded and unfolded his arms, put his hands in his pockets, took them out, and finally settled on fidgeting with the cufflinks again.

"We were good friends all through school. And we dated on and off. After what happened with Jordan, I felt an obligation to protect her. She was really shaken by it."

I nodded and asked, "Did she ever talk about Charlotte with you?"

"She only mentioned she had an American friend who used to visit in the summer. That's all I knew." He reached for my hand and placed it over his heart. "Honest."

Exhaustion draped itself over me. A heavy, three-week-pound weight hung from my shoulders. And now I don't want to play the honesty game anymore. I don't want to ask questions. I don't want any more answers.

But I need answers.

"Did you even miss me?" I asked, keenly aware I was poking a hornet's nest.

Xavier staggered backward like I'd sucker punched him. Real pain twisted through his handsome features.

"Did I *miss* you?" The question sounded incredulous coming out of his mouth.

"Did I miss you?" he repeated it, tasting the bitterness of the words on his tongue.

I shrank away from him slightly when he approached. Not out of fear. Hell, no. I shrank away out of embarrassment. How selfish was I to think I was the only one who suffered through this?

My lip trembled when he brushed his thumb over it. Goosebumps erupted on my skin as he trailed his finger down my neck to the ring hanging there.

"Did I miss you," he said softly, sliding the ring onto his thumb and dragging it up my neck to my mouth. The cool metal pressed into my lips. "I thought of nothing but you. The sound of your laugh, the radiance of your smile, your boldness, your compassion, your playfulness…" He faltered. "My God, Victoria, not a day passed when I didn't miss you."

"Why didn't you tell me you'd be here?"

He removed the ring from his thumb so he could pull me close again. "I was sworn to secrecy."

I wrapped my arms around his waist and slid my hands under his shirt. "Bennet?" I asked, lifting an eyebrow.

"Killian." He grinned.

"Killian?" I repeated, shocked. "When did my best friend become a double agent?"

The sound of Xavier's deep, throaty laugh lifted the mood in an instant.

"When I texted him at halftime and told him I was flying here after the match." He rested his forehead to mine. "He told me all about this last minute fundraiser he'd been invited to. So, we thought it would be a good idea to get you out here so I could see you. Actually, Max was in on it as well. We had a three-way text group going on."

"A three-way. Sexy," I teased.

He smiled, reaching for my face and slanting his head. I anticipated his kiss, anticipated the feel of his mouth and breath and tongue.

"I'm sorry," he whispered.

Chapter
THIRTY-FOUR

He didn't kiss me.

Color me confused.

I lightly scratched my nails on his back, down along the waistband of his tailored pants and around to his stomach.

"Am I still an asshole?" he asked, his breaths becoming more staggered as I dragged my nails across his skin.

I reached up and loosened his tie. Music and laughter from inside the event floated out to the terrace. We were still alone and unbothered in our little spot.

"Maybe," I answered, untucking the rest of his shirt and then unbuttoning it. His whole body vibrated on a groan when I caressed his chest, using both hands to touch and trace his tattoos, feel every taut muscle, stroke every corrugated line.

"Is touching you like this okay?" I asked, running my finger from his throat down to his stomach.

"Yes," he answered hoarsely, staring at me in a way I've never seen him do before. Conflicted and determined. Terrified and indifferent. "I thought maybe…maybe you'd be too upset with me to even want to see me."

"I am." I locked eyes with him. "I'm trying so hard to understand why you did this. It makes absolutely no sense."

"I know it looks that way," he murmured. "There are so many things you don't know."

"Then tell me," I demanded resting my hand on his stomach. "Tell me so neither one of us has to go through it again."

We stood like this for God knows how long. My fingers kept kneading into his skin to assure myself this was reality and not some ultra-vivid dream. He answered my internal doubts by sliding his hand down to the dip of my waist, resting it on the small of my back.

"I'll tell you everything, love. I promise. Just not tonight." He held me close. "Please, not tonight."

I moved my hand to the nape of his neck, playing with pieces of his hair. *Not tonight.* His parted lips and hooded eyes silently convinced me to heed his request, for now. And then he pulled me flush to him. I could feel every muscle, every breath, every tremor in his body. I'm so starved for him. Starved for his touch, his sounds, his affection.

I wanted all of it, right here on this terrace.

Here, tucked from view and mere feet away from the upper echelon of Manhattan society.

"Xavier." I said his name the way I've done when he's buried deep inside me. Soft and urgent and tinged with need. "Kiss me."

He blinked at me, his eyes filled with liquid heat. But he shook his head. "All I—"

"Surely you didn't fly all this way, get dressed up and conspire with my friends just to stand here and stare at me."

"You don't—"

"I don't what? Want you right here? Right now?" I pressed my hand into his chest so he had no choice but to walk backwards into a nearby wall covered in ivy. "I always want you."

"But—"

"Xavier." I repeated his name the same way as before. Soft, urgent, filled with need. I pressed into him, pleased to feel the friction of his hard length rub on me. "Kiss me."

His thighs trembled with restraint.

"Please." My eyelashes fluttered when I looked up at him.

Whatever control he'd been holding onto snapped. Whatever plan he had in place for tonight disintegrated. Insatiable, carnal need etched into his face, darkening his eyes.

"There you are," I coaxed, tracing his lower lip. "Come out and play."

I felt his hand on my bare thigh. His hand and the metal of his rings. Then, I heard *that* voice. "This is reckless, love."

"Hasn't stopped you before." I sifted my fingers through his hair, pulling gently.

He lifted me without warning, turned and pinned me to the wall. Ivy leaves tickled and caressed my neck and shoulders. The night air soothed my bare skin as soon as I wrapped my legs around his waist.

He's not there yet.

He's still holding back.

I cupped one hand behind his neck and idly scrolled lazy circles on his chest with the other.

"I'm glad you're here," I told him. "I'm glad I can congratulate you in person for today's big win."

"Yeah?"

I nodded. My eyes dropped to his mouth. His pouty, sultry, promises and sins mouth. I wanted the sins tonight.

His grip on my thighs tightened. My arousal sped up when he dragged his tongue over his lip in the slow, deliberate way that drives me crazy.

"Why are you holding back?" I asked. "Why won't you kiss me?"

"Honest answer?"

"I won't accept any other."

The muscles in his neck worked overtime when he swallowed. When his eyes met mine he said, "I don't want to fuck this up again."

I stretched my arms so each one draped over his shoulders and my hands dangled lazily. "Well, if we're keeping score, I think the technical term is…equalizer? I had my fuck up and now you have yours, so we're tied."

"Level," he corrected with a smile.

"Fine. *Level*," I repeated. "The next one who fucks up wins."

"Wins what?" He furrowed his brows. "A lifetime of regret?"

"Wow. Dude. I'm gonna need you to not be such a downer."

A little crooked grin appeared. "I don't want to disappoint you or see you as upset as you were just before."

"Hate to break it you, Maddox. That's how relationships work. We're human. We're going to fuck up and disappoint and be upset. But we're also going to get it right and satisfy and be so happy it'll outweigh the down times."

"Yeah," he sighed. "Been awhile since I've done the whole relationship thing."

I bit down on my lip to stifle a laugh. He tilted his head in this adorably confused way, staring at me like I had the audacity to call him out on something.

"Are you having a laugh over my attempt at being an actual gentleman and trying to be sensitive about your feelings?"

"Maybe." I pressed a finger to his mouth before he could get all huffy about that silly word. "I just find it a little amusing that the great Xavier Maddox, whose hands don't miss and who wins all sorts of fancy medals, is just as mortal and fallible as the rest of us when it comes to relationships."

"Hmm." He teased his fingers along my thighs, leaning his muscular frame into me. "Do you still want me to kiss you?"

"Yes."

"Is that all you want?"

My pulse raced hearing the tone of voice I loved. His whole demeanor shifted from unsure to in control.

"No."

He hovered his mouth over mine and asked, "What else do you want?"

"I want you to apologize."

He whimpered, leaning his forehead to mine. "How?"

"However you want."

"Is that all?"

"No."

"What else do you want?"

"You." I laced my fingers behind his neck. "I want you."

"How do you want me, love?"

His mouth barely touched mine. Just a faint brush of his lips. All I had to do was pull him a fraction of an inch closer. And he'd let me. I knew he would because his body, as firm and muscular as it was, would surrender to me without question.

"I want you like this, out here," I answered. "Please don't deny me."

"Does my dirty princess want to be fucked and apologized to on the terrace?" he growled.

"Yes, please."

Our mouths collided in a searing, burning, desperate kiss. I grabbed his shoulders, sinking my fingers into the jacket. He fisted his hand in my hair, moving my head sharply to the right, taking my mouth fully.

His clothed erection nestled perfectly into my three-week-sex-starved pussy. (I know, I know. Poor me.) If I rocked my hips just a little, I could create some friction and satisfy one small need.

So I did. And each time I did, he kissed me deeper and harder until he tore his mouth away with a grunt.

"I'm not coming in my pants this time. I'm coming inside of you."

I hummed with approval, my head lolling back against the wall. He let my legs slide away until my feet were firmly on the ground.

"Look at me," he ordered.

When he knelt in front of me I made a noise I don't think I've ever made before. Something between a groan and a mewl. I loved seeing him kneel. Loved it.

"Are you going to apologize to me on your knees?" I purred.

The salacious glance I received in response got me so wet I regretted wearing underwear. He licked his lip again and hiked up my dress.

"This," he murmured, running a finger along the slit, "got me hard the moment I saw you."

He eased off my panties, pulling them down, lifting my right foot and then my left so I could step out of them. With a grin, he stuffed them in his pocket.

I trembled, feeling his hands caress up my thighs, parting my legs. Using his thumbs, he opened my folds, exposing my unabashed desire for him. On a moan, he pressed his nose into my skin, inhaling my scent.

"I'm sorry," he whispered, massaging my clit in slow circles. One finger drifted inside me, curling to touch the sensitive textured spot that made me see stars. He stopped to drape my leg over his shoulder, giving him full access.

"Forgive me," I heard him say as he started to suckle and lick my clit, swirling his tongue at my entrance and dipping it inside me.

I laced my fingers in his hair, pulling him closer. He growled in appreciation, devouring me in earnest. My legs shook so hard I clutched onto his shoulders for balance. His tongue alternated in long licks and short flickers. His fingers worked me into a frenzy, rubbing me and teasing me. The combined sensations made my breathing quiver.

"Xavier," I panted, rocking my hips, bringing myself closer to the edge. "It feels so good. *Xavier.*"

My orgasm melted me from the inside out. I squirmed and gasped and shuddered. He continued swirling his tongue gently as my climax ebbed and flowed on his mouth. When my body finally went soft and pliant, he leaned back and looked up at me.

The visual of him on his knees, his mouth sucking my desire off his fingers, and his eyes bright and wild made me whimper. After carefully removing my leg from his shoulder, he stood, held my face in his hands and kissed me. A full, lush, passionate kiss. If his mouth gave me the sins I craved between my legs, it's giving me the promises I yearn for on my lips.

"Tell me," he demanded when our mouths parted.

"I love you," I said in a low, husky tone. "I love you so much I could burst. You've changed me. You make me feel whole again."

He unzipped his pants and lowered his boxer briefs enough to free his rigid cock. "What else?"

"I hated being without you." Tears pooled in my eyes. Surprising, since I'd cried an ocean on his shoulder already. "It felt like half of my heart was ripped out of me."

I wrapped my legs around his waist when he lifted me. His body shivered when his hard length pressed against my wet opening.

"Tori," he said hoarsely. "I love you. You make me come apart in the best way. And then you put me back together and make me feel more like myself than I could ever dare to imagine."

He kissed me at the same moment he thrust inside me. Our mouths and bodies joining in one motion. One perfect union. I'd always assumed my first time having sex with someone in public would be some sweaty, dirty, salacious experience.

I could not have been more wrong. This felt almost sacred.

He rocked himself into me harder and deeper, filling me and owning me. All the while, he kissed and softly bit into the delicate slope between my neck and shoulder, apologizing and praising me with every thrust.

You're my world...and please forgive me...and let me love you forever.

My head fell back into the ivy leaves as I moved my hips in rhythm with him.

"Look at me, Tori."

I clenched around him, eliciting a low groan. He said my name in *that* voice. The one I never wanted to stop hearing.

Our eyes locked. Blue to green. Sky to ground. Heaven to earth.

I wrapped my arms around him, spearing my fingers into his hair.

And now my body was nothing but sensation. Nothing but energy. Nothing but the feel of Xavier inside me and his body caged around me. His sharp breaths. His grunts and moans. His steady, deep pounding.

When his fingers roughly massaged my clit, I fell apart immediately. Writhing and coming and whispering *I love you* into the night air.

He rode through my release, spilling into me in long, hot pulses. My hands twisted in his jacket, holding him close as our bodies came down together. Shaky and sated and whole. His warm breath tickled my throat when he nuzzled into me. I responded by squeezing my legs tighter around his waist.

He kissed me slow and gentle and deep.

"Dirty princess," he spoke on my lips. "Do you accept this apology?"

I rested my elbows on his shoulders, running my hands through his hair. "I do. Can't wait to see what the other ones look like."

A full smile. Full and dimpled and crooked and happy.

"You keep breaking your policy for me."

"I have a new policy now."

"Oh?" An eyebrow arched. "Tell me."

"It's a pretty strict one," I warned. "No deviations this time."

"Sounds serious."

"Had to be done."

The silky, softness of his tongue slipped through my lips for a sweet, tender kiss. "I guess you should tell me the bad news," he said.

"The only professional athletes I date are British goalkeepers with dirty mouths and tattoos, crooked smiles and dimples, and sapphire eyes that see past all my barriers and love me for everything I am. Know anyone like that?"

With a devilish grin, he hovered his mouth over mine. "Maybe."

Chapter
THIRTY-FIVE

I never used to like surprises. I still don't if I'm being honest. They're notorious for catching a person off guard and wreaking havoc. I always preferred to control situations. And then let my impulsiveness have its way.

Now?

Oh, I'm still as impulsive as fuck. That won't ever change.

And the surprise thing?

If someone told me I'd be celebrating the 4th of July (of all things) with my best mates and my American girlfriend at a gorgeous lakeside house in New York I would have laughed my arse off.

SURPRISE. Here I am.

In fact, once this cookout is over, I plan to grab the stunning redhead over by the water in the black two piece bathing suit and emerald green cover-up and ravage her body until she gasps my name. And then do it again.

But first, hamburgers.

"Do you even know what you're doing?" Maxim derided Cade, watching over him like a hawk.

"I am a master griller, thank you very much," Cade pouted. "It's just meat patties, for fuck's sake. And what does this even have to do with American independence?"

I grabbed an ice cube from the cooler and threw it at my friend. "Did you miss that day in school, Gallagher? Something about Thomas Jefferson and a document and some bloke named Hancock moaning about there not being any food."

"Stop talking bollocks, Maddox," he shouted with a smile.

"Harden the fuck up, Cade," I retorted, lobbing another ice cube at him. It ricocheted off his arm and hit Bennet in the head.

"Would the two of you knock it off," Bennet groused from his lounger. "I'm trying to read."

Cade and I shared a glance. I reached for a plastic cup and filled it with ice and water. Cade ambled over to our prim and proper friend, blocking the sun as best he could with his tall, muscular frame.

"Gallagher, you're in the way," Bennet huffed.

"That's the point, genius."

I crept up behind the chair and waited for Cade's signal. I also pleaded silently with Hannah not to say anything. She'd been sitting in the lounger next to Bennet, observing what we were up to. She grinned and shook her blonde head.

"I think the lord of the manor got too much sun. He needs to cool off," Cade suggested.

And with those words, I dumped the cup of ice and water on Bennet's head and hoped to Christ he wouldn't flip out too much. Forgiveness instead of permission and all that.

"*Maddox*," he roared, sitting up in the sharp way people do when they're doused in something cold.

He whipped his head around and glared at me. I shrugged and feigned innocence.

"This has your name written all over it," he grumbled.

"Maddox, one. Logan, nil," Cade exclaimed.

Hannah reached over and stroked her boyfriend's leg, unable to hold in her laughter. The commotion caused Noah and Tre to stop throwing around the football and stare.

Yeah, that's right. Noah and Tre. Who's *not* a jealous boyfriend anymore?

Tracey, Victoria, and Killian wandered over from where they'd been sitting by the water.

"I can't leave you boys alone for two minutes," Victoria scolded, looking from me to Cade. She perched her sunglasses on her head, resting her dark green gaze on me.

No matter how many times I looked at her, I always had the same reaction. Her beauty weakens me. It rocks me to my core and steals my breath.

And I let it.

I surrendered to it every time. I surrendered to her every time.

I never wanted to stop surrendering to her.

Being with her in New York for the last six weeks has been glorious. Living with her, dating her, discovering her. I'd fallen in love after only knowing her for a few days. What I felt for her now was deeper than love. More profound. More consuming.

I'll do whatever it takes to keep her safe and happy. Whatever it takes, for as long as it takes.

Electricity and awareness skittered over my skin the longer I held her stare. Her eyes moved first, pausing at my mouth before admiring my bare chest, my stomach, my not-so-hidden erection protected only by these swim trunks.

"I'm just trying to make burgers for fireworks or documents or some shit like that," Cade grinned and went back to his grilling duties with Max hot on his heels.

Bennet relaxed into the chair and continued reading. I approached Victoria and reached for her hand.

"Walk with me?" I asked.

"Sure," she smiled.

"Don't get engaged or anything," Killian teased and kissed his best friend on the cheek. "I mean, get engaged but please don't have a wedding in this heat."

"Oh my God, Killian," she chuckled but looked slightly panicked.

I grinned, patting him on the back when he walked past me.

"Ready?" I squeezed her hand.

"Oookayyy," she over-enunciated the word.

"Don't look so worried. It's just a walk."

I led her down to the dock and stopped, pulling her in front of me so she can lean her back into my chest. But because it's her and because I love it when she switches shit up on me, she turned to face me, hooking her arms around my waist.

"Enjoying your first visit to Lake George?"

"I am."

"Getting into the whole Independence Day thing yet?"

I chuckled. "Maybe."

She leaned close and kissed along my collarbone. "You're hot."

"You think so?"

"No. I mean yes, but you're, like, literally hot." She touched my chest. "Your skin. Do you need to get out of the sun for a while?"

"Is this your way of coaxing me into the house for a birthday quickie?"

"This is my way of preventing sun stroke and a sunburn."

My laughter tumbled out with no effort. "Ah, Tori. Concerned about the pale English guy getting too much sun?"

"Shut up." She poked my side. "And you're not that pale."

"Mmhmm." I pulled her flush to my body so I could feel her curves. "Speaking of your birthday, I actually wanted to give you one of your presents now."

"Oh?" Her eyes widened.

"Yes, *oh*," I teased, trying to control my wildly beating heart. "I want to thank you for these last six weeks. And for the days and moments we had together in England."

I put my finger on her plump lips, stopping her from saying anything. I had to get this all out before I lost the ability to form sentences.

"I want…" I paused. My throat and chest started doing this weird thing. A different thing than before. *Get it together, Xavier. Just say it.* "Remember when you asked if I could recommend someone to fix up your cottage?"

She nodded.

"Well, I found someone."

Her whole face lit up. "You did? That's amazing. Who is it? Should I call them and start—"

I silenced her with a kiss. A deep, passionate kiss. I kept kissing her until she went pliant in my arms.

And then I told her.

"I'm doing it, Tori. I'm going to fix up the cottage."

Her eyes brimmed with tears.

"Xavier," she whispered. "I don't know what to say."

"You don't have to say anything," I breathed, nuzzling into her neck. "I want to do this for you. I want to help make what's broken, beautiful for you again."

He's willing to risk everything for her…
Xavier and Victoria's story concludes in *The Penalty*

Still to come in the Royals and Legends series…
The Legacy
The Elite
The Striker
The Trophy

Thank you so much for reading *The Keeper*. If you enjoyed it, please consider leaving a review on the platform(s) of your choice. Reviews help spread the word about our books! Every single one helps.

xo,

Lynn

AUTHOR'S NOTE

Hi reader friends. Still with me? Okay good. The Keeper pulls together a few ideas I've been toying around with for a while. Plus, I didn't want to leave you with any lingering questions.

Royal City Athletic is not a real English soccer team (excuse me, *football club*). It's inspired by several Premier League teams.

And no, the New York Legends don't actually exist either. Both teams were born in my brain and let me tell you, coming up with their names was its own adventure.

Briarcliff Village isn't a real place. It's inspired by a few real villages I've visited in Scotland and England. And since I've watched the movie *The Holiday* an embarrassing number of times, I fully admit I was inspired by the locations used from Surrey.

The "Paws for Help Sanctuary" where Victoria and Charlotte volunteered is not real. However, there are thousands of small animal shelters nationwide doing amazing work to help abandoned cats and dogs. I volunteered at one in Massachusetts called Angelcat Haven Feline Rescue. Small shelters always rely on the generous donations from every day people like you and me.

Victoria's struggle with anxiety, grief, and guilt is unique to her. Yes, she's a fictional character but she experienced the fallout from a very real trauma that affects people from all walks of life. I tried to be as delicate and real with her character arc as I could. The way Victoria handles the guilt and anxiety from Charlotte's death might not ring true for anyone else but her.

If you are experiencing mental-health related distress or are worried about a loved one who might need crisis support, help is available. Call or text 988. Or go to 988lifeline.org to connect with a trained crisis counselor.

Thank you, reader friend, for jumping into Xavier and Victoria's whirlwind romance with me. I threw a lot of stuff at you. And at them.

I hope you're all ready for more…

ACKNOWLEDGMENTS

Don't tell my other books, but The Keeper holds a special place in my heart. It's the first book I've written since 2015. I know, right?!?

The seed for this story was actually planted in 2017. It always centered around Xavier and Victoria but started out as a football romance, not soccer. Xavier was American (!!!) if you can believe it. I think being British suits him better.

Anyway, The Keeper went through quite a few births and deaths and rebirths and needed all the feedback. All of it.

Thank you to everyone who read through the early stages.

Thank you to my friends and unofficial betas who read through the later stages when I posted a desperate plea on Facebook. Your emails, words of encouragement, thoughts, and suggestions were invaluable.

A special thank you to my friend Deana, for all the calls and texts immediately after finishing each emotionally intense scene. I hope you've fully recovered.

I've never written a romance from the guy's point of view, let alone a spicy romantic scene, so a special thank you to the fine gentlemen who helped keep Xavier honest.

And thank YOU, reader friends, for being so patient and jumping on this rollercoaster with me.

Let's continue, shall we?

ABOUT THE AUTHOR

Lynn Montagano is a contemporary romance author, podcaster and unapologetic football fan. When Lynn isn't writing or recording her weekly podcast, you can find her cheering loudly for her beloved New England Patriots. She lives in the suburbs outside (way outside) of Boston with her husband and three rescue cats.

Want to know more?
www.lynnmontagano.com